June

in the

Garden

June
in the
Garden

A Novel

ELEANOR WILDE

CROWN
NEW YORK

CROWN

An imprint of the Crown Publishing Group
A division of Penguin Random House LLC
1745 Broadway
New York, NY 10019
crownpublishing.com
penguinrandomhouse.com

Flower illustration: Shutterstock.com/Rivabegum

Published in Australia by Text Publishing, Melbourne.

Library of Congress Cataloging-in-Publication Data
Names: Wilde, Eleanor author
Title: June in the garden : a novel / Eleanor Wilde.
Identifiers: LCCN 2024061250 (print) | LCCN 2024061251 (ebook) |
ISBN 9780593799598 hardcover | ISBN 9780593799789 trade paperback |
ISBN 9780593799772 ebook
Subjects: LCGFT: Novels
Classification: LCC PR6123.I53523 J86 2025 (print) |
LCC PR6123.I53523 (ebook) | DDC 823/.92—dc23/eng/20250306
LC record available at https://lccn.loc.gov/2024061250
LC ebook record available at https://lccn.loc.gov/2024061251

Hardcover ISBN 978-0-593-79959-8
Ebook ISBN 978-0-593-79977-2

Editor: Shannon Criss
Editorial assistant: Austin Parks
Production editor: Serena Wang
Text designer: Amani Shakrah
Production: Dustin Amick and Jessica Heim
Copy editor: Sibylle Kazeroid
Proofreaders: Amy Schneider and Barbara Greenberg
Publicist: Lauren Chung
Marketer: Chantelle Walker

Manufactured in the United States of America

2 4 6 8 9 7 5 3 1

First US Edition

The authorized representative in the EU for product safety and compliance
is Penguin Random House Ireland, Morrison Chambers, 32 Nassau Street,
Dublin D02 YH68, Ireland, https://eu-contact.penguin.ie.

For my son who was born on a sunny day in June,
For my daughter who slept beside me while I wrote this novel.
And for my mother, who always brings me flowers.

"

There is no true
end to a garden year.
It simply continues
into the next.

"

June and the Midafternoon Appointment

The rain falls hard on the redbrick buildings on Avenuepark Street in Maryhill, soaking into the moss that grows on the roof tiles, seeping through the cracked shingles and the gutters that already sag precariously, and dripping down the walls of the community center where I sit in the waiting room. It's afternoon on the seventh of May, a Tuesday. According to the forecast I read this morning, it should be 16 degrees Celsius outside right now, which is impressive for Scotland at this time of year, but it does not feel like 16 degrees. Not in here. The dampness in the air doesn't help either.

It wouldn't be the first time a newspaper forecast was incorrect. My *Gardener's Almanac* is far more accurate. The Royal Horticultural Society predicts a wet summer with heavy downpours, and they are not often wrong. Over 120 millimeters of precipitation for Glasgow. Even more for Exeter.

In the corner, a red plastic bucket catches stray raindrops from a leak in the ceiling, which seems to have got worse in the time I have been sitting here. The wet patch has now spread down the wall and appears to be affecting the electricity around the light switch, making the bulb flicker and splutter. My eyelids twitch and pulse to the rhythm.

The clock on the wall matches my rainbow watch perfectly: 3:32 p.m.

I squirm in the chair, the backs of my thighs numb from the metal seat. My feet tingle with pins and needles, but I am unable to cross my legs or change position as there is a small coffee table jammed against my knees. A stack of magazines with features on "summer bodies" and "flirty-thirty dating lives" sits next to a vase filled with artificial baby's breath. I know it is baby's breath because we have it on our kitchen table at home, clipped by my own hands, of course, and arranged in a ceramic jug as milky white as the flower itself. Far better than any artificial version. I refreshed the water before I left for work today, when the morning rays were streaming in through the lace curtains, making dust motes dance in the slices of sunlight. The house was quiet at that time. So incredibly quiet.

"June?"

I had clipped the baby's breath from the flower bed meticulously, approximately one inch aboveground so it would grow back for the autumnal bloom. Not many people know that baby's breath blooms twice in one year.

"June?"

Yarrows, roses, and salvias are also repeat flowerers. There is a term we use for that, a word I learned from my Royal Horticultural Society encyclopedia, one that rolls off the tongue like a foreign language only spoken in black-and-white movies.

Remontancy.

A marvelous word.

"June?"

"Yes?" My voice sounds strange, as if it has been pinched and plucked from my throat, separated from my body. I turn slowly toward Aileen, who is standing in the doorway, clutching a large brown folder in one hand and a takeaway coffee cup in the other. I frown, a surge of envy flooding my body. I requested a milky tea at exactly three o'clock, like I always have, but the receptionist told me that this is not a café and she is not a waitress. I did not assume that either of those things was true; I simply asked for a cup of tea while I waited for my caseworker, who is frequently late for our appointments and never offers me a warm beverage at 3:00 p.m. Punctuality and reliability are not Aileen's best traits. Mother soon learned to clear our entire afternoon on days of home visits, never knowing when and sometimes *if* Aileen would arrive.

"June," Aileen says again, this time in a way that makes me feel strange. "Shall we?"

I rise and follow obediently. She doesn't say anything as I trail behind her, clutching my translucent umbrella, which I won at last year's local flower show—an obvious win. Carol's petunias were overfertilized. Her stems were weak. More is not always better.

Aileen's heels squeak on the tiled floor and I startle. I want to ask her to pick up her feet a touch more to stop them from dragging, but I don't. We enter a room down the hall, and she collapses heavily into a large armchair. She takes a swig from her coffee cup, wipes the latte foam from above her top lip, then sets the cup down by her feet. She gestures for me to sit too, so I edge into a chair, leaving one seat between us. Bubble space is very important. I have a bubble and she has a bubble, and they cannot overlap. I only ever let my bubble overlap with Mother's, and that took years of practice.

Aileen clears her throat. "June, how are you?"

"Fine," I say, crossing my ankles like I am a schoolgirl sitting in the headmistress's office.

"I'm so sorry for your loss."

"Fine."

"I talked with the police again yesterday." She pauses and waits for my response. I do not say anything, so she continues: "The autopsy report doesn't mention any drugs in your mother's system—"

"Mother doesn't take drugs. Not anymore." I glance at the door, which is ajar. Voices carry in narrow hallways, and the last thing Mother would want is the whole neighborhood thinking she was a drug addict.

"There was a lot of alcohol, though."

I swallow hard, and my throat hurts.

"June, you can trust me."

Trust is a strange word. Abstract and somewhat incomprehensible. I trust my *Royal Horticultural Society Encyclopedia of Gardening*, the 2012 edition. I trust my *Gardener's Almanac* for long-range weather forecasts. I trust Mother. I do not trust short-range weather forecasts on television, in newspapers, or on mobile phone apps, nor do I trust the "Google" for its horticultural suggestions. Once I used the computer in the staff room at work to research organic at-home composting and was incorrectly advised to add fresh pine needles to balance out the matter in the mixture. The truth is, pine needles are far too acidic and need to be completely dried out before use. And they should only be incorporated if the matter contains solely non-acidic materials. I never trusted the internet after that.

"Is there anything you want to say? It's a safe space."

There are lots of things I want to say, particularly because without Mother, I have not had an opportunity to practice my social skills in real-time conversation. But I also think that Aileen is referring to something else, something that pecks at the edges of my mind. Without Mother, my head feels like a thousand-piece puzzle that has been split apart. Broken, the pieces separated, perhaps even turned upside down. Nothing fits together anymore.

Maureen at work likes to do those large puzzles. She often sets one up on the back table in the staff room and encourages everyone to have a turn. I am not allowed anymore because I cannot just do one piece. I have to finish the puzzle, all of it, even if it takes me the rest of my shift. Therefore, I no longer look at the back table. I simply sit at the first table, facing the door, and eat my packed lunch until the timer beeps on my watch, then I clean up and go back downstairs to the shop floor or the stockroom.

"When can I collect Mother?" I ask. "She'll want to be home for my birthday."

Aileen sighs and crosses her legs, knocking over her latte cup in the process. She swears under her breath, but I hear her. Mother sometimes swears too. Aileen grunts and pants with exertion as she contorts herself into an awkward position to wipe up the murky brown liquid that has seeped out from the sipping hole on the plastic lid. She glances up at me and tries to smile, but it looks wrong on her face. "As you know, the investigation into your mother's death has been closed, and you are free to proceed with her funeral whenever you want." She drops the cup into a tall black bin and it clatters to the bottom, the remaining liquid sloshing up the sides.

This appointment appears to be finished, so I nod and stand. I had been practicing nonverbal cues with Mother before everything happened.

"This may seem sudden," Aileen continues.

I sit back down, wondering how she missed my cue. Perhaps it was incorrect, like the weather forecast.

"But at some point, we need to discuss more . . . long-term arrangements."

At first I think she is referring to funeral arrangements, which is natural to discuss after someone's death. However, Mother has already written notes about how she wants the disposal of her body to be "arranged": she is to be wearing a navy dress from the autumn 2017 range at Marks & Spencer, which I got with my staff discount, along with her favorite suede heels. If there is a small gathering of neighbors and/or former Royal Mail colleagues, she wants a reading of Robert Burns's poem "To a Louse" and a buffet lunch that consists of miniature prawn cocktails in jars, triangular cheese sandwiches, and salt-and-vinegar crisps. There are no other arrangements to be considered. Mother has been very clear.

"Your neighbor has kindly offered to look in on you daily, once in the morning and once in the evening, until we can find more suitable accommodations."

"I already have accommodations," I correct her.

"Your current home was allocated to you and your mother as a family unit; since her passing, however, we might need the house for a . . . *larger* family."

I blink hard. "Where would I go?"

"We're still looking into options."

"Who's 'we'?"

"Me and my colleagues in Adult Services, and the team over at the housing association."

"I see." The room is suddenly very quiet. I hear muffled voices from out in the hallway, spilling through from the waiting room. "You mentioned that a neighbor would be checking in on me. Which neighbor?"

Aileen glances down at a yellow Post-it on the front of a beige folder. "Mrs. Maclean at number 26."

"Mother doesn't like Mrs. Maclean. She leaves her bins out for days after collection. They clutter the pavements."

"Have you considered how you'd like to bury her?"

"Mrs. Maclean?"

"No, your mother."

"Oh, yes, Mother told me her wishes."

"Well, just in case you have any questions." She wrestles out of her coat pocket a leaflet that is damp with the rain outside, the corners pulled back. It's titled "Living with Death" and there is an image of a woman sitting on a park bench alone, surrounded by daffodils. That photo must have been taken in early to mid-April, at their peak bloom.

I nod politely, tuck the leaflet under my arm, and endeavor to leave again. I wave goodbye to minimize confusion, then, avoiding a small puddle of coffee that Aileen missed while cleaning up, I walk out the door. It slams loudly behind me, echoing down the dimly lit hallway.

The bus journey home is long, and by the time I arrive back at my street, it is past six o'clock. *Past.* I haven't even started peeling the potatoes or slicing the carrots, and who will put the chicken in the oven? That was Mother's job, and it was always done on time.

Dinner won't be on time today. It'll be late. And Mother won't be there.

A wave of heat surges through me and I strike, my foot kicking over Mrs. Maclean's glass-recycling box. Small jam jars roll down the pavement, following close behind each other until one drops onto the road and shatters, fragments spilling out over the asphalt.

That reminds me, we need more strawberry jam. I'll go to the shops tomorrow after work.

Opt for locally grown flowers for a more personalized funeral tribute, and to represent the landscape of the recently deceased.

June and the Cremation

The clock in the "family room" of the crematorium is ticking loudly, each stroke of the minute hand scratching around the dial, the buzzing of the mechanism behind the glass vibrating against my cranium. We have clocks at home, but when she bought them, Mother ensured that they were the silent kind. Had she not, my erratic sleep patterns would have been even more erratic.

I am dressed in my usual attire: khaki trousers, wellies, thick navy socks, long yellow raincoat with a hood. I'm wearing a large straw sun hat even though the sun is not out. The sky is filled with thick clouds, dense with water vapor and saturated air. My wavy hair, auburn like Mother's, and always cut to shoulder-length, is pulled back in a low bun that sits at the nape of my neck, secured with an elastic band and a green ribbon. Stray locks of hair hang limply around my face until I re-tuck them behind my ears and reposition my hat.

The rainbow watch on my left wrist tells me that it is 12:17 p.m., and the empty lunch plate on my lap confirms it. The sandwiches were delicious, as was the tea, nicely brewed, but I did not touch the little prawn cocktails in jars nor the salt-and-vinegar crisps. We played

Mother's favorite tune, "Songbird" by Eva Cassidy, at the beginning of the service, while a man in a black suit stood at the podium, his hands clasped in front of his belly, his head bowed. Standing in the second pew, I copied his stance. I could not sit in the front pew as I had lined the wooden bench with tulips and delphiniums. I wanted to drape wisteria over the benches and around the casket, but I was unable to source adequate blooms in time. Carol's wisteria at the community garden, where I volunteer on weekends, was overhydrated, and the Botanic Gardens had an entry fee, and a security guard at the gates.

Due to the state of Mother's body, arrangements had to be made quickly. I didn't have time to inform others of the cremation details. I considered putting an advertisement in the newspaper, but I did not know whom to ask about that. I also contemplated sliding hand-written notes through the neighbors' letterboxes, but Mora at number 19 has a sign that says NO SOLICITATION and I did not know if a cremation invitation constituted "solicitation." Therefore, it is just me today.

The service began promptly at 11:00 a.m., as I requested, and ended at 11:45, a little later than anticipated. I struggled with the Scots tongue during my reading of "To a Louse" and had to repeat myself several times, starting from the beginning each time, of course. There were a lot of words in the poem that I did not recognize— *crowlan, blastet, grozet, flainen*—and I wasn't able to practice aloud with anyone. Mother taught me to speak like the ladies on *Downton Abbey*, not like the characters one would find in a pub in Glasgow on a Friday night.

The service was supposed to end at 11:30 a.m., thus giving me time to transport the floral arrangements back into the van the crematorium kindly organized for me before luncheon was served, but the late finish meant I had to move straight into food preparation. The man in the black suit asked me if I wanted to say goodbye to Mother before the curtains closed and the furnace was fired up, but

I said, "No, thank you." Mother and I will be reunited again soon enough.

Ah, here she is now.

"I am so sorry for your loss," the man says again, cradling my mother in his arms. The urn looks so small. I wonder how she fits in there.

I hold out my palms, ready to take her, but the man does not hand her over. Mother will not like this.

He gestures to a plastic bag by his feet. "Your mother's shoes and some personal items. Her watch and rings."

I frown. Mother would have wanted those items to be burned with her, especially her suede heels. I bought them for her at work during the Boxing Day sales, when staff get an additional 15 percent off. Cobalt blue, like delphiniums or asters. She worked an extra shift at the postal sorting offices to pay for them.

I hold out my hands again. This time, he passes Mother over as if she is a cat. I cradle her like he did, struck by the lightness of the ceramic. "Is this all of her?"

The man blinks quickly. "Sorry?"

"Is all of my mother in here, or did you have to remove anything?"

He doesn't say anything, but his mouth is agape.

"It's just so light."

He swallows loudly. "Yes, Miss. Wilson. *All* of your mother is in there."

"Excellent. I am glad she's not missing a leg or anything."

His cough sounds more like a choke, and I wonder if the prawn cocktail got him. People do not expect there to be a spice kick, but Marks & Spencer put a pinch of paprika on top of theirs. I only know that because I have been a loyal employee at their Foodhall for some time now, picking up the odd culinary fact, like how cooked chicken should have an internal temperature of 73.9 degrees Celsius and that the price of honey varies depending on how hard it is to harvest that year.

"Well, I best get home," I say with a quick shrug. "It looks like it might rain this afternoon, and I need to repot the violas on the back terrace. Thank you for my mother. And for the cheese sandwiches."

"Here, my wife can give you a lift home with the flowers." He turns to call over a woman who is standing by the open doors.

Beyond her, cars stream in to the car park, winding down the crematorium driveway in a slow procession. That must be the 12:30 service. There are a lot of vehicles here. A lot of mourners. This family must know how to advertise a service, unlike me. Perhaps they have a friend at a newspaper, or one of those online things Maureen at work always talks about, which asks you for your personal details so they can disclose them to hackers. A social media account.

Oh well. Mother and I never did like crowds. She'd have been happy with how her service turned out. Just the two of us.

"That's okay," I say. "Keep the flowers for the next service. The community garden won't miss them. I'll take the bus home. I always take the bus." I nod once and wait for him to acknowledge my non-verbal cue. He nods in return. Pleased, I gather up the plastic shopping bag of Mother's personal belongings, tuck her under my arm, and head out into the fresh air.

"

A garden in
May will present
new challenges.

"

June and the Maisonette

It is my birthday today.

Twenty-two.

I think it's a song.

Music escapes me, though. Lyrics that refer to emotions and memories, and times long gone do not make sense to me.

I sit at the round kitchen table, a cup of milky tea beside me because it is five past three in the afternoon and this is the time I have it. Mother sits opposite me, in her usual chair. I've tied blue laces around the neck of her urn, unthreaded from an old pair of shoes to represent the heels that were not cremated along with her. The carcasses have been discarded. The shoes, I mean. As they are worthless without laces.

Rather than tea, I have poured Mother a glass of Cava as it is a special occasion. Mother always said sparkling wine was for special occasions and I consider my birthday to be one of them. I had found a brown envelope in the top drawer of her dresser, beside a letter not addressed to me. I put that one somewhere safe, although I don't remember where now. Inside the brown envelope that had my name printed across it was a birthday card. On the front of the card was a large sunflower with a slim green stem. I only ever received one birthday card a year, and that was from Mother.

I did get mail today, but it was not a birthday card. It was a letter from Aileen, a follow-up on these "long-term arrangements." It explained that due to a recent change in my situation, the house in which I currently reside is to be reallocated to another family like she had mentioned. I have less than a week to pack my belongings. I have been "less" of a few things over the years—rest*less*, job*less*, friend*less*, and, according to the teachers at school, "hope*less*." But never home*less*. Until now.

My options are limited. Due to the circumstances, Mother's life insurance policy had been rendered null and void two weeks ago, leaving me with even fewer options.

Aileen had indeed spoken with her colleagues and would like me to meet her tomorrow morning at ten o'clock to view two potential homes. I have doubts about whether either of them will be appropriate for me as I enter the next stage of womanhood, inching closer to "flirty thirty," but I will try to be "flexible" as Mother always encouraged, and because it is my birthday and on special occasions we do things outside our routines.

After I finish my tea, I offer Mother a top-up on the Cava and watch it flow over the lip of the coupe glass as I pour, spilling onto the wooden table and dripping onto the tiled floor beneath. Then I clean it up, wash the dishes, and return to the garden to finish the weeding before dinner preparations.

The freezer is stocked with chicken Kievs, bags of frozen sliced carrots, and pre-chopped potatoes. I don't need to use the frozen potatoes as I will clean and slice fresh ones myself, having stopped by Asda on my way home from work this afternoon. I had meant to finish my shift at four o'clock as I usually do, but my supervisor had insisted I leave early to "grieve."

It had only been one carton of eggs. I hadn't meant to throw them and had cleaned up the mess immediately, but a customer reported me and then I was sent home. The thing is, I had overheard the staff talking about Mother in aisle three. I don't tend to eavesdrop on other people's conversations, but in this case, it related to me. I struggled to decipher exactly what was being said. The conversation was muffled, somewhat muted by the clatter of a customer's cart rolling down aisle two, full of reduced-price white wines. I had asked her to please be quiet and even paired it with the universal gesture of one finger to the lips, but she carried on down the aisle, the bottles clinking together, distorting the conversation in aisle three even more. It was then I noticed someone had discarded a carton of eggs on the shelf beside me. Eggs do not belong in the Sauce aisle, and that, along with the incomprehensible conversation about Mother in the next aisle, unsettled me.

I had wiped the egg yolk from the woman's boot; there really was no need for her to report me to Maureen.

My dinner is ready at exactly six o'clock and by half past I have finished my meal and poured Mother a Chianti. I am in my pajamas and dressing gown, ready for the BBC show *Escape to the Country* to begin at seven o'clock. By nine, I will be upstairs, preparing for bedtime. I had considered staying up a little later since it's my birthday, but routines and schedules exist for a reason. Without them we would become overwhelmed, like a garden overrun with holly and hawthorn.

The sounds of night do little to soothe me to sleep and I lie awake for a long time, with a churning in my belly. I doze somewhere between midnight and dawn, and rouse before my watch alarm goes off.

The address specified on Aileen's letter is not far from my workplace, so I take the usual bus into town. I contemplate popping in to Marks & Spencer to say hello to my colleagues but dismiss the idea after I recall Maureen's expression when I catapulted the empty egg carton off her shoulder. I was asked not to return until Monday, but perhaps I shall go in tomorrow as Maureen's off on Wednesdays and I do not like last-minute changes to my schedule. Maureen has her grandkids Rosie and Reuben on Wednesdays, while her daughter goes off with her new boyfriend. She's had three in the past year alone.

I wait on the pavement outside a small red brick building that has a buzzer. Aileen is twenty-two minutes late—the same number as my age—and again arrives with a takeaway coffee for one. She waves at me even though we are the only people on the street.

"You found it okay?" she gasps, already noticeably out of breath from the short walk here.

"Yes," I reply, although if I hadn't found it, then I wouldn't be standing here, so Aileen's question didn't really need an answer.

She balances her coffee cup, a beige folder, and a large slim mobile phone in her hands and thunders on a red door. The paint has chipped off all around the iron knocker and the doorbell has two pieces of black duct tape across it in the shape of an X. Mother disconnected our doorbell years ago, so this actually suits me just fine.

Aileen knocks again, this time louder, spilling her takeaway drink in the process. She swears and drops the folder. Papers scatter across the dirty tarmac around our feet, some upside down, others face up, covered in type and headings in bold. On the one nearest my wellies, I see a photo of a much younger me, possibly back when I lived in foster care. My hair is matted and split into two side pigtails, strands poking out from the loops, and my face is pale and gaunt. I have a sliver of a bruise running alongside my face from my temple to my jaw. There are many things I no longer recall about that time in my life, the taking of this photo being one of them.

Aileen gathers up the papers and shoves them back into the folder. As she opens her mouth to say something, the red door swings open and a man with long, dark hair and a medical bandage on one eyebrow answers.

"Yeah?" he grunts.

"My name is Aileen Macdonald. I'm from the council, and I'm here to show a tenant around the property."

He tuts and opens the door wider, but by the time I shuffle inside, he's gone. The hallway is covered in browning wallpaper and smells like the inside of my welly boots after a hot day in the garden. Aileen pretends she doesn't smell anything, but I hear her choke on an inhale. She leads me down the hallway, counting the numbers on the doors until we come to number 6.

"It's a ground-floor flat," she begins, "close to your work, as you probably know already, and has a fully equipped kitchen, a recently repaired shower, and a bedroom large enough for one person."

I edge inside the space, my boots catching on the shaggy carpet. There's a big stain beneath the coffee table. It looks like red wine. Or maybe blood. A brown sofa sits next to a small rectangular window that looks out onto the block of flats next door. The only other furniture is a TV unit with no TV and a tall, freestanding lamp with an upside-down, tasseled lampshade. I can see the kitchen from here, through a carved-out hatch in the living room. The door to the kitchen is beside that and is propped open with a gray rubber doorstop. I walk over to the window and gaze out. There's a little boy sitting at the open window opposite me. He waves. I don't wave back.

"How do you access the garden?" I ask Aileen.

"It doesn't come with a garden."

"What do you mean? Don't all houses come with a garden? Or do you have to pay extra, like an add-on? Like how you can sometimes add on a bottle of wine or Prosecco to a dinner deal at Marks & Spencer?" Mother quite enjoyed an add-on or two.

"No, sorry, I meant there is no garden here," she clarifies.

I stand back, mouth agape. My fingers twitch and tremble as the heat bubbles within me. I can feel the warmth spread to my cheeks in seconds.

"I have another property to show you that does come with a *shared* garden," she quickly adds.

I sigh deeply and close my eyes, feeling my breathing slow. Then I nod and follow her out of the ground-floor flat with the fully equipped kitchen and recently repaired shower, to the next property.

It's a flat, much like the one we viewed before, even though Aileen tells me it's a "maisonette," apparently French for—I don't remember now. It's not much bigger than what we just saw and is still close to work, within walking distance certainly. The bedroom is smaller than my current one and the kitchen is at the back of the property rather than at the front, which is quite confusing. The living room carpet is stained here too, this time brown like coffee, but the sofa is green like a Cymbidium orchid and there is a matching armchair, which is quite pleasant. I do like the color green.

Aileen's eyes widen as I shimmy Mother out of my handbag and place her urn on the armchair, slightly tilted toward the TV. I sit on the sofa and try to imagine watching the new season of *Strictly Come Dancing* here with her.

But I can't imagine it.

The image of us together but not at home is impossible to conjure in my mind and when I try, it falls apart like a withered dandelion, the seedheads tumbling to the ground. This is not my sofa, that is not the armchair Mother always sat in, and this is definitely not my house.

The world tilts and I hear someone scream. I feel a warmth inside my veins and a tightness closing in around my body. A crushing, suffocating tightness. Then, nothing.

I blink once, twice, and see Mother's urn still sitting in the green armchair.

Aileen is gone, and the door is wide open.

In the spring,
the gray partridge
will often nest under
hedges, where it is
dark and protected.

June and the Attic

The attic floor is thick with dust, disturbed only by a narrow track of my own footprints. I came up here occasionally when I was a child, when I first returned to Mother. The attic reminded me of the one at my last foster home, where I would be sent if I got angry or if I disagreed with anyone, which happened frequently because people are often wrong. Now the attic reminds me only of Mother. Many of her things are up here and it oddly smells like Merlot, her "everyday wine."

Rays of an apricot afternoon sun seep through a small window behind me, reaching along the dusty floorboards like fingers, searching. I sit down and huddle into myself, pulling my knees into my chest, and gently rock back and forth, needing movement to soothe myself. It does not work. My belly still churns; my veins still pulse. I begin doodling on the dust-covered floor, circling and looping and etching flowers and vines all around my bare feet. The dust collects at my fingertips, some particles mixing with the air and tickling my nostrils. I hum, deviating from the song's true melody, never quite remembering how Mother sung it.

Downstairs, the phone rings again.

Aileen called this morning. At first I thought it was to ask me how I was feeling, which is a standard follow-up after someone's mother passes away and when someone has a strong reaction like I had yesterday at the "maisonette." But instead, it was to discuss "supported adult living services"—shared housing with individuals similar to me, with the occasional visit from a carer or caseworker, such as Aileen. I thought she was joking, particularly because comedy tends to confuse me. Why would I want to live with other people like me?

But then she called again, and finally there was a knock at the front door, which is why I came up here, to hide in the attic with Mother. It may not have been Aileen at the door, but Mother and I don't usually have visitors or parcel deliveries from online shopping companies that require credit card details, so who else would it have been? Not Mrs. Maclean; she popped by on Monday. The milkman? No, he doesn't come anymore, not since March when Mother stopped paying him. Now we get our milk from Asda.

I can't sit up here all day. Eventually I'll need to go downstairs to prep dinner. But perhaps, just in case there's another knock at the door, I'll sit here for a few more moments surrounded by the cardboard boxes and heavy wooden chests laden with memories of Mother.

The phone rings again.

I unfurl myself from the corner and scoot over to one of the chests, sliding through the doodles in the dust until they are nothing but smears and gaps. I creak open the chest's lid, the smell of sandalwood and lemon trickles out, and press my hands deep into Mother's fabrics. Silk dresses, suede skirts, satin shirts. Mother dressed so well. I tend to dress for the garden, even when I am at work—loose-fitting khakis or shorts, occasionally an old linen sundress if I am not handling shears or a rake, a knitted cardigan for warmth, wellies and a raincoat for practicality, and of course, my gloves. There's always a pair of gardening gloves in my pocket. I wish I had inherited Mother's style. I wish many things, some of which I cannot quite remember right now as I sit here, cross-legged, my hands covered by her dresses.

I press deeper, until my fingers graze something on the bottom of the chest. When I pull back, there's a thin scrape across one of my thumbs. A globule of blood oozes out. It drops onto the dust-blanketed floor and spreads, reminding me of wisteria after a heavy rainfall. The phone rings again. I return to the chest, determined to find whatever cut me. It's an envelope—two, actually, paper-clipped together. The first is a large brown one, ripped open at the back and split on one side, filled with letters, photos, and a newspaper article. When I look closer, I see the letters are all addressed to Mother, from someone called Robert. Many of them ask something of her—to call him, to write to him, to visit him. Robert seems very demanding; no wonder she ignored him. I return the letters to the envelope and hold up the newspaper clipping to the sunlight filtering in. Three figures are illuminated, well, four if the animal is counted. The paper is stained with overlapping circles of red wine, like a Venn diagram, or like petals on an English rose. The black-and-white image of a family standing in a garden is nestled beneath a headline from two years ago: "Local Businessman Raises £200,000 for Care Homes in Clapham." I don't recognize anyone in the photo and therefore don't understand why Mother kept it. She must have grasped it for a while as the ink has mostly faded from the edges and her thumbprint lines are etched into the picture. I shall now make a point of keeping it too.

The man in the picture is much shorter than the woman who stands beside him. She has the whitest teeth I have ever seen on a human, and rests a hand on a young boy's shoulders, her skinny fingers curved at his collarbone. I shiver. I wouldn't like to be touched like that. A scruffy biscuit-colored dog sits on the ground in front of them, its thick wiry mane in desperate need of a good trim with a pair of gardening shears.

The phone rings again.

"Robert Wilson, Judith Wilson, and Henry Wilson, of Lansdowne Road, Notting Hill," I read aloud. My voice sounds strange again, separate from my throat. The phone rings again.

They all share my surname, but why?

The second envelope is much lighter but still rather bulky for the regular post. It's addressed to Robert, stamped but never sent, and Mother would never deliberately waste a stamp. She was a loyal Royal Mail employee. Until she was fired four years ago.

Perhaps she once intended to send this envelope but changed her mind at the last moment, or simply forgot. I forget things all the time, more often now that Mother is not around to remind me, and because my head feels so foggy these days. Heavy, like a rain-bearing nimbus cloud.

Inside is a small cloth bag filled with a child's teeth. My teeth, I suppose. Unless Mother collected another small human's teeth. I turn one of the teeth over in my palm, poking and prodding at the white object. It looks far too weak to have been able to cut and chew through food effectively. No wonder they fell out. There are also several drawings, a feeble attempt at "art"—sketches of daisies and daffodils, paint-splatter suns, and sequin-adorned gardens, stiff with dried-up glue patches that crack and flake off as I riffle through.

June Wilson, Age 6

June Wilson, Age 7

June Wilson, Age 8

This is my art. Pictures from almost every year of my childhood, thankfully getting progressively better over time. It doesn't surprise me that Mother kept all of these as she always was a sentimental person, proudly displaying each drawing on the wall in the kitchen. Even at age six I loved the garden. Florals and vines inching their way up the edges of my mind and spreading onto the paper through crayon and paint.

Did Mother think in color and stem too?

I gaze at her in the urn, sitting by the window in the last slivers of sunshine, and suddenly the world around me is far too heavy. Far too thick with uncertainty. A warm tingling sensation under my skin itches and spreads like the droplet of blood on the dust.

It is nightfall before I wake and my belly rumbles, knowing I have missed a mealtime. I'm confused, lying on the cold floorboards, a thick speckled cardigan around my shoulders, the stack of sketches and paintings still in my hand. The newspaper clipping sits a little farther away, near Mother, who is now shrouded in shadow and an inky darkness. My chest throbs, an indecipherable sensation I have never felt before.

I have injured myself. A paper cut, perhaps. Blood drips onto the clothes beside me, and onto the small cloth bag of hollowed teeth and forgotten memories. I crawl along the dust-covered floorboards to Mother and cradle the urn.

Downstairs, the phone keeps ringing.

"

Plant families tend
to share the same traits
and the same pests.

"

June and the Biological Relatives

The milk has curdled. It's thick and gloppy and floats on top of my morning coffee, circling on the surface and occasionally hitting the sides of the mug. I thought I'd bought a new carton yesterday, but this one has an expiration date on it that was three days ago. Wasn't it just yesterday that I went to Asda? What day is it today? Has Mrs. Maclean come already? No, she did not come this week. She hasn't come in two weeks now, not since I yelled at her and told her to bring her bins inside after collection. There's no reason not to take your bins back to the house once they've been emptied by the council. It's just laziness.

"Isn't that right, Mother?" I say.

Mother sits at the kitchen table, a black coffee in front of her, cold now. It is officially June. My month. Mother said she'd picked out my name because my due date was meant to be today, but I came early. I am always early. Punctuality is an important trait to have, which is why I try to ascertain where a clock is in each room I enter to remain aware of the time. Analog clocks are far more reliable than digital clocks, as I discovered once during a power outage.

Two letters sit beside Mother's cup of untouched coffee. One is from the electricity company demanding payment again and threatening to shut off the power, and the second is from Aileen. She has secured me a *shared* room in the residential home. According to her, I will be happier—and "safer"—in this place. A place that locks but has no key. Not for those inside, anyway.

This is not my idea of a home. How will I get outside to the garden?

I would also need to store my tools in a secured cabinet, as many gardening instruments are sharp and can be used as a weapon. I would prefer not to be decapitated by my own shears in the hands of a fellow resident upset at a schedule change. Elsbeth at the community garden almost lost her head after Carol dropped her pruning saw from the ladder while trimming the holly tree last winter. Like-minded people are often in the same location at the same time, and that is when accidents tend to happen.

Regardless of my concerns, staff from the assisted-living program will be here on Monday morning at ten o'clock to support my "transition."

I reach for my *Gardener's Almanac* on the chair beside me and retrace my days. Yesterday must have been Saturday as it rained in the morning and had winds blowing from the northeast, which means today is Sunday, with a forecast of afternoon rain and a predicted humidity level of 90 percent. The gardens will be needing the rain. I shall leave a letter for the next tenants with instructions on how to tend to the flower beds.

I have decided that today will be my last day here.

The envelopes from the attic sit on the kitchen table next to Mother. I remove the top one and shimmy out the newspaper clipping about the family, and while I wait for the milk to drain down the sink, I practice saying the name Robert, rolling my r's like all good Scottish people do. Mother had mentioned a Robert once or twice in passing, and had murmured his name many times while she slept off the Merlot on the sofa. Could this be the same man she'd dreamt about?

I press my face against the article, the smell of newsprint and tobacco filling my nostrils. Robert Wilson has my auburn hair, my crooked nose and thin lips and even a faint dimple exactly where I have one. We must be related, which means he will have to take me in if I am without a home. But what about the boy? Is he too related to me? I suppose if the boy has my surname and is a direct descendant of Robert Wilson, then yes, the stocky boy is also my relative.

I prod the remaining milk lumps down the sink drain, wash out the mug, then place it next to my bag as I will bring it with me on my journey to 16 Lansdowne Road in Notting Hill, London, England. If the Wilsons live there, there must be room for me too, because I am also a Wilson and that is how it works.

———

I get to the bus stop a little before lunchtime, stopping to wheel Mrs. Maclean's bins around to her back garden one last time. She taps on the kitchen window and tells me to stop, but I don't. Today is not a bin day and there is no need for her bins to litter the pavement. This will be my parting gift to the street.

The river thrashes and churns behind me, and a cold shiver snakes up my spine as the bus pulls around the corner. It chugs to a slow and clunky stop and the doors spring open with a sigh.

"Reduced fare to town, please. One way."

The driver does not say anything, so I engage in eye contact to proceed with the exchange. I blink hard as I realize I know him. It is Mr. Frank. I do not know what to say because I did not expect to see Mr. Frank today. All the drivers know me by name now and I know most of their names, but I don't know the weekend drivers because I never go into town on weekends. I work Monday through

Friday. Weekdays only because the weekends are for the flowers and
the soil.

"Not like you to work on a Sunday, June?" he says, adjusting the
glasses on his face.

"Y-you work Sundays?" I stutter, glancing at the empty seat behind him where I always sit. I do not like to sit at the back of the
bus. I need to be close to an exit at all times.

He nods slowly. "I do."

"But you work Thursdays, not Sundays. Today is Sunday." Mr.
Jarrett works Mondays, Tuesdays, and Wednesdays, Mr. Frank works
Thursdays and Miss Agatha works Fridays. When one is ill and there
is alternative staffing, it confuses me and sometimes I need to return
home to Mother.

"I work Thursdays *and* Sundays."

"Oh." I hadn't considered that I would see any of my usual drivers today. What if they tell someone, like Aileen?

He raises an eyebrow. "Are you coming on?"

My bag is heavy on my shoulder and if I wait for the next bus, I
will surely miss my train, so I hesitantly climb the stairs, closer to
Mr. Frank.

"One way, you said?" he asks. "Surely you mean Return?"

I nod quickly, and present my disability card for the discount,
like I always do.

He shifts in his big seat and squints at me. "Does your mum
know where you're at?"

I suck a breath in. I can't give him too much information because
he is not a stranger. Strangers you can tell anything to because you'll
never see them again, but people you know and tell things to will
always know your business from then on. That's why Mother never
had friends, never invited neighbors over for tea in the afternoon,
never joined any book clubs or craft groups or darts teams. It was
always just the two of us.

I nod again. I don't usually lie. In fact, I have never lied before, but perhaps not *saying* the words doesn't count as lying. Technically.

I drop shiny two-pound coins onto the curved yellow tray and say, "Goodbye, Mr. Frank." I sit in the second row, which feels strange. I cannot sit behind him as he may ask me more questions, but I cannot sit too far away from the exit.

The chair is stiff against my spine and one of the coils on the base is broken and splinters into the seat cushion beneath my thighs. I perch on the edge and draw hydrangeas on the empty seat beside me with my finger, looping up for the stem and circling out for the petals. I recite all the flowers I can remember that start with the letter M because M is for Maryhill until we're over the bridge, past the river, then I unclench my fist, stretch out my fingers, and sit back, watching the streets and houses and gardens of Glasgow whiz past, perhaps for the last time.

At Central Station, I do not say a word to Mr. Frank when I get off the bus, even when he calls my name.

"

Begin summer
planting early,
when opportunity
is abundant.

"

June and Edinburgh
Waverley Station

E dinburgh Waverley Railway Station is like wild bergamot on a warm summer's day. Overpopulated and difficult to tame.

The station is far busier than I'd expected for a sunny Sunday, but perhaps, in Scotland's capital, it is normal for this amount of people to be crammed into one space. Mother and I had very few occasions to venture into a city, and even fewer occasions to board a train, so this is all very new to us. I hold her up so she can see people hurrying about with bags and phones and tickets, often banging into each other like frenzied bees vying for nectar.

Some women carry miniature handbags that look far too small to fit their lunch and a book inside. Personally, I never leave home without a sizeable bag for these items, even if I am just taking the bus into town for work. Sometimes I carry two books, so space is a necessity.

Today I travel with more than a sizeable bag. I carry a duffel bag that hangs heavily on my shoulder and makes me walk slower than usual. I may have overpacked it, but after several repacks, I decided I absolutely could not part with any of the items inside, especially my books and gardening equipment. As Mother and I never spent overnights anywhere other than in our own house, we did not own a backpack or suitcase of any kind, so I had to go to TK Maxx yesterday where a shop assistant talked me into purchasing a "duffel bag," which, she explained, was half backpack, half suitcase. A hybrid, she termed it. A lovely word.

Hybrid.

I also brought into the shop—in a black bin bag—the items I wished to pack in the new bag; I wanted to test it out before any purchasing was to occur. I had sat cross-legged on the floor and attempted three different packing styles. After settling on the tried-and-tested "fold and roll," I was quite satisfied that this bag would do for my journey and completed the sale. It was only when I'd returned home for my three o'clock tea and biscuit that I remembered the pillow I had failed to account for, so now I have to carry it under my arm.

I also forgot to consider my sun hat. Therefore, I have chosen to wear it, even though I will be inside stations and train carriages for most of the day. Straw is difficult to roll.

The TK Maxx assistant had said duffels were excellent for camping, weekend "getaways," and short breaks. I'm not embarking on any of those. I won't be camping where I'm going and I certainly won't be participating in any "weekend getaway," which sounds illegal. What exactly is the difference between a weekend getaway and a short break, anyway? Does a getaway strictly have to occur on a Saturday and Sunday? What if a person wanted to leave on a Thursday evening? What if they enjoyed themself so much that they extended the break to a Monday? Does that then turn into a "short break"? And what about a "holiday"? Is this duffel not equipped to handle the length of a "holiday"? Which is what—seven days? Ten? Fourteen?

Did I lock the door when I left the house today?

I adjust the strap on the bag, which pokes into my shoulder. I had managed to squeeze in all my clothes, a visor, three books (my gardening encyclopedia, my *Gardener's Almanac*, and *Peter Pan*, a copy from my childhood), a toothbrush, toothpaste, face wash, lotion with a 20 SPF, Vaseline (in case my lips dry out with the London sun, and in case the city of London doesn't sell these products) and some important gardening tools.

And, of course, Mother. I have thankfully remembered to pack my mother.

The main hallway to the railway station is even busier than the entrances and exits. There are narrow barriers, black rubber ramps, and backpacks and cases strewn across the tiled floor. The surrounding shops offer takeaway coffee, hot pies, and a variety of sandwiches, chewing gum, and newspapers. I don't need to stop anywhere because I've also packed a digestive biscuit and thermos of milky tea for three o'clock, a double-walled insulated food flask with a chicken Kiev and a few potatoes for dinner, and a bottle of still water. Thankfully, I ate my sandwich while waiting for my connection to Edinburgh, so that's one less item to carry. Sandwiches from cafés are very expensive, even if you work in one and use the staff discount, therefore I always bring my own regardless of the situation. A person needs three meals a day, plus a good cup of coffee in the morning and a perfectly brewed tea in the late afternoon. I always carry my favorite mug for both because I don't like using other people's mugs, nor will I ever drink from a takeaway cup. If a tea is done correctly—hot as it should be—it will simply melt the cardboard. Why would I attempt to drink from soggy, flimsy cardboard?

"Isn't that right, Mother?" I snort, patting the urn.

I've never been to Edinburgh City before, but there are no trains to London from Glasgow today because of "overhead line equipment failures," according to the station attendant. I had wanted to ask her more, but she seemed preoccupied with her crossword puzzle.

Mother said Edinburgh is a city of hills, foreign tourists, and "hippie vegan cafés." Linda at work once talked of a great big castle here, up one of those hills Mother was talking about. Had I more time, and more tolerance for crowds, then I may have visited it. Castle gardens are wonderful, always so immaculate and full of bright colorful

flowers. I watched a *Countryfile* special once on the gardens at Clive-
den House in England, which has been nicknamed "the Versailles of
the UK," whatever that means. Three hundred and seventy-six acres
of pristine flower beds shaped into triangles, hedge mazes, and grass
cubes. Exquisite. Topiary is a dying art. I have tapered a hedge before, to allow more sunshine to reach the lower branches, but never
shaped it, molded it, curled and sculpted it into an animal or a music
note of some kind. That is a skill not yet natural to my fingertips.

Linda at work also said there is a big festival here in Edinburgh
every summer with theater shows and comedy performances, but I
wouldn't like that. Too many people and too much noise. And I do
not find "jokes" funny like some do.

I wasn't able to say goodbye to Linda in the end, just like I couldn't
tell Mr. Frank where I was headed. Only strangers can keep secrets.

A surge of commuters whiz past me as an announcement blasts on
the speakers about a train departing from Platform 6. I grip the shoulder straps on my duffel and cradle Mother tighter in my arms, then I
head for the ticket desk. The line is very long and snakes back onto
the floor and around the café. The line there is even longer. I expect
to see a lot of soggy dripping cardboard cups coming out of there
soon. I do not immediately take position as I am momentarily mes-
merized by the flickering light of the Information board, numbers and
letters ticking and rolling to form departure times and city names:

2:18pm Manchester
2:50pm Bristol
3:05pm Cambridge

It's only now I realize just how big the world is, and how small
Mother and I made ourselves, in order to squeeze into one tiny corner of it. But what a beautiful corner it was. A corner full of daffodils and violas and cups of tea on warm grass.

I slip out the envelope addressed to Robert Wilson, the one that was never postmarked, never sent, nor received, and stand in the queue behind a family whose children are bickering over a toy train. About twelve minutes later the conflict has been resolved and it is my turn, so I shimmy to the wooden box with a glass window and holes to speak through.

"London, please," I call through the holes.

"Where in London?"

"To Mr. Robert Wilson's."

She stares at me. "What?"

I clear my throat and read out the address on the envelope: "16 Lansdowne Road in Notting Hill, London, England. I saw a newspaper clipping of the family standing in front of the house. It appears to be a white house with a small pebble driveway and a garden path up the side that I hope leads to a spacious garden in the back."

"Are you trying to be smart?"

"Pardon?" I ask.

"King's Cross or Paddington?"

"Are they both in London?"

"Yes."

"Hmm." I drum the counter with my fingertips, while considering the options. "King's Cross or Paddington . . ." I repeat slowly. "How about you choose, then it'll be a surprise." I don't usually like surprises but Mother does. It'll be a nice treat for her.

The attendant sighs loudly. "King's Cross from Edinburgh has no changes, so we'll go with that."

"Excellent."

"Seat or bed?"

"Oh, certainly a bed as it'll be nighttime." Surely all passengers would prefer to sleep in a bed and not upright in a chair? That would be uncomfortable, and quite bad for the posture.

"And will you be needing a return ticket?"

"I don't need a return. One way, please. I'm going to live with my biological family, although they don't know yet. That's also a surprise."

66

Pollution can often
be the main cause of
plant migration, not
climate change, contrary
to popular belief.

99

June and the Train Journey

My ticket is for "Berth 6, Twin Cabin," which is very difficult to find. According to a woman clutching a half-eaten Snickers in carriage D, all the "sleeper cabins" are in carriage B. When I do finally locate my seat, I see that it is not a seat at all but more of a tiny bunk bed for infants or hobbits. It fits me just fine, but what about people bigger than me? My neighbor in Maryhill, at number 19, is two times my size, and that's just by width.

At least there is a small table beside the bunk for me to put my belongings on and for Mother to rest on. She'll want a window view. I have already eaten my dinner, of course, but it is only 7:25 p.m. and I am not quite ready for sleep. Since there is no television in my "cabin," I contemplate my options for passing the remaining two hours and five minutes:

1. Stare out the window at the countryside with Mother.

2. Doodle florals and vines on the napkins that the previous person has left on the top bunk.

3. Read one of the three books I have packed.

4. Go for a walk to (a) stretch my legs since I did not have
garden time today, and (b) explore the train as it may be
the first and last time I am on one if I am to live in
London going forward.

After much deliberation, I select the last option while it is still
light outside. I slide my duffel under the bed and scoop up Mother,
as she'll also want to explore. She always said she was an "adven-
turer" when she was my age. She lived an island once.

The hallway outside is long and narrow, with similar cabins
branching out on the left and a row of windows on the right, each
depicting a fast-moving image of grass and field and farmland. Families, businesspeople, and other solo travelers; I wonder if we are all
going to London. One cabin has its curtains drawn completely, making it impossible for me to see inside, which feels quite rude. In the
next one are three little children wearing Mickey Mouse ears on
their heads and clutching various electronic devices that buzz and
beep and blink, and make my vision flicker.

Past the toilets, which aren't particularly pleasant-smelling, is the
carriage for "Food & Drinks Services." Intrigued, I press the PUSH
button and dart in between the sliding doors before they close on
me and Mother, potentially impaling us. I don't intend to buy anything, because I already have my snacks and beverages sorted for the
journey, but I am curious about the setup of this carriage, and
whether there is a television that passengers can access. *Strictly Come
Dancing* isn't due to commence until next weekend, but at this time
of the evening I might find an episode of *Countryfile* or perhaps a
nature special of some sort.

The Food & Drinks carriage resembles the café at my work, with
rectangular tables and chairs, and the odd brown leather bench seat
that faces into the middle, forcing people to look at each other while
sipping and munching, which is quite unfortunate. A wall-mounted
menu includes three "cold snacks" (chocolate, crisps, nuts) and one

"hot food" item (a grilled cheese sandwich with or without ham), but the list of beverages is never-ending.

Beer

Cider

White wine

Red wine

Sparkling wine

Gin

Vodka

Whisky

I stand in front of the drinks menu for a moment, dazed. I can see now why railway stations are far busier than bus stations. It seems a person could get quite intoxicated on a train. In fact, I am slightly concerned about the amount of alcohol being served on a moving vehicle, but at least there are sleeper cabins in carriage B to accommodate the customers passing out in carriage A. I couldn't wake Mother for hours after she enjoyed a few of these beverages. I'm not a drinker myself, for fear it will interfere with my paroxetine medication, although I have not taken that since Mother went away. She never explained how medications are ordered, who I talk to, or whether I pay for them. Ever since she left, I have a lot of questions, and no one to ask.

I will soon, though. Because Mr. Wilson is a relative, and relatives have to answer questions honestly and in-depth.

A woman appears before me, dressed in a white shirt and navy trousers, all well-ironed. She holds a laminated paper copy of the menu in her hand and wears a money belt around her waist. "Anything you fancy from the menu?"

"Gosh, no," I reply, "but do you have a television I could access?"

"No, the Wi-Fi on here is pretty good, though. It'll be fine for streaming."

Streaming? I believe she and I are having different conversations, so I thank her for her time before turning around, then shimmy back through the carriage, where the doors almost squash me again. Back in our cabin, I position Mother at the window once more and wonder whether I should have ordered a Merlot for her. Although, it is a special occasion, us leaving Scotland, so perhaps it should have been a Chianti or some sparkling wine. Outside, the sky has darkened, thick gray clouds now pressing against the window. The harsh light of the cabin obscures the towns and fields whizzing by. What flowers grow this far south of Maryhill? What species of trees circle the farms and the valleys? Aspens? Willows? My breath fogs up the glass until I can't see myself anymore, then I crawl into the bottom bunk and fidget with the weathered strap on my waterproof rainbow watch.

8:24 p.m.

It's still too early to sleep, so I slide out *Peter Pan* and reread the chapter where Peter returns to the now grown-up Wendy, and wonders how time has passed by in such a way, leaving him both confused and saddened. I turn onto my side, away from Mother, and lightly touch the words on the page. I read the line *"I came back for my mother," he explained, "to take her to the Neverland"* over and over again until my eyelids become heavy. Until my fingers drop away, and the words in the book transform into nightmares of a churning, thrashing river. Of cold water and snakelike reeds and milky-white skin.

66

June is a good
time to tackle weeds
and to take risks.

99

June and the Arrival
in London City

The train comes to a hard stop and I bolt upright, bumping my head on the frame of the top bunk. I don't remember falling asleep, but it is no longer dark outside. In fact, it's blindingly bright. Unnaturally bright. I try to shield my eyes from the fluorescent lights streaming in through the carriage window from the platform. When I finally peel my eyes open, I see a crowd of passengers standing outside my cabin and flooding the platform beyond the glass, where a large sign reads KING'S CROSS.

I glance at my watch. 6:30 a.m. I'm here. I am in London, England: I am in a different country for the first time in my life. My chest twists and tightens, and I spin around looking for Mother. Thankfully, she still sits where I've left her, facing out to the views of the platform beyond. Then I see a man in the top bunk. A tall, portly man, in a gray suit, sleeping with his head on a laptop bag, a cable spilling out haphazardly down to my bunk below, which could have very well strangled me during the night. His chest rises and falls, pig snorts spilling out of his mouth and nose.

When had he arrived?

I clamber out of bed and quickly tuck *Peter Pan* back into my duffel bag. I scoop the pillow and Mother under my arm and yank open the carriage door to join my fellow passengers departing the train. As I slowly shuffle toward the exit door, a deep yawn escapes my lips and I groggily wipe sleep from my eyes. I had thought I'd be too nervous to sleep on a "sleeper train" since I have never been away from home before. Not since the foster care days. Perhaps it was the movements of the train that lulled me into the darkness last night, coupled with the fact that I haven't slept properly in weeks. The restless nights have left me feeling utterly exhausted, like I've come in from a long day out in the garden, where things had to be clipped, sheared, dug, dragged, and laid. It reminds me of the time Mother suggested we completely overhaul the front garden to try to grow hedges to escape the neighbors' prying eyes. After weeks of replanting, months of maintenance, and years of regrowth, she realized she preferred the garden the way it was before, blanketed in yellow flowers that reminded her of the sun. So I changed it back.

We all finally spill out of the carriage and onto the train platform, bags and maps and tickets in hand, looking for exits or connection signage. I pass the window of the sleeper cabin where I'd bunked and see the man in the gray suit still curled up on the hobbit bed. Maybe this is his stop too. I pause at the window, my tired reflection staring back at me. If this were me, if I were him, I would want to be woken and not end up in a completely different place, having slept through my intended destination. Linda at work says I'm not a good "teammate," but today I will prove her wrong and be a terrific "bunkmate." I slam my fist on the window and bang continuously until the man startles and slips off the bunk, falling to the ground and disappearing from my sight. I rise up on my tiptoes and search for him. Suddenly he pops up from the floor, his glasses half dangling from his face. His eyes are wide like those of a scared animal. He rubs his shoulder where he likely landed from the fall and finally focuses on my face. I knock on the glass again, this time softer as he is already awake, and shout, "King's Cross station!"

He blinks at me, mouth agape, glasses still diagonal across his face. Perhaps he too is from the north and needs further clarification, so I follow up with "London, England!" before turning around and rejoining the crowd looking for connecting trains.

On the escalator up, I realize I didn't give him ample time to thank me, but I'm sure he is very grateful. What a misfortune it would have been for him otherwise. He could have ended up back in Scotland and would have had to set off on the journey all over again!

The people around me are all looking down at their phones, bumping into each other. Mother and I never had one of those devices that allow the government to listen to your phone calls and track your location. Mother said it was best to live "off the grid." Another one of her expressions that I did not understand at the time. Now I think she must have been referring to an *electrical* grid.

I reach into the side pocket of my duffel and pull out my ticket. Edinburgh to London. That is where I have journeyed. Well, technically, from Glasgow to Edinburgh to London plus all the stops in between that I slept through.

I grip the ticket in my hand until my fingers become all clammy, and I look around for a station attendant of some kind, because all tickets should be verified. It's the only way to check that every person has paid the appropriate fare, but there is no one in sight. There are only metal barriers where passengers are swiping phones and tickets across a screen with ease, and confidence. Everyone here seems to have traveled on a train before. I do not know what to do, and that makes my belly flutter and my cheeks burn. I gaze hard at the ticket in my hand. It has a small barcode on it, like the items at the retailer where I work, which could mean the screens at the barriers must be like the scanners at a self-checkout. I rejoin the queue and when it's my turn, I step forward and swipe my ticket like it's a box of biscuits. But the scanner doesn't beep or blink green like at the checkout. And the barrier certainly doesn't open to let me pass through. The scanner just flashes red. I swipe again. Behind me, a line quickly forms and I feel the warmth of the crowd pressing against me from behind. I don't like it. I don't like large groups of people, and I definitely don't like broken scanners that fail to operate as they should do. If this were a real checkout, there would be tape across the barrier to indicate to customers that it is faulty. But here, no one seems to care.

I step to the next lane and try my ticket there instead. This machine also fails to beep and open. I have been sold a defunct ticket, like a retail item with a partially destroyed barcode. At my work, we put those items off to the side to be recoded, which I often did myself as I am quite good at that. But here there is no cart for defunct tickets and, as I've already established, there is no station attendant to manage this situation. Just barriers and gates and people now yelling from the back, "Hurry up, for fuck's sake!" and "What's taking so bloody long?"

I don't know what to do, so I place Mother on the floor by my feet to replace my straw sun hat with my noise-cancelling headphones. I cup the hat as best I can, so as not to break the straw, and tuck it under my arm, along with the pillow. With the headphones now on, the world around me is very quiet and still, like a television that has the volume down low. I can hear my raspy breaths and the thumping of my chest as people continue to press against me.

"I'm waiting for assistance!" I shout, scooping Mother back up into my arms.

"Assistance, please!" I call out again, recalling a time when that worked for a dropped jar of pasta sauce on Aisle 5 at the grocery store. "Assistance!" I hold Mother tighter, hugging the urn against my chest until it hurts against my skin and bones.

I feel someone tugging open my palm and when I open my eyes, I discover a young woman, with blue hair and several painful-looking piercings, trying to free the ticket from my grasp. My fingers are still clammy and the ticket slides out easily. I blink, wondering if I am a victim of thievery, but she instead swipes it, pressing more firmly on the screen. The barriers beep and open, and I stumble through them, almost dropping Mother. The blue-haired girl slides my duffel along the floor, steps over me, and then marches on.

"Thank you!" I call out to her. She waves a hand, not bothering to glance around.

The crowd has now dispersed and the air feels calm and still once again. I slide my headphones down over my hair and leave them at the nape of my neck, in case I need them again, and proceed with my journey to the Wilsons' residence.

The hallways of King's Cross station are lined with black and white wall tiles, posters of theater shows, and buskers singing about love and summertime. I follow a small group of people until I see a kiosk and, finally, a station attendant. The kiosk doesn't have the words *Information* or *Customer Service* on the side or along the top—in fact, there are no signs at all—however, there is a small desk and a man in a uniform.

"Excuse me—" I start.

"Are you going to Heathrow?"

"Sorry?"

"Are you going to Heathrow?" he asks again, in a funny accent I recognize from one of Mother's favorite shows about a pub in North London, where everyone argues and has extramarital affairs.

"Where is 'Heathrow'? Is it near Lansdowne Road?"

"No, Heathrow, as in the airport."

"The airport? No, I just got here. I don't have any intention of going back just yet, and certainly not by way of plane." Mother told me planes are for rich men. I am a woman. And not rich.

"I'm selling tickets for the Heathrow Express here," he says, look-ing away from me.

"I'm not buying tickets for the Heathrow Express. But I do want to purchase a ticket to 16 Lansdowne Road in Notting Hill, London, England."

He laughs and shakes his head. "Tourists, eh," he mutters. "Try the ticket desk."

"Aren't you a ticket desk? You just offered me tickets a moment ago?"

"Only to Heathrow. I don't sell tickets into the city."

That is very confusing, but I accept his explanation, with hesitation, and follow the crowds down the hallway until it eventually opens onto a large concourse. There are shops and toilet cubicles along the sides, and an odd metal, net-like ceiling above my head. Clusters of travelers huddle in corners, holding those unsafe cardboard coffee cups and government-monitored mobile phones.

It takes me about fifteen minutes to locate another ticket desk. The one in front of me is properly signposted and other passengers hover around it. Things look more promising than at the last ticket desk.

7:18 a.m. It is getting close to my breakfast time.

The line is about as long as the one at Edinburgh station and I wonder whether employing more staff would improve this system. I'll be sure to mention it in the feedback form, assuming there will be one, which I very much hope there will as I like to share my thoughts and opinions, having worked in retail for many years now. Three, to be exact. I used to remember the months and days too, but oddly I cannot recall that right now.

"Do you remember, Mother?" I ask her.

"Next, please," calls the man behind the glass.

I step forward, glancing at my watch. I will need to get breakfast before embarking on the next leg of my journey.

"Good morning. I want to get to 16 Lansdowne Road in Notting Hill, London, England, after 7:45 a.m. It's a white house with a small driveway and some rosebushes in the front. Does that help?"

The silver-haired man behind the glass laughs, then appears to wait for me to laugh too, but I don't join in because I don't know what is funny. He slides toward me a small piece of paper display-ing an intricate map of colored lines and station names. I don't know how to read maps. I found geography difficult as a child, and Mother didn't explain this subject very well during my homeschool lessons because she also found it quite challenging, having had lim-ited overseas opportunities.

Once I'd asked her where she'd gone after she'd left me in a brown wicker basket outside Glasgow Royal Infirmary on the morn-ing of June seventeenth, when temperatures were twelve degrees with southeast winds of six miles per hour (I'd looked this up on the "Google" at work). Mother's face suddenly became all wet and splotchy. When she finally answered, she told me, "Jura. I got the boat out to Jura and worked at the pub that sat on the edge of the sea, serving whiskies to tourists and pints of beer to fishermen."

I knew to respond with a follow-up question, as follow-up ques-tions maintain a conversation, so I asked her what kind of boat it was and whether she'd seen any ocean animals, like sharks or pen-guins or eels, while on it. She didn't respond, so I deduced that those follow-up questions were not appropriate. I then asked her about the weather and plant growth on Jura, as island foliage was not an area of horticulture that I was familiar with at that time, particularly that in the Inner Hebrides. I have read up on it since and now consider myself quite knowledgeable in that area too.

Mother didn't say too much about the vegetation either and re-quested that we change the subject, which we did. I told her all about the seventy species of flowers in the daisy family. She enjoyed this conversation, and of course asked me follow-up questions.

I had considered taking the urn to Jura, but the prospect of a boat trip was concerning, which is why Mother is here with me today in London. I also assumed she'd want to come with me for the adventure. I hope she's enjoying herself so far. She certainly seems to be.

"I don't see addresses on this map?" I say to the attendant be-hind the desk, sliding the map back to him through the small gap in the glass, which has large holes to speak through. I lean in closer. "How will I know where Lansdowne Road is?" I ask through the holes.

"Do you see Notting Hill on the map?" He slides the map back to me.

All I see are lines going across, up, and down in a variety of col-ors including yellow, pink, brown, light blue, dark blue, and green. I still do not see 16 Lansdowne Road.

He reaches for the map from the gap, circles something with his pen, then slides it back. "Take the Victoria line to Brixton, change at Oxford Circus to the Central line to Ealing Broadway, then get off five stops later at Notting Hill Gate."

"Then what?"

"Then ask someone at the station where, um . . . what was the road?"

I clear my throat and repeat, "16 Lansdowne Road in Notting Hill, London, England. A white house with—"

"Yeah, yeah, ask someone there at Notting Hill Gate to help."

"Okay. Can I buy a ticket, please?"

"Swipe your bank card at the barriers to get through."

"I don't have a bank card," I say. Mother said never to give your money to a bank as they'll spend it all, then claim they're bankrupt so they don't have to pay it back. I always requested banker's drafts from work and cashed them immediately at the post office, then we hid the money in the sugar jar by the kettle. After assessing the cof-fee jar, tea jar, fridge, freezer, cutlery drawer, and the inside of a cookery book, Mother and I had decided that the sugar jar was the safest place as neither of us took sugar in our teas and coffees.

"Okay, well we're still accepting Oyster cards at most stations, so you can add some cash to that."

Oyster cards?

That sounds like a gift certificate to an expensive seafood restaurant, not a ticket for a train.

"Can I add ten pounds onto an 'oyster,' please?"

"That won't get you far in London if you're crossing zones?"

"After today, I won't be traveling much. I intend to remain in Notting Hill with my biological relatives."

I have always been good with understanding money and tallying coins and notes. I want to ensure that I have enough to last me until I can secure retail employment. Linda will give me a good reference, I'm sure of it.

"The Oyster card is a fiver itself—"

"Five pounds!"

"Which you can get back if you return it on your way back to . . . back to . . . well, wherever you came from."

"So it's like giving a pound coin to get a trolley at the supermarket? I'll get it back when I return the trolley?"

"Exactly."

"That makes sense. Okay, add ten pounds onto that," I say, handing him fifteen in total, made up of one ten-pound note and five one-pound coins. I also show him my disability card.

He picks it up and looks at me, then goes a little white. "Sorry, I maybe should have explained it a bit better," he mutters.

"I think you explained it very well." I smile. "Thank you."

He offers me a half smile in return, then types on his keyboard. "Do you want me to register you for a Disabled Persons Railcard?"

"What's that?"

"It just means you'll get a discount on off-peak travel for the underground."

"I like discounts, so yes please. And here's a tip for you to thank you for your time: the Foodhall at Marks & Spencer offers heavily discounted food items on the clearance shelves after 5:00 p.m. on a Thursday to prepare for the arrival of the weekend stock, but don't wait until closing as it will be all gone. Discounted desserts are very popular, even on a Thursday."

He smiles and nods. "Thanks, my wife will be happy to hear that."

"You're welcome."

He slides my new Oyster card over. "Don't forget to return it for your fiver."

"I won't forget," I say, before giving him a wave goodbye.

I have an extraordinarily good memory, particularly when it involves money. I have a very good memory when it comes to other things too, such as how long it takes to boil an egg before it hardens (at least eight minutes), all previous contestants on *Strictly Come Dancing* (the good ones anyway), and all the names of flowers that begin with the letter *J*, because *J* is for June and that is my name.

Jaborosa   Jacob's ladder   Jewel orchid   Japanese bellflower
Jack-in-the-pulpit   Jacaranda   *Justicia*   Jewelweed

"

Without a good hoe,
weeds can become
unmanageable,
robbing a garden of
sunlight and nutrition.

"

June and the British Transport Police

7:50 a.m.

I stand on a little bridge, balancing my blue ceramic mug of Starbucks coffee and a brown paper bag containing a half-eaten butter croissant in one hand and the underground map in the other. Mother is tucked safely inside my duffel, wrapped in a green cardigan, while the pillow and hat are cupped awkwardly under my arm. There is a set of stairs on either side of me, one going left and the other going right. I look repeatedly between them. I can't remember all the stops the nice kiosk assistant mentioned or the station names, but there was definitely something about Victoria and something about a Circus.

The map is a little damp at the edges from my clammy hands gripping it tight.

Victoria.

Circus.

There are suddenly a lot more people in the station than when I first arrived, all coming and going, and moving in different directions like during a spring clothing clearance sale, or when you come off the M8 junction at exit 18 during peak-hour traffic. Thankfully,

Mother and I never learned how to drive, so we left the road politics to the bus drivers. After a couple of horn beeps and some choice words, the bus driver eventually just swings across a lane, assuming cars will move out of the way for them. Glasgow bus drivers are very confident on the road.

I continue looking between the two sets of stairs, contemplating the left versus the right, until my temples start to throb and my shoulders begin to tense. Mother was left-handed, so I could take the left; however, because I am right-handed, perhaps I should take the right.

"What do you think, Mother?" I say loudly to her. "Left or right?"

I don't want to go through the barriers to ask the information man again as I might have to pay to come back. I also don't want to have to add more money to the Oyster card because I will be returning it very soon for my five-pound note.

Suddenly someone clips me on the elbow and I struggle to keep my grip on the coffee mug, the croissant, and the map. I end up dropping the croissant.

"Sorry," grumbles a man in a business suit darting down the stairs on the left.

People are in a hurry in London, apparently. Thankfully, the croissant has remained in the brown paper bag and can therefore still be consumed. If it had fallen out onto the tiled floor, I may have had a dilemma to figure out. I put the saved croissant in my left coat pocket and the map in my right.

"Scuse me, you a'right, Darling?"

I turn to see another man standing a meter away from me, dressed in dirty dark jeans and a brown leather jacket. He has his hands in his pockets and he's peering out at me from under a football cap. I don't know him, therefore he is a stranger. Precaution will have to be taken. I will, however, be able to tell him all my secrets since I will never see him again.

"My name's June Wilson, not Darling," I begin. He must be confusing me for someone else. "And I'm twenty-two years old and I'm from a country called Scotland. I enjoy gardening and nature shows on the television."

He snorts, then clears his throat. "Where's it you heading?" he asks, leaning in, a little too close for my comfort.

I take a polite step back. "Notting Hill, to a white house with a—"

"So you want to take the tube to Brixton, then change at, um . . . you got a map?"

I yank the map back out from my pocket to show him, forgetting I have also stored the cash in there. Fragments of blue, brown, and purple trickle through the air and land at my feet. We both stare down at the money, most of the notes still folded, scattered around my green wellies. I quickly scoop it up, clawing at each note, no doubt dragging the station's dirt and debris with me.

"Here, I'm going the same way, darling. I'll show you which stop to get off at." He gestures to the stairs on the left and I follow him, perplexed that he is still mistaking me for someone named Darling.

The platform is long and narrow and drops steeply down to a single track. In front of me is a white-tiled wall with big framed posters featuring former *Strictly Come Dancing* celebrities who are now performing in other shows. I immediately recognize Louise Redknapp. She made it to the semifinals in her season. Her tango was excellent.

When I look down, I see that there is a thick yellow line at the edge of the platform. I know that yellow means take caution or go slow, so I move away from it quickly, but the man helping me takes me by the arm and pulls me closer until my toes shuffle past the safety line. I don't like it. Mother wouldn't approve either. Yellow means take caution and this man is not being cautious.

"Is this safe?" I ask, my eyes fixed on the yellow caution line. Perhaps the safety lines are wider in London to account for human errors like this.

"You have to get close, otherwise people push on and you won't get a space," he replies, his heels on the line, his toes almost over the edge of the platform. He is a Londoner, so he must know better than me, but before I can clarify further, a train barrels out from the dark tunnel on our right, the speed shaking the ground beneath my wellies, the framed advertisements banging against the walls. Is it an earthquake? Are we in danger? The Edinburgh railway station didn't tremble and shake and screech like this. Perhaps our railways are far more advanced than England's.

A scream erupts from my lips as a slick, bottle-nosed train whizzes past us. Strands of my hair free from the headphones cupping my neck and whip around my head, slapping my face. The train finally screeches to a halt, and I'm blinded by fluorescent lights glaring through the open doors and large windows. I heave in and out, not quite sure what I have just experienced, and gaze around at the commuters who gather around the doors. They don't look remotely affected by the high-speed machine that has just flown past us with only inches of "safety distance." This yellow line is here for a good reason, and I will never stand on it or close to it again, no matter what the locals say.

We shuffle onto the terrifying high-speed train, my breath still staggered and raspy, and shimmy through the crowd to the middle, beside the metal poles. The man helping me encourages me to hold on to one. I wrap myself around a pole, hugging it as tightly as possible. Are there not seat belts on these fast-moving trains? Beside us, a little boy eats an ice cream cone, his mother holding him as she grips a pole. The big mushy scoop on his cone is pink and I want to ask him whether it is strawberry, raspberry, or cherry flavored, but then the doors beep and we start moving. I'm relieved to find that it is much calmer and slower *on* the train than it is off.

This train is different from the one that brought me to England. It's slimmer, with far fewer seats and no sleeper cabins with little bunk beds beside windows filled with images of grazing cows, green fields, and the odd cluster of sheep. And I cannot see signage for a food and drinks carriage. I smile, knowing I have now experienced two different train journeys and that makes me "well-traveled," as Linda at work calls herself after returning from her annual "girls trip" to Benidorm. When I telephone her for a reference, assuming Mr. Wilson can help me secure employment, I will tell Linda that we finally have something "in common," which she said we would never have.

The train slows and finally comes to a stop. The man shakes his head to let me know that this is not *our* stop, so I continue hugging the pole.

"Mind the gap."

I glance up at the speaker system on the train's ceiling, where I just heard a woman's voice.

"Mind the gap," it repeats.

What gap?

Am I standing close to a hole that I might fall into like in *Alice in Wonderland*, or worse, is there a hole that leads to the tracks, where I might become impaled by the moving train?

As I search the floor around me for this undetectable and badly signposted "gap" in the ground, I suddenly feel something tickling my right side. It's gentle at first, then becomes more of a heavy tug, like someone is pulling at my jacket, like something is moving inside my right coat pocket. I don't like this. I hug the pole tighter and close my eyes.

When I open them, I see the boy beside me still licking his ice cream; his mother, who is looking intently at her phone screen; a man holding a big mint-green storage bag with the word *Deliveroo* on it; and then there is the man who calls me "Darling." The stranger. He has one hand on the railing, and the other hand is . . . inside my pocket. But why? Has he lost something and for some reason thinks I have it?

I have only three items in that pocket: (1) Mother's yellow gardening gloves, in case she wants to help me in the garden, (2) the train system map, and (3) my money.

Does he want the map to check if we are going the right way?

Before I can ask him for clarification, the train slows and we stop again. The doors beep and that same message of "Mind the gap" blasts through the carriage.

Again, what gap?

Suddenly the man removes his hand, and Mother's gloves and the map fall to the floor. Now he is rushing out the door, pushing through the crowd and fleeing up the escalator. On the floor by my feet are drips of melted pink ice cream from the little boy's cone, the gloves, and the discarded train map that the nice kiosk man handed to me.

I try to bend down to retrieve the gloves and map, but passengers surge on and cram in, knocking me over. My mug is now upside down and the coffee that was once inside all over the train floor along with the boy's pink ice cream, which I still do not know the flavor of. And Mother's gloves . . . where are her gardening gloves?

I am now on my hands and knees, avoiding the spilled coffee and the pink ice cream drips, searching the train floor. My breathing is getting heavier, raspier. My chest is tightening. All I see are shoes and socks and sandals. No yellow gloves. I reach inside my right pocket to make sure the cash is still there, but my pocket is empty. The cash is gone. All of it. My fingers graze nothing but cool fabric lining.

A crime has been committed. I have been robbed. Mugged. Burgled. He's even taken my Oyster card.

How will I get through the station barriers? I will be stuck here, trapped, unable to get to Notting Hill to see my relatives. Unable to live there. I'll have to live here, in the station, among these crowds. And Mother . . . I won't get to show her London now, nor see it for myself. See all the lovely flowers and blooms that flourish here down in the south where the climate is milder and the winters are less cruel.

My fingers tremble and I throw the blue coffee mug. Mother's mug. I hear it shatter, then watch the ceramic shell roll away. Everything around me goes blurry. Passengers turn into a sea of distorted faces. The train becomes a collage of fragmented images and splintered voices.

I hear yelling. Who's yelling?

When I blink my eyes open, the silence around me is thick, filling the carriage. I am on the floor next to the broken coffee mug that now has a broken handle and rim. My duffel is beside me, still zipped up, Mother still inside. A large space has formed around me as passengers huddle at the edges, some curling up on their seats. Everyone is looking at me. The gardening gloves are on the floor beside me. Now that I finally have space, I can see them. They sit only a few inches away, so I drag them over with a foot. My toes throb. I must have kicked something. The railing perhaps. I shove the gloves back into my pocket and pop the hat back on my head, as the speaker announces again, "Mind the gap."

With that, the doors fly open and two policemen enter the carriage. One is holding a small black baton. They grip me under my armpits and begin to pull me off the train.

"That's hers too," says one of the passengers.

The policeman with the black baton grabs my duffel bag and the pillow, ignoring the half-eaten croissant beside it, the map, and Mother's broken mug.

"The mug," I say. But they do not hear me. No one does. What is left of it remains on the floor, in a pool of murky brown coffee. As I am dragged out, the duffel swings beside me on the policeman's shoulder. Mother just inches from me.

Passengers press their faces against the glass, watching me being escorted across the platform and up the escalator.

"I don't have an Oyster card," I tell the officers, but they pull me toward an emergency exit door, completely bypassing the barriers.

"Are they allowed to do that?" I ask a station attendant standing at the railings.

Plants are best transferred in the spring to allow roots to re-establish in the new ground before the arrival of summer.

June and the Backseat of the Police Car

The temperature gauge on the vehicle's dashboard reads seventeen degrees, which is three degrees lower than the expected high for today, although it's only 9:03 a.m. The sunlight through the car window warms my face and the seat around me. I slide my palm along the soft leather, stopping at all the cracks that expose slivers of the foam beneath it. Where the leather is damaged, it curls up. It is rough and jagged. I skim my fingertips over it, playing with one frayed edge as I glance around the interior. The back of a police car is not as I expected. Not that I have a lot of experience being stuffed into emergency response vehicles prior to today. I do, however, have some earlier experience riding in the back of a car that has a fully functioning child lock on the doors, meaning I couldn't exit without someone's assistance. As an adult, my car journeys have been rare. Mother did not own one, having had her license revoked.

This car is a lot smaller than I would have imagined a police car to be and smells distinctly like a fried egg, which I conclude is a correct guess as I can now see a McDonald's breakfast wrapper stuffed into the cup holder with the word *McMuffin* written on it in yellow. I am not as familiar with the popular golden-arched franchise as my work colleagues were; they often returned with those distinctive brown paper bags during lunch breaks. I wonder if every item on the menu has a "Mc" before it, like *Mc*Burger, *Mc*Fries, *Mc*Coffee.

Police Officer #1 is in the driver's seat, slowly inputting my details from the government-issued ID I've given him. I don't drive, so I don't have a license card; Mother and I never traveled, so I don't have a passport. Officer #2 won't accept my work badge as another form of identification. According to him, the little silver badge with the words HI, I'M JUNE! HOW CAN I ASSIST YOU TODAY? is an "unacceptable form of ID."

Officer #2 has a small notepad resting on his knee and scribbles on it with a blue pen. "Okay," he mutters. "June. *J-u-n-e.*"

"Is there another way to spell June?" I ask him, truly curious.

He stops writing and looks at me through the rearview mirror. "Are you being cheeky?"

"No, I would like to know if there is another way to spell June. I only know of one way. Although I suppose one could spell it with two *o*'s, as in *J-o-o-n* but that doesn't sound as good as *J-u-n-e,* don't you think? Or it could be *J-u-n,* no *e*—short for Juniper or Juno? Which do you think is better?"

"What's her last name?" he asks the other officer, who holds my ID.

"Wilson," I shout from the back to help out. "*W-i-l-s-o-n.* Although if there's another way to spell Wilson, I'd also be very interested in that too. I'm sure in your line of work you must come across many variations of first and last names. You must know them all."

Officer #1 sighs and looks over his colleague's shoulder to check the spelling himself.

"Where are you staying in London?" he asks me.

"At my biological relatives' house," I say, handing him the envelope with the address. "Robert Wilson, my relative, lives here."

Officer #1 leans into his colleague. "So, what do we do with her?" he whispers loudly. "I don't fancy writing her up at the station all morning, do you?"

"We can't just let her go."

"Shift ends in an hour. I need my bed. We've been at it all night. Let's drop her off at her relative's with a verbal warning."

Officer #1 leans back into his seat and turns around to face me. "We're only going to give you a warning at this time, okay? No more public displays like that, all right?"

I respond with a half nod, because I can't agree to something I cannot control. That's what Aileen told Mother years back—"June cannot control her emotions." That is why I took the medication. Although I never liked it. It used to make me queasy after dairy products and my feet would go numb.

"We're going to drop you off at this address and have a quick word with them, yeah?"

"Yes, that would be ideal, thank you, as I was having terrible trouble with the trains. 16 Lansdowne Road, Notting Hill. It's a white house with a small driveway, a rosebush in the front, and hopefully, fingers crossed, a very spacious and complex garden—"

"Actually, should we take her to the hospital? She might have hit her head?" says Officer #2.

"Did you hit your head?" Officer #1 shouts back at me as I sit holding the bag that contains Mother.

"No, I don't think so?"

"What's the day today?" the other one calls back.

"Monday."

"And where are you?"

"London, England." I smile. I like quizzes. I'm often very good at them, particularly ones that involve questions about flowers and plants.

"See?" #1 says to #2. "Seems fine to me. Just take her to . . . uh . . ."

"16 Lansdowne Road, Notting Hill," I repeat, wondering why accurate memory recall is not a desired skill for the police academy.

The car shudders and heaves into gear, slowly pulling away from the pavement. I turn and look back through the window, at the train station receding in the distance. Then I lean against the window, hoping to see a glimpse of London's blooms as we drive.

———

London is an odd place. A strange mixture of concrete, gravel, and asphalt, with greens, grays, and whites. Some of the streets offer more than just chipped doorways and broken fences. Green-saturated trees line uneven cobbled paths, while clusters of weeds and wildflowers sprout up from stonewall edges. Patches of grass sit beside brick townhouses and glass buildings, and birds frantically peck at marble bird feeders perched in tiny square gardens. A meager attempt at bringing the countryside to the city, but laudable nonetheless.

Everyone on the street is just as rushed as those in the train stations, vehicles pouring out of slip roads and alleyways. Sleek black taxis, red double-level buses, compact cars. They dart frantically around each other, narrowly avoiding contact, and speed down side streets and one-way roads.

A big red bus with the words *Hop On Hop Off* emblazoned on the side pulls into the lane beside us, slowing and matching our speed. I debate whether to alert Officers #1 and #2 as the red bus appears to be suspiciously following us, and given that I was victim to a crime just hours ago, I must act efficiently this time. I mentally note the license plate of the bus and continue to observe my surroundings.

9:42 a.m.: Hop-On Hop-Off bus aligns vehicle to ours

*9:43 a.m.: Hop-On Hop-Off bus turns on left indicator
but does not take the left exit*

"Left here," Officer #2 grunts to his colleague. We take a left, appropriately using our indicator, unlike the bus, which disappears behind buildings and bridges. I cease observations.

Soon the road opens up and little shops sit side by side, racks of merchandise and clothing spilling out from their open doors. Markets advertise payphone cards, pay-as-you-go mobiles, and gold trading, whatever that is. Boutique clothing stores display dresses and skirts in bright colors and bold patterns that Mother would love. The round metal tables and chairs of cafés clutter the pavements as small clusters of consumers search for the perfect place to sit. Tourists wander mindlessly with maps in their hands and cameras around their necks.

We take a right and snake down a winding road that spills out into an intersection. Officer #2 taps the GPS system on the dashboard which appears to be a map of some kind, and also has remnants of his McMuffin smeared across it..

Where we turn next, the houses are different. The gardens are a little larger than on the street where I live—*lived*—and a little neater. Pastel roses in yellow and pink pepper the pathways up to brightly colored front doors with iron knockers. I hope the Wilsons live in one of these, but then we quickly turn a corner and continue down another street where I see a dog trotting alongside its owner, carrying its own leash in its mouth. Even the animals in London act peculiar.

The morning sun is still penetrating the glass where I rest my face, and soon I feel a burning in my cheeks. The temperature sometimes deviates from the prediction in my *Gardeners Almanac,* but it is not as wildly inaccurate as a newspaper. I think it will be much warmer than twenty degrees. Early June is the perfect month for gardens. In fact, according to my *Gardeners Almanac,* "There is no better month to be a gardener than June."

Having spent a lot of time outside in the community garden and in our own, my skin has a slight tan to it even though I regularly slather on an SPF of 20 or higher. Mother said that Agnes on our street doesn't wear sunscreen and because of that she now looks like "a shriveled raisin that's got stuck at the bottom of the box and no one wants it."

I don't want to look like Agnes.

"Here we are, number 16."

A surge of excitement shoots up my spine. I love seeing gardens for the first time. I finally lift my gaze to the white brick townhouse beside us, immediately struck by how normal it looks. I know that property in general is quite small in London, based on Mother's television soaps and my gardening programs, so I knew not to have too high expectations for my new living quarters. However, I had somehow got it into my head that my biological relatives resided in some manor like in *Downton Abbey*. I can see now that this is no manor. It is just a plain old house. There are large bay windows that overlook a gravel driveway wide enough for two cars and two cars only. A thin hedge frames the house, one that needs to be tapered to improve its health, with two large but ill-maintained rosebushes on either side of a rusty metal gate. There is a second metal gate on the left side of the house with a path that snakes around the back, which I cannot see down properly due to the big blue car parked in front.

"Number 16, yeah?" checks Officer #1.

"Yes, that's correct," I confirm. "Number 16. But is this Lansdowne Road in Notting Hill?"

"Lansdowne Road, yep." He nods.

I press my nose against the window until my breath fogs the glass, making it hard to see. Something beeps and the door swings open.

Officer #2 stands in front of me. I slowly slide out, clutching my pillow and my bag with Mother inside, and follow the two officers to the metal gate. It creaks as we open it, and I can see how rusted it is close-up. It will need a little WD-40, which I did not bring with me. Underneath my wellies are stray browning leaves and dislocated moss. The rosebushes on either side of the house are dry and bristly, lacking sufficient watering and pruning. Although roses thrive best in direct sunlight, they desperately need regular moisture and access to well-drained soil. These bushes have neither.

I'm already disappointed with my new relatives' gardening knowledge, although their negligence perhaps creates a work opportunity for me.

The front door is painted a bright red, but the topcoat is flaking off around the letterbox. The bay windows are empty, void of movement and life. I can see a large living room with a sofa, an analog clock above it on the wall, an armchair, and a big widescreen television that will be perfect for watching *Strictly Come Dancing*. I am extremely relieved that they don't have a small TV, or worse, they could be the sort of people who refuse to have one in the house altogether!

Officer #2 steps up, blocking me from seeing through the other window, and thrusts his finger into a button on the side of the door. The doorbell sounds like an instrument used to wrangle escaped cattle and makes me shiver.

When the door opens, I immediately recognize the petite woman standing in the doorway from the newspaper article that Mother kept. Her hair is much blonder now but still pulled back into a small bun. She is dressed in work clothes with high black heels and a crisp white shirt that's tucked into the rim of a tight skirt that oddly gets tighter around her knees. She has the same pinched and painful expression that she had in the article. I shiver remembering how firmly she gripped the shoulder of the boy in that photo. I hope she won't try to hug me. I do not like to be hugged.

"Mrs. Wilson?" asks Officer #1.

"Yes?" she says slowly, looking very perplexed. "Is there something wrong? Is it my husband?" she squeaks, and clutches her chest quite dramatically.

Oh no, what has happened to her husband?

"Yes, hello, Mrs. Wilson. Sorry to bother you, but we got a call to come get your relative from the station at Brixton. Apparently, there was quite a display on the train, which scared a lot of the passengers. Screaming, kicking the railing—"

"Sorry?"

"I know, but you'll be relieved to know that no one was injured.

We didn't take her down to the station, but we do have to ask, does your family member have a history of this? I mean, has this happened before? You don't necessarily need to disclose this—no one is under arrest here—but perhaps she has a history of anxiety, bipolar disorder . . . substance abuse . . . ?"

Officer #1 leans in. "Maybe she forgot to take her meds this morning?"

It's been quite a few mornings actually. I assume, however, the Wilson family will organize all that for me when I move in, along with a new doctor, a new dentist, a new caseworker, and perhaps a new cognitive behavioral therapist. I'll also need a new hairdresser at some point but nothing too fancy. I don't care if it's London or not, a trim should never cost more than £12.

"Sorry, officers," begins the pinched woman, "but I've never met this girl before."

"What?"

She throws a quick look my way, then turns back to them, whispering quite loudly, "I have no idea who she is."

"You said you lived here," Officer #1 says to me.

"What?" The pinched woman glares at me like Linda at work used to when I dragged my muddy wellies into the staff room on a Monday morning.

"Well?" he prods.

The conversation is taking longer than I expected and my bag is quite heavy, especially with Mother inside. I'm not saying she's heavy—I'd hate to insult my mother—but she does add quite a bit of weight overall to the duffel. I gently lower the bag to my feet, careful not to smash her, and straighten up. "I don't live here," I clarify to the officers, then turn to the woman still standing at the door, now with her hands on her hips. "Can I please enter to inspect your garden space before I make a decision?"

A composition of
yellow flowers can
be a great way to
greet guests as it is the
color of friendship.

June and the Tiny Porcelain Houses and Tiny Sugar Cubes

Tiny porcelain houses with tiny porcelain doors and tiny porcelain windows perch on narrow wooden shelves above our heads. On one house, a robin nestles inside the chimney, its head poking out, while another has a little boy with brown hair standing at the window. I count eight houses in total. Three above Officer #1's head, two above mine, and three above Mrs. Wilson's head. She delicately balances a teacup and saucer on her knee, mumbling under her breath. Occasionally she checks her watch, then her phone, which sits on the arm of her chair.

In front of me is a small wooden side table with tea in a teapot, milk in a jug, and sugar in a bowl. I've never had tea like this before. At home, we always had tea straight from the kettle. And our milk came from the carton in the fridge door, assuming it was still within date.

I reach for the pot and cradle it, craving some warmth. I often wear gardening gloves, so on the days I don't have them on I tend to feel the cold in my fingers more. The teapot is comforting like the fluffy yellow hot-water bottle Mother used to make for chillier evenings spent on the sofa watching winter nature shows, like *Festive*

Florals in Devonshire. At bedtime, she'd refill it with freshly boiled water and place it under my duvet. After my bath, I'd climb into bed and search for the warmth. I often slept with the hot-water bottle resting on my feet, waking in the morning to find it cold or discarded on the floor close by.

Suddenly the teapot feels very hot, scalding my thighs through the linen of my capri trousers, and I immediately stand up with a sharp squeal, letting the teapot drop to the floor. It doesn't break, thankfully, but a trickle of tea pours out the spout onto the beige rug.

Mrs. Wilson springs from her seat, leaving the faintest indent in the chair cushion where she sat, and rushes to my feet. She doesn't ask if I am okay; she simply picks up the teapot and puts it back on the tray, tutting loudly. She pauses for a moment, staring at the rug, and I wonder if she's dropped something. I crouch down and stare at the rug with her.

"Hot," I briefly clarify. Then I rub the tea stain into the carpet with my palm. My hand is now damp, so I drag it across the front of my cardigan and sit back down. Mrs. Wilson slowly turns to me, her mouth agape. The carpet stain has now become larger. I appear to have spread it, rather than eliminated it. It will dry. I gaze up at her and smile. Face still ashen, she walks slowly back to her chair.

"Is your husband far away?" asks Officer #2, also checking his watch.

"God, I hope not," she mumbles, glancing up at me.

"London traffic, eh?" Officer #1 shrugs, then stuffs a second chocolate digestive in his mouth. He reaches for a third, but this time he dunks it in his tea. I sit up, straining to see what happens to the biscuit. Will it go all mushy, or will just the top chocolate layer melt?

"Shall I pour you some tea?" Mrs. Wilson asks me, her face even more pinched.

I forgot entirely about the tea after the teapot incident. I reach for the teapot again, feeling her eyes on me, and carefully pour myself a cup. Then I add a splash of milk.

"Sugar?" she asks.

Do I take sugar? I suddenly can't remember.

"There's a spoon for it," she continues, pointing to the sugar bowl.

I lift it up and open the delicate little lid. It's so light that I'm afraid I might break it. Inside is not what I expected. "Why is the sugar in tiny squares?" I ask her, prodding the metal tip of the spoon into the mound of white sugar, crushing some of the edges.

"They're sugar cubes."

"Cubes? Did you cut them like that? If so, how do you make the sugar stick together?"

"No, I bought them like that."

"Really?"

"Yes." She sighs, checking her phone again.

"From where?"

"Marks & Spencer."

"Oh, lovely. That's where I work."

"That's nice," she mutters, gazing at the door behind her.

"I unpack cardboard boxes that come from the warehouse down south—although I guess I'm down south now—and I place the items from the boxes onto the shelves in the Foodhall."

"That's nice," she says again, still not giving me eye contact.

"I also clean up the aisles if anyone spills anything—sometimes there's the odd milk or juice that's leaking—and if I don't say anything 'untoward' to the customers, my supervisor allows me to stand at the self-checkout counter." I go back to prodding at the sugar, still wondering whether I usually take my tea with sugar. It was only yesterday that I last had tea. How could I have forgotten?

I suppose I could have one teaspoon, as that seems average. But does that equate to one cube? No, perhaps I should have half a teaspoon, just in case I'm not allowed to have sugar in my tea. "What do you think?" I ask Mother, who hides in the duffel by my feet. Mother doesn't answer, but the pinched-face lady, Mrs. Wilson, does.

"What do I think about what?"

I have decided; I will have half a teaspoon. "Can I have a knife?"

"Pardon me?" she says, her eyes widening.

"A *sharp* knife."

"Um, no, I don't think that's a good idea," she says, looking over at the two officers.

I'll just have to halve a sugar cube without a knife, then. I try first to cut the cube, but it pings off my spoon and lands on the rug near the tea stain, so then I pick one up and bite it. I spit the first half back into the sugar bowl and the other half into my cup.

Mrs. Wilson makes an odd squeaking sound and her face goes very pale.

The door suddenly swings open, hitting the hallway wall. "Judith!" cries a deep voice.

"About time, Robert. We're in here," calls out the woman, rubbing her forehead.

"Judith, what the bloody hell is going on and why is there a police car outside—" He stops at the living room door, glancing between me and the officers.

He wears a tailored navy suit; a crisp white shirt matching the lady's strikingly white teeth; and a pair of very black, very shiny loafers. His shoulders are broader than in the photo, his face is a little older, and his belly is a little rounder. His hair is graying, although it's hard to tell because it's quite fair, which must hide the gray better. This relative looks more like me. I can see now that we are definitely related. He has the same faint spattering of freckles across the bridge of the nose and cheeks, and I wonder if the sun intensifies them, like it does to mine. His eyes are different, though: dark and shiny like black marbles. Eyes that are now fixed on me. "What's going on here?" he says again. "Who's this?"

Mrs. Wilson stands. "This girl is saying she's your *relative* from Glasgow," she scoffs. "The policemen kindly escorted her from the train station where she was detained to here, *our home.*"

He looks at me, then at the lady, then at the policemen. He clears his throat. "I have no idea who she is. I don't have any relatives in Scotland anymore, not since Auntie Anne died, you know that. And Auntie Anne didn't have any children."

The policemen both stand. "Mr. Wilson, she gave us this address and said—"

"I don't care what she's saying. I'm telling you I don't know who she is. Now, if she's under arrest for something, then she's clearly dangerous. Please remove her from my house before I call your supervisor."

They're all standing and yelling, each getting louder than the next until no one can be heard over the clatter. I lean back in my armchair and start dunking a chocolate digestive into the tea. It doesn't disintegrate after all, or go mushy. In fact, the chocolate top melts into the tea perfectly. What a great idea.

"Excuse me?" Mrs. Wilson waves at me, trying to get my attention like those annoying shoppers at my work who always have questions. "Who exactly are you related to?"

"Catherine Wilson," I say, dunking my biscuit again. This time I linger and am most disappointed to find that when I pull it out, half of it has dissolved in the tea. I gaze back at the group still huddled together in the middle of the room.

Mr. Wilson has gone very white. His mouth is open and he looks frightened.

I squint at my teacup. No, I don't think I do take sugar in my tea.

"

Keep in mind, the tighter the garden space, the more encouraged wildlife will be to visit.

"

June and Mr. Wilson

We sit outside the house watching the policemen drive away, Mrs. Wilson—not the Mrs. Wilson that is my mother but another one—stays inside, in the living room, hovering near the window, staring at us. We sit side by side on the doorstep, gazing out past the rosebushes and the rusted gate to the street lined with dawn redwoods and cherry trees with pink blossoms. He is still very white.

After a heated back-and-forth between the officers and my relatives of 16 Lansdowne Road, it was finally decided that no further actions would be taken with regard to the "train station incident," the policemen having concluded that it is a "family matter."

Family.

A word that has always sounded very strange to me. I had looked it up once in a dictionary, which defined it as "descendants of a common ancestor." I am still unable to ascertain who this common ancestor of ours is.

I wonder how similar we are, being that we're "family." Perhaps Mr. Wilson too enjoys gardening, although judging by the front of the house, that's unlikely. But maybe he likes cheese sandwiches, tea with no sugar, and television shows about contestants dancing for the chance to win a glitter disco ball trophy.

Mr. Wilson leans back and slumps against the bright red door, which flakes paint onto the shoulders of his tailored suit. I am quite tired from my journey and from the scene on the train, and I'm feeling all sorts of funny sensations through my body after ingesting a cup of tea with half a sugar and a chocolate digestive. So I slump back with him, maintaining as much space between us as possible. Mother is still safely tucked inside my duffel bag, nestled between my clothes and books and gardening socks. I haven't yet reacquainted her with her relatives.

I'm not sure why Mr. Wilson and I are sitting outside the house instead of inside the house. I'd hoped to have unpacked already, or at the very least been shown to my room. Like I said, I am quite tired.

I have by this point observed some "red flags" with this new living situation. First is the state of the front garden. What kind of people are they to leave rosebushes languishing like this? Thankfully, I can remedy these mistakes, although it will take most of the summer and I haven't even seen around the back yet. Goodness knows what that looks like. Second, those porcelain houses have to go or be moved to another room. I can't have strange porcelain houses with strange porcelain children and porcelain birds staring down at me while I watch television. I'm all for a hobby, but collecting small porcelain people is very odd.

The third red flag is the most disappointing. Upon rising from my seat and following the officers and Mr. Wilson out of the house, I found myself to be completely covered in yellow fluffy hairs, which means only one thing—the dog in the photo from the newspaper cutout is still alive. I absolutely cannot live with a dog, or an animal of any kind, and that includes fish. The dog will simply have to be rehomed.

It isn't that I hate animals. In fact, wildlife is intrinsic to our eco-system. Beavers create dams, which in turn can change the water flow, helping to spread nutrients to surrounding plant systems. Birds control the insect population, which maintains soil health and re-duces tree diseases. But, rather simply, animals are not meant to be kept inside. Inside, they're unpredictable, unclean, unregulated. At my last foster home, before Mother returned from her travels, the dog bit me. The children had been chasing it, teasing it, pulling its tail. I, however, had been sitting on the floor, alone, reading a book. The dog had become restless, unsettled, and had reacted suddenly, snapping at whoever was closest, which happened to be me. I didn't need stitches in the end, but the incident left me uneasy around ani-mals. Thankfully, Mother was also not a fan of dogs, having been chased one too many times on her postal routes with the Royal Mail, when she wasn't delegated to the sorting offices.

Humans are quite fond of animals, dogs in particular. I will need to approach the rehoming conversation with caution and dis-cretion.

Mrs. Wilson begins tapping on the living room window, trying desperately to get her husband's attention. He weakly waves her away and rubs his forehead. "Sorry . . . I, um . . . ," he says eventually. Then he sighs deeply. "It's all just such a shock."

"My name is June Wilson, and I believe we are all related—"

"I know who you are," he interrupts. "You look just like her. Ex-actly like her. It's like seeing a ghost."

I wonder if that's a figure of speech or whether he does know that Mother is no longer physically with us, her ashes having been squeezed into my "weekend getaway" bag. I don't like "figures of speech." Aside from simple comparisons that use "like" or "as," I find modern expressions quite confusing, especially idioms and meta-phors; phrases that have two meanings: a literal one and a figura-tive one.

It's raining cats and dogs.
   She's as happy as a clam.
      I'll be as good as gold.
         He's a night owl.
            That was a piece of cake.

Why can't people just say exactly what they mean? Why bundle the meaning into a metaphor or a simile, making it hard for some people, like me, to decipher? Perhaps if we all just spoke clearly and plainly, the world would be a much simpler place.

"You know, I had a feeling you existed," Mr. Wilson continues. "But your mother was adamant that she wasn't pregnant and had never been. Then she just disappeared. I didn't know where she'd gone. Didn't even know she was still alive after all these years."

"Jura," I answer. "She went to Jura."

"Jura," he repeats slowly.

Mrs. Wilson taps again.

"Listen, June. My wife and son don't know I have a daughter—"

"Daughter?" I repeat. It suddenly all makes sense. Mr. Wilson is more than a biological relative. Mr. Wilson is my biological *father.*

Father. Now, that's a strange word. Do I call him that now?

And if Robert Wilson is my father, then the child in the photo might very well be my half brother. *Half brother.* Half of a brother. A brother that's been halved. Not in the physical sense, of course, because that would hurt.

Mr. Wilson continues, "Actually, they don't know anything about that part of my life, and I'd like to keep it that way for now. Just for a little bit. Things have been . . . difficult for us recently and this would be tough for my wife to understand. Are you staying in London, or will you be going back to Glasgow?"

"I was planning to stay."

"And your mother?"

I glance down at my bag. "She's here with me."

"Great." He sighs. "That's great. I was worried that you were here alone. Well, look, why don't I flag down a cab for you and you can go back to your mother for now and we can keep chatting over the summer and see where things go."

The tapping gets louder, more insistent.

"I need to handle this carefully," he adds.

"Okay." I stand up and delicately carry my bag to the front gate, not wanting to bump Mother around and upset her. We have a lot to talk about.

"Let's exchange numbers so we can keep in touch."

"I don't have a mobile phone."

"Oh. Really? I thought everyone did these days," he says. "Okay, well, here's my business card. Call me and we'll arrange something."

He steps out onto the street and waves furiously at a black cab passing by. It stops abruptly, the light on the top turning off.

"I don't have money anymore," I blurt out, staring at the black taxi, with its engine churning and pounding.

"Yes, no problem," he mutters, pulling out a silver money clip laden with notes.

"Where to, darling?" calls out the cabdriver.

Oh no, he's also calling me Darling. Will he rob me too?

"Where are you staying?" Mr. Wilson asks me.

"Um . . . I don't know." I want to say "Here," but that doesn't seem like an option anymore.

"You've not booked into a hotel yet?"

I shake my head, my cheeks flushing. Why can't I stay here?

"I know this great hotel that I think you and your mother will be comfortable at. It's got a pool."

"I don't like water."

"Well, I'm sure there's a sauna or steam room instead."

He begins ushering me into the taxi and I stumble, hit my head on the low roof and fall back into the seat. The cracked leather is warm from the sun.

"The Landmark hotel on Marylebone, please," he says to the taxi driver. Then he stuffs a bunch of notes into my hands. A couple fall by my feet and as I reach down for them, he slams the car door. The taxi pulls away abruptly, and I fall back against the seat again. With the money squashed in my sweaty palms, I turn and stare at Mr. Wilson waving to me from outside the white-brick townhouse on the street lined with dawn redwoods and cherry trees.

I have a father.

I've never had one of those before.

London has become very biodiverse, with thousands of plant species now recorded across the city.

June and the Big Fancy London Hotel

There are two entrances to the hotel and a man in a uniform with a long black coat appears to be waiting for me to choose one.

I have seen this on the television before—the theory of "tipping." Giving someone money on top of the money that you have already agreed on. But an amount isn't specified, and Linda at work told me it is calculated using percentages. I am slightly familiar with the mathematical concept from charts in my almanac and forecasts. For example, there is a 10 percent chance of rain predicted for tomorrow. Humidity will increase over the course of the summer, potentially getting to levels of 95 percent during peak heat. The issue I have is how to calculate a percentage from zero. For example, in this particular situation, entering the hotel is free; however, if the man in the uniform with the long black coat opens the door for me, thus making my entrance easier and more convenient, then I will be expected to tip him. But how much?

This is not a social situation that Mother and I rehearsed; therefore, I shall do my best to avoid tipping him altogether. And that goes for all tipping situations. At least until Mr. Wilson can participate in role-playing games. Mother and I spent a lot of time doing this before I started looking for employment. She often played the role of the customer and I was the shop assistant. Sometimes she'd ask me to direct her to the dairy aisle; other times she'd ask for a vegetable recommendation (baby potatoes for fish, Chantenay carrots for chicken, Broccolini with beef). And we did this until my responses were, as she put it, "socially appropriate."

The man in the uniform gestures to the door beside him, marked Entrance. I slowly inch up the stairs, one step at a time. He opens the door fully and smiles at me, but instead, I head for the door that is marked Exit. The man in the uniform tries to stop me, but I rush through, spilling out into the lobby beyond. Technically, I have not broken any rules. I was *exiting* the street and *entering* the hotel. I did, however, successfully avoid having to calculate a tip.

The lobby is larger than I expected, but I've only ever seen the interiors of hotels in films and on television. The floor is made of white marble, and white draped silk curtains cover the walls. Fairy lights twist and coil around marble pillars that sprout up from the floor like sunflowers. In the center of the lobby is a large dining area that is both inside and outside with garden furniture, patio tables, and a patch of Astroturf. And palm trees. Real palm trees. I have never seen anything like it before. Palm trees are native to warmer climates. I'm curious as to how they grow and thrive here in chilly England, in a hotel lobby.

I shuffle over to one in a large pot beside a couple who sip pink wine from large glasses, and place my hands on the trunk. It's rough but smooth at the same time. I tip my head back and gaze up to the top, following the rough bark up to the large leafy green palms. I imagine this is what traveling to an exotic country is like. I've always wanted to know whether I could wrap my arms around the trunk of a palm tree, so I do, and I can. How strange, and yet delightful.

A man coughs behind me. "Checking in?"

I drop my hands from the tree and turn around. "Yes, I believe I am."

"Great, just follow me. May I take your bag?"

"No, thank you. It belongs to me. I paid for it in TK Maxx last week," I reply.

He grins ever so slightly and leads me to a front desk, where a short woman with curly hair and green-rimmed glasses also wears a smile. Everyone here smiles a lot. This isn't at all like my staff room, especially on a Monday morning.

"Good morning, welcome to the Landmark hotel. Checking in?"

"Yes, I think I am meant to be doing that." But I can't remember why? Did Mr. Wilson say why?

"Name, please."

Why does she want my name?

"June Tabitha Wilson."

"Wilson . . ." She taps away at her computer. "I don't have any-thing under a Wilson for today. Would you have made the reserva-tion in another name?"

"Oh, I don't have a reservation, but I think I'm supposed to live here until the Wilsons are ready for me to move in. Is there a bed-room for me?"

"I'll see what's available. Any preferences?"

"One with a bed, please."

"Of course." She grins. "I mean, would you prefer a room with a view?"

"I suppose a view of a garden space would be nice. But please no view of the river. I'm scared of water."

She nods.

"And if it's not too much work for you, then perhaps one that's located fairly close to an emergency exit in case a situation arises in which I need to depart immediately."

She nods again.

"And one with a good-sized window to ensure adequate lighting for reading in the mornings." What else should I ask for? What else would make my stay here resemble living at home with Mother?

"And a toilet, please," I add.

She smiles at me again. She appears to like me. Perhaps she will be my first friend here in London. "Firstly, all our bedrooms come with private bathroom and shower facilities."

"Excellent."

"And I can check if we have a room beside the emergency stairs or one near an elevator—"

"Emergency stairs, please. If there's a fire, the elevator won't work. I learned that during Linda's fire drill."

"We have a room with a lovely view of Regent's Park from the top floor, or I can offer you one with a partial view that's also close to the stairs."

"Okay."

"Which would you prefer?"

A choice. Mother taught me this one well. "Choice A, please."

She nods and taps on her keyboard. "Would you like breakfast?"

I look at my watch. "No, thank you. It's almost lunchtime."

"I mean breakfast for tomorrow morning. Would you like me to add breakfast to your room rate?"

"What about my lunch for today?"

"We have an excellent restaurant on-site."

"Will they have sandwiches?"

"I'm sure the chef can do something for you." She smiles. "Now, what about breakfast for tomorrow?"

"What is for breakfast tomorrow?"

"We offer a full buffet."

"What's in this buffet?"

"Everything."

"Will there be coffee?"

"Yes."

"Orange juice without the bits in it?"

"Yes."

"Toast?"

"Yes."

"*Real* butter?"

"Yes."

"A toaster, a plate, and a knife?"

"Yes, yes, and yes." She giggles.

"Croissants? They are usually a treat, but I suppose being here in London is a treat. And finding out I have a biological father is a treat."

She frowns, then presses a smile back onto her face. "Yes to the croissants."

"Perfect."

"Breakfast is £25.95, but I can add it to your room rate."

"Pardon?"

"I can add it to your room rate," she repeats.

"It's how much?" I gasp.

"£25.95."

I take a sharp inhale and feel my chest tighten slightly. *£25.95?* Is the coffee being imported from Brazil? Does the orange juice have gold flakes in it? What warrants such an expensive first meal of the day? In Marks & Spencer, a loaf of bread is £1.10, a pint of orange juice is £1.60, and 250g of butter is £1.95. And that does the average person at least five days of breakfasts.

"No, no breakfast, thank you," I whisper, shaking my head.

She nods and types on her computer. "I just need a credit card for incidentals and deposit."

"I don't have one."

"Oh."

"I just have the cash that Mr. Wilson gave me?" I say, showing her the notes.

"Well, we can't keep banknotes behind the front desk. We'll need a card to keep on file."

"Oh," I reply, gathering the cash up. "I guess I will return to Notting Hill and let Mr. Wilson know."

"Do you have a number for Mr. Wilson? Perhaps I can call him and take his bank details over the phone?"

"That's a good idea." I slide his business card across the counter to her.

"I'll just be a moment." She disappears with his card into a small room behind the check-in desk. Beside me is a small ceramic pot with a single lily. I don't need to touch it to know that it is artificial. A real lily exudes a heady, rich scent, not too different from jasmine or gardenia. Or cat urine.

I doodle invisible lilies on the glass counter with my finger while I wait for the receptionist to return. When she does, she slides the business card back to me. "You are all set. Here is your room key. I wish you a pleasant stay with us."

I stare at the small cardboard envelope in her hand. How does a key fit in there? I open my mouth to ask her, but the man in the uniform who had been waiting for me at the entrance is suddenly standing beside me. I stare back at him. Is he here for his tip? He didn't open the door. I opened my own.

"Here, allow me, miss," he says, reaching for my bag.

"No, thank you," I quickly reply. He takes it from the floor any-way and I see the outline of the urn against the fabric. Mother won't like to be handled by a stranger, and certainly not by a strange man. I try to take the bag back, but he pulls away. I lunge for it, grabbing the handle, and we struggle for a few moments before the woman behind the desk coughs and the man in uniform lets go. I finally re-gain control of the bag and Mother, and quickly head for the elevator. I look over my shoulder to see the man in the uniform frowning. I think that's his expression, which means he's experiencing the emo-tion of sadness, anger, hunger, or confusion.

Thankfully, the elevator is straightforward. I am going to be sleep-ing twelve floors up from the lobby. I've only ever slept one floor up. This will be a first for Mother and me, unless Mother slept some-where higher when she was on the island of Jura.

By the time the elevator reaches my floor, I can feel the sugar cube and the chocolate digestive from earlier floating through my stomach.

The hallway splits off into two directions. Rooms 1201–1254 to the left and 1255–1287 to the right. I have been given a key for room 1209, so I take the left hallway, past an ice machine and a locked storage cabinet. At 1209, I carefully lay Mother down on the gray carpeted floor and open the cardboard envelope. But there is no key inside, only a card with a single black stripe up one side. I shake the envelope out, expecting the key to fall to the floor. But the envelope is empty except for this card. How do I unlock a wooden door with a piece of plastic?

I slide the plastic card into what looks like a slot in the door, but it turns out to be just a shadow. So I try to "jimmy" the door like I saw on one of Mother's television programs, but the plastic bends and almost snaps. I also try knocking, in case the man in the uniform is waiting for me on the other side. If so, perhaps he can let me in too. I'd happily attempt to calculate a tip for that gesture. But the door is still locked and Mother still sits on the gray carpet outside. Defeated, I collapse beside her and rest my head against the door. Maybe I should look for a room attendant to help me or return to 16 Lansdowne Road in Notting Hill to ask Mr. Wilson.

"Locked out?"

A thin woman wearing a blue apron stands at the other end of the hallway, beside a trolley piled with white towels and toilet rolls. She looks like Mary, our cleaner at work who used to come in before my shift ended on Thursdays. I liked Mary. She was kind to me and always asked me how Mother and I were doing. Sometimes she gave me a banana off the shelf for my bus ride home so I didn't get "peckish." I was sad when she was fired for telling Linda to "fuck off back to England."

"Are you locked out, miss?" she asks again.

"I guess so, although I was never really inside to begin with."

"Is your key not working?"

I hold up the plastic card and envelope. "I didn't get a key. This is all they gave me."

"That's your key right there," she says, walking over. "May I?"

I nod and hand her everything the woman at the desk had given me, including a ballpoint pen. She taps the top of the card to the black box beneath the handle and a green light flickers. Then I hear a click. She thrusts the door open with her hip. "There you are."

I clamber to my feet and gaze at the black box. I hadn't considered swiping at it like when using the contactless payment option at a checkout, or like the train station barriers. It makes sense now, especially that black stripe down the edge. As the towel trolley clangs and squeaks back down the hallway, I wave goodbye and slowly enter room 1209.

It's a single room—specifically a bedroom. There is a toilet, as requested, but other than that it is *one* room. There is no living room or kitchen, no stairs or hallway cupboard to store extra shoes and coats in, and definitely no garden, not this high up, anyway. But there are huge windows that overlook a park, and if I press my face against the glass, I can just about make out the Indian bean trees at the entrance. Otherwise known as cigar trees, they're named after the long cylindrical pods that hang off the branches like little silver clusters of beans.

The room is bigger than my bedroom at home, and *very* white. White bedsheets, white pillows, white walls, a white-rimmed clock, and a white desk with a white chair. Even the toilet is white—white towels, white soap, and a white vase with a single white calla lily that again is artificial.

A chime from my watch tells me it's 11:45 a.m. I place Mother on the white table beside the window so she can also see the Indian bean trees, and then pick up the receiver to call the front desk.

"Front desk, how may I assist you?" coos a female voice down the phone.

"Hello, this is June Wilson. I am in room 1209 overlooking Regent's Park. The lady at the front desk mentioned there were lunch options here, where would I find them?"

"Well, our restaurant opens at midday and offers a wonderful two-course set menu for only £35.50."

"Midday is far too late. By the time I'm seated and order, lunch will arrive far behind schedule." There's a pause. "I eat at exactly midday," I add.

"Room service is already open. Would you like me to connect you?"

"What's room service?"

"It's a food service that gets delivered to your room."

"Lunch comes to me? I don't need to leave the room at all?"

"That is correct."

"Like a takeaway?"

"Yes."

"Excellent."

"I'll connect you now."

A few seconds later, the phone rings again and a man picks up. "Hello, room service?"

"Hello, I would like to order lunch."

"Yes, what would you like?"

"A cheese sandwich on white bread with real butter and the crusts cut off."

"We only have the chicken club sandwich or the spicy Halloumi sandwich on the menu, I'm afraid."

"I don't know what either of those are."

"Well, the chicken club is sliced roasted chicken, smoked bacon, cheese—"

"Do you use real butter or margarine?"

"We have both."

"White or brown bread?"

"Again, both."

"So you have cheese, white bread, and real butter. Do you have a knife to slice the crusts off?"

"Yes," he laughs. "I will talk to the chef and see what we can do."

"Lovely, thank you. How long?"

"Thirty minutes."

"Oh," I mutter, glancing at my watch and Mother. I want to ask her what I should do.

"We will try to get it to you as soon as possible, miss."

"Thank you," I sigh. "It's room 1209, in front of the park with the Indian bean trees. Knock three times so I will know it's you and not a stranger trying to rob me again."

"Will do. Bye."

"Goodbye."

After I've paced the room several times, my sandwich arrives at exactly 12:04 p.m., later than I've ever eaten lunch before. I answer the door red-faced and panicky and quickly grab the plate off the silver cart. I don't know if the person in the uniform is expecting a tip for bringing it up to me, but I don't have time to calculate the percentage as I'm already so far off routine.

There's salad on the plate.

I open the door to call the man back, but he and his silver cart have disappeared, much to my dismay.

I sit for another minute on the edge of the bed staring at the white plate of sandwich, crisps, and salad, unsure of what to do next. I glance over to the desk by the window and wonder what Mother would do, aside from order a large glass of red wine. "What do you think, Mother?"

I nod. "Good idea."

I bring the plate to the toilet and scrape the salad into the bin under the sink. Then I rearrange the sandwich and crisps as if the salad had never been there in the first place, return to the room, and eat my lunch by the window while admiring the Indian bean trees.

"

Indian bean trees grow ovate heart-shaped leaves that gradually reduce in size as the tree matures.

"

June and the Search for Dinner

At exactly five o'clock, Mother and I go downstairs in search of dinner, which I'm worried will be a difficult undertaking in a place like London. But we always eat at six o'clock. Although now I can't remember why that is. Which of us chose that time? It must have been me. Mother was always much calmer about mealtimes, never needing the same reassurance that it would be served at a specified time. I wonder what time Mother would have eaten, had it not been for me, had she lived alone in that two-bedroom semi-detached house on Hathaway Lane in Maryhill, exactly 240 yards from the Greek restaurant we never ate at? Perhaps she would have been a late eater, grazing through the evening, then sitting down to a larger meal when most people were getting ready for bed. Maybe she would have eaten by candlelight, in her dressing gown, with the 10:30 p.m. news on in the background.

I suppose I shall never know now.

The hotel lobby is busy when the lift doors open, bustling with guests coming and going, some towing heavy suitcases on wheels and small children by the hand. It looks like a train station; a few people even carry cardboard coffee cups. I see the man in the uniform by the check-in desk, assisting a family with their luggage, likely receiving a tip at the end. I wait for a few moments to observe the tipping, but he places their bags on a silver cart and wheels it over to the elevators. There is no tipping taking place, so I leave. Sourcing dinner is far more important.

Outside, the air is mild and a soft breeze flows through my hair, which is becoming wild and unruly like stinging nettle in the late spring. I prefer my hair to rest on the shoulders, not so long that I have to style it but not so short that I cannot style it. Mother had long hair, all the way down to her waist, a rich auburn hue like a Japanese maple tree, not a dull shade like mine. She kept her hair loose, allowing it to blanket her shoulders and arms. Had she worked in a Foodhall, she would have been required to keep it tied back, like I was. Apparently, no one wants a stray human hair in among the loose apples.

I cradle Mother in my arms, and cross over to the park that I can see from my bedroom window. The Indian bean trees are even more magnificent in person. They're gathered at the entrance by the gates, then dotted around the park, lining the paths. I do not think I have seen so many Indian bean trees in one location before. How fascinating.

My ability to appreciate them is short-lived as all around me noise is pounding my ears—traffic, conversation threads, laughter, music from a car that idles at a red traffic light.

It's too loud.

When I open my eyes, I'm sitting cross-legged on the grass under a tree, Mother in my lap. I remove my headphones from my coat pocket and slip them onto my head, cupping my ears. The world is finally lulled into a perfect state of quietude. I breathe deeply in the silence. With Mother in my arms, I cross through the park to the busy streets beyond.

5:07 p.m.

I see a lit neon sign advertising "the best sushi in London," but Mother and I don't eat fish or food that's been rolled up in any way. There is an array of American burger places, pizzerias, Indian restaurants, Chinese takeaways, and Italian taverns; however, I do not see somewhere to get my usual dinner—chicken and potatoes. I carry on walking, my footsteps silent on the tarmac beneath me, the sounds of the city still dulled with my headphones.

5:18 p.m.

I pass shop owners locking doors and pulling metal shutters down, and restaurants whose signs list specials and deals like "£5 Cocktails" and "Kids Eat Free." I wish I were a kid, then I could eat a free dinner.

5:25 p.m.

Plants beginning with the letter S trail across my mind as I rattle off as many as I can recall.

Salix

   Salvia

      Sambucus

         Sage

5:32 p.m.

I have somehow returned to the same street where I started. And I am still hungry.

The man in the uniform is back at his usual post and stands outside the entrance, his gloved hand ready to yank the door open for guests. He watches me approach, smiles, and gestures to the door, but I don't ascend the stairs. Instead, I sit down on the bottom step. I wrap my raincoat around Mother in case she's cold, and check my watch again: 5:35 p.m.

Dinner will be late now, for the second time in my life. My breath gets stuck in my chest, like a blockage. My heart thumps loudly in my ears. All the worries from today—getting robbed, being escorted off the train by two policemen, meeting Mr. Wilson, navigating a hotel check-in—fade away, and all that remains is the pressing concern that today Mother and I will not eat dinner at our usual time. That our days are becoming different.

I feel a hand on me, a hand that isn't Mother's. I brush it off and swing around, knocking my headphones to the ground.

"I'm sorry, I didn't mean to startle you," stammers the man from the hotel entrance. I don't say anything. I don't know if I can. The words are also stuck in my chest, coiling and twisting around my rib cage.

What time is it?

Where's Mother?

I glance around for her, panic building, then feel a heaviness at my chest, inside my raincoat. She's here, she's with me. But what time is it?

"Are you okay, miss?" he asks.

"No," I say flatly. "It's almost dinnertime, and I can't find anywhere to eat."

"London has the best restaurants in the world." He smiles.

"No, it doesn't," I argue, the warm sensation of anger tickling my insides.

"Well, have you tried our restaurant inside the hotel? It's excellent."

I sigh. "I doubt they'll have what I'm looking for. It was hard enough to get a plain cheese sandwich this afternoon."

"What exactly do you want?"

"Chicken."

"Chicken?"

"Like a chicken Kiev, or any kind of breaded chicken, with potatoes. Maybe a few carrots, but definitely no sauce or seasonings."

"I'm sure they'll be able to do something like that for you."

"Really?"

"Yes, I'd imagine so."

"Are you sure?" I ask him again, rising to follow him.

"Yes," he says again, walking up to the door. He holds it open for me. "In fact, I'll come with you and I'll ask the host myself."

———

At exactly 6:00 p.m., I sit at a white-clothed table by a window, gazing out at the Indian bean trees and all the Londoners walking through the park, while eating a dinner of chicken, potatoes, and carrots as Mother sits opposite me with a glass of Chianti.

Foxes are becoming more common in London than in the countryside, and may be attracted to your garden.

June and the Hotel Break-In

Room service is an odd concept. Food is brought up from the kitchen to your bedroom, completely free of charge. All they ask of you is to sign your name on a piece of paper, like a celebrity signing an autograph. I don't understand how establishments like these make any money, although that's perhaps why rooms here are so expensive—to offset all the free meals. Today I ordered breakfast and despite the exorbitant cost I had been quoted downstairs upon check-in, this breakfast was apparently free. All it required was my signature.

Mother and I didn't have much need to practice signatures as we didn't often sign our names—we didn't have phone contracts or bank accounts, write checks, complete passport applications. But sometimes, when work was very dull in the warehouse and I had been removed from the shop floor because of another customer complaint, I practiced writing my name over and over again. Each time twirling, looping, or crossing the letters in a slightly different way, as I pondered the best signature to represent my personality.

June Wilson   June T. Wilson   J. Wilson   JT Wilson

Nowadays I prefer to doodle florals and vines rather than letters and a name that I now partially share with some strangers in Notting Hill.

After breakfast, I call the number on Mr. Wilson's business card; however, a woman answers. When I ask her if she's Mrs. Wilson from the day before, she giggles and says, "No, my name is Chloe. I'm Robert's personal assistant." When I ask her if Mr. Wilson is available to talk with me, she tells me that he is in a meeting with a client and will call me back. I don't have a number to give her for the callback, so I tell her I will try again at another time. I call an hour later, but he is in another meeting. I try again after that. Mr. Wilson is a very busy man, it seems. Building a caregiver relationship with him will be challenging.

After lunch, I walk through the gardens again, this time delicately picking a bunch of bluebells to brighten up my hotel room because white is a canvas, not a color. Almost half of the world's bluebells grow in the UK. They are a rare flower in other countries and other climates. I use my gardening gloves and snip them cleanly, to simulate regrowth. It's very important not to damage the stems or roots when cutting flowers. I arrange them in a glass goblet that I find by the sink in the bathroom. Immediately the room feels warmer, more colorful, just how Mother likes it. "The brighter, the better," she'd say as she sat out in a folding chair watching me in the garden. Mother liked to watch me in the garden a lot. She said it calmed her. I didn't mind as she didn't interfere with my flower beds and herb patches. She just watched, and smiled. And sipped red wine that sometimes she'd chill in the fridge on warmer days.

At dinner, I request the same table as yesterday. I order Mother a glass of Merlot this time and rotate her slightly so she has a better view of the Indian bean trees outside. A waiter approaches. "May I bring the dessert menu?"

"No, thank you. I'm quite full and I have learned that sugar unsettles me. Isn't that right, Mother?" I say, gesturing to her.

He gazes over to the urn in the chair and frowns. His cheeks redden slightly and then he turns back and nods, leaving Mother and me alone once again. After I sign my name to another piece of paper, I collect Mother and her wine and tread slowly across the lobby to the elevator. The lobby hums with energy and sounds of suitcase wheels, high heels, and polite conversations. The elevator is quiet. I press 12 and feel the elevator shudder as it ascends quickly. It beeps once, twice, then opens to the hallway.

The carpet is soft beneath my welly boots, like warm grass, and I feel a strange sensation in my belly. I stop and imagine faces on the wall—happy face, sad face, hungry face, and tired face. I draw an imaginary circle around the sad face. Sometimes I have a difficult time labeling my feelings, so the faces help. Today I feel sad. I just can't describe why. The words are foreign to me, a strange language that swirls in my mind and slips into the cracks and corners.

The door to my room makes an odd noise as I unlock it with the plastic key card and when I open the door, I gasp. Someone—other than Mother and me—has been in my room.

I have had an intruder enter my room.

The first thing I notice is that my main light has been turned off and the two lamps on either side of the bed have been turned on. I certainly did not do either before dinner. I also realize that my bed-covers are no longer pulled up and tucked underneath my pillows but are now folded down at the top revealing the crisp white fitted sheet underneath. A small wrapped milk chocolate sits on my pillow.

Why would an intruder leave chocolate?

I immediately return downstairs to the front desk.

"How can I assist you this evening?" a woman says, a wide smile on her face.

"Someone has been in my room," I whisper, gazing around. The intruder might still be here, waiting, lurking.

"Really? Well, we'll call the police immediately. Has anything been taken?"

"No. I checked the entire contents of my bag and everything is still there."

"Okay, so you're certain nothing was stolen?"

"Very certain."

"How do you know your room was broken into?"

"Well, the light was off, the lamps had been turned on, my bed-spread had been folded down, the pillows had been fluffed, and a small milk chocolate had been placed on my bed."

She raises her eyebrows, then looks at the man beside her. They smile. I may not be fully versed in emotion expressions, but I think a happy face is an inappropriate reaction when a guest has reported a crime. "That sounds like our turndown service, miss."

"Your what?"

"At this hotel, we offer a turndown service to all our guests be-tween 7:00 p.m. and 8:00 p.m."

"Why would you do that?"

"A lot of our guests enjoy this service. It makes the room ready and comfortable for a good night's sleep."

"And the chocolate?"

"Just a little treat to say goodnight from us."

"Oh." How odd—a turndown service?

"I'm not supposed to have sugar, especially at night. Can I have something else instead? Perhaps a bag of crisps or a piece of fruit?"

"Unfortunately, we don't have a selection for guests to choose from."

An apple would have been nice, or maybe some berries.

"If you don't want the turndown service, then just pop the DO NOT DISTURB sign on the door handle," she adds.

I nod, and return to the elevator.

First a woman entered my room while I was in the shower this morning, shouting "Housekeeping!" repeatedly through the bath-room door while I hid behind it in silence and a towel, and now this? How many people in this building have access to my room? How many others will enter?

It's bad enough that I was kept awake all night with the voices, slamming doors, footsteps, and giggling from guests coming home late, but now this? At home, no one disturbed us, so there was no need to hang a sign on a door handle.

"What do you think, Mother?" I ask her in the elevator.

She's not happy.

We can't stay here. It is not safe, and Mother taught me to remain cautious and alert. Tomorrow we will return to Lansdowne Road in Notting Hill, examine the garden space, and make a final decision about our living arrangements.

A new garden is a blank canvas for a painter. The opportunity to explore color, texture, and shape is vast.

June and the Spacious Back Garden

My duffel has transitioned from being a "weekend getaway" bag to a "short break" bag since I have packed it full with a free blanket and a robe that I was kindly gifted by the hotel. It was left in my room, nicely folded at the bottom of my bed with a glossy tag that read: "Enjoy your stay, Mrs. Wilson." Mrs. is Mother's title, but she doesn't like robes, or "housecoats" as Linda call them. Mother prefers pretty things like silk dresses and suede heels. I could barely get the bag's zipper closed and now I fear I have done damage to this duffel, but I couldn't refuse a gift as that would be rude. I also accepted the miniature items lined up in the hotel bathroom, including a small tube of hand cream, which is an ideal gift as my hands often callus and sting after exposure to the summer sun, thorny bushes, and thin gardening gloves.

I was handed an invoice upon returning the key card, the money already having been deducted from Mr. Wilson's credit card, which confused me immensely. It listed the free meals along with a 12.5 percent "gratuity service" on each. It must be an error, but I am sure Mr. Wilson will rectify it. Thank goodness the robe and blanket were free.

I walk to Notting Hill as I don't know how to converse with a taxi driver and I have recently learned that trains are not safe. It only takes me forty-two minutes. My feet are quite warm in my welly boots with my thick blister-preventing gardening socks, and my shoulder itches under the duffel strap, which is pulled taut with the new weight of the free hotel items. Mother is rolled in the blanket.

Even though I am an early riser, by the time I get to 16 Lansdowne Road, it is empty. I knock three times and even call out through the letterbox. An animal barks at me. It appears the Wilsons have left. I stand in the empty driveway, heat building under my skin. What do I do now?

I can't go back to the hotel. And if I go home, they'll lock me in a residential home with other people like me. They might take Mother from me too. Warmth floods my body and I need to sit down. I need . . .

———————

When I open my eyes, I'm curled up on the crushed-gravel beneath a dehydrated hedge, pebbles pressing into my moist palm. It hurts to sit up. I pick stones from my skin and watch them fall, small indentations remaining on my hand. All I smell is sweat and sulfur and I long to smell petunias or bluebells instead. My fingertips are desperate to graze wet grass, warm soil and the cold metal handle of a gardening shovel.

I stagger to my feet and push through the second metal gate on the side of the house, continuing down a path paved with slabs of copper-colored sandstone. I smell the garden before I see it, wafts of summer filling my nostrils, my pulse immediately slowing.

My toes stop where stone meets grass.

Oh my, this garden isn't spacious at all.

It's certainly bigger than our garden back home and of course bigger than my flower patch at the community garden. But it isn't as big as, say, Kelvingrove Park in Glasgow or Kew Gardens here in London, not that I've ever been to the latter. Too many crowds, I'm sure. The garden at Lansdowne Road is of a modest size with high whitewashed fences, the occasional branch from the neighbor's dawn redwood tree leaning on them. The fences are a positive, because I prefer my privacy these days. People just don't respect it.

In the middle of the garden is a large yellow shed, which looks like it has been painted in the past year. The yellow hue really pops against the greenery of this space. It's a good choice. A bold one, but good. Surrounding the shed and the perimeter of the grass are ceramic pots of all different sizes and shapes, filled with perennials, which befuddles me. A gardener tends to *pot* annuals and *plant* perennials. But pot perennials? The thought of it makes me laugh out loud. How silly. Clearly my new relatives know nothing about horticulture. That's Londoners for you. Mother used to say only Suits, Hippies, and Manicures live in London.

Potted perennials.

After another few belly laughs, I clear my throat and make a mental note to:

(1) Plant the perennials

(2) Switch the annuals to the pots when I move in

I also add:

(3) Oil the hinges in the gates

(4) Restore the rosebushes

Suddenly something tall and luminous glints from the corner of the garden, delicately touched by the morning sun. Is that a Persian silk tree? I move quickly, my hands already outstretched. The bark is smooth under my palms, and cool given the warm weather today. It's a delicate hazel color that reminds me of Mother's eyes, not quite green and not quite brown. That was Mother, never one to be labeled easily or slotted into one category. She was many things.

I remember that she is still underneath the hedge at the front of the house and return for her, scooping her up along with my duffel bag. When I return to the garden, I unwrap her from the hotel blanket and allow her a glimpse of this magnificent tree. Another good month and the Persian silk will be in full bloom, cascades of fluffy pink blossoms resting on feathery green limbs spreading wide.

What if I'm not here to see it?

My head pounds and I press my hands against the bark again harder, rougher, to take the edge off the thoughts that hurt. When I turn around, the yellow shed shines bright in the morning sun.

The door to the shed is open, the key left in the lock for anyone to take. Curious to see what the Wilsons have in their yellow garden shed, I walk to it, opening the door wide and stepping inside. Dust is everywhere, as if it has not been used in a long time. There's a blue kid's bike in the back corner beside a lawn mower and some folded tarp. There are shelves on my left, large enough to hold plastic storage boxes with black lids, each marked with a label.

- Christmas Ornaments
- Christmas Wrappings
- Christmas Tableware
- Shoes

I'm struck by the amount of Christmas-themed décor they keep in here. I immediately open all the boxes, lining them up side by side to inspect the various items, colors, and textures that this family enjoys at Christmas. Given the sharp minimal interior of their house, I half expected them to not celebrate it at all, or if they did acknowledge the holiday, then for the decorations to be quotidian, mostly matte and white to match their rooms and personality. But in my hands are magnificent plumy garlands with ivy scattered along the edges, sparkly holly wreaths with ruby-red berries, brightly colored glass ornaments with jewels, and even lace fabric. Some ornaments tinkle like wind chimes.

I like wind chimes. Mother hung one in my bedroom by the window when I struggled to sleep. I'd crack the window open slightly and let the breeze drift through the chimes and lull me into a dream of forests and flowers. It was only after she hung one that I was able to reduce the dosage of zolpidem.

I gaze at Mother, who still sits under the branches of the tree. I wish I had remembered to bring the chimes with me when I left. How will I fall asleep in this new place without them?

My fingers fumble inside boxes and find more ornaments, candleholders, small *'Tis the Season* door plaques, and a wispy strip of silver tinsel at the bottom of one tub. Mother's favorite. We didn't decorate much for Christmas; we aren't "Christmas people," as she liked to say. We prefer the summer with real plants and organic scents, and trees that grow from soil and live outside. But we partook in the societal tradition nonetheless and put up a small artificial tree in the living room beside a wine rack that was always empty and a bookcase that was always full.

When the fairy lights broke, we never replaced them; we just blanketed them in more tinsel to cover the wires and dead bulbs. Mother liked tinsel for some reason. She'd take it from the Christmas tree in the Royal Mail staff room at the end of her shift when everyone else had gone home. And when they'd replace it, she'd take it again. We had so many ribbons of tinsel by the end, in all varieties and colors. I'd considered wrapping one around the neck of the urn, but I was worried that it would look cheap and tacky, two things that Mother was not.

I reorganize the contents of the plastic storage tubs, then place them back on the shelves, pulling inspiration from my days of stacking at my workplace, and continue browsing the contents of the shed. On the floor is a small toolbox, an even smaller gardening kit, camping gear still in its box from the store. Clearly three areas my relatives have no interest in.

Overall, the garden shed is a fair bit larger than what I was expecting, especially from the outside. Not that much smaller than my bedroom at home, in fact. The foundation seems solid, well-constructed, with minimal moisture from the grass getting in, and the walls are strong. The structure can probably hold tight against the rare bout of wind and rain that blows through London.

I am impressed. If I don't like my new bedroom at the Wilsons', I might very well sleep here.

"

Bold contrast makes a garden interesting.

"

June and the Exploration of the House

Around ten, I'm hit with a sensation that I can no longer ignore. A feeling that is building and becoming crippling.

I need to use the toilet.

Mother always said, "Know where your nearest toilet is." Wise words. I, however, have not adhered to that rule and now I stand outside the yellow shed staring desperately into a house that I cannot get into. Unlike the shed's, this door is actually locked.

I wander around the garden like an indoor cat let outside for the first time, sniffing out all the hidden corners and edges; but as the need grows greater, and far less manageable, I have to make a rather unfortunate choice. First, I select the area sheltered by the Persian silk as it's private and I can hide my mess in the soil, adding further nutrition to the vastly growing tree. But as I dig a shallow hole around the base, I see the Wilsons' dog staring at me from inside the kitchen. Can I really toilet in the same place a dog does?

I cover up the small hole I've made and dart over to the pots instead. I position myself neatly over a cluster of black-eyed Susans looking in much need of a watering and squat down. Something shiny flickers in the flowers and when I stand to examine it, I see a single house key. I turn it over slowly in my hands. A spare key. One just for me.

Cautiously, I edge to the back door and stand facing a set of glass sliding doors. The dog stares back at me. I slide the key into the lock and turn it. It clicks and the dog goes crazy, leaping from side to side in a frenzy. I gently lift a small plant pot from the ground, unearthing wood lice and silverfish as I do so, forcing them out into the morning sun when they seek the cool moisture of the dark. Hovering the pot above my head for protection, I slide one door open. The animal explodes out, like fizzy juice from a can that's been shaken, knocking past me and circling back around. But rather than foam at the mouth, snarl, or snap, this animal proceeds to lick me from head to toe, pushing its wet snout into me and getting my clothes covered in slimy drool and golden hairs.

"No, dog! Sit, dog!" I command. The animal does not listen. Unable to wait a moment longer, I push past it and dart inside.

The first door in the hallway is a storage cupboard, and the second on the left is the living room, which I am familiar with, having sat in it with the transport police. I race up the stairs in my welly boots, past a kid's room and a very white bedroom that resembles the one I stayed in at the hotel I just left. At the base of the stairs, which seem to lead up to a third level, is another door.

The toilet.

I run in, closing the door so the animal can't follow me, and breathe a deep and loud sigh of relief as I sit on the toilet. Afterward, I wash my hands and pocket a tiny bar of soap that sits on the shelf in a white wicker basket, because it smells like marguerite daisies in a field speckled with morning dew. Then curious, I climb the stairs to the top floor. Instead of an attic, there are more rooms. The first room on the right is the primary bedroom, where my biological father and his second wife sleep. I know that because there is a pair of tartan slippers on the left side of the oversized bed, while the other side holds a glass bottle of Evian, a large selection of variously sized multivitamins, and a stack of books with titles such as *Take Control of Your Destiny*, *Veganism Is the Future*, and *How Not to Die: Discover the Foods Scientifically Proven to Reverse Ageing*.

Off their room is a well-sized toilet with a deep bathtub and a glass-lined shower, with more baskets of tiny soaps and lotions.

In the only other room up here, beams of sunlight stream in from the large windows surrounding an old wooden desk that holds three computer screens, a stack of file folders, and lots of thin ceramic vases filled with different-colored pens. The blue vase holds blue pens and the black vase holds black pens, but the green vase contains red pens, which upsets me and almost causes me to knock the vase over.

The desk chair shifts under my touch, swaying from side to side. I collapse into it and swivel around and around until I feel light-headed. When I stop, I find that I'm staring into a framed photo of Mr. and Mrs. Wilson on their wedding day. He's a lot younger, and surprisingly has hair. Mrs. Wilson looks very much the same, although her hair is down, loose around her shoulders, like how Mother used to wear hers.

Beside that is another framed photo, a holiday picture of them with a child, somewhere hot and sandy. In it, Mr. Wilson sits beside a poorly constructed sandcastle while a young boy stands behind it holding a shovel up high, identifying himself as the incompetent creator. Mrs. Wilson crouches next to them with a pearl-white smile and a sunset-hued drink, garnished with speared fruit and a paper umbrella.

I've never been on a holiday before, certainly not one like this where the sun shines all summer long, people wear minimal cloth-ing, and you can eat ice cream if you're hot. I'm not sure if I'd like that. I don't like minimal clothing or ice cream, and although I am a summer girl, I prefer a landscape of lush greens, not sandy yellows. And if there is a time difference, which I heard from Linda at work is very common when you travel to exotic places, then my meal-times would be completely off. Would I eat lunch at midday UK time

or midday local time? What if it was lunchtime where I was but dinnertime back home? Would I then eat a cheese sandwich or chicken
and potatoes? How would I navigate such challenging times? And
without Mother. I push the frames away, and begin opening the
drawers in the desk one at a time. This must be Mr. Wilson's study.
What does my biological father keep in his drawers?

Papers, mostly. Presumably work correspondence. Along with
envelopes, a stapler, a hole punch, printer ink and blank paper. At
the bottom of the drawer is a large stack of brown file folders that
crinkles when I prod them with my finger. Curious, I poke them
again, and a crackle and rustle of plastic breaks through the silence.
When I lift the top folder, I see that there are no more folders underneath, just packets of crisps, chocolates, and biscuits. Mr. Wilson
has a hidden snack drawer! I wonder why he doesn't just keep his
snacks in the kitchen cupboards, where most people keep them;
however, perhaps being two flights up makes this a necessity. Although gentle exercise is essential, traveling up and down the stairs
in a multilevel townhouse several times a day for refreshments is
maybe too much for some. That I understand. I get my daily work-
out from gardening—all that squatting and lifting and reaching.
Gardening is a wonderful form of aerobic exercise, and free. No
expensive gym membership needed.

I decide to create my own snack collection—in the side pocket
of my duffel bag, for now—and remove from the drawer one of
Mr. Wilson's bags of crisps, a Wispa bar, even though I don't eat
chocolate, and half a packet of plain biscuits that has been twisted
and closed with an elastic band. I also liberate a few sheets of
printer paper, along with one pen from each colored vase, even
from the green one, for doodling florals and vines in the evenings.

It's getting close to morning teatime, so I wander back down the
stairs to explore the kitchen. It's a large open-plan room that faces
out onto the garden. A white dining table is positioned in front of
the double sliding doors, with an excellent view of the Persian silk

tree and the neighbor's dawn redwood. In the center of the room is a rectangular island made from what looks like dazzling marbled stone with iridescent swirls of black. It's immaculately clean, not a speck of crumb remaining from breakfast, which is commendable. Definitely a preferred trait. Above the island is a rack of cast-iron skillets and copper pots that hang precariously from the ceiling, waiting to fall on someone's head. Do all Londoners hang their cookware like this? Will I find a floating utensil jar somewhere above too? Plates? Coffee mugs?

The dog sits at the patio doors, projecting an annoying high-pitched whine through the glass doors and into the kitchen. For hygiene reasons, I would prefer not to have it in here while I make my tea, so I ignore its pleas and leave it outside.

The cabinets are well-sized and extremely organized. Some hold glass jars of odd-colored pasta shells and grains, while others are practically empty bar a couple of boxes and trays. I slide out one plastic box labeled "Snacks" and read the contents.

Dehydrated Chickpeas
Chia Power Bars
Quinoa Puffs
Lentil Cakes
Gluten-Free Flaxseed Crackers
Sulfur-Free Dehydrated Papaya
Cacao Goji Berries
Dehydrated Kale
Soya Bites
Hemp Clusters

These are snacks? Why is everything dehydrated? There is nothing in these cabinets that I recognize or even understand, and I work at Marks & Spencer!

My fingers hover over the handle of the fridge, afraid of what I will find in there. I take a deep breath and swing it open. Cartons of hemp milk are pressed tightly against pots of chia pudding, tubs of vegan margarine, and plastic packets of soya "bacon" strips. And there are bottles of something white and curdled called "probiotic kefir."

Who are these people?

A wild garden
can be more
enchanting than
a structured one.

June and the Chocolate Bar

After my morning tea, I reread a chapter from my almanac on how to protect summer blooms from foxes and birds, then decide to explore Notting Hill for lunch options. I want to give myself plenty of time to choose wisely. Given the Wilsons' questionable kitchen ingredients, the neighborhood of Notting Hill may not be familiar with how to prepare a cheese sandwich.

I have concluded that 16 Lansdowne Road is like one of those "retreats" on reality television where people sign up to be dared into eating peculiar foods like fried beetles and donkey testicles. Mother used to watch those shows, like *I'm a Celebrity . . . Get Me Out of Here!* and laugh heartily as she poured another Merlot and sucked on a strawberry sherbet lace.

Thankfully, by 11:37 a.m. I have located a small café offering "light lunches" and "specialty coffees," squeezed between graffiti-covered bus stops and secondhand clothing boutiques. After much negotiation, I manage to get the girl behind the counter to make me a plain cheese sandwich on white bread with real butter, crusts cut off. After paying her an astonishing £4.40 for the sandwich, I hurry back down the cherry tree–lined street to the house, where I sit cross-legged in the garden by the yellow shed. I eat facing the Persian silk tree with Mother by my side, and the dog back inside. I consume two chapters of my encyclopedia before trimming the front hedges. I don't cut them too short in case anyone notices but just enough that gives me something to do. My fingers have been itching to be back inside my gardening gloves. I have never had this much time away from gardening before. Now, as I trim, the world around me becomes clearer, calmer. More predictable.

Around 2:55 p.m., I let the dog out again while I go in for afternoon teatime and as I wait for the kettle to boil, I reach into my duffel for a biscuit from Mr. Wilson's stash. My fingers tickle something with a purple crinkly wrapper. I shimmy it out and hold it up. It's the Wispa bar. I don't know why I took it, but it interested me at the time. I make my tea and go back outside, swapping places with the animal. I sit at the patio table, steam rising from my mug, and slowly peel open the purple wrapping, exposing the brown chocolate beneath.

I hold it up and turn it over, assessing every edge and corner and bubbly dent. It's creamy, dense but also light. Airy, with tiny pockets visible in the center. I snap it in half and watch as small shards tumble onto the table like crumbling soil and scatters of stone. It smells sweet, milky sweet like lily of the valley, with a slight aroma of an evergreen coffee shrub, specifically the *Coffea arabica*. The robusta shrub is a tad too bitter to be likened to such a caramelized and nutty scent. Vanilla can be detected, like in the delicate white star-shaped flowers of a clematis vine in spring, with a hint of white jasmine and English lavender. Both of which grow exceptionally well at this time of year. June really is an exquisite month for blooming and blossoming—two terms commonly misunderstood to mean the same thing. While blooming refers to finally being "in flower," such as *Gardenia jasminoides,* blossoming speaks to the peak of a plant's bloom. For example, bell heather blooms in late July but doesn't fully blossom until August. Bell heather is very popular with the bee population. I saw a few bees in the garden today, even though the Wilsons don't have any bell heather in the flower beds. The silly dog tried to eat a bee and then got chased around the Persian silk by it. Animals are not smart.

Have I tried chocolate before? Yes, I have; in fact, I had dunked a chocolate digestive into my tea here in this very house. Days are becoming hazy without Mother, all bleeding into each other, distorting and disappearing. Like Snowdonia hawkweed, which once blanketed valleys and mountains in Wales before it vanished completely. That is my memory. Hawkweed.

I remember now that Mother and I had found that sugar affects my moods, leading me into a heightened state of animation and ebullience, and then stripping me almost immediately of that energy, sending me hurling down into a fitful rage followed by a restless, groggy sleep. That's how the pediatrician described it to us, anyway. After that, we decided to avoid sugar altogether. Mother still ate it as a treat from time to time, usually a chocolate praline or a sherbet lace, but it didn't bother me.

I hold the chocolate up to my face, wondering if it smells different from the chocolate biscuit that I had yesterday. But then a car door slams causing the dog to bark wildly from inside, and me to check my watch.

3:25 p.m.

Surely it's too early for the Wilsons to return from work? Unless Londoners work fewer office hours than us back up north? We Scots are hard workers.

Shrill laughter rings out and I freeze. Then I hear a child. A young boy, but not too young. Maybe around twelve or thirteen.

I don't know what to do. I had hoped to talk with Mr. Wilson first, as he will be my primary caregiver; he can speak to Aileen and tell her that Mother and I will not be staying in that residential home. He'll vouch for me. And Linda from work will too. They'll tell adult services that I'm fine to live by myself or at least live here in

London in the Wilsons' strange house. Those food choices will have to go, though, because I eat *normal* food.

But it's Mrs. Wilson that's here, not him. I don't know what to say to her. She might use language that I don't understand like idioms and figures of speech. I could perhaps hide over by the Persian silk tree, but I've just witnessed the dog toileting over there and I don't fancy accidentally stepping in anything. Perhaps I could make a dash for it along the side of the house and out the garden gate while they come through the front door. Teacup still in hand, I grab my duffel and Mother, and walk briskly to the side, but then I hear voices and footsteps coming closer. They're coming in through the back! Why don't these people use front doors? That is what they are designed for—to be entered. The back door is for garden access, everyone knows that.

I dance around the patio, unsure of where to go. The yellow shed sits open, blanketed by the heavy afternoon sun. I dart inside and quickly close the door. Seconds later, I hear them in the garden.

I press my face into the thin gap down the side of the door, straining to fully see them. A child marches into the garden, a tight-bunned and frown-wearing Mrs. Wilson following close behind, carrying both his schoolbag and her oversized handbag. They chat for a few moments about homework, politics, and someone called Boris, then finally go inside.

I take a deep breath and crack open the shed door, letting a small breeze trickle in along with the scent of neatly potted petunias, but as I shimmy a leg out to make an escape, the animal comes lunging toward me.

I stumble back in and shut the door again.

"Tilly!" coos the young boy. "Go pee."

But Tilly doesn't go pee as instructed. Tilly presses her annoying little snout against the shed door and sniffs wildly.

"Tilly! Tills!" calls the child again. The dog continues to lunge at the shed.

"Tilly! Toilet! Now!" screams the woman, her voice threatening to shatter the glass sliding doors and all the windows. The dog scampers away, a loud whine echoing around the garden.

I turn back to the shed and gaze around, the shelves now neat and organized thanks to my earlier efforts, although I hadn't expected to be here. I had hoped to be standing inside the house, not inside the *shed*.

"What do you think, Mother?" I whisper to her. She's nestled below a box of Christmas ornaments, her favorite.

I nod slowly. She's right: The shed is comfortable and warm. We could just hang out here for a bit, read, and wait for the two Wilsons to retreat inside for dinner, at which point Mother and I can quietly exit the garden. But where to? I've left the hotel, so where would we go next? If we wait for Mr. Wilson to come home, I can try to have a private conversation with him. He'll then call Aileen, tell her to stop looking for me, and Mother and I will live here for the rest of our lives. Caregiver and child, like it's meant to be. Even though I'm technically not a child anymore. A caregiver and adult child, I suppose.

"It's such a lovely evening," sighs Mrs. Wilson, "we should have dinner outside."

Getting out of here will be harder than I thought.

"What is this?" she suddenly shrieks, her voice scraping down the walls of the shed. "Henry!"

"What?"

"What is this?"

"Chocolate, I think."

"I know it's chocolate, but what is it doing *here?*"

"I don't know."

"Tilly could have eaten it and died! And you know I don't like this kind of junk food in the house."

"It's not mine. Maybe it's Dad's?"

"It's not your father's. He knows better," she snaps.

"Maybe it's those kids from school again?"

Another sigh. "If this doesn't stop, I'll be talking to the head-mistress again. First the eggs off the front door, now this. Disgust-ing," she says. "Come on, Tilly! Don't eat that!"

A collection of clatter breaks the silence that follows and their voices become muffled. My chocolate might be gone. I peer through the gap in the door again. Yes, Mrs. Wilson has removed it. That's a shame. I was slightly curious about what would happen if I left it outside in the sun for longer. How much of it would melt over a period of time?

I slide out *Peter Pan* as quietly as I can, and read the opening chap-ter, titled "Peter Breaks Through." After an hour, the woman and the child are back outside, this time with silverware and dishes, making a lot of noise. The dog whines and begs and is shooed away periodi-cally by Mrs. Wilson. It hasn't taken them long to prepare dinner, so I wonder what they're eating. I squint just enough to make out a bowl of leafy greens and some silver tongs. They're eating *salad* for dinner. Like rabbits. I don't see or smell chicken, or potatoes, which is unfortunate.

Goodness, I hope they are prepared to change their eating ways for me.

As they scrape the last of the salad onto a third plate, presumably for Mr. Wilson, my legs begin to get tired from standing, so I retreat farther into the shed. I unfold a large sheet of tarp from the back corner onto the floor, and place the hotel robe and blanket on top for extra padding. Then I lie down on my back, staring up at the shed ceiling, at the tiny slivers of early-evening sun seeping in. It's warm in here, but I don't mind the heat. I let my knees knock to-gether and close my eyes, hearing the hum of my mother's voice in the kitchen as she slices carrots and boils potatoes, singing softly to herself and to me.

When the sun
goes down, night-time
feeders will descend
on the garden.

June and the Night in the Shed

I awake groggily, unsure of where I am. I'm shrouded in a deep darkness I don't recognize. I know I'm not at home in bed because where I lie now is much firmer than my usual mattress. These aren't my bedsheets and the feeling of whatever is on top of me is an unfamiliar weight. The air is silent, with no gentle tinkling of wind chimes, or my mother's voice, to lull me back to slumber. And instead of the usual breeze that floats in through my open window, there is a noticeable smell of musk, sawdust, and birdseed.

"Mother?" I call out.

Wherever I am, the room is small and cramped, as my voice sounds contained, like the walls are padded or lined. I slowly lift myself up to a seated position and rub my eyes, adjusting to the darkness that surrounds me. Then I see my duffel on the floor near my feet, a small bike tire, half a bag of birdseed, shelves, and finally a small brown vase with a lid. An urn.

Mother.

I blink hard and remember the snowdrops and dew under my feet on the last day I saw her. I do not remember much after that. I never do.

I squeeze my eyes shut and open them again; Mother still sits quietly below the box of Christmas ornaments on a shelf cloaked in shadow and sleep haze. I remember where I am now. I am on the floor of the yellow garden shed at 16 Lansdowne Road, where I'd come to see Mr. Wilson. I don't recall hearing him return. Or hearing Mrs. Wilson and the child return inside.

I rub sleep from my eyes and carefully open the door. A wonderful breeze flows in, filling my nose with a crisp freshness. I gulp in the air and sluggishly stagger out into the garden. My feet are bare, and the moist grass slides over them, cooling them like a puddle in a wide-open field. The sound of traffic has dulled and all that remains is the distant chatter of nocturnal birds, the wind in the branches of trees, and the odd hum from nearby houses.

Lansdowne Road is different at night, as most places are. Less bright, less harsh. In its place is a softer side of London, one akin to countryside living back home. Garden smells emerge at night. After the buds have been warmed by the sun, the scents trickle through the grass and blend with the moonlit air. I can smell the petunias again, but also the rosemary and mint from the back by the Persian silk. Although muted, the colors of the garden are still visible. The pearly pinks of the petunias and sunshine yellow of the black-eyed Susans stand out in the darkness.

I walk to the center of the garden, and sit cross-legged on the grass facing the house. It's completely dark. I can just about make out a mobile of sorts from the window on the left. That must be where the boy sleeps. I didn't go in his room today—or rather, yesterday. I wonder if the animal sleeps with him. I hope not because then it might expect to sleep with me when I move in, and that will not be happening. Animals are for outside, not inside. Although I'm outside at the moment, so maybe *I* am the animal.

Being with the grass and the flowers and the trees and the soil, everything is suddenly less complicated, simpler, easier for me to understand. My brain doesn't hurt, I don't feel foggy, and my thoughts aren't muddled. The garden speaks to me and it is a language that I understand, for once. A language that many do not try to learn.

I stay outside for another hour or two, just sitting on the grass, listening to the quiet of the city. And when sleep clouds my vision and presses on my eyelids, I return to the shed, close the door, and let the darkness swallow me once again.

"

Some plant species
can camouflage with
other plants or rocks,
to hide in plain sight.

"

June and the Big Plan

It is a garish sign. Deep dark blue set within a coral and gold rectangular frame, with a partially painted *A*. It resembles more of a cheap plastic photo frame than a shop sign. I've never been to an Aldi before; Mother and I got most of our shopping needs fulfilled at Asda for cost-efficiency, or at Marks & Spencer because of my staff discount and my knowledge of when certain perishable items were going on the reduced shelf. But for today Aldi will have to do.

After a surprisingly adequate sleep in the shed last night, even without chimes, I awoke early this morning with a genius idea. As I still have not managed to have a conversation with Mr. Wilson about my accommodations, I thought why would I spend the money on a hotel in a city that offers many garden spaces? I could camp in a park or garden somewhere! Then it occurred to me that I am in a garden already, and one close to Mr. Wilson, making it easier for me to grab him when he walks by. Why not live in his shed?

That will also provide me with more time to address some issues I have noted before I formally accept the request to move in. There are many differences between my relatives' London lifestyle and my preferred routines, particularly their eating habits; and again, the dog simply has to go.

I understand that it perhaps sounds unusual for a grown woman to be living in a garden shed. However, I need somewhere to stay for the interim, somewhere physically close to my biological father, and with a garden, so this arrangement makes perfect sense for now. Mother agrees. We conversed in great detail about it this morning.

It's not like the Wilsons use the shed, judging by the dust that has accumulated on the shelves and floor. It is not Christmas for another six months, so they won't be needing their boxes of decorations. They don't seem like the camping or biking type. And in my professional opinion, they're not gardeners, so they likely won't be visiting the shed for any "tools," none of which here are even suitable for a simple gardening task. I had a look in Mrs. Wilson's kit this morning before I left and found a pink polka-dot hand shovel. Therefore, I am fairly confident that I have the shed to myself for at least the next week or so. And that is all I will need. At that point, Mr. Wilson and I will have come to some sort of a living agreement and we'll have notified Aileen back home so she can reassign my room at that home to someone else. Someone less capable than me, perhaps. I am functioning very well in the world, on my own, and without my medication. My social skills are progressing well and I have not gotten angry recently. There are still some memory issues, but I am sure that is temporary.

Even though I don't anticipate being in the shed for long, I still need to make it more livable. I can't continue sleeping on the floor on a tarp and a hotel blanket. First, I need to address the sparsity of the decor, then I can focus my attention on the overall "vibe" of the inside. Mother talked a lot about "vibe," eventually delving into books about room psychology and feng shui, most of which she had to specially request through the library's online catalog as they were not available at our local branch. This did not surprise me in the slightest. Our librarian is often distracted, getting caught up with the more trivial demands of the library, like banning my mother after she failed to return the feng shui books.

I listened intently while Mother talked about "essence" and "energy," held her ladder while she dismantled a light fixture that gave her "bad vibes," and painted alongside her as we went from room to room. The living room was repainted yellow because, she said, "yellow makes people cheery," and the kitchen became a vibrant red to "engage the senses and stimulate passion," whatever that meant. When she asked me what color I wanted for my bedroom, I answered quickly: "Green." Green like zinnias, mint chrysanthemums, and "Limelight" hydrangeas. Green like a garden in June.

And so we painted my room green.

And it was beautiful and peaceful and turned out exactly how I'd pictured it. The following spring, we used permanent markers and acrylic paints to draw small flowers that grew from the baseboards and flourished up the green walls.

I am here today for that. Not just the paints to decorate the shed walls, but everything else that I had in my bedroom back home. I am here to inject some "positive energy" into the shed.

As I wheel my trolley down the homeware aisle, I mentally tally up my findings to be sure I have enough money left over from Mr. Wilson's hotel fund to cover me.

1 yoga mat in forest green . . . £4.99

1 small analog alarm clock . . . £2.99

1 beanbag chair . . . £7.99

1 rug (striped with tassels) . . . £10.99

1 slim bedside table in white oak . . . £15.99

Estimated total.. . . . . £40ish

My total comes to £42.95, so I wasn't far off, but still, it is a bit more than I intended to spend. As I slowly walk back to Lansdowne Road, I can't help but wonder if I have enough to last me over the next week or so, especially if I also have to buy my meals given that the Wilsons are incapable of stocking their cupboards like a regular family.

"Can I give you a hand?"

I stop and slowly turn to face a young man pushing a green bike down the street.

"Pardon me?" Perhaps I look like I am struggling a bit; dragging a bedside table for two and a half miles isn't the most fun a person could be having on a sunny summer's day. And the bag with the remaining items keeps swinging off my hip. But he is wheeling a bike with both hands, so where is this *spare* hand he is offering?

"The table looks heavy. Can I help you?" he says again.

"I don't think that's a good idea."

"Why's that?"

I pause and think back to the tragic train situation on day one. "Because if I give it to you, you might not give it back."

He laughs. "You think I'm going to steal it?"

"Possibly. And you have the means to do it. I won't be able to keep up with your bike."

He laughs again, like I'm purposefully being funny even though I am very serious. How can I chase him if he's on a bike and I'm in welly boots?

"Okay, how about I promise *not* to steal it?" he says, holding out his hand to shake mine.

I gaze around at the crowds as they march up and down the street, everyone with their head down, eyes on their phone screen. He wouldn't get very far with this foot traffic if he did try to make off with the table.

I nod and eventually shake his hand. We have made a pact, and

I intend to take it very seriously. I will not have another train situation. I don't know if Mr. Wilson will give me more money if there's another incident.

The young man gingerly takes the table from me and positions it under an arm. He walks alongside me, pushing his bike with the other hand. He balances the items well and I am initially impressed.

"Good finds in Aldi today?" he asks, stopping to awkwardly scratch at his shaggy dark beard, which hides the bottom half of his face. His hair is long and could do with a trim, much like mine. I might ask him what hair salon he visits.

"Yes, I found what I needed." I frown and gaze at the bags—did I find what I needed? I suddenly can't remember now what I came for and why.

"Glad to hear it."

His bike squeaks beside us and I wonder why he isn't riding it like most cyclists do.

"What's your name?" he asks.

"Um . . ." I want to ask Mother if I'm allowed to give my name to strangers because I can't remember, but I did not take her with me. I was worried I would drop her while carrying bags.

"I just thought we might engage in a little conversation while we walked?"

I suppose engaging in conversation would allow me to practice my social skills, perhaps even learn something new.

"My name is June Wilson and I am twenty-two years of age," I answer.

"June?"

"June, like the month. And what is your name?" Returning with a question is apparently polite, and preferred.

"William, or Will for short."

I shrug. "I don't get called anything 'for short.' It's just June."

"Like the month."

"Like the month." I nod.

"You're not from London, are you? Scottish?"

"Glasgow."

"Ah, so properly Scottish?" he laughs. I don't know what he means by that, so I don't laugh with him. "What brings you to London?"

"I'm going to live with my biological relatives."

He frowns slightly, then nods. "That's cool. Family's important."

Family.

There's that word again. I thought all I needed was Mother. But now I need a place to live. So yes, I guess in this particular circumstance, family is important.

We carry on walking in silence, the way I would have preferred it in the beginning, but as we wait to cross the road, with the tour buses and taxis whizzing past us, he strikes up a conversation again. Two social opportunities in one day. Mother will be happy.

"So, June, what do you do?"

"What do you mean?" He is beginning to use "fuzzy language."

"I mean, what do you do in your spare time? Do you play any team sports, or maybe you enjoy horse riding, swimming, stuff like that?"

Now his question is clearer. "I do not play any sports because my PE teacher once told me I'm not a 'team player,' I don't horse ride because I don't like animals, and I don't swim because . . ." I swallow hard. "Because I don't like the water."

"Why not?"

"I just don't," I say firmly, remembering the river beside my house. The churning, thrashing river.

"Well, I enjoy swimming. I also play cricket and as you can see, I love to cycle."

"Don't most cyclists *ride* their bikes rather than walk them?"

He laughs and stops to shift the table to the other arm. "I got a puncture just before I saw you. Typical, first time out on the bike this summer and I get a flat tire within the first ten minutes."

"That is unfortunate."

"It certainly is."

We head down toward the little shop that sells tea-stained antique maps and the coffee place that advertises overpriced beverages. The sun pokes out from a cloud, momentarily shining down on us, then slips away again.

"So, how are you enjoying London?" he asks as we pass the coffee shop. I gaze in and see a small cluster of people cooing over a vintage chalkboard adorned with latte specials such as "Summer Berry," which sounds very unappealing for a coffee flavor.

"It's okay," I answer. "It's different than Glasgow. The people here are odd."

"*We're* odd?" he scoffs.

"Yes."

"Well, I hope it grows on you. London's really fun in the summer. There's a lot going on. There's a great festival in Hyde Park coming up and—"

"This will do," I announce, stopping under the Lansdowne Road sign. The conversation has been surprisingly pleasant, a lovely opportunity indeed, but now I am feeling quite tired from having to think so hard before I respond.

"You live here?" he asks.

"I live near here, but if I go any farther then it might give away my exact address and then you'll know where I live, and then you won't be a stranger and we can't talk like this again."

"Okay." He grins.

"Thank you very much for assisting me."

"Well, 'June like the Month,' it was lovely to meet you. If you ever need a tour guide to show you a bit of London, I can give you my number?"

"I don't have a mobile phone."

"Oh, okay. Really?"

"Really. I never had a need to call anyone other than my mother and I used the landline for that."

"Well, I work down at Canary Wharf at the aquarium, not that you'll be spending much time there since you don't like water, but come find me if you want a friend."

Friend.

I've never had one of those before. What does having a friend entail? Frequent conversations, regular meetups, dining together? I am intrigued by his offer, of course.

"I'll think about it," I say, placing the Aldi carrier bag down by my feet. I hold out my hands to take the bedside table from him, hoping he hasn't scratched it against his bike frame on the walk here. "Thank you again for your help. I enjoyed this conversation."

"You're very welcome. I did too." He smiles, then ambles alongside his bike up the road, heading back in the direction of Aldi. He must have forgotten something there, perhaps.

"

Even the most
experienced gardener
will make a mistake.
Turn these errors
into lessons.

"

June and the Boy in the Window

I know I shouldn't have napped this afternoon. But after tidying, rearranging, lifting, dusting, and sweeping, I was so physically tired that I thought a quick power nap would help take the edge off my unsettledness. It did not. I awoke groggy and grumpy and hungry, and now it is affecting my ability to sleep at night.

There is a definite change in the air tonight compared to last night, when I slept so soundly. First, there is a small stone underneath the yoga mat I am using as a thin mattress and it's causing me great discomfort. And then there are the sounds from outside. New noises I didn't hear last night. Cars on the road, late-night buses pulling into the stop across the street, voices from other gardens, couples sitting outside and clinking glasses, dogs barking, cats meowing.

Our street at home is quite busy at times, but those are noises I am accustomed to. These are new noises, and along with a new bed, a new room, and a new city, there are a lot of *new* factors affecting my sleep. And I do not do well with "new." Mother told Aileen that when she tried to relocate us to another property in Shawlands.

Still restless, I stagger to my feet and open the shed door to the garden beyond. Perhaps I just need to feel the moist grass beneath my toes and the moonlight on my face again. It's cooler outside the shed. I already know there is a full moon in the sky tonight, because I checked the lunar chart in my almanac earlier today. I can even see a few streetlamps over the top of the fence and a couple of outdoor bulbs accidentally left on. Perhaps I need a night-light in the shed to aid my REM cycle, but I don't know where I would find one. Frustratingly, I forgot my night-light, along with the wind chimes. Although had I brought it along, I'd have had difficulty locating a socket for it. There is an outdoor plug by the patio table near the back door, but Mr. Wilson may return home late one evening and accidentally trip on the cable.

For safety reasons, I will simply sleep with the shed door slightly ajar so that the moonlight and light from the streetlamps can seep in. It will also let some fresh air flow in; it gets very stuffy throughout the night and will only get worse as the summer warms up.

I sit cross-legged on the grass facing the house like before and gaze into the dark windows. The blinds in the kitchen haven't been drawn and I can still see the remnants of dinner on the dining table. A bottle of wine, two glasses, a vase of flowers, a couple of small candles, some unused silverware, and a water glass.

Earlier, I observed their dinner from the side of the house. My newfound relatives sat at the white table, mundanely passing white dishes back and forth. Unfortunately, I couldn't hear the little conversation that passed between them. I would have liked to know what they talked about over their meal. Mother and I often used the time to practice social conversations; for example, she'd ask me about my day and I would reply, then return the question and wait for her reply, sometimes nodding animatedly to indicate that I was listening and engaging. Dinnertime was very productive in my house, whereas this exchange looked less constructive.

The child had his head in a book for most of the dinner hour, setting his fork down to turn the page every so often, while Mr. Wilson regularly glanced at his phone before being reprimanded by the stern-faced Mrs. Wilson, who sat quietly beside him staring at her manicure. He had put the phone down eventually, but he'd hid it on his lap and was glancing under the table at it every so often until he was caught once again by Mrs. Wilson. She took the phone from him and carried it over to the kitchen counter, where he couldn't reach it. I've never participated in a dinnertime ritual quite like that one.

Mother and I cooked together, beginning at exactly 5:15 p.m. We sliced the potatoes and carrots together and then she put the chicken in the oven. While the potatoes simmered in a pot on the stove, she poured herself a large glass of Merlot and put the radio on. We listened to Radio 2, the soft rhythmic beats trickling out from the speakers while tiny water bubbles danced above the potatoes, soon turning to a roaring boil. At 6:00 p.m., when everything was ready, Mother would top up her wine goblet and we'd carry our plates to the living room, balancing them on our knees while we watched television. There we would engage in our social lessons during the adverts. We only ate one meal a day at the small round dining table we'd got from the Salvation Army shop, and that was breakfast, purely because we needed the table space for the butter, jam, coffee mugs, and so on. Lunch we had separately on our respective work breaks.

Dinnertime was always our time.

Now it is a confusing time for me, where I watch them partake in a meal while I eat cooled potatoes and carrots that I have cooked in the afternoon, before the Wilsons return from work/school, and pre-cooked chicken pieces from a packet that I purchase from the grocery store in Shepherd's Court, which is a seventeen-minute walk from the shed. I have considered walking across the street to that McDonald's place to check if they sell chicken, but I'm slightly worried that I will see those transport police officers from the train station as they had McDonald's wrappers in their car that day and might frequent there. They might ask me questions and if I don't answer correctly, then they might return me to Scotland, to Aileen.

I wonder if when I join the Wilsons I could persuade them to bring their plates through to the living room so we can watch television while we eat dinner. I wonder a lot of things now. New thoughts press into my mind until my head pounds. And when I ask Mother questions, she doesn't answer like she used to. There's just silence. A deep heavy silence that hurts my bones.

Where is Mother?

Where am I?

I gaze around and remember that she is inside the shed, and that I am outside in the garden.

The moisture from the grass tickles my knees and shins as I wrap the blanket around my shoulders. My bedtime clothes are thin and do little to keep out the cool night air.

All of a sudden, I see something moving in the top left window.

I freeze, my body stiffening like goldenrods in winter. If I run back to the shed now, perhaps they will see me. And then they will know that I am living in their shed. I shall remain frozen, as still as I can be, and hope that from up there I blend in with the grass and the trees.

But I don't. Because seconds later, a face presses into the glass, a face with round-rimmed glasses and hair that sticks up. It's the child. He appears to be in red pajamas. He stares at me intently, at this stranger in his garden in the middle of the night who is also dressed in pajamas.

I stay still, not sure what to do now that I have been spotted. Will he tell his parents? Is my time in London already over and will I be immediately bused back up north? After all that cleaning and organizing I did today? What will I do now with the bedside table and rug? I haven't even sat in the beanbag chair yet.

The boy in the window continues to stare, and then slowly lifts his hand to the glass. I wait for him to start knocking and yelling for his mother, who will certainly tell me to leave, but instead, he waves.

I blink hard and stare back.

He waves again, this time more enthusiastically and with a smile.

I wave back.

"

Boquila trifoliolata is probably the world's most surprising plant; it spreads along a forest floor and attaches itself onto host plants.

"

June and the Vegan Roll

A small golden bread roll sits on a silver-rimmed white ceramic plate, with a generous dollop of some strange yellow emulsion that's pretending to be butter but clearly isn't butter.

I heard footsteps outside the shed earlier today. The crunch of grass blades bending and snapping under boots. The steps were too slow and controlled to be those of the animal, who erratically bounds around the garden like she has consumed too much sugar.

After the footsteps receded, followed by car doors slamming, I had unlocked the shed door and peered out. It was then that I noticed the plate. Had I not, I may have stood directly in it, and got the lemon-colored artificial margarine in between my toes and under my nails.

At first I assumed someone must have left it there by accident while hurrying out the door to work or school. But when I saw the note underneath it, scribbled on a white disposable napkin, I knew that this was a meal not forgotten but deliberately left.

The note read:

FOR THE PERSON IN MY GARDEN

The note and roll have to be for me unless another person is living out here, and they have to be from the boy at the window from last night. He's the only one who knows I'm here. I assumed he'd be telling his parents this morning, not leaving me a roll, but I'm not one to turn down breakfast. It's not my usual, but it's bread, so it falls under the same category as Toast or Croissant.

I step out into the garden. The morning sun touches only the top half of the garden while the trees at the bottom are still blanketed in darkness. It's an odd feeling to wake up in someone's garden, but more so in someone's shed. It's a feeling I'll have to get used to, I suppose. The alternative is a residential home in Glasgow with other adults who can't name their feelings.

The bread roll tastes strange. It's unnaturally dense yet slightly doughy in the middle, as if it hasn't baked properly. As if it's not made with real flour. Is this one of the Wilsons' trick foods, like non-flour bread or dehydrated something?

It makes me flush with warmth and I throw it down. I close my eyes and imagine four faces dancing in the air in front of me: HAPPY, SAD, ANGRY, TIRED. I hover above TIRED but eventually circle SAD in the air. Yes, that is it. I am sad, I conclude. I want my usual breakfast, because this is different and I don't like different.

"Is that correct, Mother? Am I sad? Or is it angry?"

She sits in silence and solitude beneath the bottom shelf beside my welly boots, which I hosed down in the garden yesterday and wiped clean.

I throw the roll in the bin marked "General Waste" at the side of the house, beside the path, then I let myself in using the spare key. I wash the plate in warm soapy water and place it with the others, make a coffee, and use the bathroom. After "breakfast," I go for a brisk walk to stretch my legs and engage in a bit of exercise, which is good for the heart and the lungs. I haven't been as active in the garden since traveling down south. I'm worried I'll start to look like Mora, our old neighbor at number 19 with the "No Solicitation" sign.

She waddles when she walks, and her clothes look incredibly tight and uncomfortable on her body. She lives alone now that her husband, George, has passed away. Mother said Mora must have eaten him. I asked Mother if we should call the police and she just laughed, then hugged me and said, "My sweet June, don't ever change."

When I return to the garden, radiant sunlight fills the space between the patio doors and the redwoods, and spreads to the herb patch in the far corner. It nourishes the buds and warms the grass under my bare feet. I hold my boots in my hand, having slipped them off a couple of streets away. I had thought that in a neighborhood this rich in green shrubs and vibrant perennials, the concrete just beyond that paradise would feel warm and clean underneath my feet. I was wrong. Along the two streets I took to walk back here, I'd stepped on someone's chewing gum and had to avoid a shattered beer bottle. The pavement is warm, sure, but clean? Absolutely not. London is a *dirty* place.

I eat lunch in the back with a book on my lap, under the branches of the Persian silk and in the shadow of the neighbor's dawn redwood. Afterward, I go inside to clean and dry my dishes. I tend to the rosebush in the afternoon, clipping back the dead stems and stimulating the regrowth of the healthy ones. Red was a good choice. Once I restore the bushes, the crimson color will really pop against the gray of the city.

In the afternoon, I return inside for my tea break and to boil the potatoes for dinner. As the kettle and the small copper pot bubble away, my fingers skim the glass cabinets on the other side of the kitchen island. Inside are rows of neatly placed wineglasses, goblets, and flutes. Marks & Spencer has a good selection of glassware, which is how I learned the difference between a tulip and a coupe, but these are lovely. Heavy, with thick crystal stems and sturdy bases. Some flicker and dazzle in the afternoon sun when I hold them up to the window. Mother would like these.

On another shelf are teacups and saucers, and a beautiful teapot with yellow roses. Mother and I had a tea party once in the garden. We sat on blankets with the sun on our backs and ate small triangular sandwiches from tiered trays using paper plates and butterfly napkins. I had cheese in my sandwiches, but Mother had made hers with thinly sliced cucumber pressed gently into the butter. She asked me to try one. I said no, but she asked again and I pushed the meal tray away. I hadn't meant to thrust it into her so forcefully. I hadn't meant for it to hit her bottom lip and make her bleed. I hadn't meant to ruin the tea party. After that, she never asked me to try new foods.

Something presses at my mind again. A memory. A fragment or a broken image. Of Mother. Of a wild raging river. Of crushed snowdrops beneath the soles of bare feet. I try to hold on to the memory, grasp it firmly, but then it's gone and I cannot remember what it is that I am forgetting. Every time that happens, a small piece of another memory is tugged into the darkness with it—Mother's favorite color, the last television show we watched together, how many rings she wore on her fingers.

I blink away a flicker of a memory and pour myself a strong tea, then wander into the living room. The sofa is well-proportioned to the space and the coffee table is adequate to hold cups of tea and glasses of Merlot. A set of circular, white marble coasters is stacked on the table. I've never used a coaster before. I wash a palm over the coffee table. The wood must be expensive if there are coasters. The porcelain houses are still here, as is the small boy who stares down from the window of one of the houses. Beneath them is a shelf of books with lovely untouched spines and crisp hardbacks. I slide out one in the middle and turn it over in my hands. *War and Peace*. I thought my encyclopedia was gigantic, but this is even bigger. It is in immaculate condition. All the books on our shelves at home were frayed and their spines broken. Mother was a fervent reader. She had read all the books. She preferred stories about forbidden romances and tragic fates, but sometimes she read ones that made her laugh aloud.

I open *War and Peace* as wide as I can, bending the pages back until

I hear the spine crack and break, then I close it again and place it back on the shelf with the other books. Lines run up the spine, like branches on a birch. Now it's perfect. I smile and take a seat with my tea.

A television guide is open on the table, beneath the remote controls. I shimmy it free and skim this weekend's highlights. Suddenly my hand quivers, splashing hot tea onto my thumb. Shakily, I place the mug down on the table, forgoing the coaster, and bring the TV guide closer to my face. A familiar warmth fills my belly and spreads to my cheeks. In all the busyness of coming here and setting up the shed for my stay, I've completely forgotten that there's a special edition series of *Strictly Come Dancing* starting this Saturday.

Our show.

Mother and I would watch it together every Saturday evening. We never missed it. If it was cancelled or delayed due to a breaking news special or a sports game that ran into overtime, I became extremely upset. Things would get broken, thrown. None of which I would remember afterward; Mother would have to tell me. Nonetheless, it was not a particularly pleasant experience for either of us. And now I won't be able to watch it at all because there's no television in the shed, and even if I could source one in the next forty-eight hours, there is nowhere inconspicuous to plug it in. And there's no one to tune it, to find the correct channel at the correct time, to position the screen so very minimal head movement is needed to take in the whole screen.

No. This won't do at all.

Heat and anger flood my body.

It takes me a few moments to realize that I'm wet. And that I'm standing in a puddle of milky tea and broken ceramic. The hot liquid scalds my skin through my trousers, and I stand there for a few moments longer to feel the burning sensation. Then I clean up and return to the garden, and try to remember the name of one of Mother's books.

Bridget something.

"

A yellow-necked mouse will often graze on young seedlings in the garden, threatening their development.

"

June and the Letter Exchange

Huddled in the shadows of the shed over an entry in my RHS encyclopedia titled "Assessing Your Site and Soil" somewhere between dusk and evening, I hear the crunching of shoes on gravel.

The tiny hairs on my arms prick up as I wait in silence, unsure of what exactly I am waiting for. The footsteps get louder, closer, until a dark blanket of a silhouette appears under the door. The small brass knob shifts slightly but doesn't turn as it's locked from the inside with the key, which now sits on the edge of a shelf beside a box marked *Christmas Ornaments*. I close the book. I had expected this to happen at some point, though not quite this early on in my stay. Aside from today's "disturbance" over the TV guide, I have been rather careful not to disturb too much inside or outside the house, beyond some light gardening and grass cutting. I am very confident that Mrs. Wilson will not have noticed that given the state of the flower beds, her poor choice of gardening tools, and her decision to pot perennials.

I clutch my encyclopedia to my chest and wait for the door to swing open and reveal the Wilsons standing there with Aileen and the police. But instead, a loud knock cuts through the silence. I am no expert on the ways of Londoners, but nobody knocks on a garden shed unless they know it's not empty. Still, I let the silence build a wall between us and bite my lip to stop from saying "Hello," which is what a person does when someone knocks on their front door.

After another very uncomfortable moment of silence, I hear more rustling. A folded-up piece of white paper shoots under the door toward me. It lands at my bare feet, smearing dust in its path. Then the footsteps recede and I hear the whoosh and click of the kitchen sliding doors as they close. I exhale deeply, not realizing I had been holding my breath. That explains why I suddenly feel so lightheaded. I sit down, pulling my legs into my chest, and unfold the note.

> *Dear person in my shed,*
>
> *How are you?*
> *I just wanted to let you know that tomorrow's*
> *forecast shows heavy rain and that shed is known to leak.*
>
> *Yours sincerely,*
> *Henry*
> *(The boy inside the house)*

I know this, of course. The long-range weather forecasts in my *Gardener's Almanac* are quite accurate, and I've been reading the newspaper in the morning after everyone leaves for the day while I wait for the kettle to boil. There's a weather section in there too, along with a TV guide and a column titled "Ask Helen Anything." Yesterday someone asked Helen if she should leave her husband because he's gained weight. The day before someone asked Helen for advice on removing a pet stain from an antique rug. Helen was quite knowledgeable in both areas. I may decide to write to her myself: "Dear Helen, what is the process for rehoming a dog?" "Dear Helen, how can I establish an emotional bond with a caregiver in three days?" "Dear Helen, do all biscuits melt when dunked into hot tea, or just the ones coated in chocolate?"

I don't tend to read the remainder of the newspaper, the headlines or featured articles, mostly because I find politics and sport irrelevant to my lifestyle.

Does the boy not mind that I am in here, sleeping in his garden? Is he going to keep my accommodation a secret? He must want something in return. There's always a "but" or an "if" when it comes to random acts of "kindness." Mother taught me that, and she is usually correct.

If residing in a
location where
rainfall is frequent,
fill a garden with plants
that can withstand
water logging.

June and the Rainstorm

It is indeed raining. In fact, ever since I woke up this morning, it has been raining and raining, and raining some more. And just when it seems to ease off, it starts again.

Rain batters the sides of the shed and pelts the yellow roof, like angry fists above my head. I do not mind the rain; it's never bothered me before. I've always quite happily popped on my wellies and gone outside regardless of a shower. Gardens always need tending to, and I can't afford to be known as a "fair-weather gardener." I'm aghast even thinking about it now. Sunshine or rain, or sleet in some cases, I am out there—pruning, shearing, clipping, planting, fertilizing, plotting, and planning. As long as there isn't any standing water, gardening in the rain is quite fun and can be efficient if I'm planting new seedlings. It saves me having to loop back around with the watering can, particularly the rusty one at the community patch that Elsbeth sliced her thumb on last autumn.

But I'm not home, and this isn't my garden or the community patch I share with ten others including Elsbeth and Carol. This is someone else's garden, which I am reminded of every time I catch sight of the untouched gardening equipment, and the equally unused black wellies in a ginormous ladies size 9. I'm not pointing fingers—the owner could be anyone—but Mrs. Wilson does not look like the dainty-feet kind.

At home, I kept my wellies beside the door on the white rack, next to Mother's high heels and work boots. Mother wore brown water-resistant walking boots, frayed at the rim and with the rubber traction on the soles slightly coming away, for her long days at the sorting office in town. On the occasions she had to take Mr. Pete's postal shift, the boots suited her just fine and provided enough comfort for walking up and down the streets. And they were light enough to manage a quick dash out the front gate in the event that someone had let their dog out in the garden, which happened more often than not. Hence her distaste of animals.

On the days of her long shifts, she'd come home, shimmy out of her boots and place them on the shoe rack beside mine, and then rather than slide her sore feet into soft slippers, she'd slip on a pair of heels for the evening. When I asked why she'd change into heels for an evening spent bathing in TV light and Merlot, she said, "Because when else would I wear heels?" She loved pretty things, but she was always barefoot in the garden. Like one should be. Unless they're working in it. Then it is welly boots.

Mother was a ladies size 5, just like me. Those welly boots in the shed corner are a better fit for a mountain bear. They're also very plush for a rainy day such as this. On the side is a small crest of two swords and a lion's head, which seems very bizarre to me as lions are mostly found on the continent of Africa, not in the suburb of Notting Hill.

The boots are useful for something, though—I use them as a makeshift seal, lining them up along the bottom of the door just in case the water starts to seep in underneath. Around 7:20 a.m., it does. Not a lot but enough to spill around the boots, which haven't worked well as a seal, and to warrant the upheaval of my bedding onto a shelf and the relocation of other items on the floor, including my books and alarm clock. I have already concluded that the thickness and height of the foundation of the shed is to blame for this.

Around 7:45 a.m., everyone finally leaves the house and I am able to open the door and release some of the humidity that has built up inside the shed. Rain lashes down on the patio and washes away any remnants of the chocolate bar. I slip on my raincoat for the short trip across the patio to the kitchen, my clothes for the day tucked inside to keep dry. I block the animal from getting too close and manage to guide her outside into the garden and the rain. I check the newspaper forecast while the kettle boils to ensure that it matches my almanac—"heavy rainfall" and "chances of flooding." The newspaper has aligned itself well. After a slice of toast and a mug of milky coffee, I take a quick shower and dress accordingly for a day in the rain—waterproofs and wellies.

Outside, the deluged flowerbeds are struggling, water skirting around the stems of cornflowers and primroses. There is a slight accumulation of standing water in the herb pots, so I drain those and shift them back slightly, under the shelter of the shed's roof. The planter box at the edge of the garden is too heavy to be lifted, so I tip it instead and let the water run out onto the grass by my feet. It trickles through the blades like a river, passing over a daisy, and reminds me of the small white flowers that grow wild on the river shingles by our house. The small white flowers are not native to the riverbank, nor are most blooms around water edges. They are called "garden escapes" because their roots spread far beyond the fences that struggle to contain them. That was Mother—a garden escape. She could not be contained.

I gaze up at the child's empty window and see a gray bunny rabbit sitting on the sill staring down at me in his absence. It reminds me of a task I wanted to complete this morning before my tea break, so I return to the shed and start writing him a reply using paper and a pen that I took from Mr. Wilson's study. While there, I also took a new pack of gingerbread biscuits for my tea break.

Dear Boy in the House,

Thank you kindly for your weather warning. In the event that you are keeping tabs on the shed's longevity and durability, please note that the roof is holding up well. There is a minor drip from the back-left corner, but it is easily managed so far. However, water has entered under the door, which I believe is a construction flaw. Upon entering the shed initially, I estimated the foundation to be only five inches high and typically garden sheds are eight or nine inches high to avoid weather-related issues such as this.

I understand that I am in no position to ask, as I have nothing to offer in return, but I have a couple of minor requests, which are as follows:

A. *Next time you leave out breakfast for me, can you leave something a bit more edible, like toast or a croissant with* real butter and real flour? *Strawberry jam would be lovely too for the weekends as a treat, but sugar-free and seedless, please, as I find the seeds terribly annoying to remove from my teeth. They make the bread taste grainy like I'm eating sand.*

B. *Tomorrow evening is a big night for me. I'm not sure if you're aware of this, but it's the opening episode for the all-stars special of* Strictly Come Dancing. *I have noticed that there is an interior sliding door between the kitchen and the living room. Can you please* leave it open at 6:55 p.m. *so that I can see the TV screen from the kitchen patio? This will mean you'll need to have your dinner eaten and cleared away by 6:50 p.m. at the latest. I have*

made the decision to fully support KONNIE HUQ, *the
Blue Peter presenter, for the following reasons:*

* She has a kind face

** She read my letter about conservation and environmental
growth on-air on a Tuesday afternoon. I did not win the
green badge due to being significantly older than the
9–15 years old entry requirement, which I was most
disappointed about. However, to be recognized nonetheless
was a joy and I wish to repay her.*

** She looks like she could tackle a paso doble and certainly
a Viennese waltz. She may not be robust enough for a jive,
but only time will tell.*

*I have contemplated where would be the most efficient place
for our letter exchange and have concluded that the plant pot
with the lemon thyme would be ideal. I will place all future
correspondence under the pot. You are free to do the same or slide
your letters under my door. If raining, I will place my letters
inside a shoe on the rack.*

Yours sincerely, the Girl in the Shed

After completing the letter, and reviewing it twice to ensure that
there are no spelling errors, I fold up the paper and let myself in
through the back door. I am immediately assaulted once again by
the dog, who does not seem to get my nonverbal cues. Perhaps the
animal and I have more in common than I first thought.

"Shoo! Shoo!" I yell at her, but that seems to excite her more.

"Do you want a gingerbread biscuit?" I ask.

She yelps and wags her tail exuberantly against the kitchen
table leg.

"Follow me, then."

Being the loyal but stupid mammal that she is, she follows me blindly into the living room, while I fist my hand pretending that I suddenly have a biscuit inside. "Sit," I command. To my complete amazement, she sits. Then a big sticky, oozy pool of saliva bubbles at her lips and pours over onto the carpet beneath. I walk out and close the door, trapping her inside. I have no biscuit.

Since it's raining, I slide my letter inside the boy's trainers, which I assume are his as the other shoes are women's heels or men's loafers.

I pick up the pair of red heels closest to me and flip them over, exposing the soles: *Ladies Size 9.*

I knew it.

Water fountains,
sculptures, and
fairy houses create a
garden full of surprises
for children.

June and the Coffee Shop

The next morning, sunlight pokes through the gap under the shed door and stretches toward me, like long spiky talons of a dracaena plant. It strikes me in the eyes, waking me from a rather restless slumber on the yoga mat and hotel blanket.

It is only 6:02 a.m., far earlier than my usual waking time, and I feel quite dazed and confused about what to do. Should I rise? And if I do, will this become my new waketime, and then will all my mealtimes need to be adjusted in accordance?

I have tried hard to accept the new routines since arriving here, pushing back my breakfast time by a whole five minutes while the last of the Wilsons trickle out the door to work/school. At home, I was always downstairs for my breakfast by 7:45 a.m. I'd make my own coffee, which I had to learn to do from an early age due to Mother's early work shifts at the post office. Over the years, and after many mistrials, I came to realize that my ideal coffee was 1.5 teaspoons of Marks & Spencer instant coffee, of a number 3 strength, with a generous splash of milk. I'd tried it several times in the staff room at lunchtime and had become familiar with the taste. Breakfast was usually completed by 8:05, shower by 8:20, and my boots were on at 8:30. I had to get the 8:40 bus into town for work. My shift was not until 9:30, but I liked to read the newspaper in the staff room before I started.

I was never late for work, not once. Some staff members sauntered in way past their start times, and some had the audacity to take a longer lunch break than the designated time, blaming it on the line at the sandwich truck or the slow-boiling kettle in our staff room. One reason why I always took a packed lunch and a thermos of tea from home. I had suggested that be made compulsory for all staff, but Linda had dismissed my suggestion. Linda dismissed a lot of my suggestions over the years, including ditching Christmas Sweater Day in lieu of Gardening Sweater Day, and requesting that all staff use a closed-lid container to store their food items in the fridge. I certainly did not want Maureen's smelly tuna baguette touching my cheese sandwich. I also requested that the containers be color-coded so I could visually locate my own with ease. That was also dismissed.

I glance at the clock on the shelf again: 6:12 a.m.

Confusion still clouds my thoughts and hurts my head. I roll over and grab the notepad from beside my boots and make a list, drawing a vertical line down the middle to separate the Pros and Cons. "Changes to an established and proven successful routine" goes under Cons and "More time in the day to tend to the garden" goes under Pros.

Routine is so important, according to Mother and my caseworker, who rarely agreed on anything except that. But it's not 7:45 a.m., and this is not my usual mattress or my bedroom. This is not my house, and when I go inside to make my coffee, it won't be my kitchen. This is all different and my routine is getting lost, alongside everything that made my life, *my life*. Mother included.

Heat churns in my belly, bubbling and boiling loudly like the kettle in my old house. The gray quick-boil kettle with the missing top handle because I'd thrown it against the wall one morning when I'd awoken to a power outage. I'd come downstairs to find blank clockfaces on the oven, the microwave, and the dishwasher. There were no lights and no electricity, which meant no breakfast. Everything was wrong with the day after that. I didn't make it to work for my shift and they'd called Mother. She'd come home immediately to find the kettle on the floor and me under the kitchen table drawing chrysanthemums on the wall with a black marker. After that, we had to fill the kettle with water directly through the spout and not through the top, as without the handle it was sealed shut, which at first was a terrible inconvenience but which I did get used to after seven and a half weeks.

Mother made sure the electricity bills were paid on time after that.

I take a sharp inhale as fragments of memories in my old kitchen and coffee mornings with Mother become heavy in the space behind my eyes, distracting me from my wake-up confusion. I gingerly inch open the shed door, and gaze into the kitchen beyond the glass. It's empty. The Wilsons don't tend to rise until closer to seven and for the forty-five minutes after that, the sounds of breakfast dishes, barking, and hurried conversations about homework and PE kits vibrate against the sliding doors and into the shed.

I gaze up one more time at the dark vacant windows, then stagger onto the moist grass, sleep still in my eyes. Dewy blades poke at my palms and the smells of summer and sunlight fill my nose. The neighbor's lavender bushes are now in full bloom and the scent wafts in through the slats in the tall fence. I can't go back to sleep, not now, so I pull on my boots and my long raincoat, only partially covering my ladybird pajamas. My hair is still knotted into a scrunchie at the top of my head like a pineapple. I can't go inside to make myself a coffee at this time; I have to go elsewhere for it. I take Mother, even though this is early for her too, and walk down the street, eyes flitting between the drawn curtains of sleeping neighbors and the glossy serrated leaves of the Japanese Yoshinos that line the other streets of Notting Hill. Sadly, I have missed the Yoshinos' short-lived bloom, which is usually no more than the first two weeks of early spring.

Most gardening enthusiasts love spring, but I am more partial to summer's long days and short nights, the higher temperatures, and the blooms—geraniums, bee balm, hydrangeas, and hibiscus. Winter, on the other hand, is not my favorite time of year at all. In fact, it's not particularly kind to me. The dark mornings confuse me and make me tired even though I go to bed at the same time and get up at the same time. And the cold biting wind destroys my summer efforts in the garden. Winter is a time for trimming back the dead and tending to the withered. Winter was also a time when Mother became small and quiet, choosing to spend evenings in her bedroom with a bottle of red wine, her pills, and her photo albums. Winter wasn't kind to Mother either.

Clutching her tight, I stop at the beginning of the next street, gazing down at the array of brightly colored shop doors and café canopies. I pass a little antiquarian dealer with more tea-stained maps in the window and a printing shop that boasts, "We print everything under the sun." Surely this is a figure of speech because everything that exists under the sun cannot be printed.

Beside the print shop of ambitious claims is a small café. Its door is wedged open and scents of cinnamon and vanilla waft out onto the concrete. I wiggle my hands into my pockets and find a crisp five-pound note, then I push open the door, which tinkles above my head. The sickly-sweet aromas are even stronger inside, and they tickle the inside of my head and behind my eyes. I resist an urge to sneeze.

A young woman around my age approaches the counter, a mint-green apron around her waist. "Good morning. Can I help you?"

"Good morning," I say back, pleased that I remember my manners even at this time of day. "Can I have a coffee, please."

"Sure. We have latte, cappuccino, Americano, espresso, macchiato, mocha, flat white, or just a filter? We also have an excellent selection of cold brews and nitros?"

I blink. "Pardon me?"

She names them all again, each word an exotic concoction of consonants and vowels. Is she speaking to me in a different language? Italian, perhaps. I do enjoy a bite of pizza every now and then, but I am more of a chicken and potatoes type of person, none of this European stuff.

"What's a nitro?" I ask tentatively.

"It's our classic cold brew coffee infused with nitrogen."

"My god, nitrogen? Why?"

"It gives the beverage a smooth and velvety texture."

Eyes wide and mouth agape, I glance around at the empty café wondering if the lack of customers is due to a significant safety concern over the nitrogen use.

She clicks her tongue and points to an old machine behind her. "Are you more of a filter person?"

"Susan at work says I have no filter?"

She clears her throat. "How do you take your coffee normally?"

I rattle off my tried-and-tested formula, emphasizing that the milk has to be made into a paste with the coffee granules before the water goes in. A couple of minutes later, she appears with a green speckled ceramic mug, steam rising from the hot liquid inside. I thank her and transfer the coffee into Mrs. Wilson's floral mug, which I have brought with me. Aromas of chocolate and oak seep into the air around me. I choose a small round table by the window that looks out onto the street lined with Yoshinos and aspens and gently position Mother on the table opposite me.

I take a long slow sip of coffee and check my watch again.

Conifers are a popular choice for patio spaces, but position them at a sensible distance from the house to allow room for growth.

June and the Season Opener of
Strictly Come Dancing

That evening, with the sun still high in the sky, I get a full view of everyone eating dinner inside the house. Dinner in the Wilson household appears to again consist of a large leafy green salad better fit for a garden animal, like a rabbit or mouse, the kind that are bothersome when composting or growing strawberry patches. Occasionally I have observed the Wilsons indulge in pasta. For example, yesterday they had spaghetti.

Londoners really seem to enjoy Italian cuisine and coffee. It might be difficult to convince the Wilsons that a frozen chicken Kiev and some boiled plain potatoes will be equally satisfying. Mrs. Wilson in particular will be hard to persuade, assuming she is still around come my move-in day.

When I first tried to envision life with my new caregiver, which was extremely difficult to do, I saw Mr. Wilson and myself out in the garden tending to the seedlings and the soil while the sun bathed us in its warmth. I did not see a pinched-face woman, a boy, and an animal in my vision. I saw myself and Father. And Mother too. But perhaps I will have to allow some leeway. Be "flexible," as one

caseworker told me to be once after another incident at the foster
home with the other kids. I told her that I was very flexible, that I
could touch my toes with my pointer fingers, unlike the other children in the house. She told me that one day I would understand what
she meant, but I am twenty-two years old and I still don't fully understand. I can, however, still touch my toes with my pointer fingers.

I got another note from the child inside this morning. I have not
opened it yet as I have had a very busy day. I had to clean up the
mutt's business over by the Persian silk. I may need to put a fence
around that at some point. The animal will eventually destroy the
soil around the roots.

The paper crinkles in my hands as I unfold it and begin to read.

Dear Girl in the Shed,

I received your letter safely, and was not aware that Strictly
Come Dancing *is showing on TV tonight. Usually we watch*
Ant & Dec's Saturday Night Takeaway *unless there's a good
movie on. Tonight Channel 4 is showing* Jurassic Park, *however,
I have seen it once before and found it quite scary, so I'm fine to
insist we watch* Strictly.

*I've had most of the day to give a lot of thought to the best
TV angle and I think if I turn the TV to the left (my left), you'll
get a better view of the screen from the patio. The only problem is
if Dad sits in the armchair in front of it, then his big head will
block the bottom left of the screen. I'll need to make sure I get
there first.*

*I'm not allowed to use the internet, so I'll see who the
contestants are tonight and then pick my favorite after, if that's
okay?*

*I have a favor to ask in return—I'm doing a survey for a
school assignment, but I don't know who else to ask except for*

myself, Mum, Dad, and our neighbor Camille. Will you do it too?
I've included it below if you can.
  And if you can, then thank you very much.

Yours truly,
Henry

I gaze at his survey, perplexed at the questions and the means of keeping score. I can only assume that the questions are not his idea nor is the expectation that he use only tallies to count and not real numbers. Mother and I didn't study tallies much in our homeschool lessons, but the boy must be covering tallies in math, so I play along:

This or That		
1. Dogs or Cats?	Dogs: III	Cats: I
2. Summer or Winter?	Summer: IIII	Winter: I
3. Water or Juice?	Water: IIII	Juice: I
4. Chelsea or Crystal Palace?	Chelsea: II	CP: II
5. Television or Cinema?	TV: I	Cinema: IIII

I don't answer question 1 because I dislike animals or question 4 because I have never heard of either of those political parties. I add my name to the list of participants, next to someone called Camille Hargreaves, draw a flower beside it, fold the survey back up, and slide it within the pages of my almanac for safekeeping.

It is now 6:52 p.m. I want to ensure a good viewing spot for the season premiere, so I quietly leave the shed and tiptoe across the grass. It's still wet from a day of rainfall and mist, and I am glad for my wellies. I've considered investing in a pair of slippers for the shed, but perhaps I'll save that purchase for when I move into the house so they don't get dirty or dusty from being outside.

The kitchen is empty, and the dining table has been stripped clean of the meal. The chairs are tucked back in and the place mats have been wiped down and stored in the wire rack in the middle of the table, along with a large stack of frilly napkins. A very efficient cleanup. A dim bulb still shines over the cooker, potentially draining energy, and a red light flickers on the dishwasher.

I kneel beside the potted plant to the side of the glass patio doors. Above, a small window is propped open, likely to allow me to hear better. Tucked behind the ceramic pot is a tartan cushion from the living room. I am impressed. The child has exceeded my expectations for tonight's viewing. The cushion is a nice addition. I place it under my bottom and sit cross-legged, Mother beside me. I check my watch again. 6:59 p.m.

Through the kitchen is another set of sliding doors, which the child has thankfully remembered to pull all the way open. As promised, he sits in the armchair facing the TV, which has been angled toward the patio doors. Mrs. Wilson perches on the sofa opposite him with a book in her lap and a glass of white wine on the coffee table. She checks her watch and glances behind her, to the hallway and front door. Mr. Wilson is nowhere to be seen. The living room chandeliers are dimmed, and the light from the TV screen illuminates the room and Mrs. Wilson's face. The image of the silver disco ball spins and spins on the TV as the opening music trickles out the open window into the garden space. I smile and glance down at Mother.

It feels familiar.

First up are the judges' introductions. Mother's favorite. And then the professional dancers saunter onstage, twirling and leaping in sequins, tulle, glitter, hardened hairspray, and sparkly makeup.

And finally, the contestants. All twelve of them. Some I have never seen before, likely coming from the fields of sports or politics.

I watch them, each parading across the screen with their assigned dance partner. All twelve . . . but where is Konnie Huq? My eyes dart between the contestants, wondering if my selected favorite is styled beyond recognition, but even through the orange makeup and hair extensions I cannot spot her.

I press my face harder against the glass. I don't recognize anyone else in this moment, and so far no one has wowed me with their quickstep or winning smile. I had spent time choosing Konnie when the names of the contestants first got released to the media earlier this year. Mother and I had picked her together.

And now Mother is not here to help me pick again.

Everything is wrong about this evening, suddenly.

A warmth builds in my belly, as familiar as the silver glittering disco ball on the screen. My hands grip the edge of the terra-cotta pot beside me, fingernails digging into the soil that sits beyond the lip. A loud beeping in the corner inside jerks my head to the left. A sound of churning and a hiss of rushing water rips through the kitchen and the garden.

It's the dishwasher.

They have put the dishwasher on, right as *Strictly* is starting!

The chugging and sloshing drowns out the voices and music from the TV. I can't hear anything.

There is a flicker of gray in the hallway and suddenly Mr. Wilson is standing between the kitchen and the living room, his back to me, hands in his pockets, chatting to his wife—blocking the television screen. I fight the urge to scream through the glass, "Move!" I bite down on my bottom lip until I pierce through it and a trickle of metallic blood hits my tongue.

He does not move. In fact, he turns and closes the sliding doors, the television screen disappearing behind a wall of oak and frosted glass. Then everything goes dark and quiet. A swirling swishing sound fills my eardrums until they throb. My fingertips sting, my palms are red, and I become aware of a gritty pebbly residue on my hands.

When I open my eyes, I am on my hands and knees, panting. There is a droplet of blood on the stone beneath me. Mother is on her side, thankfully intact, but the terra-cotta pot is cracked open, shattered across the patio. Fragments of orange clay surround me. There is soil everywhere. The roots of a small conifer are strewn on the ground. Torn and exposed.

The kitchen is empty, silent except for the chugging of the dish-washer. And I am outside, alone.

A companion planting chart can show which vegetables benefit from being paired together in a bed.

June and the Boy in the Garden

I remain in the shed for most of the next day as the rain starts again. Beads of water tap against the wood outside as if someone is gently knocking. The air inside has become stuffy and suffocating, and I wish for nothing more than a small window to crack open to let a breeze in to wash away the mugginess and the heaviness from last night. But no air flows in under the door, and the walls become increasingly warm and claggy throughout the day.

Because of the rain, or perhaps because it's a Sunday, the Wilsons have also remained inside. I have had to source my meals and teas outside at cafés. If it rains like this often in London, then the money Mr. Wilson gave me will not last much longer. I now have a loyalty card for the Coffee Project, so at least I can look forward to discounted coffee. Their staff was most disappointed that I didn't have a phone to download the "app." If I had, I would have got a free coffee. That's a shame. Mother would have said it was a scam, though, and if I did have a phone to download the app, then the government would steal my private information and use it against me to sway political votes. Mother is more experienced in the world than I am, so she probably would have been right.

At 4:12 p.m., it finally stops raining and a sliver of sunshine seeps in under the shed door. It tickles my fingers as I dance my hand in front, casting small shadows on the shelves beside me. The air outside is quiet, still, as if everyone has finally gone out, but as I reach up to unlock the shed, I hear the back door of the house slide open. The shrill voice of Mrs. Wilson erupts through the garden, likely shaking the branches of the Persian silk and terrifying the cat at number 14.

"My conifer!" she screeches. "What happened out here? Robert, did you see this? . . . Robert? . . . *Robert!*"

"Yes, dear?" he grumbles, the sliding door whooshing open further. I haven't heard Mr. Wilson's voice since the day he escorted me into a taxi with a handful of money and his business card.

"It's those bloody kids again!"

I listen to her clean up the pot from last night, the scraping and dragging of broken ceramic on the wet stone. I wonder if her brush will be wet now because of the rain on the patio.

"What was that, dear?" Mr. Wilson asks, although I am not sure why, as the entire street is likely to have heard her.

Heavy footsteps slap down on the wet patio stone, making the tiny hairs on my arms bristle and stand up.

"I said, it's those kids again, vandalizing the gardens. I'm calling the police. I'm not having this. Look, Robert, my favorite pot! Ruined!"

"I could try gluing it?"

"Don't be ridiculous. You can't glue this. Besides, you'd see all the white bubbly glue lines afterward and people would think we just couldn't *afford* to buy a new one."

"I don't think people care that much about our plant pots, Judith."

"Of course they do—it's London!" she snaps.

The door clicks open again. "What's all the shouting about?"

Now the child has joined. The only one missing is—

"Tilly, down!"

The sound of an aggressive tail wag thumps through the air, followed by a scraping of metal on stone. I think the patio furniture is being rearranged. I shall have to move it back as I'm used to its position by now and any change may affect me.

"Henry, get Tilly inside. I don't want her getting shards of this pot in her paws."

"But she has to go to the toilet," he argues.

"Okay, quickly, then. Take her over to the back corner."

No, not by the Persian silk tree again.

As they head back inside, Mr. and Mrs. Wilson continue discussing the possibilities of gluing the terra-cotta pot back together without their neighbor Camille noticing. There's a swift thud of the door as it closes behind them and their voices soon fade. Suddenly a rustling of bushes and a snapping of twigs cuts through the silence. A small silhouette covers the gap in the shed door, extinguishing the light from the sun that had trickled in. From the size of the shadow it appears to be the child, so I shift closer and wait for his note to be slid under the door, but all I hear is heavy breathing.

"Did you do that to the pot?" he asks.

"Yes," I reply because Mother told me never to lie.

"Why?"

I don't answer.

"I won't tell anyone."

I press a finger into the dusty wall of the shed and draw three faces, one with an upturned mouth, one with a downturned mouth, and one with an open mouth, teeth bared. I circle the last face. "Because I was angry," I finally say.

"Why were you angry?"

No one except Mother has ever asked me why I am angry. Not even my old teachers at school. All they were concerned about was the damage that had been inflicted as a result of such anger. It was Mother who made me write down on paper why I was angry and what would help me next time so that I wouldn't become angry again. And then she started with the faces—a smiley face, a sad face, a hungry face, a tired face, a confused face—and she'd ask me to circle the one that best represented how I felt inside. That was often easier than putting it into words and so we carried on with that. But Mother is no longer here to draw those faces, so I have to do it myself. At least until I move in, then Mr. Wilson can do it for me. That will be much quicker and will shorten my response time to questions about my emotions.

"Konnie Huq wasn't on and she was my favorite. I didn't recognize the other contestants, except for the TV presenter who was arrested last year for indecent exposure, and so I didn't know who else to choose," I reply, my voicing strained and unsure.

"The presenter said—"

"Claudia or Tess?" I question. If the boy is to be my new *Strictly* viewing partner, then he must learn the names and the dances and the judges and the meanings behind the scores.

"Um, the lady with the black hair and scary eye makeup."

"Claudia." I nod.

"She said Konnie Huq had broken her leg in rehearsal—"

"I knew she wasn't robust enough for the jive," I sigh. Perhaps Konnie had been the wrong choice to begin with, even if Mother and I had chosen her together. We did doubt her jiving strength even back then. The jive isn't for everyone. It takes a certain level of stamina and flexibility.

"There's the singer, Aled?"

"No. Not him."

"Why not?"

"Because I don't know any of his songs and because his name is spelt incorrectly."

"How about the chef, then?" he suggests, his feet shuffling closer. I can see a sliver of his blue trainers through the crack at the bottom of the door. Cobalt-blue like lobelias and delphiniums. Like Mother's suede heels. My chest cavity aches.

"His waltz looked quite good, not that I'm an expert like you."

I stand up straight. He's right—I am an expert. I know all the dances, the correct techniques, and I can usually guess the judges' score based on the contestants' performances. Just because Konnie has let Mother and me down, it doesn't mean the entire season is unwatchable. I can choose another contestant, like the child is suggesting. I can be *flexible*, unlike Konnie Huq, apparently.

"Okay. The chef will do. I remember him now. I think I do know him. Sometimes his Sunday-morning cooking shows were on in the background when I came downstairs. He looked like he made good pancakes once. Nicely shaped, anyway."

"Okay, the chef it is. We can support him together."

Together.

The child sounds pleased. His dog sounds hungry, her wet snout sniffing the door.

"I have a couple more requests for next week's episode," I add, also shuffling closer.

"Okay."

"The dishwasher was on last night, so I could barely hear the television over it. You have a very loud dishwasher."

"I don't think I can buy a new one by next week," he says quietly. "I believe they're quite expensive."

"No, my question is, why was it on at seven, during the show?"

"That was Mum."

"Of course it was," I grumble.

"But I'll ask her not to put it on until after the episode."

"And then when my biological father came in, he closed the door, completely blocking me out," I snap, shrilly, sounding a bit too similar to Mrs. Wilson.

"What?"

"You were probably so engrossed in the show that you didn't notice. It's understandable given that I often find myself completely captivated, especially when at the opening episode. Don't get me started on the season finale. Sometimes I forget to eat that day, or use the toilet."

"You called my dad your 'biological father,'" he says, drawing even closer.

"Yes, I believe he is my biological father, as does he. Although perhaps one day we should take a DNA test just to be sure."

"So . . . so does that make you my sister?"

"I suppose, but only *half* a sister as we only share one parent," I emphasize, not wanting to lead him on into thinking we are one *whole* of anything.

The boy doesn't speak for a few moments. He just stands there, his mutt loudly rummaging around the herb pots behind the shed. She better not be defecating in the lemon thyme. I'm hoping to use it in a fruit salad. The fragrance is lovely when it's sprinkled on watermelon and green apple slices.

"Cool," he finally says.

"Cool," I reply, the corners of my mouth pulling up. I press a fingertip into the shed wall again and this time circle the face with the upturned mouth. HAPPY.

"

Careful consideration of distance and depth when planting can greatly lower the risk of disease spreading in beds.

"

June and the School Bullies

The next morning, after I have put on a pair of red capri trousers and knotted the top half of my hair to pull it away from my face, I open the shed door and discover a real croissant is sitting out for me. Even better, it has been warmed and wrapped in tinfoil, along with a good dollop of seedless jam. It's not seedless *strawberry* jam, but it is of a berry origin and is certainly better than the flourless bread roll and fake margarine I had been given the last time. Someone must have gone shopping. If I had known, I would have requested M&S Gold instant coffee of a number 3 strength, as I am running low.

I have continued to rise earlier than my usual time and without my usual coffee, things have been slightly hazy and confusing. I make coffee inside after everyone leaves, but recently they seem to be leaving a few minutes later each morning. On Sundays, they do not leave until after 10:30 a.m., which means I have to sneak out of the shed and the garden and head over to the Coffee Project, which even with my discount card is still expensive. And I'm not sure why they term it a loyalty card as it seems that every person who enters either has one or is offered one.

Back home, I was always outside on the weekends, either in my garden or at the community one, working alongside Elsbeth or Carol, our knees on mats, trowels heavy in our palms, hats or visors dipped low, as the shared patch was often in direct sunlight. I certainly wasn't indoors lounging on the sofa like the Wilsons tend to do on weekends. I once overheard a conversation in the staff room at work, when Maureen said she enjoyed being a "couch potato" on Sundays, and I remember wondering what role the root vegetable had in her weekend pursuit. I could understand it if she were a gardener like me, but she was referring to a piece of furniture at the time and I could not make the connection. Couch. Potato.

I am still uncertain of that one.

The rate of my breathing increases as fragments of the life I left in Maryhill make their way back into my thoughts. It makes my skin tingle. Memories of work, of home, of the community patch with Carol's overfertilised petunias, Elsbeth's stories about her husband's backpacking trips in Peru, and the verbena I'd pluck only moments from finishing, so I could immediately bag it and bring it home for Mother to steep in her tea.

Mother.

I haven't seen much of Mr. Wilson over the past couple of days, except for a brief glimpse of him this morning as he let the dog out. He was dressed in his work clothes already, his tie hanging off his shirt collar like a leash. He held a large coffee mug and I could smell the aromas through a crack in the shed door where I watch the unfolding of the household on most days. He moved slowly, his shoulders slumped and sagging. He kept checking his phone, then he went back inside with the dog, the door slamming behind them.

At 11:50 a.m., I enter the house with the hideaway key, make myself a sandwich with a packet of cheese slices that I hide in the bottom fridge drawer under the bag of kale, and sit outside in the garden, cross-legged in the middle of the grass with the blades poking at my shins and a mug of milky tea cradled in my hands. The sun is high in the afternoon sky, a cloudless canvas of clear blue. Afterward, I wash and put away my dishes, tend to the lemon thyme in the planter box, and clip back the clusters of mint. Mint can be both an enemy and a friend, giving the garden a wonderful cool scent yet growing more rapidly and wildly than any common weed in just the blink of an eye. Mint always has to be scaled back, always clipped and trimmed, and never allowed to wander freely, otherwise it's the end for the garden.

At afternoon break time, I make myself another cup of tea and again sit on the grass to enjoy it, beneath the shade of the Persian silk and the street's dawn redwoods, the encyclopedia on my lap, open to "How to Propagate Shrubs," the pages flapping in the mild breeze. If I close my eyes and let my mind wander free like the mint, I can bring myself back to my old garden at home in Maryhill. I can feel the same breeze across my cheeks and shoulders, hear the same birdsong floating from the trees. For a moment, however fleeting, I am home. And if I close my eyes really tight and pretend really hard, then Mother is home with me too. I can faintly hear her inside the kitchen, rustling food shopping from bags or clinking dinnerware over the sink. And humming, always humming. While cooking, tidying, and sometimes while sipping her red wine in front of the TV during the adverts.

Suddenly I cannot remember her favorite song. I believe there was "bird" in the title.

I remember the tune, though. I can still hear it, even over the traffic, the neighbor's radio, and—

The laughter. The cruel laughter, and the taunting of schoolkids. I flicker my eyelids open, the garden of 16 Lansdowne Road coming back into focus and the familiarity of home fading fast. Mother's song abruptly silenced. It trickles out of my ears and away from my memories, and I am left with an odd sensation in my chest, a sort of coldness, perhaps.

I slowly climb to my feet and edge to the bottom of the garden, where grass meets crushed stone. There, I hear the kids' name-calling and whistles, their taunts and jibes. I peer around the side of the wall and see a group of schoolboys laughing and pointing, while the Wilson child hunches in the middle, his face red and his eyes low on the ground as they ask him if his mum and dad are also "spastics," whatever that means.

I listen to it go on for a bit, curious but not concerned. Concern is for full siblings, not for *half* brothers and *half* sisters. I wait for the child to get angry and scare them off, throw a plant pot or a shoe, or swing his backpack at them. The things that normally work. But he doesn't do anything other than stand there and idly receive their insults. I wish he had someone like Mother. When I was bullied, Mother stormed out of the house, her nightgown flapping in the wind behind her, screaming murderous threats while she swung an empty wine bottle at the kids. They never came past my house again, and I was never bullied again. I was also promptly removed from school, Mother suddenly favoring the benefits of homeschooling. My caseworker came around more often after that too.

Eventually, it becomes quiet and the sounds of the breeze in the branches trickle back in around me. I glance at the shed, the door swinging open to let the wind in and the smells out, wondering if I should dart inside, but then the stones crunch and shift as the child meanders down the garden path. He startles when he sees me, his cheeks reddening. He stands rigid like a garden statue, hands down by his sides, eyes wide, through thick-rimmed glasses barely blinking. He wears a school uniform, a very boring combination of dull navy and matte beige. The shirt's collar has a little bit of a red trim, but all in all, it isn't exactly a very summery outfit for the month of June. But perhaps "dull" is London's dress code. All I've seen Mrs. Wilson wear is beige and black, while Mr. Wilson regularly opts for gray. Most of the dresses or capris I own are either patterned in florals or brightly colored like the buds I tend to in the garden. Mother was the same. She loved the colors and patterns of the season. Mother was summer all year long. Except for in winter. Mother wasn't even Mother in winter.

"You look different to what I imagined," the boy eventually says.

"You look the same." I shrug. "Although I have seen a photo of you already."

"You're out of the shed."

"Yes, I'm out of the shed."

He walks slightly closer and glances around. "What are you doing?"

"Standing on the grass."

"Why are you in the garden without shoes?"

"Because it's soft and warm on the grass."

His eyes twitch, and he comes closer again.

I take a step back and he stops. I sink onto the grass and sit cross-legged, grass tickling my ankles.

"What are you doing now?" he asks, his eyes wide.

"Now I'm sitting on the grass." I lean back on my hands and continue staring at him, a strange familiarity between us.

He walks a couple more steps toward me, his hard shiny black school shoes crushing the blades of grass. He slowly sits down opposite me. He crosses his legs and leans back like me. I don't say so, but I'm immediately taken aback by how similar his eyes are to mine. Green and shaped like an almond-lobed leaf from a *Prunus triloba* shrub. His thin pursed, disapproving lips come from his mother.

We spend the rest of the afternoon like this, neither of us in the mood for further conversation. Occasionally he sweeps his palm over the grass that is thickly blanketed in the afternoon sun, confirming he agrees that it is both soft and warm. He watches me lie back, eyes closed, face tilted up to the sun, and soon joins me, our heads slightly touching.

Surprisingly, it doesn't bother me.

When my rainbow watch beeps at 4:55 p.m., I stand up and go back to the shed, locking the door behind me. I don't say goodbye or glance back at the child. A few minutes later, I hear his mother's car pull into the driveway, the five o'clock news blasting from her radio, followed by the unnecessary loud slamming of a car door. I curl my knees into my chest as I sit quietly on the floor, on top of my bedding. Moments later, Mrs. Wilson's sharp voice cuts through the once peaceful air, the shrillness slicing through my door.

"Henry, what on earth are you doing out here? Why are you sitting in the middle of the garden? We do own chairs, you know?"

"

Forget-Me-Nots are edible, delicious when candied, and are known to soothe anxiety and alleviate stress.

"

June and the Return of Mother

The caseworker said it must be fragments of a conversation I had overheard later on, but I think I remember the first time I met my mother. Not the *first* first time, when I was born, but after that, when she returned from "finding herself."

I was almost seven years old and had been with my third foster family for about two years by then, and my old caseworker, Aileen, had orchestrated a meeting in a park opposite the house, near Irvine. I was never one for noise and chaos, two things closely associated with the average playground, so by the time Mother had arrived to meet us, I was being dragged out of the sandbox for apparently striking another child with a toy truck.

Mother stood under a weeping willow tree, her hands clasped in front of her, and watched as I was led away from the sandy pit of destruction, through the gates, and out to the grassy field. I remember how slow she walked from that tree to where I stood and how fast she blinked her eyes as she gazed down at me. I remember thinking there was something wrong with her eyes, that perhaps she too had had sand flicked into them by some nasty little boy with red hair and a toy truck.

She gave the caseworker a cursory greeting, then bent to her knees. She held out her arms, her palms up to the blue sky above us that was suddenly filled with blackbirds. Aileen nudged me forward into this woman's embrace, and before I could stop it, her arms tightened around me. I didn't like hugs, even back then. As I wriggled in her bony arms, which struggled to hold me in place, she said to me, "I'm better now, June."

Then she held me tighter.

That was the first and only time I wet myself. The warmth spread through me and over me in seconds, and trickled down my leg onto my white socks and yellow trainers, the kind that lit up and sparkled when I walked.

I hadn't even realized that Mother had been away until the day she returned.

That was the first day of summer, the twenty-first of June. It was a Thursday. I looked it up when I was much older and when I became interested in forecasts, long range and short range. It was overcast with low winds and humidity, and the temperature didn't get over fourteen degrees that day.

We didn't talk about that day again, and there were only brief mentions of her years away from me. I asked minimal questions and she gave me minimal answers. We were strangers to each other for a very long time, but then we became something else. Something akin to what I'd seen on television shows or from watching the kids at school greeting their mothers at the end of the school day.

We become familiar with one another.

Mother didn't have any family she still talked to, and she didn't make friends easily. For me, she was the only family I had, and the only friend I could make too. Other than the times at our respective workplaces, I had my gardening and Mother had her television soaps and her red wine, but we spent evenings and weekends together. And I even grew to not mind brief hugs from her, not that she gave them as freely as she did in the beginning. She typically reserved them for special occasions like Christmas Day, birthdays, and the opening episodes of *Strictly Come Dancing*.

I had missed her hug at the weekend, missed the smell of her perfume, the tickle of her long wavy hair against my cheek, and the sound of her voice as she said my name. "June."

And no matter how hard I try, I can't seem to stop those memories from wilting and fading, like tulips on a hot summer's day.

Gardens can provide refuge to plants and wildlife escaping an increase in property development and a decline in wild countryside.

June and the Garden Chat

Today is an odd weather day. Only seventeen degrees, much milder than the previous one. It feels more like spring than summer. I'm wearing a cardigan the color of rusted copper and green-print trousers, and a thicker pair of socks inside my welly boots. I have spent most of the early afternoon prodding the earthworms around the Persian silk, to make sure the soil-dwelling detritivores are doing their job. A buildup of decomposing plant matter around the roots of a Persian silk can be very detrimental to their growth. Thankfully, the worms are behaving, so I let them be.

At 2:55 p.m., I make my way back into the kitchen for my tea break, this time sampling one of the Wilsons' gluten-free, dairy-free biscuits, which is very much bordering on being taste-free too. Given the cooler conditions, I drape a blanket over my shoulders before I sit on the grass, again needing to air out the shed. Around 3:25 p.m., the child returns and joins me in the garden. Once more, he sits cross-legged facing me, eyeing the mug I cradle in my hands.

"How often do you go into the house when no one's home?" he eventually asks, after twelve whole minutes of silence.

"Four times during a weekday, but weekends vary, depending on the weather and your mother's plans. Sometimes I need to source my meals and teas at the café at Notting Hill Gate. It's incredibly inconvenient."

"What do you do when you're inside my house?"

"I make my meals and teas in the kitchen, and I use your bathroom."

"I knew it," he says, shaking his head. "You don't wipe down the sink after you wash your hands, and Mum blames Dad for it. Why are you living in our shed?"

"Because it's warm and sheltered from the rain. It's also free."

"Do you not have any money?"

"I have some."

"I have £8.57 in my piggy bank upstairs if you want it?"

"That's not going to get me very far, but I appreciate your efforts. Thank you."

"I can get more."

"We'll see."

"How do you know for sure that my dad is also your dad?"

"I don't, but he seems to think so. I also found an envelope addressed to him by my mother that had my things inside: old drawings, some teeth—"

"Teeth?"

"Baby teeth."

"Right." He scratches his nose, drawing my attention to the freckles around it, like mine. "Will you live with us one day, *inside* the house I mean?"

I suddenly become aware of the birdsong over my shoulder, the sound of the breeze in the branches, and the passing of a large vehicle of some kind on the roads behind. I want to ask him if he wants me to live inside the house one day. But instead, I say, "My turn for questions."

He shrugs. "Okay."

"Why would I wipe down a sink after I wash my hands?"

"To dry it."

"Isn't the point of a sink to wet it?"

He shrugs again.

"Why do you own an animal?"

"Tilly's our pet."

"So?"

"She's part of our family."

"She can't be. She's an animal. Only humans form families."

"I disagree."

"Noted."

"Any more questions?"

"Favorite color?"

"Blue."

"Favorite flower?"

"Daisy."

"That's a weed, not a flower."

"I disagree, again."

"Noted, again. Who tends to your garden? I haven't seen anyone come out here in the three weeks I've been here."

"You've been here for three weeks?"

"It's my turn for questions, remember?"

"We had a gardener, Sally. But then Mum called Sally a cow and she stopped coming around. Mum says she's better at gardening than Sally anyway."

"Sally must be really bad, then."

"Anything else you want to know?"

"Why does your mother buy sugar in cube form?"

"I'm not sure. You'd have to ask her yourself."

I take a final slurp of tea, which has now cooled beyond the point of taste and comfort, and gently place the mug down in a nest of grass and daisies. Weeds. "Why do you let those boys call you names and make fun of you?"

He shrugs again, and plucks a daisy from beside the mug. "What else can I do?" he mutters.

"Hit them."

His eyes flicker up, a smile forming on his face, then it fades as he realizes I am very serious.

"Hit them," I say again.

"Mum says just to ignore them and they'll go away."

"That advice is incorrect. They don't go away."

"I know."

"When I was called names, ridiculed for my interest in flowers and plants and insects, and my passion for brightly colored jumpers and summery accessories, such as visors and sunglasses even in the winter months, I tried ignoring them too. It only made them shout louder. The only thing that silenced them was Mother swinging a bottle of Chianti Reserva at them. That shut them up."

"Your mother sounds way cooler than mine."

"She was." That coldness in my chest is back, tugging and pulling at my insides.

"Only three days left of school, then it's the summer holidays. Hopefully they'll find a new target by September."

"Doubtful."

He uncrosses his legs and rises to stand, blocking the light from the sky.

"Where are you going?" I ask.

"It's almost five o'clock. Mum will be home soon."

I glance at my watch. The child is correct. I haven't even noticed the passing of time, which is very unusual for me.

"Goodbye, then," he says.

"Goodbye, then."

He walks away, then turns when he gets to the patio. "One last question: What's your name?"

"June."

"June like the month?"

"June like the month." I smile. The child and I might get on after all.

"I'm Henry."

"I know."

"Well, bye for now, June."

"Goodbye, Henry."

He enters the house through the sliding doors, closing them with a click. Then he walks through the kitchen and disappears around the corner, into the hallway. His mother's car pulls into the driveway minutes after that.

A successful garden needs careful consideration and planning.

June and the Ready-Made Birthday Cake

It's been another restless night, with sleep coming but never quite staying. I have already awoken several times to find the shed still blanketed in nighttime. The hands on the small analog clock scrape slowly around the barrel and bezel, reluctantly edging forward. When sleep comes, my dreams are a fog of old beginnings and new endings. I dream of the day Mother died, and of long grass and knots of weeds, muddy riverbanks, flashing police sirens, and blood on my hands. Then I wake and stare at the clock dial again. And it continues on like this for most of the night.

I consider wandering the garden, perhaps even entering the house to make myself a cup of warm honeyed milk like Mother used to make for me before the wind chimes, but my body feels too heavy to rise from my bed on the floor. And I worry that the Wilsons will hear me from their bedrooms. I wonder how they sleep. It can't be deeply. All that dehydrated kale and probiotic kefir must be very difficult to digest. I expect them to be up several times through the night with bloating.

When I finally do surface from the shed, the house is quiet, empty, all traces of human chatter and breakfast clatter gone. I hadn't heard the family leave this morning, having been too engrossed in a chapter about soluble aluminum and stunted root growth. I unlock and slide open the patio doors. The dog bounds out into the garden, her tail whipping too close to the flower beds. She immediately circles and squats by the Persian silk, a look of triumph on her furry face. I sigh loudly. The grass around the roots will never be the same.

When I turn back to the kitchen, I pause, surveying the space before me. Brightly colored streamers and balloons explode from corners and wall edges and even from the fridge door. Above the living room archway is a long silver banner emblazoned with red lettering:

Happy Birthday, Dad

It appears to be Mr. Wilson's birthday today, although I have not been informed of this fact. Birthdays were a very big deal in my house. Mother would dress in her finest, layers of satin and tulle cascading down her lithe frame, while she danced around the kitchen, sifting flour into ceramic bowls and whipping egg whites into stiff, snowy peaks. The granite counter was cluttered with baking instruments, an array of mismatching bargain finds. She was an expert "thrifter." She would often pass thrift stores on her walk back from work and return home laden with bags and boxes. Glassware with intricate designs coiling and curling up the stems, hand-painted bowls, teacups with exotic prints.

After the beating of eggs and the folding of white sugar into yellow butter, the cake batter was delicately placed onto the oven rack, a timer set for sixteen minutes. I never ate the cake in the end. Even in the earlier days, I didn't stray too far from my everyday dietary choices. Mother ate it herself, washing it down with a bottle of sparkling wine that she'd won in the staff raffle earlier that year. Mother always seemed to win in the raffle. Mother was very lucky. Sadly, her colleagues didn't see it that way and reassigned the task of organizing the Royal Mail raffle to someone else. After that, she was forced to source her own sparkling wine, which she was most upset about. They didn't sell wine in our local thrift stores, but I wonder if they do in London. England seems to have its own way of doing things. Thankfully, the English do adhere to some universal rules such as "Don't lie" and "Acknowledge birthdays."

Mother's birthday is October . . . October . . . why can't I remember the day?

The nineteenth, perhaps. Or maybe the eighteenth. Details seem to be escaping me more and more lately, my head becoming heavier with thoughts that never plagued me before—mealtimes, daily routines, sleep patterns. Even these decorations bother me. They are excessive, and the streamers hanging from the cooker hood are certainly a fire hazard. Each balloon is tied with a thin ribbon and secured to a surface with thick strips of gift-wrapping tape. And the decorations continue through to the living room, around the television set, into the hallway, and up the stairs, winding along the banister. They're everywhere. Every wall corner and available edge is occupied with a glittery shiny decoration of some kind, which strangely makes me desire a strong mug of coffee even more.

As the kettle splutters and roars to a boil, I swing open the fridge door, the balloons on it bouncing around. On the middle shelf of the fridge is a large white box. Always the curious one, I slide it out and onto the table for further inspection. Inside is a cake—a square buttercream-lathered sponge cake with the same basic and somewhat predictable lettering: HAPPY BIRTHDAY, DAD.

I can't believe it—the Wilsons have *bought* a birthday cake. They have paid money for someone else to bake it. Where is the effort and thought in that? Have they also hired someone to shop for, select, and wrap the birthday present? Are they going to pay someone to cut the cake later too? Where does it end?

Once I drain my mug and refill it, I return to the shed to gather my belongings for my first trip to London's famous shopping district.

I don't know what Londoners wear on a weekday outing to the stores, so I dress conservatively in loose-fitting linen shorts, a daisy-print top, and my usual gardening boots. I throw on my raincoat and loosely tie my hair back with a ribbon that I've stolen from a birthday centerpiece on the dining table, hoping that the Wilsons will blame the dog and her insatiable hunger for inanimate objects.

A slight chill hovers in the air, the weather threatening to turn at any moment. I zip up my coat and follow my map to Notting Hill's underground station, where I will have to purchase another Oyster card if I am to board a train. I haven't been on public transport since the day a man took my money and I kicked the railing so hard my toes bruised a shade of purple, like crocuses. If I see the man again, I'll ask him to return everything immediately.

I pop on my headphones and stand at the top of the stairs beneath a giant circular sign:

UNDERGROUND

At the bottom, a small number of people bustle about. Everyone bumps into each other, phones in hand, eyes down. I take a deep breath and descend one step, reminding myself that this birthday predicament has to be rectified, beginning with a carefully chosen gift and the purchase of ingredients to bake a *real* cake. But my feet cannot move past the first step. I am frozen, commuters bumping into me as they pass, forcing me to clutch the handrail until my knuckles turn bone white. I shimmy back up the step and immediately feel my shoulders relax.

No, I cannot.

I have legs. Two of them. I can walk.

Foliage plants add
color and texture
to any urban space
and can thrive
in shady areas.

June and the Trip to Harrods

The walk to Knightsbridge takes me a little under an hour, but outside in the daylight where it is safe, there are no bad men or thieves or police officers, which is always good news even for the most seasoned city traveler. But just to err on the side of caution, I've hid my money in my left welly boot.

I asked the woman at the Coffee Project to direct me to the best shop in London to pick out a gift for a maximum of £10 for the man I recently discovered is my biological father. She has sent me to a place called

HARRODS

The building is gigantic. Dozens of windows are dotted between brown brick and flagpoles, and there is a large glass revolving door. In my experience, these doors can be a safety hazard for easily distracted consumers. At my workplace, shoppers come and go through a one-way pull door, which is far more efficient.

Past the door is a large easel displaying the general "guidelines" for shopping at Harrods, which include refraining from "wearing clothing which may reveal intimate parts of the body." I am not wearing revealing clothing that showcases "intimate parts of the body," so I feel comfortable proceeding with the shopping task.

At my work, there are four departments: Men's, Women's, Accessories, and my department and area of expertise, the Foodhall.

Technically, "Accessories" can be broken down into further sub-departments if someone counts shoes and handbags as separate, but in general, the departments are fairly easy to find and to navigate. Here at Harrods, there are 330 departments.

How am I ever going to find a gift for my biological father in the allotted ninety minutes?

I decide to visit Personal Shopping, even though I am not entirely sure of its purpose. It does, however, display a large sign of comparable size to the "guidelines" boasting "immediate shopping success," with confident statements such as: "We'll find you exactly what you need."

I plop down on the plush armchair and await assistance.

A tall blond woman in a skirt suit approaches me from the side and sits in the leather chair opposite me. "Good morning."

"Good *afternoon*," I correct her. Already a bad sign.

"Sorry, *afternoon*. How can I assist you today?"

"I'm here to buy a present for my biological father. I just found out it's his birthday today."

She blinks a couple of times, then smiles. "Lovely. And what does he usually like?"

"I'm not sure. I only met him three weeks ago."

"Okay. Do you know about his interests, what he likes to do, what his favorite colors are, and so on?"

"Like I said, I only found out it's his birthday today, so I didn't have time to ask his son, my half brother, which I understand now would have narrowed my search significantly."

"Of course." She smiles. "In the past, what have you generally bought for people on their birthdays?"

"I only buy presents for my mother, and only on three occasions:

Christmas Day, her birthday, and Mother's Day. And I always bought her a bottle of wine, and sometimes a box of pralines too if I had money left over from the wine purchase."

"Have you perused our Food & Wine department downstairs?"

I tilt my head. What a fantastic word that is, *peruse*. I'll be sure to add it to my vocabulary. I am always looking to expand it. "No, I have not *perused* it."

"Would you like me to take you down there now? I'm also a Master of Wine, specializing in old-world reds, but if you're after a new-world bottle, then I can point out a few of our finest. Personally, if it has to be a new-world wine, I'm partial to South American regions such as Chile."

I hold my hand up before she delves any deeper. "That's okay, but thank you kindly. You see, I'm a bit of a wine master myself—I work at Marks & Spencer." I wink because I saw Linda at work do that once when she boasted of a skill. In her case, it was soap carving. She tried to gift me a bar once, when she first started, as she said she'd infused it with lily petals and wanted my opinion. I declined the soap as it was unfamiliar and told her an aroma of cat urine would not be favorable to her marketing efforts. I suggested rose or gardenia petals instead.

I thank the woman again and follow the signs to the escalator. Several minutes of confusion and misnavigation later, I am in the Harrods Food & Wine department, which is larger than my entire house was back in Maryhill. The chocolate section alone is four times the size of the Wilsons' shed. Everywhere I look, there are shiny gold gift-wrapped boxes and sparkling silver canisters of chocolate made with every variation of international ingredients imaginable. There are chocolate bars with Peruvian chili flakes, Icelandic sea salt, and Brazilian goji berries. And the wines! Aisles of green and black bottles, organized by region of country and then by grape. I don't know where to begin!

Again, I ask a staff member. I really hate doing this as I don't like it when people approach me at Marks & Spencer asking me where the gluten-free muffins are located or why wine isn't included in the Dine

In for Two deal of the week. I have a lot of tasks to complete on a typical workday and answering customer questions is not one of them. I do my best to help, of course, but if there are follow-up questions, I politely inform them that I am very busy with more important things. They don't like that answer very much and sometimes complain to Linda, but it is the truth and I like to be honest whenever possible.

Kneeling on the floor at Harrods is a woman not much older than me, with mousy brown hair that's tied very tightly into a bun at the top of her head a bit like Mrs. Wilson's style and resembling a small ant mound. "Excuse me, sorry to bother you while you stack the Brazil nuts, but I'm looking for a recommendation for a red wine for a birthday present?"

"Of course." The attendant smiles, pulling herself up. "Would you prefer old-world or new-world?"

Again, I'm hearing this confusing concept of wine originating from places classed as either "old-world" or "new-world" when all I want is a bottle of red wine from this *current* world.

"How about a lovely Cabernet from the Napa Valley?" she says, walking over to the shelves labeled "USA." She slides out a sleek burgundy bottle with a silver and green label. It certainly looks pretty, and I like the name of the region—*Napa*. I open my mouth and practice saying it. "Napa." I roll in my tongue for the *N* and puff out my lips for the *p*. "Naaaapaaaa."

She looks at me, then smiles again. "It's a nice region, I know."

I take the bottle from her and weigh it in my hands. The glass is heavy, well-made. "How much is it?"

"That one is priced very reasonably at £96."

"Sorry?" I splutter. Is that reasonable for Londoners?

"Napa Valley had a very bad season with the harvest due to the weather conditions and drought, so their prices are a little higher than usual, but I guarantee you that this bottle is worth it. It's exquisite."

"Perhaps we should find a bottle from a region that isn't suffering from poor crops and bad weather. Maybe a less sunny region where drought isn't a factor?" I suggest, handing the bottle back to her. "How about the UK?"

"Actually, there's a lovely Pinot Noir from a vineyard in Devonshire, now you mention it. But as wine production in the UK is low compared to the rest of Europe, the retail cost of wines from smaller, more independent, British vineyards tends to be in the £70 to £80 price range too."

"What is the most *common* wine region? The one with the biggest vineyards that churn out bottles on a conveyor belt like that," I say, snapping my fingers.

"Well, um, Italy is quite popular."

"Fantastic. Italy it is!"

"We have a nice Chianti?"

That was Mother's favorite. She said it's for special occasions, while everyday wine is Merlot from Asda. That needed to be cheap, as sometimes she'd go through two or three bottles a night, especially if she'd finished her work shift before 2:00 p.m. that day. Buying Mr. Wilson a Chianti will be like bringing a piece of Mother to him. He'll like that. "Chianti is perfect." I nod. "I'll take a £10 one. Actually, £8 would be better as I'd like to throw in a box of pralines too."

She squints, then glances around the aisle suspiciously like she's checking to see who is listening to us. "I'm so sorry, but I don't think we have any wines here that are £10 or under."

"Oh, really?" And Harrods boasts of catering to all shoppers' needs! All shoppers except me, it seems. Clearly, Harrods doesn't need my business, so I thank her, as it's not her fault, and leave. I march out of the department, up two sets of elevators, along several aisles, past hundreds of shoppers, and out the glass swing doors. And I head straight for the nearest Marks & Spencer, where I purchase a bottle of Chianti for £6 and a box of pralines for £2.

£10–£6 = £4

£4–£2 = £2

Which leaves me enough change for a cheese sandwich from the Foodhall.

"

Any effort in the garden will always be recognized and appreciated.

"

June and the Birthday Party

My shopping expedition took longer than expected, and I lost yet more time navigating my way back to the yellow shed on foot, but when I return to the garden, I am pleased to find the Wilsons are not home yet. This gives me a little time to sift, mix, fold, and whip the cake ingredients using Mother's very own recipe, taken from *Women's Weekly*:

Ingredients

200g soft butter, plus extra for greasing
200g self-raising flour
1 tsp baking powder
200g golden caster sugar
4 eggs
2 tbsp milk

For the filling:

142ml double cream
50g golden caster sugar
1/2 tsp vanilla extract

100g strawberry conserve

Icing sugar, for dusting

Method

Heat the oven to 180C (160C fan, Gas 4). Grease and
base-line two 2 x 20cm nonstick round sandwich tins with
baking parchment, then lightly grease the parchment. Sift the
flour and baking powder into a large bowl, then tip in all the
other sponge ingredients. Using an electric whisk, beat
everything together until smooth. Divide the mix between
the cake tins, then bake for 20–25 mins until cooked and
golden. When cool enough to handle, remove the cakes from
the tins, then leave to cool completely on a rack.

To make the filling, whip the cream with the caster
sugar and vanilla until it holds its shape. Build the cake by
spreading one sponge with jam and the other with cream.
Sandwich the whole thing together, then dust with icing
sugar.

Next up is the birthday present. Wrapping a bottle is actually
quite difficult and it isn't a technique I have practiced much over the
years as I usually use a gold bottle bag, which also fits a slim tube of
Marks & Spencer's hazelnut pralines at the side. I am always very
careful not to overstretch or tear the bag as after Mother removes
her gifts she gives it back to me, neatly folded for the next time.
However, in my haste to pack up, I have forgotten to bring that gold
gift bag with me, so something in the Christmas wrapping box will
have to do. I slide it onto the shed floor, pushing aside the floral
mug that I still haven't returned. The lid pops off the box and I begin
rummaging through pearl garlands and bubble-wrapped glass bau-
bles until I find two sheets of gift wrap at the bottom. One is blue
with snowmen and the other is rose gold with foil lettering wishing

everyone a "Very Merry Christmas." I opt for the sheet with snowmen, which I think is slightly more subtle than the latter, but after folding it over the base and body of the bottle I realize that it only covers half. The label and neck still stick out. So I use the second sheet of paper and secure it with some black duct tape I find on the shelf. Perfect.

But something is missing, wrong. I turn the bottle over in my hands. It sloshes, the deep red liquid traveling up the sides to the neck. Red, sanguine, like blood.

I have forgotten to buy Mr. Wilson a birthday card! How will he know the gift is from me? I dig out the sales receipt and scribble a simple but effective message on the back:

DEAR MR. WILSON. HAPPY BIRTHDAY.

FROM YOUR BIOLOGICAL DAUGHTER
FROM SCOTLAND, JUNE WILSON

I attach the note to the wrapped gift and gently place it on the doorstep. Then I return to the shed and await his arrival. Around 5:25 p.m., Mrs. Wilson and Henry finally arrive home, notably later than usual. I peer through the crack in the door at the big red balloon the child tows down the garden path, while his sullen-faced mother stomps behind rabbiting on about a latex allergy. "None of my colleagues at the consultancy firm believe me, even after I got that rash at John's retirement party with those silly bon voyage balloons. And now the GP doesn't believe me, or the allergist. Your father certainly doesn't."

"I believe you, Mum."

"Thanks, Henry—" She gasps loudly. "What is this?"

I press my face against the warm wood of the shed, eyeing them as they stand at the back door gazing into the kitchen. I didn't have time to tidy the kitchen *and* wrap the present, so I prioritized the wrapping, naturally.

"What a mess! There's flour everywhere, and my eggs! I bought that carton of eggs yesterday and all six are gone . . . uh, there's one on the floor. Henry, what is this? Did you do this?"

My face aches from pushing into the wood as I wait for the boy's response, which is taking a lot longer than it should.

"Um . . . ," he splutters. The red balloon dances and bobs in the air over him.

"Well?" demands his mother, standing over a mound of flour that had unfortunately poured out of the bag when I held it upside down, unaware that it had already been opened on one side. At my house, Mother always sealed opened food bags with brown parcel tape. Here, Mrs. Wilson has simply folded over the lip of the paper bag, like that is a foolproof way to contain the food inside.

"It was me," he finally says.

"You? When? You've been at school all day, then we went to the florist to pick up the balloons."

"I came home on my lunch break to make Dad a cake."

"We have a cake. It's in the fridge next to the kefir bottles. Giovanni's specially made Dad's favorite."

What is Mr. Wilson's favorite? And why is Giovanni privy to this information? Is Giovanni family too?

"I know, but I just wanted to make him one myself . . . or at least try."

Mrs. Wilson sighs loudly, her moan trickling out the open kitchen doors to the garden. "Well, that was nice of you, I suppose. But just because you're in high school now doesn't mean you can sign yourself out at lunchtime. Your father and I pay a lot of money to send you to a private school. Lunches aren't cheap. Now, where is it?"

"My school lunch?"

She tuts. "The cake you made?"

"Oh, yes . . . um . . ." I hear a lot of shuffling around in the kitchen, cabinets opening and closing, drawers slamming on their hinges. Why would the cake I baked be in the silverware drawer? Finally he realizes that it's still in the oven. I had to frost it while it was still warm, sadly, due to a lack of time. There wasn't enough room in the fridge, so I had to put it back in the oven. Houseflies are terrible this time of year. The summer humidity is an ideal climate in which to reproduce.

"The oven? Oh, Henry, the icing's all melted off and has made such a mess of the wire racks," she complains.

"Sorry, I— Dad's home!" he yells.

A strange sensation flutters in my belly as I await the opening and closing of the car door, and the sound of Mr. Wilson's expensive shiny loafers on the gravel.

"What's all this?" Mr. Wilson exclaims as he trudges up the path. I press an eye into the crack even more. He holds my birthday gift in his hands.

"Your son decided to make a cake—and a complete mess of the kitchen—on his lunch break," she sighs.

"Lovely, well done! A homemade cake, yum! Can't wait to try it." He wraps his arms around the boy, who looks back at the yellow shed where I stand. The sensation I feel begins to simmer in my belly. The cake was *my* effort, and I should be getting the credit.

"What's that?" Mrs. Wilson asks her husband, pointing to the bottle-shaped parcel.

"I'm not sure," he says, slowly turning it over to read the label. He stops, his shoulders stiffening.

"Well, who's it from?"

"Uh, a colleague at work. He'd messaged to say he'd missed me at the office and would drop it off on his way home."

"That's nice of him. What's his name?"

"Carl," he says quickly.

"I don't know any Carls in your office."

"He's new."

"New? Nice of him to be giving out gifts if he's new," she scoffs. "Very generous indeed. You're obviously paying him too much. Is that Christmas paper? Who would use Christmas paper to wrap a birthday gift in June?" She laughs.

My insides burn. There is no rule forbidding the use of snowman gift wrap outside of December. This must be an English thing.

"Come on, you can help us tidy the kitchen," she instructs. The child is already standing over the flour patch with a brush in hand.

Mr. Wilson hovers outside on the patio stone while his wife goes in, his eyes still on my present. He turns it over in his hands once more, then gazes up at the garden. He looks around, his eyes darting from the potted lilacs and mustards on his right, to the Persian silk at the back, to the planter box whose contents I've trimmed this morning, and finally to the yellow wooden shed.

My jaw aches as I clench my teeth, my eyes fixed on him. He stares back, not looking at anything in particular. Not looking at me. Then his eyes rest upon the gift in his hands. My gift. He slumps over to the bin by the side of the garden path and drops the present inside.

The shattering of glass cuts through the silence.

"What was that, Robert?" Mrs. Wilson calls out from the kitchen.

"Nothing, darling," he replies.

July is the final month to sow runner beans in the UK, and only in the south of England.

June and Summer Term

Since the garden shed is turning into more of a long-term accommodation, I decide another shopping trip is needed to make the place even more hospitable. I return to the market, thankfully not bumping into any chatty cyclists this time, to collect the following items:

1 box of colored markers . . . £1.00
5 cans of spray paint in "India Green," #54 . . . £2.75 each
1 box of amateur acrylic paints . . . £1.50
2 art paintbrushes . . . 40p each
1 silver photo frame . . . £2.99
1 white shoe rack . . . £5.99
1 small red vase to house Mr. Wilson's red pens . . . £2.50

I also stop by the shops to buy more of the bread I like—plain white, not the brown seedy kind—a jar of coffee, and some cheddar slices. I don't need to buy biscuits for my tea breaks because Mr. Wilson replenishes his snack drawer regularly. I drink my late-afternoon tea from a thermos I brought with me and saunter back to the garden. When I arrive, the boy is already waiting for me on the grass, a schoolbag by his side.

"There you are. I was worried when I got back and couldn't find you. You're always here."

"I went shopping," I say.

"Shopping? For what?"

"For things to make the shed look more like my house back home," I answer, dropping the shopping bags by my feet and reaching in for the shed key. Mother said it was always best to lock up and test the handle at least three times to ensure that it was secure before leaving. I always do.

He rises to his feet and joins me at the shed door. "What did your house back in Scotland look like?"

"You'll see soon enough. I'm about to redecorate."

The shed door swings open, battering off the wall.

"Can I help?" he asks eagerly.

"No, thank you."

His shoulders sag.

"Please?" he asks again.

"How can you help if you don't know what my house looked like?"

"You can tell me."

I nod reluctantly and assign him some simple tasks to keep him busy and out of my way, including shifting clutter to the back corner, relocating the sheet of tarp, and sweeping.

4:15 p.m.

I will paint and decorate the walls another day when we have more time before Mrs. Wilson's return.

"Are you excited for *Strictly* tomorrow?" he asks as he unfolds some extra tarp out on the grass.

"Week 3 is movie week. It's a good one," I say with a nod, carrying one of the Christmas boxes to the back. "On season seventeen, Kelvin and Oti did the Charleston to 'Trip a Little Light Fantastic' from *Mary Poppins Returns*. It was fantastic."

Mother and I ate popcorn while sitting on the living room floor, which she'd covered with a garden blanket like we were having a picnic outside. She draped fairy lights over the bookshelves. It was wonderful. I have never had popcorn again. Or an inside picnic.

"I'm looking forward to watching it."

"Will there be popcorn?" I ask him.

"For tomorrow? Probably not. My mum doesn't allow things like that in the house."

"Really? Our biological father keeps a stash of crisps, chocolates, and Haribo gummy bears in the third drawer of his study, underneath the brown envelope labeled *Wills and Power of Attorney*."

His eyes widen. "Mum won't like that at all."

I reposition the rug, this time aligning the tassels with the opposite walls, brushing them out with my fingernails. With the boy's help, I set up the bedding against the right wall at the back where I had my bed frame at home and position the bedside table beside the pillow. I will sleep facing south, like I did at home. The shelves are dusted and my new paint set is organized and laid out for the next time. My gardening boots and gloves are placed on the new rack to the left of the door, like at home. In Maryhill, they sat beside Mother's blue suede heels, but here they sit next to a red pair of Mrs. Wilson's, which I hope she hasn't yet noticed are missing.

The last piece is the photo frame.

At home, I had a framed photo of Mother and me, the only one we had of ourselves, taken by my old caseworker Aileen the day we were "reunited." Mother said she hated that photo, but she never asked me to remove it, knowing I had no others to replace it with. Here my frame is empty as I forgot to take the photo with me the day I left, so I'll have to keep the picture it came with, a color print of a smiling family next to the words "5 x 7 silver frame. Only £2.99."

"You don't have a photo for your frame?" he says.

"No. I did not bring it with me."

"What was it of?"

"My mother and me. She was young then, but she always looked the same to me."

"What will you put in it instead?"

I shrug. "I'll leave it as is."

"I can draw you a picture if you want? Maybe I can draw your mother? Then you'll have a picture of her for your frame?"

"You don't know what she looks like."

"Tell me."

He hurries inside, and when he returns he is hugging a notepad and a silver tin to his chest. We sit on the floor of the shed, where he positions a sketch pad next to a tin of coloring pencils and an eraser that looks brand new.

"Hair color?"

"Brown with flecks of dark red, like a copper leaf."

"I don't know what that is."

I slide my encyclopedia off the bedside table and skim the pages for "Autumnal Blooms and Foliage." "Here," I say, pointing to a large photo of a copper leaf. "It needs direct sunlight at all times and blooms best in temperatures above fifteen degrees."

"Eye color?"

I point to the picture on the next page, still under "Autumnal Blooms." "Calycanthus 'Burgundy Spice.'"

He carries on drawing, taking much longer than I had scheduled for. I glance periodically at the clock, reminding him that his mother sometimes returns from work early on a Friday to pour herself a glass of Australian chardonnay. He hands me the picture and waits for my critique.

"The eyes need to be rounder, more like mine, and the lips need to be thinner. And her hair is too flat. It was wavy like mine, but longer, down to her waist."

He tries again, but the eyes are still not right. Perhaps it's more the eyebrows that are off, so I take the pencil from him and correct them myself.

"Better," I mutter. I walk over to the open shed door and hold the drawing up to the light. His art skills are definitely questionable even for a twelve-year-old, but all the basic features are there and if I squint and tilt my head to the side, I can see elements of my mother in the picture.

It will do.

The next evening as I wait for the dish clatter to fade and the droning of Mrs. Wilson to die down, I find myself staring at the child's picture in the frame.

"What do you think, Mother?" I ask her.

I think she likes it.

The air shifts and I suddenly become aware of a clamminess in my palms. I look back at Mother, who now sits on a newly cleaned shelf beside my books. I glance at my watch. It's almost time for *Strictly*. I don't know many movie titles as I don't tend to watch much television other than this show and anything gardening-related. I often needed Mother to help me match the songs with the movies. She stayed up much later than me, and enjoyed watching late-night movies, so she was more clued up on the names of films.

What if I don't know the movies selected for tonight? Who will help me?

My breathing becomes heavier, sharper, almost loud enough to drown out the familiar tune of the opening credits. I unlatch the shed door and shakily take a seat at the side of the patio doors by the new terra-cotta pots. Mr. Wilson is nowhere in sight and Mrs. Wilson is in the armchair with her back to me. The child stares out, looking for me. I wave. A smile stretches tight across his freckled face. He quickly glances at his mother, then gestures to the pot beside me.

Inside, nestled under the leaves of the Acer, is a small bag of popcorn.

An experienced gardener will plant colorful beds that flower in succession.

June and the Invitation
to Kew Gardens

"I have tickets," the boy exclaims with a smile so wide I wonder if it hurts his cheeks. He waves a piece of paper at me. It's still warm from the printer and I can see images and dots and lines of different colors, some smudged and faded at the bottom to indicate that the ink needs to be replaced.

"Tickets to what?"

"To one of the biggest tourist attractions in London . . . the UK . . . probably the world!"

"No thanks," I quickly reply, getting back to my weeding. The growth around the planter box is particularly bad. Perhaps Mrs. Wilson shouldn't have sacked Sally.

"Why not?" His smile is now gone, an upside-down one in its place.

I sit back and sigh. "Because you say it's one of the *biggest* tourist attractions in London and probably the world, which implies that due to its size, it will be a fair distance outside of London, which likely means a long train ride, and that doesn't appeal to me. Plus, trains are not very safe; people steal your money and Oyster card on trains and then the police come. And if 'biggest' doesn't refer to the size of this attraction, then it must mean big in popularity, which means large crowds, long queues, and toilets you have to pay 20p to use, which also doesn't appeal to me." I continue with the weeding.

He kneels down beside me, peering over my shoulder as I firmly pull the roots out from the soil, dragging murky green threads over the dirt. "What are you doing?" he asks.

"Weeding is a very important step in regular garden maintenance. Without it, the weeds will slowly drain nutrients from the soil, pulling life from the plants and flowers around them. They also compete for sunlight and water, and if you're not careful, they can harbor pests that destroy the garden."

"Common Weeds" is chapter 3 in my encyclopedia. If you can identify them, then you'll know what you are dealing with and, moreover, how to get rid of them. Even Mother occasionally engaged in a few moments of weeding with me while the potatoes were boiling for dinner. She wore her own gloves, yellow like the daffodils I planted for her in the front garden after the hedges were removed. Even though I did not tell her they are nicknamed "Lent lilies" because they only bloom between Ash Wednesday and Easter Sunday. We are not the religious type. We never went to church, and Mother regularly engaged in profanity and blasphemy.

I informed her that daffodils need direct and full sunlight, which we lacked in the front garden; however, I agreed to plant bulbs nonetheless because she wanted to see daffodils every time she came home from work. Because they made her happy, and when she was happy, I felt something similar occur deep inside me. My plan was to replant them every year knowing they'd only survive one season in our poorly lit garden. I wonder who they have reallocated the house to. And that maisonette, the one above the Indian restaurant and the pawnshop, with the green armchair. I'm fairly certain nobody will want the flat without the garden. I'm sure it is still empty.

I am pleased that I managed to retrieve Mother's gardening gloves from the train floor before I was escorted out of Brixton. I have become quite fond of them. The yellow is very bright and occasionally catches the sunlight, flickering into my eyes, but I cannot part with them for some reason even though I know they are more fashion gardening gloves than anything else. I don't usually keep items that have no purpose or value, so it's odd that I have kept those.

"Imagine how much work it takes to maintain Kew Gardens," sighs the boy dramatically, his eyes darting to mine briefly.

"Kew Gardens?"

"That's what these tickets are for. I thought you'd want to see the fifty thousand plants there, but I guess I was wrong," he says, getting up and slowly walking away. He swings his arms by his side. The printed tickets flap in the breeze.

"*Fifty thousand?*" I stand up, my gardening tools sliding from my hands onto the grass.

"Fifty thousand," he repeats, standing in front of the garden gate, a slight smile creeping onto his face.

I shimmy my hands out from the gloves and start tidying up my tools. "You didn't say it was Kew Gardens. Had you led the conversation with that fact, we could have saved some time," I mutter, shaking my head. I tuck the gloves into the pocket of my raincoat, just in case the staff at Kew Gardens needs some assistance from a visitor today, especially someone as skilled in the garden as me.

We trudge out the gate, my wellies still on. The forecast predicts sunshine and afternoon clouds, but you can never fully trust weather predictions as they're often calculated by "meteorologists" and "supercomputers." Not real gardeners like myself.

———————

The line for the Royal Botanic Gardens in Kew zigzags down the street and curls around the corner. Thankfully, the child's foresight to prebook has allowed us to skip the main queue and instead join a much smaller one on the right.

The taxi ride here was quick and efficient. And free. Turns out Mr.

Wilson gave the boy a small amount of cash to buy new school shoes, which he gave the cabdriver instead. His current school shoes look just fine to me, so I don't see a problem with that decision. The twenty-minute journey had gone by rather quick, which I chalked up to the Wilson child's mildly engaging conversation about steam engines, and the fact that the cabdriver was speeding on at least three occasions. At times, the boy's conversation was almost interesting, and though I am not a train person—more so because of recent events—I did find myself attending to the information. The boy is very excited about trains. I'm sure he learns a lot more from my dialogue about horticulture and *Strictly* episodes than I do from his chatter, being that I am so much older and more experienced with the world.

As we get nearer the entrance, I notice a man and a woman standing at the gate asking to see inside people's bags and coat pockets. They wear gray uniforms and have name badges pinned to their chests, not too dissimilar to my old work name tag.

"What are they doing?" I ask the child as we inch closer.

"Who? Them?" he says, pointing rather indiscreetly. "They're just checking people's bags, for security, you know."

"Why?"

"I suppose to make sure we're not terrorists." He shrugs.

I gaze at him, eyes wide. I have been preparing myself for crowds and noise, but an act of *terrorism*? I had not considered that, and therefore I am extremely unprepared.

The queue gets shorter, and I begin to feel the moisture forming on my palms.

It's our turn next.

"I'm not a terrorist!" I scream at the pair of security guards as they motion us forward. A heavy silence fills the space around us, then whispers begin. I hadn't intended to proclaim the statement so suddenly and so loudly; however, the idea of strangers putting their hands on me and inside my coat pockets, again, is instantly overwhelming. Even my breathing is erratic.

The guards pause, look at one another with an expression that escapes my emotional repertoire, and continue with their protocols. I don't have a bag, thankfully, but they still pat down my raincoat and sweep a palm over my back. I bite down on my bottom lip as they do so until I taste a metallic tang on my tongue. They eventually step away from me and I feel the breath return to my lungs. I take a deep inhale and stagger through the entrance.

The boy is looking at me oddly, his eyebrows raised high. "Are you okay?"

I nod quickly, and blot my lip with a tissue. It stains a fresh bright red like that of a cardinal flower.

"You know, you don't have to say you're not a terrorist? I think they decide that on their own," he says with a shrug.

That makes sense. I suppose that's their job. And all in all, the exchange took less than thirty seconds. I take another inhale and feel ready to commence with the outing.

"Where to first?" he asks. He's suddenly clutching a brightly colored map, possibly one that he's taken from an information stand that I frustratingly failed to notice coming in.

"Where did you get that?" I ask him.

He ignores me. "Would you like to do the garden walk first?"

Where are the maps? I look over his shoulder, but I can't see the shaded areas and dotted lines on the paper clearly; he's holding it too far away. I edge closer and reach for the map. I don't want to be guided around Kew Gardens by a schoolboy. He shifts slightly, casually moving it out of my grasp.

He continues, "Or we could visit the ar . . . bo . . . ?"

"Arboretum," I sigh. This is why I want to hold the map. "It's a botanical garden consisting exclusively of trees. The garden walk first, please."

He nods, then folds the map and places it in his pocket, where I can't get to it. He points left toward a small entrance, pauses, looks around, then shakes his head. "No, it's this way, I think."

After several minutes of map reading, sign navigation, and possible guesses, he finally leads me through a large stone archway onto a promenade of exquisitely lined paths and circular flower beds. And it keeps on going. I stop. I am very rarely awestruck or impressed in any sort of way—Mother said I had a "poker face that could rival Doyle Brunson's," whatever that means—but the view from where I stand takes my breath away.

The range of plant families on display is incredible. Pastel pink roses climb up trellises, evergreen shrubs twist around towering obelisks, tightly clipped yews are shaped into Egyptian pyramids. My head whips around quickly, my neck already aching. I don't know where to look first, or where to start, so I wander down the path, past two girls taking photos of themselves in front of the sunflowers, each taking a turn pretending to smell a flower. I glance at the boy and am satisfied by his expression that he too is perplexed by this activity. I stop in the center of the path and breathe deeply, making a very audible grunt as I do so, startling him.

"What are you doing?" he whispers.

"Close your eyes," I say. "And smell properly, not like those people back there pretending. Really *smell*."

He closes his eyes, reluctantly at first, breathes in, and also makes a snorting sound. Then he breaks out into a cough, heaving over and clearing his throat.

"Do you know what that is?" I ask him when he's finished and straightened up, his eyes still watery and pink.

"No," he splutters. "I don't think so." He takes another sniff, gentler this time, thankfully. "Smells like . . . toothpaste."

I nod. "It's mint. You can do a lot with mint—in teas, foods, drinks, soaps, scrubs."

"Do we have mint?"

"Yes, in the back, but mint is not for the novice gardener. In one blink of an eye, mint can grow and spread and take over the entire garden. It's hard to contain, impossible to tame, as it's wild."

Mother often referred to herself as mint.

"Glad we have you, then." He grins.

"And over there," I continue, "is white milk parsley. There's Turkish sage, chives, and lemon thyme, and see all those tall purple feathery spikes? Lavender."

"Smells like my mother's perfume," he says, walking to the edge of the lavender patch. I edge closer to him and together we gaze out at the sweeping drifts of purple and green that flow from where we stand to the pond of creamy white water lilies.

"Did you know lavender is actually part of the mint family, so another one to watch if you're planting it in small gardens. And lavender first blooms in my favorite month."

He smiles. "June."

"June." I nod.

"You know a lot about plants and flowers. Did you have a big garden at home?"

"We had a small garden with sunlight in the back during the summer months. I grew clematis, salvias, Angelonia, and lavender. The community garden where I volunteered was bigger and my patch was in direct sunlight, so I was able to grow so much more, including herbs for Mother's teas, like chamomile and lemon balm. Some people use lemon balm for their Sunday roast as it goes very well with chicken."

"We don't eat chicken."

"Why not?"

"We're vegetarians."

"What?" I scrunch up my nose at the word—a *vegetarian*? "Do you just eat vegetables?"

"Legumes too."

"What about that time I watched you all eat lasagna at the kitchen table?"

"Fake beef," he shrugs.

Fake beef?

Perhaps I'll need to rethink this living arrangement. Do I really want to live with people who eat fake meat, buy factory-made birthday cakes, pot perennials, and collect porcelain houses?

I shake my head in disbelief and then go back to smelling the clusters of herbs, all twisting and coiling around one another, creating a mixed fragrance of citrus, wood, and earth.

"Will you teach me about plants and flowers? Show me how to garden?" he asks quietly.

"I prefer to garden alone."

"Oh." His shoulders sink and his walking slows. "It's just, I don't really have much else to do this summer. I . . . I don't really have many friends."

"You don't need friends," I say. "I didn't have any and look how I turned out."

He nods slowly and walks on.

A twinge of something unfamiliar begins curling inside me, growing rapidly like the wild mint beside us. "Okay, fine. I can show you some beginner gardening skills," I sigh. I suppose some company in the garden wouldn't be so bad. I'll just pretend I'm back at the community patch in Glasgow.

He grins. "Really?"

"Yes, but don't touch anything in the garden without asking me first, and never ever touch the yellow gardening gloves or my books."

"Deal."

We continue down the path, toward the flower beds that boast blankets of bluebells and bellflowers, smelling, seeing, and touching, even though there are large signs asking visitors not to touch. I am no *visitor*. I am a gardener, and gardeners experience the garden with their hands, so the sign does not apply to me. And I suppose now that the child is my new assistant, the sign does not technically apply to him either.

As we walk, I point out mottled purple crocuses, periwinkle hydrangeas, and Heleniums the color of a deep coral sunset on a perfectly clear summer sky, and the boy listens, nodding, seeming to take in the information well. He is already a good student. I identify gerbera daisies with heads bigger than my palm, white-tipped yarrows that look like snowy mountain peaks, and flame-orange hibiscuses that are swarmed with butterflies.

And Lent lilies. Rows and rows of perfectly neat daffodil bulbs, all awaiting their next Easter bloom. They're long gone now—summer is never their friend—but by next year's Ash Wednesday their yellow trumpet heads will peek out, ready to take the spotlight in Kew's spring flower beds.

I stand at the edge of the patch, which has been taped off. There is nothing more than earth and stem beyond this point, not particularly pretty to the eye, and I feel a churning deep inside. Soon the churning turns into a bitter fiery twist that makes my belly hurt.

I no longer see a withered and abandoned patch before us; I see daffodils in the garden, snowdrops on the riverbank. Reeds in the water, swirling and coiling.

"June?"

I turn and find the child still beside me, his palm out facing the sky like he's trying to take my hand but thankfully respecting the unspoken rule that I do not like to be touched. "Nothing. My tummy feels funny. I must be hungry," I reply quietly.

"Do you want to get lunch? There's a café here?"

"I only eat cheese sandwiches," I say, looking back over my shoulder at the dark empty field of bulbs and roots.

"Really? Me too."

I look at him and he smiles. I hope he knows I mean real cheese and not the vegan stuff his mother buys. He then guides me onto the main path, back under the stone archway and toward the entrance where we'd come in. I follow slowly behind him, my hands digging deep into my pockets until I feel Mother's yellow gardening gloves. The pain in my chest lessens.

When I glance up to find the boy, I see a small kiosk with brightly colored maps. I smile and grab a handful.

Moisture is key for
maintaining grass in the
summer. Water at least
two to three times
a week.

June and the Little White Lie

The maps create a nice collage on the south wall of the shed, with brightly colored shapes, dotted lines, and arrows pointing out little grass patches. Kew Gardens in person is much nicer than the computer drawings on this information leaflet, but for purposes of wall décor, it'll do.

Mr. and Mrs. Wilson are long gone, off to work in shades of beige and gray, carrying black leather satchels and flasks of filtered coffee. The boy has cleverly convinced them that he's signed up for a summer program at the local library and that he'll be back at lunchtime to let the animal out for a widdle. Truth is, he has been in here with me since they left and the animal has done many, many widdles.

I dip my paintbrush into the plastic art tray, swirling it into the mound of white, which has the same consistency as the double cream that curdled when Mother forgot to unpack a grocery bag. She had tried to persuade me it would still be okay, but the overpowering sour vinegar smell that filled my nostrils told me otherwise.

With much reluctance, I have finally relented and tasked the child with the painting of the grass, which will run along the north-facing wall of the shed, providing a nice foundation from which to build my flower beds of painted daisies and tulips among moss-green vines that will reach up high to the ceiling. Apparently, the boy thinks that grass grows in perfect singular straight lines like the tally sheet from his math lesson. There is no movement, no breeze, no freedom in the growth.

I wince as he paints another ghastly straight line onto what was once going to be my best wall design yet. Now that goal is unattainable.

"I like your daffodils," he says, edging closer to me until his knee almost touches mine.

I inch away, leaving a gap. "They're tulips."

"Oh. I like your tulips, then."

"Thank you." He continues to look at me. Perhaps he is waiting for me to return the compliment on his grass. I do not, as there is no praise to be given.

"Should I draw a tree?" he asks eagerly, sloshing his brush into the brown clumsily.

"No, that's probably not a good idea."

"Why not?"

"Because . . . well, it might look a little like that grass."

His shoulders sag and he drops the paintbrush onto the plastic tray.

"What?"

"You could *pretend* my grass is good?"

"Pretend? You mean lie?"

"It's not a lie as such."

"I'd be saying something that wasn't true. That's a lie and that would be wrong."

"Sometimes lies, or 'little white lies' as my mother calls them, are okay if they make the other person happy."

I stop painting the stem on my tulip and turn to look at him. He isn't kidding. He looks very serious about this "little white lie" fact. At a work review meeting once, my supervisor had lightly discussed this idea of telling a white lie to customers to encourage a sale; however, I had disagreed at the time, arguing that if I were a customer, I would want to know if an item of clothing I was trying on looked unflattering on my body type or if a food item in the Dine In for Two deal was grossly overpriced. It was never discussed again. I was also moved to the stockroom after that.

"So if I was to say, 'Your drawing is good,' then that would make you happy?"

"Yes."

"Even if that meant you went on to always draw grass like that and there was no improvement in your art skills because you had been told no improvement was needed?"

"Yes."

"That's a little white lie?"

"Yes."

"Okay." It really doesn't make any sense to me, but oddly I am willing to try. For the child.

"I've been thinking, it's July now. How long do you intend on living here?"

"In London?"

"In our garden shed."

I shrug. I have become strangely comfortable here in this shed. It is now a familiar space. I know where everything is and with these wall drawings, it is looking more and more like my bedroom at home. Mother agrees. Perhaps we could live here in this garden shed forever? Ideally, we'd have a room inside too, for the days of rain and snow, but this could be our home. And this time, there would be no one to take it from us.

"I heard Dad on the phone just after you moved in." The boy shifts uncomfortably, again flopping a bit too close to my side of the floor space. "He was talking to someone at a hotel, I think. He was asking when you'd 'checked out.' He looked worried."

"How do you know? 'Worried' is a difficult emotion to convey."

"He was rubbing his forehead. And pacing. Maybe you should call him or write him a letter?"

A letter.

I haven't written many letters in my lifetime. When I was six, my caseworker made me write a pretend one to Mother when she was "finding herself." I was asked to write as if she would receive it, which I'd later learn was impossible as we didn't know where she lived. Mother taught me all about the importance of correct addresses, postcodes, and stamps when she returned and got a job at the post office. But I complied nonetheless, perhaps slightly intrigued by such an exercise. With her help, I titled it "Dear Mother" and went on to introduce myself and tell her my age, height, weight, and current interests. Some of these included sitting on the grass in the garden, making daisy necklaces for the other kids in the home, folding socks, and looking at analog clocks. There isn't much to do in foster care other than that. There are never enough toys, and when you do get your hands on one, it will be swiftly taken by a child of larger size. I did like one toy where I wound up the handle and out popped a yellow bear. I wound and wound and wound, even though I knew every time the result would be the same. But one day I wound and wound and wound, and out popped a thin metal coil. One of the bigger kids had pulled out the bear. I was relocated to another foster home after that. I was never sure if it was the finger biting or the eye gouging that had me removed so promptly.

"What kind of a letter?" I eventually ask, as he leans across me for more green paint.

"Oh, you know, 'Hi, it's June. How are you? How is your summer going?'—something like that?"

"I know how his summer is going. I watch you all through the windows every day."

"Maybe don't mention that."

"What else could I say, then?"

"Well, you could tell him a bit more about yourself? Tell him you like to paint and you like to garden. And maybe you can ask to meet?"

"Why?"

"Because it's going to start getting chilly in the evenings soon and there are no heaters in the shed."

"I've only ever written three letters before."

"Really? We were assigned pen pals at a school exchange once but mine never replied to me. I can help you if you want?"

I watch him carefully draw a straight line down, his hand quivering slightly but the brush firm between his fingers. The oak wall is now looking greener and more alive with the outdoors, flowers, vines, and nature. With each paint stroke, my insides calm and my breathing slows.

"Okay," I finally say.

"Great. I'll finish this off and get a notepad from inside."

"We can do it after lunch. It's already 11:45."

"Okay. Will you make my cheese sandwich again today? I like how you make it. It's better than Mum's."

"It's because I use actual cheese. Real butter too."

"We don't have those things in the fridge, do we?"

"Yes we do. I hide them behind the probiotic kefir bottles because no one ever seems to drink those."

"Oh." He shrugs, leaning into me again. "I like your vines."

I glance at him, wondering if he is applying this notion of a little white lie. His face gives nothing away, so I add a few more tiny pink flowers before I follow him into the kitchen to make lunch.

66

Very few garden
plants will survive
excessive waterlogging.

99

June and the Trip to Canary Wharf

"Tomorrow we'll begin our lessons in the garden," I announce in the taxi to South Bank the following day. The child was keen on another day trip, and since the outing to Kew Gardens was so successful, I have agreed. He hasn't yet told me where exactly we are going in South Bank. I am becoming quite a seasoned traveler here in London, exploring many different parts of the city. The boy suggested we take the underground train today. I said no and suggested we walk the two-hour distance. It was the child's turn to say no. In the end, a taxi was the compromise.

"Can I plant something, like a tree?" he asks eagerly, clutching his seat belt as the driver takes a quick turn around the corner, sending us soaring to the left.

"Of course not. Our first lesson will be about soil."

"Dirt."

"No. *Soil.*"

I am beginning to regret my decision already.

"I wrote our biological father a letter like you suggested," I add.

"What did you say?"

"I asked him to meet me in Hyde Park on Friday."

"That's good." He nods. "Hope the weather is better than this."

The taxi pulls up outside the tallest and biggest clocktower I have ever seen. I stumble out, my head tipped back, rain on my face, gazing up the magnificent dial as the child counts out cash for the driver. He will need to ask Mr. Wilson for more after today.

"Is this your first time seeing Big Ben?" the boy asks me, as he slams the taxi door.

"There is an illustration of it in my book," I say, remembering the embossed golden figure of Peter Pan dancing in front of the clockface, swirling in a sea of pixie dust, Wendy and Michael not far behind him.

I gesture for the child to lead on, afraid he will ask to borrow it if I don't end the conversation.

The rain peppers down, creating shallow puddles on the pavements. Commuters holding large black umbrellas rush by, occasionally bumping into each other. I don't need an umbrella; my raincoat is "proofed" in every sense of the word—rainproof, showerproof, waterproof. Spending so much time outdoors, I have had to invest in decent outerwear. Some of the "coats" I see here are flimsy fabric with an odd bit of fur on the collar. No wonder the people here need umbrellas. Those coats are certainly not proofed. One teenager scampers down the street with a floral umbrella that juts up and out awkwardly, the metal ribs broken. The rain drips down onto her shoulders and hair. The child also huddles under an umbrella, likely given to him by his mother. But she hasn't equipped him with adequate outerwear or footwear. He has on a flimsy anorak that already looks like it is leaking and very polished black loafers. Whereas I have on my usual wellies, suitable for a day like this. In fact, I seem to be the only person in London that has dressed appropriately for the weather.

The boy stops outside a large gray stone building that's nestled under the bridge. He bounds up the steps beneath a bright blue canopy that has the words *Sea Life* written on it.

"Sea life" = animals that live in the sea, that survive in *water*.

"No," I murmur, shaking my head.

"No? I thought you'd love the aquarium since you like nature so much. There are sharks, penguins, jellyfish, a rainforest exhibition, and a—"

"No," I say again, before I turn and walk away.

The boy hurries after me, his stupid green umbrella bobbing around in the air and hitting people's shoulders. "Why not?"

"Because nature is not found in an aquarium; there's nothing natural about large tanks of heated water filled with mammals not native to the UK. And secondly, I don't like sharks or penguins or jellyfish."

He lets his umbrella drop down by his side, the rain quickly dampening his hair. I watch it trickle down his cheeks and into his coat collar. I lift the umbrella back up over him. I don't want him sneezing around the garden if he catches a cold. Vegetarians don't tend to have strong immune systems.

"Sorry," he says quietly, looking down at his shoes. "I thought you would like aquariums. I thought maybe you hadn't been to one before, being from Scotland and all that. Have you been to one before?"

"No. I do not like water."

"But you shower?"

"Yes."

"And you don't mind being outside in the rain?"

"No."

"So how is that different?"

"It is very different. I don't like *large* amounts of water like in swimming pools, oceans, aquariums, and . . ." I swallow hard. "Rivers."

"Sorry," he says again. He bites his lip and gazes up at me, eyes wide. "Maybe we could go in for a few minutes? I already bought the tickets and they're nonrefundable."

I look back at the gray stone building filled with water, facing a river also filled with water, while the rain lashes down on us. There seems to be no escaping the water today. Perhaps I could go in, just so the child doesn't pout or worse, cry. Children's cries can be piercing, and persistent. "Okay, just for a few minutes. But mostly because I have to use their facilities. The morning tea is going right through me."

He smiles and tugs on my arm, annoyingly, leading us back to the stairs and the little canopy that is a bright rich blue like *Lithodora*. I take inventory—clammy palms, elevated heart rate, beads of sweat forming along my hairline. I know this sensation well, but I cannot label it.

As we edge closer to the entrance, I try not to imagine the swirling, churning waters behind the doors. Perhaps the glass will be matted, obscuring the tanks and volumes of water beyond.

Thankfully "security" here is hands-off. Instead, there is a large structural device at the entrance that scans us as we enter, which is quite fascinating. I gaze over the security man's shoulder, wondering if a still image of my skeletal framework remains on his screen. Sadly, it does not and he ushers me along before I can observe what happens with the next customer who enters through the metal contraption.

I then excuse myself and find the ladies' facilities, which are filled with children on their summer holidays and exhausted, grouchy mothers. I wash my hands at the sink, staring at the water as it sloshes around the basin and flows over my skin. The hand dryer startles me and I quickly turn off the tap and sweep my hands across my coat. When I come back out, the boy is waiting for me with another brightly colored map in his hands. This time I know to look for an information kiosk or leaflet stand. I find one by the toilet entrances and take six maps.

"Wallpaper for the shed?" he asks me as I stuff them into my pockets next to my gardening gloves.

Before I can respond, I see a man waving at me. "June?"

It is the cyclist from Aldi. He has on a blue Sea Life T-shirt and is wearing a name badge stating: "HI, I'M WILL." I wore a similar one at Marks & Spencer back in Maryhill. Today he is without the bicycle.

"What happened to your bike?" I ask.

He laughs and runs a hand through his hair. It is dark blond like a cymbidium orchid. "It's in my bedroom."

"Why is it in your bedroom?"

"Because I share a flat and I don't have a garage or a shed. Where are your rug and bedside table?"

"They're in the shed. We have one of those," I answer.

"No good, were they?"

"No, they were very suitable. They were always intended for the shed."

The Wilson child steps in front of me and holds his hand out like strangers do on television when meeting for the first time. "Hello, I'm Henry. June's brother."

"*Half* brother," I correct.

"I'm Will," the cyclist says, taking the child's hand. They shake for a very long time. At least seven seconds.

"What are you doing here?" he asks me.

"We've got tickets for the aquarium," the child answers for us.

"Ah, of course. For a second I thought you were here to see me." He grins.

"Of course not. I'd actually forgotten you work here," I say.

"Well, you're here now. I can give you a quick tour if you want?"

The child excitedly jumps up and down. "Really?"

"Yeah, I've got to feed the stingrays at eleven o'clock."

"Cool! Can we watch?" squeals the child.

"We're not staying long, remember?" I remind him.

The cyclist smiles and beckons for us to follow him. I try to keep my eyes on the floor, occasionally glancing up as he leads us through a tunnel that has the words **Sea Life, Sea Happy** written above the stone archway. We encounter a large orange vessel entrance with a DIVE sign beside it. I freeze. I am neither prepared nor willing to dive into anything today, most certainly not a large body of water.

"Don't worry, no diving is involved," the cyclist laughs, flicking the sign with his hand.

The ground is wet and solid beneath my boots, like in a cave. Past the incorrectly posted sign is the penguin exhibition. The child grunts excitedly as small penguins waddle around and jump headfirst into pools of ice-cold water. Perhaps the DIVE sign would be better relocated here.

Penguins are an oddity. They have wings but cannot fly; a

confusing fact, like flowering dogwood, which is native to Asia and North America, yet grows wild on the edges of British woodland.

"Would you like to feed some stingrays now?" the cyclist asks us.

I shake my head while the child animatedly screams, "Yes!"

We follow the cyclist around the penguin area and down past the octopus exhibit. The stingray pool is up a set of stairs and underneath a ceiling of wooden panels and bright lights. The pool is filled with large flat fish with pincer tails. The fish soar and glide through the water, cutting through it like gardening shears.

I suddenly feel cold.

The cyclist produces a large metal pail from under the stingray pool and the child and I peer inside at the squirming clams and wriggling worms.

"Yuck! Is that what they eat?" The child grimaces. I wonder whether to remind him that at home he eats dehydrated chickpeas and drinks something called kefir.

"This is fine dining to them," the cyclist smirks, looking at me. He picks up a worm with metal tongs and holds it over the pool. It squirms against the metal and frantically darts for an escape. Down below, the frenzied stingrays gather, crashing into each other, causing the water to churn and thrash—

A splash of cold water hits my face and I startle, stumbling back from the edge of the pool. My hands shake wildly and my shoulders tremble. The water is cold, wet, and slightly salty, not warm like a shower or familiar like raindrops. This is like a swimming pool or a large open ocean, or . . . or a river. A rushing, roiling river. A river that pulls you under, so deep that the light from the sky fades. A river that pulls you down until you're in a place where the sun can't reach, where no one can reach. Until there is nothing but darkness and decay. Until there is death.

I can hear the child and the cyclist calling my name as I run, my boots slapping on the concrete floor clumsily. I am not used to running in wellies or indoors on hard surfaces like this.

"June!"

I do not turn back. I lose my way with the crowds and the noise, and find myself in a long glass tunnel, the exit so far away from me. Above, sharks zip past behind the glass, visitors squealing in excitement, bumping into me, frantically taking photos. I don't see the sharks and the stingrays and all the little fish. All I see is the water. It is everywhere. It suffocates me, pulls me under—

"June?"

I feel the child's hand on my arm, squeezing tightly. Pressing into my skin. I blink hard and look around. I no longer see water. I only see him. His freckled nose, his thick-rimmed glasses and almond-shaped eyes. Then I see the faces of families, scared and confused. And staring. My right hand is still balled into a fist, throbbing now. The toes on my right foot are also sore, already bruising beneath my socks, and I know then that I must have been kicking at the wall. Beating at the glass with my hand. Trying to get out.

The child's face is ashen, his eyebrows going in a down direction along with the corners of his mouth, which had been upward at the stingray pool. If I could draw on the walls here, I would circle the sad face for him. I take a deep breath and simply nod in acknowledgment. Then I stand slowly and follow the boy as he leads us through the tunnel and out the exit. I see the cyclist at the reception desk looking around for us, metal tongs still in his hand. He doesn't see us leave, and we don't say goodbye.

When we get outside, the air hits me and I take a deep inhale. It is no longer raining. The sky has finally stilled and the clouds have cleared, a speckle of bright sunshine piercing through the gray. The boy marches on in front, his head down, his cheeks flushed the color of a Peruvian lily. I remove the aquarium maps from my bag and toss them into a bin. I do not want them in the shed, or anywhere near Mother. I hurry to catch up to the child, and we walk in silence back over the bridge, over the river where I don't glance down, and to the nearest taxi rank. I make us lunch when we return to the garden, but the child eats alone at the dining table.

"

New gardeners should invest in a good encyclopedia to learn the basic principles of creating and maintaining a garden.

"

June and the Beginner's Guide to Gardening

"Here," I say, pouring soil into the boy's open palm, the grit crumbling onto his skin. "Feel that? Dried out, dehydrated, not tended to during a particularly hot summer."

"This is ours?"

"No, that's from your neighbor's garden. Perhaps if he spent less time drinking beer and watching the tennis, the soil in his flower beds wouldn't be so dry and cracked, like a broken plate that's been glued back together."

"Is it dead, forever? Or can it be saved?" the child asks as we stand in the middle of the garden, surrounded by small pails of soil, metal gardening tools, and my encyclopedia open to the first chapter.

I sweep the bad soil from his palm and back into the pail. "It takes some work, but with a lot of watering and mixing in of other organic materials like compost, manure, and peat moss, the soil's moisture retention will eventually improve. Organic matter like that also attracts worms, and they help water flow through the soil."

"Worms? Like the ones we fed to the stingrays yesterday?"

I nod, the sloshing and swirling and dark murkiness of the water inside the aquarium coming back to me, flooding my brain and my insides.

He wipes his palm on his shorts. A few remaining soil crumbs fall onto the grass between us. "Can I ask you a question?"

"Of course. I hope you ask lots of questions. I don't usually like questions, but that's the only way you're going to learn about all this and in such a short time."

"It's about yesterday."

"Okay."

"What happened?"

"We saw some stingrays, jellyfish, and sharks, like you wanted."

"No, I mean, you were yelling and kicking the walls in the shark tunnel. You were . . . very angry."

I sit cross-legged on the grass, the warm blades scratching at my bare shins. The boy and I are both wearing khaki green shorts, too alike. "I don't know."

"You must know," he says, sitting opposite me.

"I don't know how to describe it."

"Has it happened before?"

I nod. "It used to happen all the time, especially when I was younger. And then it stopped. Because of my mother." Mother became very good at following routines. Every day was the same, and that makes sense to me. I know what is going to happen; nothing is a surprise and that is how it should be.

"What's it like to get angry like that?"

"I don't like it," I say quietly. "Sometimes I don't know it's happened. It's like I go to sleep, and when I wake I'm myself again. Sometimes bleeding, always sore."

"That sounds . . . scary." He bites his lip and I wonder if the fear he talks about is what he feels now. What he felt yesterday at the aquarium.

Fear is a difficult emotion to understand, and to recognize in others, but I think I am becoming more aware of it and the signs to look for. Eyebrows elevated, eyes wide, face pale.

"Did *I* make you angry yesterday?" he asks quietly, playing with a blade of grass with his fingers. "Was it my fault?"

"No." I tilt back, my spine pressing into the grassy floor. The sky above is a pale creamy blue, the color of forget-me-nots, filled with large chalky clouds. "Mother said it was her fault, because she left me when I was a baby and didn't come back for years." I remember those early days when we were learning how to live together again. Mother used to say the house was too big for us, but for me, as a child, it always felt too small. There was never a room I could be in where I didn't hear her voice. But when I was in the garden, I didn't hear her in the house. Out there, the smells overpowered the sounds. Out there, I let the stems and petals and grass graze against me. And it didn't bother me. And eventually, when Mother became familiar to me, I didn't mind when she came into the garden to join me. Because her voice became birdsong, and I grew to listen to it, to need it.

I don't hear her voice now. Not anymore. I don't hear her words, "My sweet June."

"Where's your mother now?" he asks me.

"Gone," I whisper, the clouds drifting across my vision.

"Is she coming back?"

"No."

I never said things like "I love you" to Mother, because those words sounded strange, foreign. Aileen always said I had a problem with "attachment," which is silly, because I am attached to many things. My books, my welly boots, Mother's yellow gardening gloves, Mrs. Wilson's coffee mug, which I haven't returned yet. At home, I was attached to the television remote, Mother's suede heels, and the blue ceramic mug that broke on the train. At the foster home, I had an attachment to the sage-green blanket that Mother had swaddled me in when she dropped me off at the hospital because she thought that was where unwanted babies went.

I think I was also attached to Mother. I wonder if she knew that. Perhaps if I had said that to her, things would have been different.

The child lies down beside me, our heads slightly touching. I allow it to happen.

"I get upset sometimes too," he says. "And I cry. People make fun of me at school. I don't have friends."

"Me neither." I shrug. "You get used to it. Sometimes you only need one person."

He rolls onto his side, propping himself up on an elbow. "Do you want to be each other's person?"

"Can't," I say. "I'm already Mother's person and she's mine."

"Oh."

My rainbow watch beeps once.

"It's afternoon tea."

He clambers up. "I'll put the kettle on then and see if Dad has any shortbread left in his drawer." He stands at the patio doors, his fingers on the handle. Inside, the dog foams and froths at the mouth in anticipation. "June?"

"Yeah?"

"Even though I'm not your person, can you still be mine?"

I prop myself up on my elbows to get a better look at him. His eyes are wide and waiting, like those of the dog beyond the glass.

"Sure," I say. "I guess that would be fine."

He grins and slides open the door, the dog leaping out onto the warm grass, her tongue flopping out to one side.

While the kettle roars to life, I lie back down on the grass, watching the clouds pass by in the sky, wondering if this cold sensation behind my rib cage will ever go away.

66

Encourage a butterfly
to visit by planting
brightly colored,
nectar-rich flowers.

99

June and the Hyde Park Meeting

The park is crowded, brimming with bums on blankets, picnickers on pashminas, and sunbathers under sun hats that resemble those edible flying saucers filled with sherbet that tumbles out of your mouth when you bite into them. I've never had one, but I've watched Maureen at work stuff them into her mouth in the staff room at lunchtime. Her black skirt would be a mess afterward. Sherbet smears the shape of prickly berberis.

The sounds of birds in the sky and the breeze in the branches are masked almost completely by the drone of London's lunchtime traffic and the blasting of wireless speakers that hang on the edges of blankets. Lazy tourists and workers on their break bake themselves an unnatural and unappealing shade of rusty orange.

It was me who had suggested Mr. Wilson and I meet at Hyde Park, but with all the bodies crammed into one green space, I am now worried that he'll have difficulty finding me. After looking at the child's London travel guide, I chose the Peter Pan statue as a meeting point, given its connection to both me and Mr. Wilson. I carry the book with me, placing it on the bench beside me like I once saw someone do in a movie Mother was watching. In it, two strangers were meeting for the first time and the woman used a book to identify herself. It worked in the movie, so hopefully it will work now. Although I suppose Mr. Wilson knows what I look like, so maybe I didn't need to walk the thirty-seven minutes with a hardback novel in my hand.

My thighs itch under my pants and I squirm slightly. I don't know if Mr. Wilson is coming today as I didn't offer a way for him to respond to the letter. I don't have a return address to put down other than "Your Garden Shed," and the child told me not to write that. I gave Mr. Wilson a day, a time, and a location near his office and asked if he could meet me. I hadn't considered until now that he might be unavailable today due to (1) work demands or (2) a lack of interest in meeting at all.

So far, I have been waiting ten minutes. I came early to get acclimatized to my surroundings before he arrives. The child suggested that too, although he didn't use the word *acclimatized*. That's my word. Like how plants with deep root systems can acclimatize to structural changes.

The sun warms my skin underneath the green linen capris that I have paired with my usual wellies, and the raincoat to shield my shoulders from the rays. I am slightly too warm, but most days I prefer to be too warm rather than too cold.

I've arranged the meeting for immediately after lunch so that it doesn't interfere with my mealtime and teatime. I was still able to have my cheese sandwich at noon, outside in the garden, on the grass with the boy. It is now becoming our thing, except for at weekends, when he is expected to have his lunch inside at the kitchen table with his sullen-faced mother hovering around. He doesn't get real butter on those days. He gets organic, vegan, cholesterol-reducing margarine. And he doesn't get real cheese either. He gets one slice of something labeled *Cheese-Flavored Soy Protein*. When I make our sandwiches, I put a generous smear of slightly salted butter on the bread and use two slices of cheese because that's how

Mother did it for me. She'd say, "Why eat cheese if you can't taste the cheese."

I pick at a stray piece of skin beside my thumbnail. When it starts bleeding, I put it in my mouth and suck hard.

"June?"

I look up and see Mr. Wilson approaching, briefcase in hand. He has on a heavy suit. It appears that neither of us is dressed appropriately for the weather today. I stand and extend a hand, like the child did when meeting the cyclist at the aquarium. Mr. Wilson accepts my hand, laughing oddly like I have just told a joke. I shake firmly, startling him, then sit back down, resting my book in my lap.

After a moment, he sits beside me, facing the bronze statue of a little boy who has no parents and lives in the wild among the flowers and the fairies.

"How are you?" he eventually asks, his eyes still fixed on the statue.

"Well, thank you. And you?"

"I'm okay. I mean, I've been thinking about you and our first meeting." He clears his throat. "I'm sorry if that went differently to how you thought it would go. I was caught off guard and didn't know how to respond. It was a shock seeing you like that, in my living room . . . with my wife."

"And the police."

"And yes, the police too." He clenches his jaw and stares on.

"Crown imperials."

He snaps his head to me. "Sorry?"

"The flowers over there. I couldn't identify them immediately when I first sat down and now I remember, they're crown imperials. Their scent keeps rodents away, apparently mimics the smell of fox fur."

"Oh, right, very interesting," he mutters. "So, you enjoy flowers and plants and all that?"

"Very much so. I spent most days in the garden at home and at a community patch in town. I won an award at the community flower show two years ago for my okra. They're very difficult to grow. The trick is to harvest them three days after the first blooms fade." I suppose I won't win this year as I am not in Maryhill anymore. I am in London. Perhaps there are flower shows here I can compete in.

"Right, very interesting," he mutters again. "And do you have any plans to return home to your garden? I mean . . . will you be in London for long?"

"As long as my accommodation stays dry. It's hard to tell whether it's adequately weatherproof at the moment. Some structural issues emerged earlier in the summer during a bout of heavy rain."

"Where are you staying now?"

"I'm living at more of a private residence, but the owners are very nice, although I'm not sure about the wife."

"It's in a safe area?"

"Yes, it's in a very good area of London. Very *upscale*."

"Good, and you're comfortable there?"

"Quite, actually. I have a nice neighbor, a young boy who's helped me move in."

"Oh, good." He clears his throat. "And your mother, where is she?"

I take a sharp inhalation, suddenly unable to gather words for a response. So I simply say, "She's with me, although not here in the park right now." Mother is back in the shed as she prefers to be warm. On that note, I wonder now if the petunias I planted on the morning of her cremation are getting enough sunlight.

Mr. Wilson turns slowly to look at me, then his eyes flicker down to the book on my lap. He blinks hard, and cocks his head. "I recognize that book."

"*Peter Pan*. I think it's yours."

"Really?"

"I found it in the attic years ago. It has initials scribbled on the inside, although I didn't think anything of it at the time." I hand it to him. "See." He stares down at the curling R and the flick of the

W. "Mother was angry I found it, but when I got upset, she let me keep it."

"Oh," he says quietly, his eyes dropping to the ground.

"I brought it with me to London in case you want it back. Do you?" My chest tightens as I await his response. "I suppose it belongs to you, not me, so if I keep it, then that would be stealing and stealing is wrong." My belly flips.

"No, it's fine, June. You can keep it," he says, sliding the book back into my hands.

My chest loosens again.

He clears his throat and checks his watch. It's much nicer than mine. Gold, with a shiny face that sparkles in the afternoon sun. "Listen, I should get back to the office. Sorry it's been so short. I have a meeting with the partners at half two that I wasn't able to rearrange, but I wanted to see you. Perhaps we can do this again?"

"Okay."

"How can I reach you?"

"I don't have a mobile. And my current residence lacks a proper letterbox or mailing system of any kind."

"Why don't we just set a date now then?" He reaches inside his briefcase and pulls out a brown leather planner. The pages are bent slightly like those in the horticultural books that I read often, and are filled with scribbles in various pen colors outlining what looks like a very busy schedule. No wonder he keeps a secret stash of snacks in his home office drawers. No one with a schedule like that can subsist on lentil puffs and chickpeas. "How about next Monday? No, wait, I have that client lunch. Hmm, maybe Tuesday after . . . no, that won't work." He takes a deep inhale. "Okay." He nods. "How about next Friday? We could meet for lunch?"

"I eat my lunch at noon sharp," I say. I have never organized anything over lunchtime before.

"Right, noon, that's okay with me."

"Can we meet at half eleven, to give us adequate time to *peruse* the menu and order?" I smile, happy I can once again find an opportunity to drop the recently acquired *peruse* into a sentence.

"Half eleven, next Friday. Meet at Zelman's? Do you know where that is?"

I shake my head.

"Take the tube to Knightsbridge and it's on the fifth floor of Harvey Nichols."

"Harvey Nichols?"

"It's a department store, like Harrods."

I furrow my brow, thinking back to my shopping experience in Harrods with their overpriced wines and imported chocolates. Can Harvey Nichols be trusted with my lunch order?

"Is that okay?" he asks.

"Yes, that's fine," I sigh, unable to offer an alternative restaurant as I know none.

He nods, then slides off the bench, briefcase in hand. "Goodbye, then. See you next Friday."

"See you next Friday," I repeat.

He begins to walk away, then turns back and gestures to the book in my lap. "My father gave that to me on my sixth birthday. I wrote my initials inside straightaway. I used to carry it with me all the time as a child. I thought I'd lost it." He smiles. "I'm glad it's you that found it."

"I'm not one for simple children's stories or books about nonsensical worlds and adventures, but I like this one a lot. I reread it almost every year. I also always carry it with me. I suppose we share that trait."

Suddenly his smile drops and his face softens. Then he clenches his jaw again and walks away, checking his watch.

Remove the wilted petals from a wishbone flower to encourage a second bloom.

June and Lesson 2 of the Garden

"It's called a *dawn redwood?*" the child asks, pointing to the large bristly tree looming over the fence in the back corner. The sunlight pokes through the branches and spills onto the grass around us, warming the soles of our bare feet.

"It's fast-growing and can reach up to a hundred feet tall when fully matured, so of course it will need to be relocated in the next three years."

"Ripped out?"

"No, just replanted somewhere else, somewhere more suitable, like a larger community space. Not a small London back garden."

"Then why plant it here to begin with?"

"Exactly. Believe me, this isn't the only confusing aspect of your city," I say as I shake my head.

"And we have a—?"

"Persian silk." I point to the fluffy pink blossoms and feathery greens of the tree beside us.

"Mum said it was a cherry tree?"

"Your mother isn't a gardener," I answer sharply.

"Was yours?"

Mother knew the basics. How to weed, when to water, but not how to maintain. When it came to choosing what to grow and what to remove, she often needed my advice. She liked bright colors in the garden, said it made her happier, so often I chose the brightest buds I could find in the local garden center and tended to them night and day. But by the end, not even the brightest tulip or the most colorful rosebush made a difference.

"She knew a bit," I say quietly.

"Tell me about these," he says, pointing to the contents of the planter box over on the left.

"These are your mother's failed attempt at growing herbs for your meatless dinners. This one is lemon thyme, this is basil, and here is where I removed the mint. You absolutely cannot pot mint. It needs to grow freely."

"Where did you replant it?"

"In the back flower beds, but it needs constant attention. I may decide to remove it altogether."

He bends over and takes a loud inhale that ends with a snort.

"Pinch a stem," I say. "Rub it between your fingers. You'll smell it better."

He plucks a couple of stems of the lemon thyme and breathes in the citrus-earthy scent filling the air around us.

"When I arrived, they were overwatered and desperately lacking sun exposure, so I clipped back some branches of your neighbor's birch tree and that redwood, drained most of the water, and replaced the overhydrated soil, and I managed to bring them back to life."

"Mum really isn't very good in the garden, is she?"

"No."

Tires crunch up the gravel driveway, cutting through our peaceful afternoon in the garden. I quickly gather up the tools, stuffing the handheld shovels back into my gardening belt, and duck into the shed. The clock only reads a quarter to five, which confuses me.

Mrs. Wilson is sometimes home from work five minutes early, but never a full fifteen minutes. I'll need to readjust my timings so we aren't cutting it this close again.

I sit cross-legged on the floor, Mother beside me, and open up my RHS encyclopedia to page 206, "Annuals and Biennials." I often reread important chapters until dinnertime. Occasionally, I hear the Wilsons eating inside at this time too. It's like we're eating together, but at different tables. My table has better food. The child has offered me their leftovers before but I refused, fearing an upset stomach would give away my location. I can't imagine soy protein would sit well with me. On some evenings, the child leaves dessert by the shed door. If it's fruit, I'll bring it in and eat it, but if it's vegan rice pudding or gluten-free flapjacks, then I'll usually leave it out for the dog to find. I don't mind some fresh fruit after dinner, but Mother would have been most unhappy with a sliced banana or some dairy-free soggy rice for her dessert.

She had such a sweet tooth.

"Isn't that right, Mother?"

We didn't keep sugar in the house, but she would ask me to bring home whatever pudding remained at the end of the day on the "reduced and discounted" shelves at work. This sometimes consisted of fluffy buttery profiteroles topped with chilled chewy dark chocolate, dense white chocolate mousse, a crumbly lemon tart, or Mother's favorite—something with hazelnuts.

I raise my head at the sound of footsteps coming down the garden path from the driveway. These are not the clacking of Mrs. Wilson's heels; these are the heavy tread of Mr. Wilson's loafers.

"Henry?"

"Oh, hi, Dad. I thought you were Mum."

"No, I think she's not far behind me, though. What are you doing out here?"

"Oh, you know, just enjoying the garden. Did you know that's a Persian silk tree in the back, not a cherry tree?"

"What? No, I didn't. Anyway, what's this charge on my credit card for Sea Life London?"

"Oh, that. I took the train in for the day for a rainforest exhibition."

"Aren't you still going to that summer thing at the library?"

"Uh, yes, but it was a day off."

"Okay. But you know your mother doesn't like you going into the city alone. It can be a very dangerous place—"

"I wasn't alone. I went with a friend. And their mum."

"A friend? I didn't know you had any . . . well, I don't mean it like that, I mean you've never mentioned him before. What's his name?"

"Um . . . Jude."

"Jude?"

"Yes, Jude. He's new, just moved here."

"Oh, how interesting. Well, that's absolutely fantastic. Do you see him often?"

"Almost every day. He lives *very* close by."

"Great. Maybe we can meet him one day, perhaps have his parents over for a drink in the garden?"

"Eh, yeah, maybe."

The crushing of stone fills the air around me as another car pulls into the driveway.

"That'll be Mum. I better get washed up to help with dinner," the child says, before heading inside. He glances back at the shed. A few moments later, Mrs. Wilson trudges up the side path, her high heels pecking at the pebbled path like little birds.

"You're home early?" she says, her voice raising at the end.

"I still have some work to do tonight, but I figured I could do it in the study after Henry is in bed."

"You were late last night? I didn't hear you come in."

"I had to prepare for today's presentation. I hope I didn't wake you."

"And Friday afternoon?"

"Friday?"

"I called the office and they said you had gone out for a *walk?*"

"Oh, yes," he murmurs.

"A walk where?"

"Uh . . . Hyde Park."

"Do you often take time off for strolls around Hyde Park?" she asks curtly.

"No, not really . . . I just, um, needed some air after my meeting."

"Hmm."

A heavy silence spreads through the garden and into the shed. I press my ear against the wood to hear better.

"Well," she continues, "since you're home early, you can help Henry and me in the kitchen, for once."

"What's for dinner?"

"Lentils and couscous."

Lentils and couscous?

"Delicious," he coughs.

Heels nip at the patio slab again, then march onto the kitchen tiles. Mr. Wilson's heavy footsteps follow close behind. Then the doors slide closed and all other sounds are muffled, no longer available to me. I sit back down and continue reading.

Around 6:55 p.m., the child quietly opens the patio doors again. He leaves a small plastic box of mango spears by the shed and hurries back inside. I take the box and sit by the terra-cotta pots at the edge of the patio. The child pushes open the kitchen window and living room door, just in time for a BBC Two special on England's best botanical gardens. I eat the deliciously sweet mango, sprinkled in lemon thyme from the garden, while the camera pans across the various flower beds and trellises in Kew Gardens. When I've finished the last bite of mango, I have to resist knocking on the window and asking the boy to shift the TV slightly to the right for a better viewing angle.

If the roots of a
plant are rotted,
it's unlikely it
can be saved.

June and TV Themes Week

Today is Saturday and, more importantly, TV Themes Week on *Strictly Come Dancing*. Mother and I used to do fairly well identifying the soundtracks on this particular week, Mother being somewhat of an expert when it came to soaps, British favorites, and popular BBC dramas. She often didn't sleep well and stayed up most of the night catching up on any missed programs from the week, neglected because of her erratic work shifts or in lieu of my preferred television shows. For that reason, she recorded hers and would watch them later when I went to bed or if I was tending to the garden outside. Other than that, she never once asked to watch anything of her own.

Because of that our storage space tended to operate at a 98 to 99 percent capacity, Mother reluctantly having to juggle firm favorites like *River City* with one-off TV dramas and celebrity biographies. She'd also record the odd show for me to soothe any anxieties or anger occurring from unforeseen technical problems or schedule disruptions, like the time we lost power halfway through *Strictly* during a storm and she needed to replay a *Countryfile* episode to calm me afterward. Or when a football game ran into extra time and interfered with *Britain's Flower Show*.

Yes, I am looking forward to TV Themes Week, very much indeed.

There are only seven hours and fifty-two minutes until it starts, so I will need to schedule my time wisely. Mr. Wilson is spending his Saturday in the office, it seems, and Mrs. Wilson and the boy left twenty minutes ago. Zelman's with my biological father next week will be a change to my usual routine, so I decide to prepare myself with a practice session today. I pack a lunch box, fill a water bottle, and head out to find a picnic spot in London.

It's a particularly balmy July day, and I don't fancy being indoors in the shed waiting for the Wilsons to come home. I could sit outside, and continue gardening, but I don't know their schedule as well on weekends and wouldn't want to be caught outside.

By the time I get organized, I have approximately forty-eight minutes to find the perfect picnic spot before lunch, so I walk down Bayswater Road and head back to Hyde Park. It is an ideal location for today's lesson, albeit a risky one. London on a sunny Saturday afternoon in the middle of July reminds me of the time Mother took me to the zoo. It was during our earlier years when she was still very unfamiliar to me, and I to her. She coaxed me gently onto the bus with promises of sunshine and happiness. It rained the entire time we were at the zoo, but the weather was not what spoiled my day, nor what broke Mother's promises. It was the people. The shoving and bumping to get the best view of the animals, the line-cutting to get to the toilets first, and the raucous squeals of excited tourists who acted as if they had never seen an animal moving before. It would take years of trial and error and hours of research for Mother to eventually discover noise-cancelling headphones.

I wear them now as I stand on the edge of Hyde Park, which is blanketed with sunbathers, lunch-goers, and the occasional reader resting on a patch of grass, on their belly, face in a novel.

I have entered at a different section of the park, where I can see its true size. The park is enormous, which is rather odd as I consider things in London to be much smaller when compared to the rest of the country: sheds, houses and their gardens, bedrooms, coffee cups, meal portions. Even the cars stuck in traffic jams are smaller here, as are the dogs being walked around me, and the phones people carry, perpetually glued to their hands or ears. Linda from work has a mobile and it's almost twice the size of the ones down here. Even my train cabin to London was hobbit-sized. London is a very big place with very small things.

I dance around picnic blankets and muted conversations until I find a shaded spot by the pond where swans swim and ducks hover near the verge for food. Unfortunately, there is nowhere else to sit. I shimmy out of my raincoat and lay it down on the grass, then sit facing the crowds, with my back to the water and my feet bare on the ground. I eat slowly, hearing myself chew with the headphones still on. The cheese between the buttered slices of bread is slightly moist and not as crumbly as this morning, but it tastes fine and eventually I no longer notice.

This is going okay. Even though I am not in the garden of 16 Lansdowne Road or with the child, whom I have grown very used to, I am still eating a cheese sandwich on warm grass. This is a change I am handling relatively well. I glance at the urn that peeks out from the top of my bag. Mother agrees.

I slide out my RHS encyclopedia and review one of the later sections on cacti and succulents. The odd crumb from my sandwich falls from my mouth onto the pages as I skim the names with my fingertips.

Aeonium

> *Echeveria*

>> *Rhipsalis*

>>> *Sinocrassula*

Like me, succulents prefer the summer days when sunlight simmers for at least fifteen hours and, also like me, they don't mind a shower of rain but don't fare well in deep water.

A jogger in bright clothing catches my attention and I gaze out at the clusters of people all over the park, basking in the warm sun. A

few have flasks of what I'm sure is not juice or water, while others
openly pour from sparkling wine bottles into plastic flutes. Londoners enjoy drinking in parks on hot days, it seems. Glaswegians enjoy
drinking in parks too, but the people near our house tend to wait
until after dark and then litter the cans about the gardens.

As my head drops back to my book, I see a flicker of wild cop-
pery wavy hair floating in the breeze. A pale-yellow pashmina draped
over her shoulders, her body slightly hunched with age, the woman
drifts over the grass, her back to me. Everything about her is so
familiar—unnervingly familiar.

I stumble up to my feet quickly, knocking the headphones off my
head. The sounds rush back in, pressing on my eardrums, but in this
moment I do not care. My sandwich has dropped to the ground and
I am stepping over it, edging slowly toward this woman. She is
walking away, her hair bouncing on her back, tassels from the pashmina trailing behind her in the wind. The long green floral dress
and sandals she wears are also familiar. I follow her, my steps slowing as I realize she is walking toward the water. My chest heaves in
and out as I find my voice to call out to her.

"Mother!" I yell across the park.

The man and woman in front of me gaze up, then return to their
conversation.

"Mother!"

They glance at me again.

I stumble after her, quickening my pace, my hand slightly out as
if to touch her, to grab her.

Soon she stands only meters from me, her sandals at the edge of
the pond. Her hair sits at her waist, with the familiar curl at the
ends. She readjusts the shawl around her, pulling it tight across her
shoulders. I inch forward, my breath hitching. The grass crunches
under my bare feet, my soles squashing the tiny white daisies and
yellow buttercups that catch between my toes.

"Mother?" I whisper.

She turns. Her eyes are smaller than Mother's. Her nose is larger, her lips are thinner, and her eyebrows are a touch too thick. Her facial structure is all wrong.

"S-sorry," I stutter. "I thought you were someone else."

She smiles and turns back to the water, waving to a couple of kids who pedal in a small red boat not far from us.

I exhale sharply, feeling a warmth rise from my belly into my throat until bile burns my insides. I swallow hard. I have suddenly lost my bearings completely. Why am I here?

"June?"

I whip around and see the cyclist from Aldi/Sea Life standing behind me.

"I thought it was you." He grins.

I glance back at the woman who definitely isn't Mother, and then walk toward him, back in the direction of my half-eaten sandwich and open book.

"Where are your shoes?" he asks.

"There," I say, pointing toward my coat.

"Funny bumping into you again."

"Why is that funny?"

"It's just a saying, I suppose. Have you been here long?"

"No, not long," I say, crossing my arms at my chest. I feel cold, a shiver snaking up my spine. "Why aren't you at the aquarium? Won't the stingrays need you? How will they eat?"

"It's my day off. There are other staff to feed the stingrays, don't worry. And the aquarium isn't all I do. I go to university too."

"What do you study?"

"Environmental management. Are you studying anything at the moment?"

"No. I haven't been to a school in a very long time," I mutter. "There's a lot you can't learn in a classroom."

"There's a lot you *can* learn in a classroom," he gently argues, his mouth pulling up into a wide grin.

I don't bother coming back with a counterargument as my insides still tingle and churn.

"Are you busy?" he asks.

"Um . . . I . . ."

"We could rent pedal boats?"

"Boats? No."

"Oh." His face wears an expression not too dissimilar to the child's when I refuse something. I remember what I'm meant to do—clarify and expand, rather than just say no.

"I don't like water. I'm scared of ponds and oceans and things like that," I add.

"Ah, explains what happened at the aquarium," he nods. "Was that some kind of a panic attack?"

"Kind of." I don't want to say anymore. I have already clarified and expanded. "I should get back." I start gathering up my belongings, sliding my bare feet into my wellies. I had hoped to stay a little longer, but I don't want to engage in conversation with the cyclist all afternoon, for fear that I'll run out of things to say or that I'll lose track of time. It's an important day, with the *Strictly* episode and all. I'm also worried that the Wilsons will return while I'm gone and it'll be challenging to get back to the shed without being seen.

On Saturdays, the child leaves a flower on the garden path to warn me that they are home and possibly wandering around. On those days, I have to sneak into the garden and wait until all sounds have faded from the kitchen before I can make for the shed. On the days I return home first, I'm the one that leaves a flower on the path.

"Well, enjoy your day," I say to the cyclist.

"Are you leaving already? Sorry—is that because of me?" His smile fades.

"No, I have to get back. I have something important this evening to prepare for."

He nods. "Look, you probably don't know many people in London, so if you ever want to hang out, maybe get a coffee, I work Thursdays, Fridays, and Sundays at the aquarium."

"I won't be going back to the aquarium."

"No, but I take my lunch break at midday, if you're ever in the area. We can do something non–water related. Food-related, preferably." He grins.

I doubt I'll ever be in the area of Sea Life again, but I nod in agreement anyway.

"Enjoy your evening then, June. Say hi to your brother."

"*Half* brother," I correct. "And goodbye."

I watch him leave, then I stuff the remainder of my sandwich into my pocket next to the yellow gardening gloves. I have never left a meal uneaten. It feels wrong. Wasteful. I glance one more time at the woman standing at the water's edge, then walk slowly back to 16 Lansdowne Road, images of wild flowing hair crowding my mind, my body tingling with the memory of battered, bloodied knuckles and a throat red raw from screaming.

Geraniums are very versatile and are great for new gardeners to experiment with.

June and the Lobster Croquettes

Strictly was particularly good that evening, with four identifiable TV themes, including a fabulous paso doble to the opening-credits music of *EastEnders* and an impressive Argentine tango to the theme of Mother's favorite drama, *Line of Duty*. There were a few themes I didn't recognize, of course, such as the ones for the waltz and the American Smooth, but overall, it wasn't a bad episode for me and the contestants. The average score was a 7, with an occasional 9. The child seemed to enjoy it too, occasionally turning around to grin when he recognized a theme. At one point, I was worried that his mother would catch on, but she seemed distracted, looking down at her phone screen and frequently glancing up toward the front door, which didn't open until after 9:00 p.m. She and Mr. Wilson exchanged some brief words and then he went upstairs and didn't return.

Unfortunately, I couldn't hear what was said and, for obvious reasons, wasn't able to ask them to speak louder, but Mr. Wilson looked angry and Mrs. Wilson looked . . . well, I'm not sure how she looked. Her facial expressions are still indistinguishable to me. She appears to have the same look for HAPPY, SAD, ANGRY, and CONFUSED. Not like Mother at all. Mother's feelings were always easy to identify, even when she tried to mask them with another emotion. I was momentarily tricked, and unsettled by the lie, but I eventually figured it out.

Throughout the week, Mr. and Mrs. Wilson continued to converse only briefly, mostly exchanging the occasional comment about house chores or bills. On Wednesday, for example, Mrs. Wilson reminded her husband that the council tax was due. That was the extent of their interaction for the day. At least this morning they conversed for slightly longer, and in the garden, where I could hear them better. Mrs. Wilson asked him to stop by the florist on his way home from work to pick up flowers for their neighbor Camille, whose husband just left her. I had circled the CONFUSED face on the shed door when I heard this conversation. Not because Camille's husband was gone—anyone could have seen that coming, particularly me as I have had all summer to people-watch. I have spotted Camille's husband getting increasingly thinner, more tanned, and reluctant to give her a kiss goodbye in the mornings before work. So, no, this is not a surprise at all. But I was confused upon hearing Mrs. Wilson's request because we have a whole garden of flowers here. All she has to do is clip a few stems and tie them together with some string or ribbon. Actually, all she has to do is ask me to do it as I don't trust her with a pair of clippers in the garden. But at least Mr. and Mrs. Wilson were conversing in longer sentences today, as I wouldn't want him to be distracted before our big lunch meeting.

I haven't been sleeping well since seeing that woman in the park, so dark shadows sit under my eyes, but I dress as best I can for the occasion and head out into the drizzly rain. After a long deliberation, I decided to leave Mother in the shed. A reunion with two family members is perhaps too much in one day. I shall reacquaint Mr. Wilson with Mother another time.

The walk to Knightsbridge takes me a little under an hour but it's a pleasant stroll through Kensington Gardens, the rain sprinkling the hood of my yellow raincoat. When I put my headphones on, I don't hear the rain at all, but feel the tiny vibrations on the crown of my head. Everything is hushed, and tranquil. Until I arrive at Harvey Nichols.

The multistory terraced townhouse expands along the street, each property bleeding into the next. I don't know how many houses comprise this one shop as it's hard to see where one ends and another begins. I try to make myself as small as possible to avoid being brushed against, and ascend the five floors in the department store that is not Harrods but looks nearly identical with its gold-framed revolving entrance door, concierge desk, and large range of departments from cosmetics and clothing to footwear and luxury foods. However, unlike the one at Harrods, the Harvey Nichols dress code is rather vague, simply recommending "smart casual wear."

I take the escalator this time, enjoying the views as it rises above the sea of clothing racks and white shelves of designer handbags, and finally over the heads of customers, their arms filled with shopping bags and plastic clothes hangers, rectangular price tags swaying from the fabrics.

Zelman's is tucked away beside a food market and a wine shop, and seems to be one of many choices for eating. I glance down at my green wellies and raincoat, sufficiently confident I am adhering to the "smart casual wear" guidance, emphasis on the *smart,* for I am the only one in Zelman's dressed for the weather outside.

Mr. Wilson is at a table near a window, chattering away on his phone as his laptop sits clumsily on top of his silverware and napkin. He gestures me over before I can answer the host, who wants to know if I have a reservation, then ends the phone conversation quickly and tucks the tiny device into his suit coat pocket.

"June, glad you found this place okay," he says, closing his laptop. He slides it off the table, bringing a fork with it, and puts it in his briefcase. Then he calls a waiter over for a new fork. "You're right on time," he adds, as the waiter returns promptly with a shiny new piece of cutlery.

I blink hard, not sure why me being here on time would even be in question. Of course I am here on time. Punctuality is essential in any situation. Perhaps he is talking to the waiter, who hovers near our table.

"Can I start you off with drinks?" he asks, in a sharp accent that I can't quite place.

Mr. Wilson allows me to answer first.

I have practiced this in the shed. I clear my throat and say, "Water, please."

"And I'll have a glass of the Chianti," Mr. Wilson adds.

Mother would have been pleased with his selection.

Mr. Wilson gestures down to the black-and-white menu that sits in front of me, then slips on some glasses and starts skimming the page with his index finger. At first I am confused, because the menu isn't a menu at all, more of an enforced choice between two dishes: steak and sea bass. That is it.

I glance up at Mr. Wilson, who seems to be nodding as he reads, although I am not sure what he is reading. If he has the same menu as me, there aren't many words on the page.

"The cuts here are delicious," he murmurs.

Before I can ask him what a "cut" is, the waiter is back with his Chianti and my water.

"Have you had a chance to peruse the menu?" the waiter asks us, pulling out a small white notepad and a pen.

Peruse. That's one of my words.

"June?" asks Mr. Wilson.

"Um . . . yes." There isn't much to *peruse.* "I'll have . . . a cheese sandwich, please." I hand my menu to the waiter and smile to indicate my order is over.

"Sorry? I don't believe there's a 'cheese sandwich' on the menu?"

"No, there's not," I say slowly, "but I'm hoping the chef could make something different, something that's not on the menu?"

The waiter and Mr. Wilson are silent. I have chosen incorrectly. I have not been "flexible" in my thinking. But I always eat a cheese sandwich on white bread, crusts cut off, at this time. Always. They continue to stare at me, hoping for further clarification on my order. My belly starts to twist and turn. I wish I had brought Mother with me, as she'd know what to do. I glance back at the kitchen, the sounds of chopping and clanging and slicing echoing out.

"Is there something else you may wish to order instead?" the waiter prompts.

"No," I reply. Mr. Wilson is blinking quickly, but not saying anything. My mind is heavy with possibilities. I could, perhaps, have an opposites day, where I eat dinner for lunch and lunch for dinner. This evening, I could have a cheese sandwich on white bread instead, crusts off. It's not ideal, but it seems to be the best solution for this predicament. "I'll have chicken, then," I say firmly, holding out my menu. "A Kiev would be ideal, but I'll take any kind of breaded chicken. No sauces or garnishes. And with some boiled potatoes and carrots, please?"

"Sorry," says the waiter, slowly. "But Zelman Meats sells only meats."

"Chicken is a meat," I say, my eyebrows sinking low to my eyes. Isn't it?

"Meats, in this case, refers to cuts."

There's that word again, *cuts*.

"The steaks are out of this world."

"Yes, they really are," my biological father agrees.

"We have an excellent striploin from Brazil, or a three-hundred-gram rib-eye from New South Wales. Or my favorite, a fillet from Uruguay aged for thirty months."

"Or fish?" adds Mr. Wilson. "The sea bass is divine."

I am beginning to wonder whether Mr. Wilson is also working for Zelman Meats.

"I thought you were a vegetarian?" I ask him.

He laughs, and glances awkwardly at the waiter. The smile quickly fades from his face and his cheeks turn a deep red color much like that of a cockscomb, a flower that gets its name from its rooster-shaped head. "How do you know that?" he asks. "I eat meat sometimes."

The waiter clears his throat, and I realize he is still standing beside me with his pen at the ready.

"So, no chicken?" I clarify.

"No chicken."

I feel hot and itchy, and begin squirming under my clothes. I don't usually feel the heat like this, but my raincoat and wellies are suddenly stifling. I had thought reversing lunch and dinner would solve everything, but I was wrong. I am still without an option for lunch and time is running out.

"How about you share my fillet and an order of the roasted root vegetables as that will have carrots, and then perhaps the chef would be so kind to boil up some potatoes for us too?" Mr. Wilson suggests. "And then if you don't like the fillet, you'll at least have the potatoes and carrots?"

"We only have the triple-cooked chips," tuts the waiter.

Mr. Wilson turns in his chair, the metal legs scraping on the tiled flooring. "Then you'll definitely have potatoes in the kitchen. I'm sure if the chef knows how to slice and triple cook potatoes, he'll know how to slice and *boil* them?"

The waiter clenches his jaw but nods.

"No seasoning on the potatoes," I add. "Just plain, please."

"And we'll have some lobster croquettes for the table," Mr. Wilson pipes in.

I am glad to see the "menu" taken away, never wanting to see another one quite like it again. Tonight for dinner I will have to have a cheese sandwich and a piece of chicken. That's the only way to rectify this day.

"Sorry, I didn't realize you didn't eat steak or fish," he says, taking a sip from his glass. He grunts and closes his eyes momentarily, savoring the wine. Just like Mother used to. She really did enjoy a Chianti.

"Mother cooked chicken every night. It was just what we ate, and I like to eat the same thing every day."

He nods slowly, his eyebrows pinching, and I worry I have said the wrong thing. "But," I quickly add, "occasionally, she'd come home from work with a fish supper to share. I ate the chips and she ate the fish."

He nods again, this time more quickly and with a gentle smile. "I love fish-and-chips. There's a great place around the corner from us; maybe one day I can show you." He stops, his eyebrows pressing into the bridge of his nose. Then he softens his face, takes a deep breath, and gazes up at me. "Did you do well at school?"

"Mother homeschooled me from the age of eight. Said it was better that way."

"Did you pass your standard grades? Highers?"

"What's that?"

"They're exams you should have taken in Scotland, even when homeschooled."

"I don't remember taking any tests? Except the ones the caseworker gave me."

He leans forward. "What kinds of tests did a caseworker give you?"

"She'd give me scenarios and I had to tell her what I'd do. For example, if someone approaches you and asks you for money, what should you say? Or sometimes I had to rate myself."

Would you congratulate someone for an achievement?	Very Likely	Maybe	Not Likely
Would you hold a door open for the person behind you?	Very Likely	Maybe	Not Likely
Could you recognize when someone needs help?	Very Likely	Maybe	Not Likely

"I see," he says slowly, taking a bigger sip of his wine.

"Mother told me to always circle Maybe as Maybe's couldn't be adequately judged."

Our food arrives just as Mr. Wilson opens his mouth to speak. It's placed on the table between us. The steak sizzles and crackles like a fireplace, while steam rises and billows from the boiled potatoes and roasted vegetables. Unfortunately, it looks like they have been salted and peppered. I will have to forgo the top layer to find the unseasoned ones underneath. As Mr. Wilson requests another Chianti, the lobster croquettes come. How fancy they are. Little golden pillows of breadcrumbs and cheese, surrounding a small ramekin of reddish sauce topped with a single stem of Italian basil. Although most people grow basil from the seed, it's an herb that can actually grow from a clipping. Not just any clipping, though, a nonflowering shoot, snipped just below the leaf.

Mr. Wilson spears a croquette and places it on his shiny white plate, then he breaks into it with a swift movement of his fork. I lean in and watch white fluff and gooey cheese ooze out of the breadcrumbed shell. He lifts his fork to his mouth, hesitates, then goes back for the sauce. After a quick dip into the ceramic ramekin, the croquette disappears fully into his mouth. I watch as his eyes roll upward in delight like Mother's used to when she broke into the box of pralines on her birthday.

"Mmm," he purrs. "Delicious. Do you want to try one?"

"No, thanks. It's not chicken."

"It tastes like chicken."

"Really?"

I don't try new foods. Not since I was a child. But this afternoon is beyond my standard routine anyway, so I decide to impress my biological father and try one, "step outside my comfort zone" like Aileen used to encourage me to do. I thrust my fork into a croquette and bring it up to my lips for a sniff. It smells okay, but I decide against the unknown reddish sauce. That is a tad too adventurous and bold, even for today.

My hand quivers slightly as I bite into the croquette. Buttery mashed potato explodes in my mouth and it's quite a pleasant experience. The breaded crumb is garlicky and very akin to the coating of a Kiev, and Mr. Wilson isn't entirely wrong; the taste of lobster isn't too far off that of chicken. Thankfully, the lobster is chopped very fine because if that wasn't the case, then the texture of the lobster would be very wrong. All in all, I am surprised. I have tried a new food, and it's very pleasant indeed. In fact, this "croquette" is absolutely delicious. Once I finish it, I take another and then another until the plate is clean, leaving only the strange sauce and some meager salad garnish. After Mr. Wilson orders a second plate, I realize that I haven't even touched the boiled potatoes and vegetables, instead filling up on this newfound favorite—lobster croquettes. How fancy I have become since moving to London!

As I slide out the insulated food container I have brought with me for leftovers, I decide to quiz Mr. Wilson as a means of conversation, which died out as I feasted so passionately on the croquettes. "How likely are you to hold a door open for the person behind you?" I ask, spooning in the last of the carrots.

"Sorry?" he says as he polishes off his last piece of steak.

"Very Likely, Maybe, or Not Likely?" I clarify.

"Oh, I see, like your test." He nods eventually. "Um . . . Very Likely."

"Would you recognize when the person you are conversing with is bored and a change of topic is needed?"

"Very Likely."

"Would you be able to resolve a conflict without losing your temper, defined by yelling or getting angry?"

He takes a deep inhale. "Honestly, it would be a tie between Maybe and Not Likely."

"Would you recognize when someone needs help?"

He lowers his wineglass to the table, and drops his eyes down.

"Would you recognize when someone needs help?" I repeat, not sure why he has suddenly stopped playing the game.

"Maybe we should get the bill, June. I have a lot of work on this afternoon if you don't mind."

"Okay," I say, snapping the lid onto my container. The leftovers should keep warm for a couple of hours, giving me the perfect accompaniment to my cheese sandwich and chicken.

After he flags down the waiter and pops his credit card into the little silver card machine, he asks for his coat, which baffles me as I don't know why the waiter would have taken it to begin with. I still have possession of mine. Where has his gone?

We move back onto the shop floor as he wrestles with his coat and laptop bag.

"How likely are we to do this again?" I ask him when he's successfully got his coat on.

He smiles, his face softening. "Very Likely."

Prevent injury with a
hardy pair of gardening
gloves when using
secateurs.

June and the Planting
of the Snowdrops

And *Very Likely* we were.

In fact, Mr. Wilson and I meet the following week, this time for a morning stroll around Hyde Park, where I get to see more of it and what it has to offer the city of London, which includes lovely flower beds filled with rosebushes and herbaceous perennials such as purple torches and "Brunettes." He brings with him two scones with *real butter* and two teas in takeaway cups, and we meet at exactly 10:30 a.m., my usual tea break time.

We don't talk much, which is how I like it. I point out all the blooms in the seasonal beds surrounding the rose arbor while he names all the statues. We walk past the yew hedges and watch tourists throw pennies into a fountain called the Joy of Life. And while I am tempted to fish them out and save them for later, he suggests joining in on this peculiar tradition. Of course, I decline. I am not one to literally throw away money. Our meeting only lasts an hour, but it is a very pleasant hour indeed, and it goes by fast, which means I am back to the garden before midday, right on time for lunch, which the child has prepared ahead of time, and rather well. He's remembered my extra cheese slice.

The boy has been rather annoyed at me for missing lunch last Friday, but today he sits on the grass beside the plant pots, two plates beside him. He rests his chin on his hand and flicks blades of grass as he waits for me. When he hears my boots on the garden path, he immediately looks up.

"You're late," he scowls, making me check my watch.

"No, it's not quite midday yet. One minute left."

"Tea's probably cold by now," he mutters, sliding a mug over to me.

Now, that is a problem. A cold sandwich that is already cold to start with is fine, but a hot tea that's now cooled? That's not okay. I kneel in front of him and reach for the mug that I know is mine because it's Mrs. Wilson's. When I bring it up to my lips, I am relieved to find that the tea is still warm and manageable for the occasion.

"It's not too bad," I say, sitting cross-legged beside him.

He slides a plate over to me and we eat in silence, bar the squelching of buttered bread in our mouths and the slurping of tea. When we're done, we wipe our mouths with the backs of our hands and slowly finish the tea.

"How was it?" he asks me, finally cutting through the silence.

"Not bad at all. You got the second slice of cheese, but the butter could be a slightly finer smear."

"No, I mean how was the park with Dad?"

"Oh, that. It was fine, thank you. Our biological father certainly knows a lot about the metal structures and marble statues in Hyde Park."

"Does he? I wouldn't know. He's never taken me to Hyde Park before."

"It's nice. You should go with him."

"I'll ask him, but he'll probably say he's too busy. He's always too busy."

He doesn't seem too busy to me; in fact, he's arranged to meet up with me again next week. But something tells me not to mention that to the child. Instead, I sip my tea until the last milky drop hits my belly.

"I have something to tell you," he mutters, looking down at his feet.

"What?"

"That letter you wrote Dad, well, I found it in the bin in the downstairs toilet. It was ripped into lots of pieces, but I recognized your writing."

"Oh."

"Perhaps he didn't want Mum to see it." He shrugs, playing with a crust on his plate.

"Perhaps you're right."

I shift to stand and take my plate into the kitchen so we can begin our work in the garden. The lemon thyme in the back planter needs tending to today.

"I have something else to tell you," he says.

I sit back down.

"Mum's planning to garden this weekend."

"She doesn't need to. I've done it all for her, so she'll be hard-pressed to find anything that needs to be done. In fact, I'd really rather she not touch the garden," I snap, the heat stirring in my belly, tossing around the partially digested sandwich.

"She'll probably need to get into the shed," he says, biting his lip.

"What?" I gasp.

"Her gardening tools are there."

"She doesn't own proper tools. Everything on the shelf was either brought from home by me or bought here, also by me."

"I tried to stop her. I asked if she wanted to do something else, maybe go to the park or take a day trip to visit my aunt Kay, but she's got her mind set on planting snowdrops."

I rise to my feet. "What?" I scream, my voice dancing in the air and hitting off the tree branches. "It's too early to plant snowdrops! Bulbs only thrive when planted in the late autumn or early spring. They'll die in this heat! Tomorrow is August!"

The child's eyes open wide, his cheeks flushing.

"She's not been in the garden all summer, why start now?"

"I don't know." He shrugs, rather unhelpfully. "She yanks out weeds when she's stressed."

"Why is she stressed? Other than for reasons related to being a vegetarian, having very large feet, and being incompetent in both the garden and the kitchen?"

He shrugs again, making me wonder why I am asking him questions at all. Clearly, his knowledge is as limited as mine.

I huddle into a ball and wrap my arms around myself. I can feel the heat building. "If she goes into the shed, she'll find all my stuff."

The child shifts closer, which is not a good idea. "We'll just have to move your things. We can hide your bedding upstairs in my room; there's heaps of space under my bed. And everything else we can hide in my cupboard."

Air seeps out of my lungs at a pace so fast I can't inhale. "But—" My jaw hurts and suddenly I feel all tingly all over. "What about me? Where can I hide?"

"I don't think you can stay here, June. At least not for the weekend."

And just like that, the garden around me spins, tossing and churning until dirt clumps under my fingernails and the metallic taste of blood lingers on my tongue.

When I finally come to, heaving and panting, the child is inside, staring at me from behind the glass doors. His eyes are filled with a look I know all too well, having seen it many times on strangers' faces and once on Mother's. I don't ask if he is okay. I just stand up and readjust myself, smoothing my hair down and tugging at my clothes. Then I begin pulling out my belongings from the shed, stacking, piling, and folding what I can. After a few minutes, the child comes out and helps. But he doesn't say anything for the rest of the afternoon, and moves slowly and cautiously around me.

August is a time for planning. Cast a critical eye over the garden and decide what has been successful this summer and what has failed.

June and the
Gray-Haired Bookseller

The following morning as I lie curled up in what little bedding remains on the shed floor, the child slides a note under the door.

Dear June,

I have talked with Mum and it seems she's planning to start gardening around 9. I have left a croissant outside your door and a thermos of coffee for breakfast, and a cheese sandwich wrapped in tinfoil. I have tried to go lighter on the butter based on your last feedback.
Don't forget about it or Tilly will get it all.
She's made plans to meet a friend all day tomorrow so you should be able to come back tonight, in time for Strictly. I've done some research and the chef is doing the rumba to a Queen song.
Dad has to work late again, so Mum's letting us order takeaway from a new vegetarian café. I'll see if they have potatoes and vegetables for you. I'll tell Mum I'm really hungry.
I'll leave a flower on the path when it's all clear to come into the garden.

Don't worry, we'll put the shed back how it was
as soon as possible. Signing off for now.

Sincerely,
Henry

I glance at the clock. I have ninety minutes to eat breakfast, read, then remove myself and the rest of my belongings from the shed. I sip on the coffee while turning the pages of *Peter Pan*, hoping the words will soothe me. They do not. Instead, stories of young children living in forests, wishing they had a mother, only give me a headache. I pack the book into my duffel bag, which is bulging at the zip again, and leave, Mother cradled in my arms. I lock the shed door and leave the key hanging, the way I found it several weeks ago.

I can't believe so much time has passed and now August has arrived, pushing me closer to the autumn months. Mr. Wilson and I have met again, this time for a coffee near his office in the late afternoon, but he still hasn't mentioned me moving in. The child is back to moping around the garden after another run-in with the bullies from school on his way to the shops the other day, reminding him that they will be waiting for him come September.

He has been talking more about it recently, a sad, defeated look crossing his face when he does so. The same look, in fact, as the dog when she finishes her meals and realizes there is no more food left.

The animal and I have become somewhat acquaintances over the last fortnight, agreeing to stay out of each other's way, but with me also occasionally allowing her to rest beside me as long as she is not touching me. Yet I still find her little golden hairs on my capris and shorts, in my hair, and sometimes inside my bra. My nostrils are also becoming desensitized to the smell of the animal, except on rainy days. When the dog is wet, a strong smell emanates from her fur and I have to sit farther away from her.

I stand at the edge of the yard, where grass flows into crushed gravel, and gaze around the garden one last time before Mrs. Wilson destroys it. All those days and weeks of hard work—gone. At least I will have something to do to keep myself occupied when the child returns to school.

My feet drag slowly along Lansdowne Road, weighed down by the duffel that is back on my shoulder, stuffed with my books and clothes and Mother. I have left what I could part with at the house, in the boy's wardrobe, nestled beside his old Spider-Man comics, and have taken only the essentials. Yet the duffel is heavy and beneath the dawn redwoods and the cherry trees with their pink blossoms, my walk feels weighted down by its burden.

I waste two hours in the overpriced coffee shop sipping on one coffee and reading my encyclopedia until I am prompted to leave as a line forms of hungry customers waiting for tables. After that, I wander through the streets and the alleyways and all the spaces that Londoners call "green" to distract myself from the fact that someone is currently destroying my beautiful flower beds.

Covent Garden is a cluster of tourists, designer shops, and restaurants offering "meal deals" that are nothing like the Marks & Spencer meal deals that I am used to at work. These ones are much more expensive and have fewer choices. I wonder if these dining establishments are also owned by Zelman's, given their limited menu options and price range. The thought of Zelman's makes my stomach churn and flip as the tiny fluffy, buttery, gooey oozy lobster croquettes burn in my mind. I sit on a bench in a marbled courtyard surrounded by planter boxes filled with verbena. When it is midday, I eat my cheese sandwich. Afterward, I get my clippers from my duffel bag and snip some sprigs to show the boy when I return. Perhaps I can replant them in the back of the garden. Verbena can grow from either seeds or cuttings, and attracts pollinating insects, although it doesn't often survive the first frost of autumn.

I bag the trimmings and then begin soaking the soil and compost with the remainder of my water bottle, being careful to avoid the leaves as dampness can cause fungal diseases. When the shop owner comes out and shouts at me in a very angry voice, I pack my gardening tools away and hurry along the street. I turn up an alleyway to get away from him and from the crowds, which seem to be growing as the day goes on.

The cobblestone alley is narrow and lined with cast-iron lampposts like something out of a period film. Shop signs dangle from poles, hanging over my head, each advertising an antique of some kind—maps, lamps, and my favorite, books. Lots and lots of antique books. These tiny little bookshops with their chipping wooden doorframes and flaking red paint sit neatly side by side all the way up the cobbled street. I glance back at the street sign so I'll know what to look for next time I visit Covent Garden. CECIL COURT.

I saunter up the street, being mindful of the dips in between the bricks where the mortar has receded. The first shop has faded maps in the window showing what Great Britain used to look like back when it was known as Britannia. The next few shops on either side are selling secondhand weathered-looking books. A familiar cover catches my eye and I wander into the shop, cradling Mother and my bag. The bell tinkles overhead as I push open the door. Almost immediately, an old man with a gray beard and tiny spectacle glasses pops up from behind a stack of dust jackets and frayed paperbacks.

"Hello!" he loudly calls to me, a wide smile stretching tight on his face, like I am the first and only customer to have ever entered his shop.

"Hello!" I reply, matching his volume and robustness, because that is the polite thing to do and I've passed enough tests with the caseworker to know that.

"Can I help you find anything?"

"Actually, yes. That book in the window, can I have a look at it?"

"Which one?" he asks, shuffling out from the obstacles he's created in his path.

"The illustrated *Peter Pan*."

"Ah yes, a lovely children's classic."

He squeezes his thin body between a table and a small wooden bookcase to grab the book, but instead of handing it to me as I requested, he carries it with him to the checkout like I am ready to purchase it immediately.

"I just want to look at it," I quickly add. With all the coffee purchases and cheese sandwiches, Mr. Wilson's money is almost coins now.

"Of course." He slides it over to me, carefully, and watches as I place my hands around the binding and open it. It crackles like a fireplace when I turn the pages, which pleases me immensely.

Every page is beautifully written in cursive, and adorned with vines and florals growing up the sides like a wild garden. Pencil drawings of Peter and Wendy fill some of the earlier chapters, while funny images of Captain Hook and Mr. Smee and a hungry-looking crocodile are scattered through the later pages.

It is just incredible.

My version is fine, but this one is spectacular. Almost as impressive as the lobster croquettes. And that says something.

"Have you read the story?"

"Oh yes," I smile. "I have my own edition, but it's very old and doesn't have as many illustrations as this one."

"Do you have it with you?"

I nod, and slide the duffel off my shoulder. I didn't dare hide the book in the boy's cupboard for fear it would be lost to the school uniforms, T-shirts, and knitted jumpers. My hands find the weathered spine and I slip the book out. It is considerably older and more "distressed looking" than the other.

"May I?" he asks.

I agree, as it seems only fair given that he's allowed me to explore his copy. He turns it over gently and lifts the front cover. He turns a few pages, then holds the book up to his face, meticulously reading each small print letter like it is an optical test.

"Oh my, this is a fine edition. Gosh, what a delight to see. Have you considered selling it?"

"Selling it? No, I hadn't considered that. It was given to me by my biological father, whose biological father gave it to him."

"It's a family heirloom? Even more valuable."

I hadn't really considered that before. A family heirloom. I have something that belonged to Mr. Wilson's own childhood, something that belonged to his family. Mr. Wilson and I do not simply share blood and genetics, we share a family history. Part of it is right here before me, constructed from words, parchment, green cloth, and gilt.

Family.

The word buzzes in my mind, tingles on my tongue, as I desire to say it aloud.

"Family," I whisper, my voice light and fluffy like the cascading branches of the Persian silk at 16 Lansdowne Road.

"What was that?" asks the bookseller, leaning in.

"Nothing," I mutter. "I better go now. It's almost teatime." I sweep a palm over his copy, my fingertips skimming the floral etchings one last time, then hand it back.

He slides a business card across the desk, along with my copy of the book. "I know it must be very special to you, but in the chance you decide to sell, let me know. I can offer you a very good price," he says.

"Thank you." I gently place Peter Pan and Tinker Bell next to Mother's urn, and lift the duffel back onto my shoulder. "Goodbye for now"—I glance at the business card—"Mr. Sawyer."

"Apologies, I didn't catch your name?"

"June. Like the month."

"Have a lovely afternoon, June."

The bell above the door tinkles again when I leave and I can still hear the echo of the chime as I make my way back along Cecil Court, which is now my new favorite place in London. And the strange thing is, it isn't a place filled with petals and stem and green grass. It is a place filled with clothbound books, colorful characters, and whimsical storyworlds.

"

Rose petals are at
their most fragrant
in the early hours
of morning.

"

June and the Single Red Rose

It's a terrible evening, followed by a restless night of sleep deprivation caused by (1) the elimination of my favorite contestant from *Strictly* after a disastrous and poorly timed rumba, and (2) the appearance of the shed, which now resembles nothing more than the dusty dirty carcass it was at the beginning of the summer. The place I have spent weeks organizing and making look like my bedroom at home now looks like a plain old everyday garden shed again. All thanks to the woman inside with large feet and sloppy garden management.

I've alternated between extreme tiredness, hunger, and anger, and by the time morning comes, I've barely slept. I can't even enjoy the coffee and buttery croissant that the child has left outside for me. And to top it off, the planting of the snowdrops came out even worse than I had imagined. They've not only been planted at the back beside the Persian silk tree, leaving it to compete for root space and soil nutrition, but it looks like Mrs. Wilson has simply tossed the bulbs about in a disorganized fashion. As opposed to mapping and plotting their location carefully, which is what any real gardener would do. And she's planted them on another scorcher of a day. She'll be lucky if these bulbs survive the week, let alone the month.

I'll have to redo everything she's done, including replanting the snowdrop bulbs in the winter, making my work even harder.

I pick at my croissant, and eventually throw the plate down, not even slightly concerned about the noise it makes. Snowdrops, really!

A light knock on the door startles me, and I pull my legs into my chest.

The next time, the knock is louder, harder on the wood. "June, it's me."

I open the door. The child stands a meter away, my shed furniture by his feet on the grass, a black bag of my other belongings behind him. "Mum's gone to get a manicure after all that garden work before she meets with Camille. We can put your shed back together now, if you want?"

I step aside to allow him into my space, and he slowly enters. He points to our wall designs that we painted earlier. His pin-straight grass lines no longer bother me.

"You should have heard Mum yesterday when she saw all that painting on the wall. She was furious at first. Then she said she liked it."

"She did?"

"Yeah, she said the flowers were really well-drawn. Said I should think about art school." He smiles.

"But you didn't do the flowers, I did. You did the grass. Did she say she liked the grass?"

"She didn't mention the grass, actually," he mutters, furrowing his brow.

I start reorganizing the shelves as he makes up the bed and after a few minor instructions and some physical assistance, it is exactly where it was before. Facing south like at home. I reposition the bedside table, with the lamp and books on it, while he arranges the footwear. My boots beside his mother's heels. We are slowly getting there.

Other than a quick tea break, we stop for lunch at 11:40 to allow for bathroom breaks and for the sandwich-making process. The child boils the kettle and begins gathering the sandwich items. He passes the bread to me and I begin buttering it, a fine smear on each slice.

"Oh" is what I hear next from him as he stands at the open fridge, the bottom drawer pulled out wide. He holds the white packet of cheese slices in his hand, slowly turning it over.

"What is it?"

"There are only two slices left."

I march over and take the packet from him. He is correct: Only two slices of the cheese remain.

"Where's the rest?"

"We probably ate it. We're the only ones that eat cheese here."

"I wonder if our biological father has been sneaking some. He eats cheese too," I scoff, wondering if he is the culprit.

"He does?"

"And he's not a vegetarian either."

"He's not?" he gasps.

"In fact, we're supposed to meet at a place next week that has lots of chicken options on the menu."

"You're meeting him again?"

"For dinner this time."

"Oh."

"What?"

"It's just . . . never mind."

"What?" I do not like it when people trail off in a sentence as I cannot fill in the gaps myself. I need the words clearly verbalized. Mother said I couldn't understood "subtext," which I once thought to be the dialogue that came up on the TV when you couldn't hear or understand what the characters were saying. Mother said that was subtitles, not subtext.

"I asked Dad if we could go for pizza next week when Mum has book club, but he said he didn't have the time. And now he's taking you out for dinner."

"Perhaps he found the time in the end, like a work meeting was cancelled."

"Yeah, perhaps."

I slide the cheese packet out of his grasp and he raises his eyebrows.

I should have told him at the beginning of the summer that I once answered Not Likely to the caseworker's question of: How likely are you to share a preferred item with someone else?

He watches me as I position the two slices of cheese on my bread and carefully press the two sides down. I slice it into two perfect halves, with a flick of the knife. Then I place both halves on my plate and turn to go outside. He slams the fridge closed and storms upstairs. A moment later, his bedroom door also slams shut.

I check my watch one last time to ensure that it is exactly midday before I walk back out the kitchen door, being careful not to let the dog out with me. I then sit and eat my sandwich and drink my tea on the grass with the sun on my face and the breeze at my back.

The boy's facial expression itches in my mind and I trace a circle around an imaginary ANGRY face on the grass beside me. I have not seen this behavior from him before. Why is he angry?

I eat slowly in case he decides to join me, but he does not. Afterward, I continue working in the garden, alone. By the afternoon tea break, the child still has not returned. In fact, he has pulled his curtains closed. Around 4:00 p.m., I go inside to make my dinner, arrange it into the insulated container to keep it warm, and head back out into the garden just as it begins to drizzle. I gaze up one last time at the boy's window before I close the shed door, that same feeling of coldness pressing on my ribs.

Later, I eat my dinner in silence, waiting for voices in the garden, but none come. I hear Mrs. Wilson's shrill voice in the kitchen during the meal, but other than that it is silent inside 16 Lansdowne Road. Around 7:15 p.m., there is a light tap on the shed door, followed by some quick steps back into the house. When I open the door, I see a small glass dish of cut strawberries.

I sit back down on the bedding on the floor, the berries nestled in my lap, mentally revisiting the exchange in the kitchen. And his facial expression when I took the cheese for my own sandwich. Surely he understands that I always have *two* slices of cheese in my sandwich? He only ever had one before he met me. But yet I suppose me taking both of them meant he had none. I consider this carefully as I pop a strawberry slice into my mouth, the tart juice bursting out onto my tongue.

Choosing my sandwich needs over his meant he did without lunch today. How would I feel if *he* had taken both the cheese slices? I pretend to draw three faces on the floor beside the fruit bowl, and circle the one with teeth bared. ANGRY, of course. I would feel angry too.

I suddenly feel strange, and tingly all over. I feel . . . I'm not sure what emotion this is.

I think about the book beside me, the one the bookseller wanted to buy, and how when Tinker Bell made Peter angry, she drank poison to save him, almost as an act of apology for harboring such anger and jealousy toward his and Wendy's friendship. Now, there is no poison lying around the shed, thankfully, but I contemplate what the next best thing would be.

I wait until the sky has darkened and slip out of the shed into the evening air. The lights are almost completely out in the house, except for a lamp on in the hallway for when Mr. Wilson returns, and the dinner has been cleared away from the table and sink area. The night air is cool, noticeably cooler than last month, hinting that autumn is not too far away. The odd car passing and bird chirping nips at the air, as I walk barefoot to the red rose bushes in the front, clasping my secateurs. The gravel is sharp underneath my soles and pinches at my toes. When I get to the rosebush, I clip a stem, being careful not to wrap my fingers over a thorn. The roses have all bloomed perfectly and finding a good one is easy as each is exquisite.

I walk quietly to the patio, and peer inside. The hallway is empty, still absent of Mr. Wilson's black loafers and briefcase. He is still at work. I bend down and place the single red rose on the patio step beside the glass sliding doors. I hope the child will like it. I think it's better than poison.

I don't like to think of myself as Tinker Bell, but in this case, I have upset someone and although it is not Mother, I suddenly find myself unsettled by that fact.

Plants can
be competitive
and sometimes kill
for survival.

June and the Extramarital Affair

I awake the next morning to the raised voices of Mr. and Mrs. Wilson seeping in under the shed door. At first I think I'm dreaming, as my dreams can often be quite loud, but soon I realize this noise is coming from inside the kitchen and not from the cracks in my memories.

I rub the sleep from my eyes, the sounds of anger spoiling the morning sunlight. My fingers find the latch on the shed and my feet drift over the dewy grass, until I reach the side of the house. I can hear better from here, just behind the terra-cotta pots where the child occasionally leaves me a television snack for the evening.

Raised voices are not new or unfamiliar to me as I often heard them at home with Mother frequently falling out with neighbors, colleagues, the milkman, the city council, and the binmen on Mondays. There are a lot of people Mother added to her ANGRY list over the years, funneling most of that energy toward the binmen. In the end they simply refused to take our glass-recycling box, which to be fair was often overflowing, with the occasional bottle rolling down the street on a windy day. It didn't help that Mother only drank one particular brand of wine, so everyone knew which box belonged to our house even when she had scribbled out our house number.

I inch closer to the Wilsons' kitchen, tilting my head up to hear the words spat out by Mrs. Wilson, who sounds very cross, and much like Mother in this case. I wonder if she too is addressing the street's waste management system.

"You're telling me you have no idea how that got there?" she yells.

"No!" replies Mr. Wilson, rather loudly.

"You just woke up and a red rose was sitting on our doorstep for you?"

"Who said it was for me?"

"Who else would it be for?"

"There are two other people who live in this house too, you know . . . plus Tilly."

"You think someone left a romantic gesture on the doorstep for the *dog*, Robert?"

"Well, I didn't say that exactly, what I was getting at was—"

"I know what you were getting at, but what I'm getting at is your *indiscretion*!"

"What does that mean?"

"You're out late all the time—"

"Working!"

"I call the office and you're taking walks in Hyde Park, going out for lunches or coffees. You're meeting someone!"

"That's ridiculous."

"I found a receipt in your suit pocket for Zelman's."

"I went outside the office for lunch to get some peace to work on a presentation for the partners."

"The receipt had drinks for *two* people, food for *two* people, and even said at the top, 'Table for *two*'!"

"Oh yes, now I remember, I uh, had a business lunch that day with a client."

"Oh, it's a client now. Your story's changing."

"It's true."

"A client that ordered three expensive sides of lobster croquettes?"

Oh, I didn't realize they were expensive. Now, that's disappointing. With what little money I have left, I had hoped to revisit Zelman's for those croquettes to retest the theory that I can in fact sample new foods from time to time. Maybe take the child with me, just to see the look on his face when he realizes how absolutely delicious and genius they are.

"And don't think I haven't noticed all the notes that have been left on the doorstep for you, which magically disappear soon after."

"That's just the post, Judith," he pleads.

"The postman puts the letters and bills through the letterbox, not hidden away on the back step or at the front door, but if you say it's him, then I'll be sure to ask him why he does that, next time I see him."

Is she referring to *my* letters to Mr. Wilson? Perhaps I should have considered more carefully where to leave the letters for him, rather than on the doorstep or on the patio as that has obviously caught her attention.

"What are you accusing me of, Judith?"

"Are you having an affair, Robert?" she croaks, her voice a little quieter.

"I am bloody well not!"

Now *he* sounds angry.

"Then who is this woman Camille across the street has been seeing coming in and out of our driveway while I am at work?"

"What? Who's coming in and out of our house?"

"Yes, Robert. Even our neighbors know you're having an affair. Do you know how embarrassing that is for me?"

"I promise you, I am not having an affair," he says again. "Camille is obviously mistaken."

"I don't believe you! You've changed. You're distracted. You've not spent any time with Henry or me all summer, and you know he needs you right now. He's been begging me to move him to a different school, homeschool him, anything not to return to that school. Term begins on Monday and he's terrified to go back. Have you even noticed? Do you even care?"

"Of course I care!"

"So show it! Because for the past few years, you've spent more time at the office than at home. You've been an absent father and an absent husband—"

"I am trying to keep us afloat, Judith! London is bloody well expensive—"

"And now you're a lying cheating husband!"

"How dare you? I am trying my best here—"

"Your best? If this is your best, Robert, then . . . then . . ."

"Then what?"

"Then I think we need some time apart, because I cannot continue on like this," she splutters.

A thick silence descends upon the house, then spills out into the garden like a dense fog closing in on me.

"What? Judith!" he cries.

"Robert, I'm sorry, I just don't believe you. You're lying to me—to us. I know you are. Something's changed with you. I don't know who you are anymore."

"Can't we just talk about this calmly?"

"Why? You're not being honest with me, so what's the point?"

"So what, you want me to move out?"

"Yes."

"Move out?" he gasps.

"Yes, I want you to leave. I don't think you'll have trouble finding somewhere to go."

"For the last time, I am not having an affair."

"But there is *someone*. And until we can start communicating like we used to, until I can trust you, I can't have you here with us. We can't argue like this in front of Henry. It's not healthy for him."

"He's probably already heard us. The whole street has probably heard us, Judith," Mr. Wilson sighs.

He's likely correct on that matter. London is a big city, but small and nosy, much like my street back home. Neighbors are the same wherever you go, and people want to know your business, which is why Mother said never to trust neighbors, especially when they ask you how you are.

The silence is interrupted by a shuffling of feet, so I hurry back to the shed. The patio doors open just a few moments later, followed by the tread of two sets of footsteps.

"Dad? Are you leaving?" I hear the child call out.

"Sorry, Henry, um . . . I'll be going away for a few days. There's nothing to worry about. I'll be back at the weekend, no doubt."

Mrs. Wilson clears her throat like she is about to cough.

"Bye for now, Henry. Judith, I'll be back later for a bag. I hope we can talk more then."

His footsteps crunch into the gravel path as he leaves. And soon I hear the screech of tires as his car pulls out of the driveway and hurls down the street. A few moments later, a second car leaves, this time much slower and more cautious. Mrs. Wilson is now gone too.

The child and I are alone, again.

I unlatch the shed door and it creaks open, letting in the warm morning sun that casts a harsh spotlight on the garden. The boy stands on the patio staring at me, his face ashen and puffy.

There is suddenly a strange distance between us. One that can't be explained by where we stand. This distance feels much deeper, more noticeable than mere lack of proximity, and it's something I have not felt before. I don't like it. It makes me feel cold, again, but this time the sensation has spread from my ribs up past my heart to my throat. It's uncomfortable.

"Is there any butter left?" I ask, finally breaking the silence between us, but not closing the distance.

"What?"

"Butter—is there any left? The tub was almost empty yesterday, but I'm hoping there's at least enough for my toast, then I can go out and get some more for our sandwiches later."

He looks at me, eyes wide, with an expression that's not part of my social repertoire.

"Did your mother already get more? Because if she did, it'll be that fake neon-yellow margarine stuff again and—"

"Didn't you hear any of that?" he interrupts.

"The raised voices? Yes, I did, why?"

"Dad's gone."

"I know, I heard. Sounds like he'll be back later to pack a bag."

"He's . . . *gone.*"

"I know," I say again, not quite sure why we are talking about this. We were just talking about butter a moment ago and now the subject has been changed but the initial one has not been fully addressed, nor resolved. We are still low on butter.

"Mum thinks Dad's having an affair because he's meeting with you, and because you've been leaving notes and roses on the doorstep for him."

"That rose last night was for you," I correct.

"Me?"

"Yes."

"But Mum thought it was for Dad. And then what Camille said . . . June, the neighbors have been seeing *you*. You're the woman coming in and out of the house."

"Oh, that makes sense now."

"You have to say something!"

"To who?"

"You have to tell Mum and Dad that it's you, that you've been living here, sending those notes, meeting with Dad . . . You have to tell them everything!"

The air suddenly feels warm around me. "Well, I can't do that.

Mr. Wilson hasn't asked me to move in yet. It's too soon to tell them. The caregiver and I need more time to connect." That's what caseworkers frequently told Mother. It took us years. Mr. Wilson and I have only been trying for one summer.

"This was a bad idea," the child says, pacing on the patio stones.

"It was *your* idea for me to start writing to our biological father, to meet up with him, spend time with him. In fact, a lot of what's happened over the summer was your idea," I say, my voice getting sharper.

"I never told you to move into our garden shed," he argues. "That was *you.*"

"It's not *your* garden shed." My skin is warm and tingling.

"Yes it is. This is my home!"

"It's *my* shed."

"It's not!" His voice bounces off the fence and hedges, and I take a step back. I have witnessed ANGER followed by a door slam and now the child is raising his voice at me. This sensation of distance and discomfort is getting stronger, more unmanageable. He has to stop.

"This all started when you arrived."

"No, I heard Mrs. Wilson say this is because of our biological father's work schedule." I rub my temples, coaxing away the waves of anger that surge through me.

"If he leaves forever, if they divorce, we'll probably sell the house, including the garden and shed—"

"Stop," I whisper, my temples throbbing and pulsing, the blood warming in my veins, pressing against my skin.

"I might never see you again . . . you might never see Dad again—"

"Don't say that!" I scream, not sure what's upsetting me more, the thought of losing another caregiver, of any sense of a home slipping away too, or the thought of never seeing this annoying, freckled-nosed child again. Why do I care so much whether I see him again? He is nothing to me, except an embodiment of some shared genetics.

No, I don't care. I shouldn't care. Because when you care, you lose things and you don't get them back. They are just gone forever. *Mother.*

"June?" he asks, his breathing shallow, his eyes wide, and waiting. But for what?

"This was not the plan. You're all not following the plan. You're all ruining everything," I mutter, rubbing my forehead hard until it tingles slightly.

The child begins to cry, and with that something inside me shifts. Slowly at first, then that familiar warmth surges and ripples through me, pulsing like the slow steady beat of music. The tingling is back, the anger building inside me. Suddenly I can label what it is I am feeling. What I have been feeling all summer is what I have seen on the faces of others; it is the expression I saw that afternoon in the garden at home in Maryhill when I pushed the metal tray of sandwiches into Mother's lip.

FEAR.

Yes, fear.

I am afraid.

I am afraid of my emotions, of unleashing them. I am afraid of harming the child who is standing too close to me. And I am afraid that, if I do, I will have to leave this place and he will fade into a place of darkness and forgotten memories, like Mother.

"Go away!" I scream at him, longing to grab something, to throw something, to break something.

He startles and takes a step back.

"Go away!" I yell again as his face gets paler, his eyes grow wider.

"I wish you'd never come here! I wish I'd never met you!" he hurls back at me, then he turns and runs into the kitchen, the doors locking behind him. Inside, the dog barks and howls, and throws herself against the glass.

I rush back into the shed and slam my fists against the walls, over and over again.

Thump.

Thump.

Somewhere, heavily blanketed under my anger and urges, I can hear the shattering of Christmas ornaments and the ringing of the clock as it falls from the bedside table. I hear my books scatter across the floor, a page of my encyclopedia tearing as it slides. I hear the thumping of my fists on the wall. And I hear my mother's voice.

"My sweet June."

I turn and scream at the urn with everything I have. How could she leave me? This is all her fault!

My voice escalates until it burns my throat and bile comes up. I fall to my knees and pant, my lungs twisting and coiling, like the dark green reeds that knotted around her hair that day.

Then a silence sets in, a deep, dark silence that hides me from the yellow shed, and from the Persian silk tree and the rosebushes and the lemon thyme. And from the child. A silence that tells me to remember the lines of Mother's face, the long wavy copper hair that bounced off her back as she walked, the sound of the blue suede heels on our kitchen floor. And the shallow pop of the uncorking of a bottle of Merlot as she turned and smiled at me, and softly said my name.

I close my eyes and suddenly remember that day, the last day I saw her. A day I have not been able to remember until now.

I scream, but I can't hear my voice. I can only hear a river.

"

A gardener needs to be resilient to tackle the hottest summers and the cruelest winters.

"

June and That Day

It was not a Sunday. And I didn't know why, but I had been plagued with the odd feeling all morning at work that I had to leave for home early that day.

It had been a strange morning already. First Linda had called in sick, which never happened, then Maureen called in, which always happened, and then all of a sudden, I was being asked to operate a checkout on the shop floor. I preferred the stockroom, signing for deliveries, counting the merchandise, preparing the stock trolley, what Linda called the "behind-the-scenes" stuff. That day, one person had told management I was "rude." I am not rude, I am *honest*. If more people were honest about what they're thinking and how they're feeling, then perhaps the world would make sense to me.

Once I heard a customer saying to her friend that she was on a diet for a cruise that she'd booked and wanted to lose fifteen pounds, so as she browsed the microwave meal section, which I was replenishing at the time, I merely pointed out that the current selection in her hands, a four-cheese lasagna, was high in both fat and calories. And when she picked up the cheesy garlic bread to go with it, I pointed out the same thing. And again when she tried to choose a dessert. It was then that she and her friend marched off to talk to management.

So for me to be manning checkout alone, talking directly to customers, was very rare. I was, however, occasionally allowed to *observe*. But with both Linda and Maureen off, and now Angus in the Meats section needing to go home early to collect his son, who had chicken pox, from school, the acting manager had no choice but to temporarily reassign me. She went over the mechanics of the machine for several minutes, then initiated a fake sale to show me how it would work when the time came. It was very interesting, actually. Tills are fascinating devices, and quite fun. If only there wasn't that element of customer interaction involved.

I stood at the checkout at Marks & Spencer, pushing the plastic keys on the cash register until it clicked and pinged and popped, the drawer opening to reveal coins of silver and bronze, crisp violet £20 notes, and blue £5 ones. *Open. Close. Open*—that was when I had the strangest feeling. A feeling that I had to go home that very second. So I did.

I first closed the register—so as not to leave it vulnerable to thieves—and went to find the manager, who looked extremely cross when I told her that, like Angus, I also had to leave early. She asked me why, and because I never lie, I said, "Because I have a funny feeling in my belly," which she deduced as being a stomach bug and therefore allowed it.

After standing in a queue at the bus station for almost a half hour, I decided to walk home, which was roughly a fifty-minute journey.

It was April, a time for new beginnings in the world of gardening. As I walked through the park near our house, I was embraced by snowdrops, the first signs of the season. It was an exceptional bloom for April time, certainly better than in the previous three years. Snowdrops in Scotland bloom best in March, their tiny white heads blanketing the ground like a thick white duvet on a freshly made bed.

When I reached the edge of the park, I bent down and plucked a handful to bring to Mother, wrapping them in my scarf to protect the delicate blooms from the wind. I was home exactly two hours and thirty-two minutes earlier than usual. Mother hadn't expected that.

The house was quiet, the front door unlocked and slightly ajar, letting a cold wind float through to the living room. The curtains were pulled closed, cabinets shut tight, doors sealed. The television was off, the remote control on top of the DVD player where it belonged.

After a few glasses of Merlot and some late-night television, Mother often left the TV remote discarded on the rug or sometimes shoved behind a pillow, where it subsequently got sat on. It upset me greatly as I'd never know where the remote was when it came time to put on an evening program. It would be in a different place each time. Once it was in the fridge. Of course I hadn't thought to look there—most people wouldn't—and it caused me to miss the first three minutes of a nature documentary. I was extremely unsettled, and from that day on, Mother made a special effort to put the remote back in the same place every night before she fell asleep.

I stood in the middle of the freshly hoovered living room, and glanced back at the kitchen, which had also been recently cleaned, but with the incorrect product, as indicated by the cloudy streaks across the granite countertop. Mother's wineglass was drying in the rack by the sink, the dishwasher had been emptied, the knives had all been returned to their correct place in the knife block. A small ceramic jug holding white baby's breath, ripped out from the neighbor's garden by Mother, not me, sat in the middle of the kitchen table on top of a coaster to catch any remaining water droplets. Beside it was my encyclopedia. Mother never touched that. She knew not to.

Other than the kitchen counter, the place was immaculately clean and Mother only cleaned on Sundays. But as I said, that day was

not a Sunday. I placed the snowdrops on the coffee table and as-
cended the stairs. Perhaps Mother was napping, having done all that
cleaning.

The hallway was dark, the light held captive in the closed bedrooms. I opened my own door first. My bed had been stripped and
remade with washed sheets, and there was a pile of washed and
ironed clothes on my dresser. My slippers had been paired up
and set on the floor at the head of the bed, my curtains opened, and
the drawers closed. The room smelled of furniture polish and
Febreze air-freshener.

Mother's room didn't look like the rest of the house. The duvets
were bundled at the bottom of the mattress, dirty laundry covered the rug, and an empty wine bottle was on its side by the leg
of the bed.

I gazed out the window which looked out onto the street below.
She said she'd chosen the front bedroom because she liked to keep
an eye on her neighbors as they often kept an eye on her.

My bedroom looked out onto the back garden, and the fence that
separated our house from the train tracks. I liked facing the garden,
onto the blush-pink clematis, violet-hued salvias, and soft purple
Angelonia. I liked the scent of lavender wafting into my room and
tickling the wind chimes.

Beyond the lilac silk fabric of Mother's curtains, the street below
was quiet. The neighbor's cat crawled nimbly under the red car
parked in front of number 24. The plastic recycling bin belonging to
Mrs. Maclean at number 26 was still positioned by the pavement,
almost three days after collection. Mother wouldn't be happy about
that.

I saw a blue car drive up the street and a supermarket delivery
van parked between numbers 28 and 30, although I wasn't sure
which was receiving the delivery.

And Mother, standing outside number 27 on the other side of
the street. She was barefoot and wearing a pale yellow nightdress that

flapped in the wind behind her. Her hair was loose and wild and flowed down her partially covered back.

I knocked loudly on the window, but Mother didn't turn around. She walked past house number 27, then 29, 31, and 33, until she wound around the corner and I couldn't see her anymore.

Worried she might be cold, I had grabbed her coat on the way out, ran out of the open back door, and crossed the street toward number 33. By the time I reached the corner, Mother was already at the end of the next street.

I followed her with the coat, down the street, over the main road that looked down onto the motorway, past the primary school where I had gone before I'd been homeschooled, and onto the riverbank. Cars honked and slowed to watch her, but she didn't stop, didn't glance around or turn back. She kept on walking.

By the time Mother reached the river, she was unsteady on her feet like she'd had too much Merlot, like most evenings. I started running to catch up to her. If she got any closer to the water, she might get wet, and in barely any clothes she would surely catch a cold or the flu and be incapable of completing her tasks around the house, like buying boxes of chicken for the freezer.

"Mother!" I yelled, darting between cars.

Mother swayed at the water's edge for a brief moment, then waded in. Her fingers grazed the reeds at the edge as the water swallowed her calves and then her thighs. By the time I reached the riverbank, the river had consumed her up to her belly, then her breasts, her collarbone.

I tripped over the long grass and wild weeds that grew in among the daisies and beer cans, and called to her again. But all I could do was watch her from the edge as she floated downstream. The fabric of her yellow nightgown tangled in the water as the current tugged at her. Her pale body sparkled under the bright afternoon sun as she twisted and coiled in the water as the current strengthened.

I raised my hand high to the sky, hoping she'd see me. Her hand shot up too, straight up like she was trying to touch the sun, then it disappeared back under the water, along with her neck, her chin, her nose, and finally the crown of her head. For a moment, a split second, she popped back up, gasping for breath, her long hair snaking behind her, then she went down again.

She didn't resurface.

I stood at the water's edge, feet covered in daisies and dew, staring into the current as it thrashed, until the sun set and the darkness crept in. Then I walked home, closed the kitchen door, removed my boots and placed them on the shoe rack next to Mother's cobalt blue heels, and turned on all the lights.

I punched the walls so hard that my knuckles split. The neighbors heard and called the police, who found her body shortly after that. They dredged her up like a lost object, or better, like a handful of weeds.

When the weather suddenly changes or a perfected technique fails, a gardener should never get discouraged.

June and the Emotions Chart

The next morning starts off slow and groggily, with rain lightly trickling down the sides of the shed and seeping in under the door. Now that it's late August, the colder and rainier autumn days don't seem too far off.

It's been two days since Mr. Wilson left, and two days since I have last seen or conversed with the boy. He doesn't come by anymore, doesn't write me letters or leave out things that he thinks I'll like. He doesn't wave from his window either; in fact, his curtains have been drawn since that day. He's away most days now, probably at the summer program he was meant to be attending, so I still go into the house and make my meals and sort my tea breaks, but lunchtimes are much different without him. I didn't realize how much I enjoyed our lunches together until now. I still sit on the grass with my back to the house, staring at the Persian silk, but now it feels different. I no longer take Mother out onto the grass with me. She stays inside the shed, beneath the shelves, beside my boots.

Everything feels different.

Just after my morning tea, I decide to walk to the shop to buy more cheese slices and butter, and a new bandage for my knuckles, which are healing just fine. I have to stand in a very long queue at the checkout, and I use the time to count the remainder of my money. I will need to come up with a plan for September, perhaps exploring employment. I can talk to the local Marks & Spencer here, explain that I am a former employee of the Maryhill branch. I will also need to investigate insulation for the shed for the winter months. I don't know when the child will start speaking to me again, but we still have a lot to cover in the garden before autumn truly sets in, including soil maintenance and weed prevention.

The walk back to the garden feels long, as images of the child standing there crying scratches away in my mind. The coldness of the memory constricts my chest, so I start reciting all the flowers and plants that start with the letter *J* because *J* is for *June.*

Jaborosa

Jacob's Ladder

Jewel Orchid

Japanese Bellflower

I freeze.

Mr. Wilson is standing in the garden, outside the yellow shed. He slowly turns toward me, the door of the shed wide open, the make-shift mattress on the floor, blankets still rumpled from this morning, my belongings on the shelves, my books on the bedside table. Punch marks in the shed wall. Blood smeared across the wood.

I had locked the shed before I left, testing the handle three times. I didn't consider that the Wilsons would have a second key for it.

His suit jacket is discarded clumsily on the grass. His tie is undone but still wrapped around his collar, and the top button of his shirt is unfastened. In his hand is a piece of paper.

"It's you," he gasps, his eyes wide, the hint of a frown creeping onto his face. "All this, all this time—it's been you." He waves the piece of paper at me. I edge forward and take it from him.

It's the "This or That" survey the child had done with me at the beginning of the summer when he'd been learning about tallies in math, and had asked me to vote. Dogs or cats, television or cinema, summer or winter. I had written my name on the bottom under Participants, next to the neighbor Camille's. Beside my name I had drawn a sunflower, like I had on the notes I had written to Mr. Wilson all summer.

"The woman that Camille saw going in and out of the house, Henry's new friend 'Jude' he's been talking about, and you . . . you said you had moved to a 'private residence' where your neighbor was a young boy who was helping you move in . . ." He shakes his head, his eyes dropping down to the grass by his feet. "Jesus, what an idiot I feel now. It was all so obvious."

I swallow hard, the lump in my throat getting large, protruding until it hurts.

He straightens up, his jaw hardening. "How long have you been living in my garden shed?"

"Ten weeks."

"*Ten* weeks?" He chokes on the words. "How could I have missed this?"

"It's not your fault, really. I wait until you leave for work, see to myself for breakfast, unless it's the weekend, and then the child leaves something for me outside the shed. Then I spend the day in the garden or go for a walk, and recently I have been showing the child how to tend to the flower beds and herb patches." I try to smile, but the expression feels odd on my face and pulls too tightly at my cheeks.

"The child? Henry? You've been spending time with my son?"

"Every day."

"Every day," he repeats, scratching at his chin. He shakes his head. "June, where is your mother? We need to call her. Now. This . . . all of this . . . is *strange*."

"You can't call her," I say quietly, feeling the heaviness of the food shopping in my hands.

"We have to. Does she even know you're here? Your mother and I had our differences, sure, but knowing her, she'd be worried."

"She's not worried, trust me." I glance behind him at the urn that sits on the floor by the bedside table. Why didn't I bring her with me to the shop? She feels so far away now.

Mr. Wilson stands firmly in my path, blocking me from her. "June, please, give me her number."

"I told you, you can't call her," I say again, the heat building inside me.

"Then tell me how to reach her." His face is getting redder and I recognize these facial expressions as ANGER. It took me a while to learn the three basic emotions, but I now understand that they follow a predictable pattern and can be easy to identify and label:

HAPPY	Common clues include: A smile/upturned mouth, laughter, eyes that light up, relaxed shoulders, sometimes affection.	Examples: Being told you received an A on a school assignment; doing something you enjoy, such as painting or planting.
SAD	Common clues include: A frown/downturned mouth, a quiet voice, eyes that gaze down or look away, eyes that water, tense shoulders.	Examples: Losing a favorite toy; not being allowed to do a preferred activity such as reading or playing outside.

ANGRY	Common clues include: A frown/ downturned or open mouth, red face, clenched jaw, loud raised voice/shouting, tense shoulders, closed fists, or arms waving about.	Examples: Someone says something mean to you; someone takes your favorite toy from you; a teacher or caregiver tells you no.

I struggled with the more complex emotions such as HUNGRY, CONFUSED, and TIRED, which were much harder to decipher, but now I can often recognize them, more specifically right before I "black out." This tends to happen when my routine is disrupted, not having my meals at a regular time makes me hungry, thus angry; or not understanding people's cues when they don't verbalize them makes me confused, thus angry; and also not going to bed at my usual time or having my sleep disrupted by a loud noise outside makes me tired, and again, angry. Once caseworkers highlighted these patterns with Mother, she tried really hard to keep everything the same for me. And it worked, along with the medication. I was able to maintain a job, volunteer without supervision at the community garden, and even go to the shops myself to buy the odd item such as milk or butter or jam. It worked, until she was gone. Then it didn't work.

The anger I've felt since April is unsettling, and I long for someone to help me identify what I am feeling and then give me a solution to fix it. I can't call Aileen because her solution will be to put me in a place where I can't get out, where there will be others who are just like me, who get angry like me. And what if I'm not allowed to bring Mother with me? Where will she go? I can't lose her. Not again.

"June," Mr. Wilson pleads. "If I can't call your mother, then I need to call someone. You mentioned a caseworker? Give me her number."

"No."

"June, I need her number—"

"No!" I scream, the panic rising. No, I need to be here with my biological father, my secondary caregiver, because that's how it works. That's what worked last time.

"Then give me your mother's number!"

"No! No! No!" I yell, my voice bouncing off the house and fence, off the branches of the Persian silk tree at the back of the garden. "No!"

He steps back, his face pale and taut like the child's was when I yelled at him in the garden. The expression on Mr. Wilson's face is one I can decipher now.

FEAR.

Mr. Wilson looks frightened. Just as the child did.

I drop the groceries by my feet. As I hear the butter tub crack on the stone, I run.

"

Allow wildflowers to seed and spread naturally.

"

June and the Night in the Park

The flower bed in front of me is shredded by the strips of sunlight that blast through the iron gates. It looks like the tasseled garland I made for Mother on her last birthday out of printer paper and takeaway leaflets.

In an effort not to remember why I am on a park bench in Ladbroke Square Garden, having scaled the iron gates to get in, I count the heads of pink petunias, purple crocuses, and white baby's breath before me. I count each one slowly, and when I have finished, I try recalling the principles of color theory from my Royal Horticultural Society encyclopedia, essential for selecting the best colors for garden beds and borders:

Primary	Red, Blue, Yellow	E.g., Roses, Asters, Yarrows
Secondary	Green, Orange, Purple	E.g., Cymbidium Orchids
Tertiary	E.g., Teal, Fuchsia, Mauve	E.g., Wisteria

But even after all that, I still cannot block out the kinds of thoughts that make the corners of my eyes prick with warmth. I clutch the bench with my fingers and squeeze my eyes shut.

Sad is not a feeling I easily identify or know how to rectify. But I have accidentally left Mother in the shed, along with my encyclopedia, Mr. Wilson's rare copy of *Peter Pan,* and all the things I have brought from home that remind me of the life I used to have with Mother. A life that is now gone, and replaced with empty garden space and floral vines that climb up dusty shed walls but don't lead to a real home.

I have also left a small cluster of dried baby's breath, which I use as a bookmark. When I'd returned home from the hospital after identifying Mother's body, the baby's breath she'd picked was dehydrated. Withered from a lack of fresh water and from the stifling heat in the house. But flowers can easily be preserved if they're hung upside down in a well-ventilated room for at least two weeks and sprayed lightly with hairspray for protection.

Thankfully, when I ran from Mr. Wilson, I was wearing my raincoat, so at least I will be warm this evening. I wonder if he's still standing outside the shed, waiting for me to come back.

I realize now I had left too many clues along the way for someone as smart as him to not piece together. But why did it have to happen now? Nothing about this London trip is going to plan. Mr. Wilson was supposed to offer me a place in his house, a room of my own to paint and decorate. I shouldn't have had to hide in the shed. Now I have nothing. I have lost Mother, my home in Scotland, Mr. Wilson, the shed. And I have lost the child. My *brother.*

I don't mind so much about Mrs. Wilson or the dog.

I dig my hands into my pockets and tickle the zip of my coin purse. I won't have enough for a hotel room tonight or for a restaurant to get a chicken dinner. I have no clothes with me, no books, no pillow to sleep on, no mug to drink coffee from in the morning. My belly gurgles and churns. I swallow hard, bile stinging my throat, and start reciting the names of all the flowers I know that begin with the letter *C*. Because *C* is for *Catherine*—Mother's name.

Calendula

California poppy

Cardinal flower

Carnation

Catchfly

I do that until the sun dips behind the clouds. As voices carry down the street into the balmy evening, I hug my knees into my chest and lie down on the cold bench. It's hard and uneven, and the metal slats press into my hips, stopping sleep from coming. I have never slept outside like this before. Mother and I camped once, in the garden at home, where I could still enter the house to use the bathroom if needed. It was in late July and the weather was exceptionally glorious for Glasgow. "London weather," our neighbor Mora said to us. We opened all the windows in the house to let the cool air in and the warm stuffiness out, but I still felt congested with the heat, which was when Mother had a solution—we'd drag our bedding down the stairs and out onto the grass, and watch the stars peek through the city smog and feel the cold air dance on our skin.

It sounded strange at first. *Sleep outside?*

I knew I wouldn't be bothered by the usual things that deterred people from sleeping outdoors like itchy grass against my back and tiny insects crawling across my face, but I did worry that the change in sleeping arrangements would be too much of a disruption for me. And what if I was thirsty in the middle of the night or had to use the toilet? Would the darkness consume me? Therefore, Mother suggested we leave the back door slightly open and the kitchen lights on, like a night-light. And after that, it didn't seem so strange or disruptive anymore. After that, I was intrigued.

It was that night as we lay on our backs, our heads touching, gazing up at the stars, that Mother first told me her plans for "after." I hadn't heard her talk about the After before and felt very confused.

She was in good health, not plagued by bowel cancer like Maureen at work, and still young. The chances of Mother being gone were minimal, and yet she talked at great length about what would happen when she was. She said I would be okay, that I would be left here alone in the house but that she trusted me to take care of it, to shop for myself and prepare my meals adequately. She had taught me so many things already, like how to check that a chicken is cooked thoroughly and how long to leave potatoes on to boil. I had a job and a steady salary, and I knew the basics of saving and spending. She said I was ready. But when I left the crematorium in Daldowie that day, clutching the urn they'd handed me with the charred remains of my mother, I knew that I wasn't ready. I'm still not. There's still so much I have to ask her, so much she needs to teach me. For example, I don't know what to do with her ashes. I had considered scattering them in the community patch, around the asters and cosmos, the seeds I'd just planted. They'll be blooming about now, although with no one to tend to them, they may not have fared well. I could have traveled to Jura since she seemed to enjoy it there so much, but the journey required a boat ride across water. I could have climbed a hill or tossed the ashes in a glen somewhere where the flowers grow free and the grass is wild. She also liked Merlot, so I could have sprinkled her ashes into a bottle or perhaps scattered them in the car park of the Majestic Wine shop. And then when Aileen told me they were taking back the house for a larger family, I had suddenly wanted more time. More time to decide, more time with Mother—just *more*.

A warmth pinches my eyes again, and I squeeze them shut, willing sleep to come and take me. But it will not. For this is not my garden at home. I am not sleeping on the grass, my house still in view, lying on my back, my head touching Mother's, hearing her steady breaths in and out. I am here in London, alone.

Mother.

The pinch turns to a single drop in the corner of an eye, which soon runs down my cheek. It tickles my skin and lands on the bench beside me. I press my finger into it and feel it disperse on the varnished wood. I have never cried before. Sadness is not in my repertoire. But neither is death.

I close my eyes again and continue reciting plants, this time with those beginning with the letter *J*, picking up where I left off earlier.

Juglans

   Juniperus

      Jungle flame—

A scattering of male voices reverberates around the park, startling me and interrupting my list. I haven't got to Justica yet, a cantaloupe-colored floret that blooms in spiky clusters in Asia, with veins coursing deep in the leaves. As I try to remember whether it is a spring or summer blossom, four or five teens appear at the park gates, outfitted in camouflage and black, with hoods up or hats on. The taller guy at the back pushes a bike by his hip, and for a moment I think he is the cyclist but when I straighten up and narrow my gaze, I realize he definitely is not him. I wonder why everyone in London chooses to walk their bikes and not ride them.

The guy at the back suddenly glances my way and stops. I scoot back on the bench, trying to make myself very small so he won't see me.

He sees me.

"Oi, oi!" he yells through the iron posts.

I don't know what "oi" is. I haven't come across "oi" as a type of greeting before. Am I supposed to say "Oi" back or "Hello"?

I don't say anything at all.

"What's wrong, love? Don't feel like chatting?" he calls.

His friends turn and soon all of them are interested in this exchange, if that's even what it is.

I ignore him, and his friends too, but that just seems to make them more insistent on getting my attention, and soon they are clawing at the iron gates like wild animals, howling and whistling and shouting.

My skin tingles and my bones throb as the cacophony of deafening sounds tears through the once quiet, peaceful park, shaking the dahlias and rippling through the stark branches of the cherry trees whose blossoms patiently wait for spring. My chest pounds and thumps.

The boys yell louder.

I press my hands into my ears. I have forgotten my headphones. The noise, it's too loud. I push my palms into my ears until it hurts—

A movement in my peripheral vision jerks me up and I see the tall guy with the bike start to climb the gate, much like I did, his foot slotting through the first slat.

They are coming in.

The darkness pushes against me as I heave myself up and run. Damp dewy blades of grass squelch and bend under my boots as I pull myself up and over the back gate. A sharp tug in my left thigh muscle makes me wince as I run.

The guys call to me, telling me to come back, as I continue running down the street, through Ladbroke Grove, onto Kensington Park Road, finally hitting Portobello Road, where the buildings are still lit up and taxis glide through the darkened streets searching for revelers. I am no reveler and I have no money, so I collapse against one of the shuttered secondhand shops selling replicas of designer handbags I've seen previously, and clutch my chest. My heart races.

I am definitely not home, and never will be again.

66

Use the early signs
of autumn to improve
soil health and prepare
the beds for the
new season.

99

June and the Aquarium Trip:
Part 2

I sit on a bench outside the aquarium, my back to the thrashing, swirling river. The entrance to Sea Life looks smaller than I remember, the door closing in on unknowing visitors thinking they are there to see jellyfish and sharks. But really they are about to be cocooned in a giant subterranean water trap.

I shiver and check my watch. It's just after midday and the cyclist is nowhere to be seen. Perhaps he is off work due to sickness or injury. Perhaps one of the stingrays got him. I will give it another ten minutes, then leave. My stomach gurgles and I hunger desperately for my usual cheese sandwich. I have never gone this long without food, but everything is different, and rather than feeling anger or confusion or loss, I just feel numb.

My fingers ache for the urn and I yearn to hold the cold ceramic close to my chest, but all I have to hold are her yellow gardening gloves, which are still in my pocket. They are my comfort today.

"June?"

The cyclist strides toward me, still wearing his Sea Life T-shirt and name tag, carrying his very small mobile in his hand.

I wave awkwardly, having already forgotten my much-practiced

social skills, then quickly follow up with a more appropriate greeting of "Good afternoon."

" 'Good afternoon'—very formal." He grins. "What brings you here?"

"You said you had your lunch break at midday?"

"Do you want to get lunch?"

"It's 12:10 p.m.," I mutter, checking my watch again. 12:10 . . .

"I had a fight with a hungry stingray," he laughs. "So, lunch?"

"I suppose I could eat late," I say slowly, the words sounding foreign to me.

He gestures to begin walking, so I do. We head past a small outdoor café where couples smoke cigarettes and drink pink wine, then
loop under a small bridge.

"How have you been?"

"Okay," I answer. I usually say "Well" or "Fine, thank you." But
not today. Why not today?

"You don't sound okay?"

"I had a fight with a child."

"Okay," he says, his voice going up at the end. "Any particular
child?" He laughs uncomfortably.

"My brother."

"Oh, sorry to hear. What about?"

"He wanted me to tell someone something but I refused, but
then that person found out anyway and now . . ." I trail off, imagin-
ing Mr. Wilson at the shed. Did he search it afterward, prod through
my things, find Mother?

"Now you wish you had just told them yourself?"

"I'm not sure," I say. "Do you think that was what I should have
done?"

He shrugs and digs his hands into his pockets, looking off slightly
toward the river. "I don't know. I can't tell you what was best, because I don't know the people or the situation, but what I can tell
you is, the truth is usually the best option."

"Mother said never to lie."

"Did you lie?"

"I don't think so. But I don't know now." I check my watch again. 12:16 p.m. "Where are we going, by the way?" I ask as we pass another café with more people sitting outside drinking wine and funny little drinks with teeny tiny umbrellas and straws. Is that all people do here in the summer? Sit around in the sunshine and drink?

"There's a great pop-up fish van over here."

"A pop-up van? The only pop-ups I've seen are cardboard cutouts of children's characters springing out of book pages."

"London has a lot of pop-up places in the summer—pop-up cafés, bars, food trucks. They set up for the summer and then break everything down at the end. Most of these places have larger venues in the city. This is just for Southbank."

"Oh" is all I can say, as I don't really understand what he means. Where do the "broken-down" places go during the rest of the year?

"Here it is," he says, pointing to a white van that's parked in a large open space surrounded by tables and chairs. It appears to be situated in what should be a car park. "What can I get you?"

Oh no, another menu to *peruse*.

"The fish-and-chips is really good here. The best."

I sigh in relief. I know a fish supper and thus don't need to look at the menu and make any rushed decisions about my lunch. It's already past 12:20 p.m. I may be numb now, but for how long? Soon the realization of a missed lunchtime is going to hit. "A fish supper is fine with me. But can I have mine without the fish? Mother always had the fish while I had the chips."

"So should I just order you some chips?"

"Oh, I never thought of that. That way I won't have to waste the fish."

He leans into the fish van's window and asks a big burly man in a white apron and football cap for two portions of chips.

"No salt or vinegar, please," I quickly add.

The man nods and turns away from us, shoveling and spooning

some freshly fried chips into two cardboard trays with tiny black forks poking out.

"Drink?"

"I don't drink," I reply. Mother encouraged me not to drink, said I would turn out like her because addiction is in the blood.

"I mean a soft drink or a water?"

"A water, please."

"Two waters, please," he asks the man.

I reach into my pocket to count the pennies I have left in the coin purse, hoping it will cost the same as at the local chippie around the corner from us back home, but the cyclist lightly touches my arm, startling me.

"It's my treat. You came all this way."

I don't clarify that I've actually been walking the streets up and down ever since the Ladbroke Square ordeal. I had not initially intended to come here to see him or to have lunch with him, but as the man in the food truck hands me a tray of hot steaming chips that instantly reminds me of home and of Mother, I am extremely thankful to have ended up here.

"Thank you," I say to the cyclist as we sit down at one of the tables that shields the sun from our faces with a tall coral-colored parasol.

The chips are delicious. Not on the same taste level as the lobster croquettes, but after two missed meals, they are exactly what I need. I inhale the greasy smell and begin wolfing them down.

"You're hungry."

"It's been a while," I choke, the end of a stray chip falling from my mouth.

"Since you've had a fish supper—without the fish?"

I nod and carry on hungrily feeding my empty belly.

Mother and I never ordered takeaways from the odd exotic restaurant that came to Maryhill, though they were always busy when we passed. Mother wasn't one for spice, but on the rare evening we would share some fish-and-chips, we'd make it an occasion, dress in our finest, cobalt blue suede heels for her and a cardigan not dusted in soil from the garden for me. And we'd sit on the living room floor on a blanket like we were having a picnic. It was a good time to practice my conversational skills too, everything I'd learned that week from Mother or Aileen, or from the television.

How was your day?	Appropriate Response: Good, thanks. And yours?
Terrible rain today.	Appropriate Response: Yes, awful. Is rain expected for tomorrow?
Did you see the news?	Appropriate Response: No, I didn't. What's happened?
I like your shoes.	Appropriate Response: Thank you. They were on sale at M&S. Do you shop there?

The fish-and-chips is different today. It does not appear to be a special occasion. There is no blanket to sit on, no fine clothes to dine in, and no Mother to dine with. There's just me and the cyclist, and given everything that has happened in the last twenty-four hours, I am not particularly in the mood to practice my conversational skills. Mindless small talk about the weather or television programs seems empty today. Instead I say, "My mother's dead. I watched her drown herself in the river beside our house, then I cremated her body. She's in an urn in the garden shed where I've been living, if you want to meet her." Then I carry on eating. The cyclist stops, his mouth still open, a chip poking out. The words feel okay, rolling off my tongue and out of my mouth quite smoothly, even though it is the first time I have ever said them. My mother is dead.

The cyclist slowly wipes his mouth with a paper napkin and lays his tray down on the table between us. He swallows hard and looks at me.

"S-sorry," he stutters finally.

I shrug, having nothing more to share.

"Does your brother know?"

"No."

"Perhaps this is one of those times where the truth is better?"

I pause, and let the fork drop down to the tray. "But I didn't lie?"

"But did you tell the truth?"

"I don't know the difference now," I say quietly.

"Why don't you go talk to him?"

"I suppose I have to go back to get my things and to get Mother. She won't be happy sitting in the warm shed by herself, especially on a day like this. She likes to be outside too."

He nods, then starts fingering his leftover chips. I copy him and do the same, but my belly gurgles and refuses any more. "Thank you again for the chips and water."

"You're welcome, June."

I smile and slide away from the table. If I leave now, it'll be afternoon tea break and we can have tea in the garden together. I can finally introduce him to Mother.

"June?"

I turn back. "Yes?"

"Would you like to do this again sometime?"

"Eat pop-up chips?"

"No," he laughs. "Hang out. Talk."

"Well, I don't think I'll be here much longer."

"Oh."

I have only "hung out" with one other person on a regular basis, aside from Mother, and that was the child. I don't know if I am ready to add another person to that list, but I feel indifferent to the cyclist. He is neither a stranger nor a "safe" person yet. Perhaps I will need more time to figure that out, assuming my stay in London has not come to an end.

"But if I do stay, then maybe." I shrug, tossing my tray into the open black bin.

"I'll take that." He grins. "Bye for now, June."

"Bye for now, *William*."

He looks at me: a smile/upturned mouth, laughter, eyes that light up, relaxed shoulders—William is visibly showing signs of HAPPY.

September is a good time to enjoy some breathing space before the garden comes alive again.

June's Return to the Garden Shed

Whenen I return to Lansdowne Road, walking under the familiar branches of the dawn redwoods and cherry blossoms, I see the driveway at number 16 is empty, and both Mr. and Mrs. Wilson's cars are gone.

It is almost three p.m.; and I wonder if the boy will be home now. There are three schoolboys standing opposite number 16. I recognize them from before, when they taunted the child. It seems the summer break did little to refocus their attention. I wonder if they are waiting for him. For my brother. I cross the road to find out.

"Are you here for Henry Wilson?" I ask them.

They turn slowly, sneering as they take me in, lips curling up in a smirk.

"What's it to you?" one snaps, leaning against the lamppost and crossing his arms.

"If you are, then it's best you leave before he returns and don't come back."

They laugh at my suggestion, as if it is completely ridiculous. As if I have asked them to plant snowdrops in August or pot perennials

in a tight container or eat tofu at dinner. I smile at the memory, of
how I will remember the Wilsons once I'm gone.

One schoolboy takes a step forward, threatening to enter my
bubble space. "And why would we do that?"

I too take a step forward; today, my bubble space can be slightly
smaller. "Because I often carry gardening instruments that are sharper
than a butcher's knife and because my caseworker calls me 'emotion-
ally unstable.'" I turn my palms over, showing them my bloodied
knuckles. "This is what happened last time I became *unstablized.*"

The one who talked to me stumbles back, then his eyes flit to his
friends who also seem to be shifting farther away from me. I stand
and wait for them to quickly turn and leave, and then I watch them
from the driveway of 16 Lansdowne Road until they fade into
specks in the distance, behind the cherry blossom trees.

When I walk up the side of the house, I see that the garden is
empty, the shed door closed, the branches of the Persian silk quiet
and still. The crushed stone from the garden path cracks and shifts
under the soles of my wellies as I creep slowly toward the grass.

The house beside me lies quiet. When I get to the corner, I carefully peer around. The patio furniture is untouched and the kitchen
doors are closed. The Wilsons are nowhere in sight. I walk over to
the shed and open the door. It's unlocked. Inside, my bedding is still
on the floor, my clock is on the shelf, the gardening tools are where
they should be, and Mother is where I left her. My chest loosens slightly.

I begin to quietly pack, folding my clothes neatly into my bag,
adding the clock and all the other items that I can fit inside the duffel. I grab my books off the table, which will have to stay, sadly,
along with the rug and the lamp. I won't be able to take furniture
with me. I lift the copy of *Peter Pan* up to my face and sigh. I have
already used a telephone box at Notting Hill Gate to call the nice old
man with gray hair from the bookshop in Cecil Court. Mr. Sawyer.
I am to come by his shop this afternoon to exchange the book for

money, then make my way to Victoria Coach Station for the next Megabus departure. I am headed home.

It will be a long journey back to Scotland. Ten hours and five minutes, assuming the bus departs on time. I wonder how I will hold my bladder for such a long time. Perhaps they give you little cups to widdle in as you board the bus. I doubt there will be a fully functioning toilet, like the train has. Or a hot food and beverages carriage. I also wonder what makes this bus so *"mega,"* compared to other buses, like the one I took from Maryhill to work. But I will find out soon enough, and then I'll be equipped with the knowledge to tell others what I have learned. The ladies at work will be very interested, assuming I still have my old job when I return.

The book feels so familiar in my palms, with the paper slightly yellowed at the edges. I flick through the pages, each one skimming the air and landing with the others. A white corner pokes out from the back. When I turn the page, I see a white envelope that's been placed behind the back cover, just after the final page. On the front are the words **"To the person who will live with/work with June Wilson."** It's Mother's handwriting. I would recognize it anywhere. I skim the words, my fingertips caressing the indentations from the pen.

I had forgotten about this letter until now. I forget a lot of things since Mother died. This envelope had been in Mother's bedside drawer along with my birthday card. I had taken both with me, but since the letter is not addressed to me, I did not open it.

The patio doors suddenly slide open and I startle, dropping the book and the envelope to the floor. High heels march across the patio stone toward me, each footstep careful and slow. Before I can decide where to hide, Mrs. Wilson stands at the shed door in front of me. She's dressed in a pair of loose-fitting beige trousers with a white shirt and a shawl of some kind draped over her shoulders. Her hair is tightly pulled back in a bun, her face taut with the force. She is the complete opposite of Mother, but she wears earrings that are the same color as Mother's cobalt blue suede heels. Blue like wind-flowers and sea holly.

"I was hoping you'd come back," she says eventually. "I parked down the street in case my car scared you off."

I just blink at her.

"I don't know you, June, and you don't know me, but it appears my husband and my son have become quite fond of you."

I'm numb, not sure what to say or how to respond. My conversational skill sessions have not covered situations like this.

"I'm sorry," she sighs. She walks over to the patio table and sits in a chair. "I didn't know Robert had a child before we met. Neither did he, it sounds like, and I believe him. You came here to meet your father and neither of us was all that welcoming. We responded terribly, but I'm listening now. What is it that you've come for, June?"

I edge over and sit in the chair opposite her, clutching my hands in my lap. I have never said the words out loud. "A home." I clear my throat and continue. "I want a family," I say, my voice strangely calm.

She nods. "Understandable. I'm truly sorry for your loss. When did she die?"

"Spring, when the snowdrops bloom. How do you know?"

"We saw the urn on the shed floor. It has your mother's name engraved on it."

"Oh."

"Robert's trying to speak to someone in adult services at Glasgow City Council."

"Why?"

"Just to talk to someone, to learn more about you, your situation. He was really worried about you when you left yesterday. We were up most of the night talking. He showed me photos of your mother when they were kids at school. She was very beautiful."

"She was."

"You look just like her."

"Will I see the child—I mean *Henry*—again?" My jaw clenches as the warmth tugs at the corners of my eyes again. I haven't come back to the garden only for my things, my books, or perhaps not even just for Mother. I realize in that moment that I have come back for *him*. For my brother.

"Of course you can—he's at the library, but he'll be home any minute. We have all been waiting for you to come back, hoping you would."

I lean forward, resting my hands on the warm patio table. "What happens now?"

"Honestly, I don't know."

I lower my head. The summer is almost at an end and I am still seeking answers to my questions. I wonder if the Wilsons will let me stay on in their shed, be the friendly girl in the garden that every London home should have. A live-in gardener. All I request are cheese sandwiches at midday and tea breaks at 10:30 a.m. and 3:00 p.m.

"But what I do know is that we won't be able to solve anything right now or today, so why don't you come inside for a cup of tea? I hear you tend to have one about this time?"

I snap my head up, and gaze at Mrs. Wilson.

"Then maybe later you can help me make dinner? And we can take it from there," she adds.

A huge wave floods over me, soaked with emotions I can't even begin to describe. My skin pricks and comes alive. Am I being invited in? After all these weeks? No more hiding. "Uh . . um . . . ," I stutter, in complete disbelief. In only a couple of hours, I will be sitting at that dining table, eating dinner with everyone. "Yes. Yes please."

She smiles, her eyes softening, and pushes herself out of the chair effortlessly. I start to follow her, then pause, my feet not yet inside. "What are we having for dinner?"

She marches over to the kettle, flicking it on with a quick hand movement. "Quinoa and marinated seitan."

A beautiful garden should never be enjoyed alone.

June in the House

Tiny yellow stickers are scattered across Henry's ceiling. Stars. Some with the corners fraying, the stickiness long gone, others with a point missing as if someone has tried to reposition them, and failed. I painted vines and florals on my bedroom walls back home, but I never considered putting stickers on the wall like this. What a clever idea. I wonder if there are floral adhesives available to buy somewhere.

Henry snores gently in the bunk bed below me. I check my watch; it's just after 7:00 a.m. I slept peacefully in the bunk above him, the street noise much quieter in here than outside in the shed. These walls are much thicker, thankfully. Insulated and leakproof. A real duvet is nice and I brought my own pillow in from the shed, along with my books and Mother, who now sits on the windowsill facing out into the familiar garden, where I have spent most of the summer.

A little cough cuts through the morning quiet. "Are you awake?"

"Yes." I didn't realize he was.

"I've never had a sleepover before."

"Me neither."

"Do I snore?"

"Yes."

"So do you."

"No I don't," I scoff. The covers rustle and the bunk creaks as he shifts around below me. "I like your stickers."

"If you move in, you can put up your own if you like? Or we can paint the ceiling? You can do the grass this time."

I stare at the stars above, counting the ones closest to the wall edge. After I get to twenty, I clear my throat. "Would you want me to move in?"

I count another three stars while I wait for his response.

"I think I would. I think I would like that a lot."

I stop counting the stars and draw a circle in the air around the face with the smile. "Me too."

While he showers, I ease myself out of the top bunk and down the small wooden ladder, which digs into my bare feet. I remove the *Peter Pan* book from my bag and place it gently on his pillow. We can share it. I am okay with that. My feet touch down on the soft plush carpet and I follow it out of the room, closing the door behind me and walking down the hallway to the stairs. Upstairs, the main bedroom door is closed; Mr. and Mrs. Wilson must still be sleeping.

I had waited up as long as I could, but Mr. Wilson had returned home from work very late. I had heard some muffled exchanges with his wife in the kitchen below us but couldn't make out what was said. The acoustics in these bedrooms are awful compared to those in the garden.

When I reach the bottom of the stairs, the dog runs toward me, pushing her wet nose into my crotch. I touch her once on the head, then wipe my palm on my pajama trousers. She has left a residue. I shoo her away back to the living room and tiptoe through to the kitchen to put the kettle on. I shall start my morning a little earlier today, so I don't miss Mr. Wilson going to work.

When I push open the kitchen door, I see him already sitting at the dining table, a pot of coffee beside him and Mother's letter, the envelope having been ripped open.

"Good morning," he says softly.

"Good morning," I echo, my tone matching his.

He gestures for me to join him at the table, so I do. He pours me a cup of coffee from a blue ceramic pot and pushes the milk jug toward me. He doesn't offer me sugar. He knows how I take my coffee, it seems. Perhaps Henry told him.

I settle into the chair, the steam from the mug billowing and wafting in front of me.

"Judith tells me you two had a nice conversation yesterday and enjoyed some dinner and TV later?"

"Yes, she made me potatoes and carrots as requested and then we watched a David Attenborough special on cacti on *Green Planet*."

He nods. "Sounds interesting." He takes a sip of his coffee and puts it down. "June, I talked to your caseworker yesterday and she seems quite worried about you. She said she hasn't heard from you since you left Glasgow. There's a missing persons file open on you because you're a . . . 'vulnerable person.'" He pauses. Is he trying to decipher my facial cues?

"I didn't have a phone while I was here," I begin. "And I didn't want her knowing where I was in case she came for me."

"You're twenty-two years old. She can't come for you. You're free to live your life. She's there to offer financial and accommodation support since your mother's deceased. She's there to help if you need it."

I nod. "She tried to send me to a residential home."

"Is that what you want?"

I shake my head fervently.

"I don't think she can legally enforce that."

I take a sip of my coffee. It's a little strong for my liking, but I don't say so. It'll do. "Should I go back to Scotland now?"

"Do you want to go home?" he asks.

"Should I? Is that what Mother says in the letter? That I shouldn't be here?"

"You hadn't read it?"

"It isn't addressed to me, it's addressed to the person who will live or work with me and you shouldn't open other people's mail."

"Well, I opened it, so I suppose that person who will live with you could be me."

A heavy silence sets in around us, and I became aware of the birds outside, nesting in the Persian silk.

"I fear I might be quite difficult to live with," I whisper.

"I fear the same," he says, raising an eyebrow.

"What happens now?"

"That's up to you. What is it that you want to do with your life, June?"

"I don't know yet," I say. "I don't really know who I am, or what I do best, other than gardening?"

"Then maybe that's it exactly," he says, pointing to the vase on the kitchen counter, filled with milky white baby's breath, blue-tinted hydrangea stems, and dark purple phlox. I didn't pick those myself and Mrs. Wilson certainly didn't either. They have been too neatly clipped. It must have been the boy. I have taught him well. I want to smile, but the coldness in my chest is too heavy. Too much weight for my body to carry any longer.

"Why do I feel like this?" I ask quietly.

"It's called grief, and I think you'll be feeling like this for a long time, June. And that's okay."

"Does the letter say why she wanted to die?"

He frowns. "I don't think she wanted to leave you, June. She loved you very much." He slides the letter to me across the table, slowly, cautiously. I stare at it, the folded edges curling up, Mother's handwriting facing up to the sun. "Read the letter," he continues, "and I think you'll see that too." He gets up, coffee mug in hand. "I'll give you some time alone."

The autumnal morning pecks at the window, the copper-stained leaves in the back rustling in the breeze. I pick up the letter and head for the patio door. The animal bounds past me and launches herself into the garden. I walk gently across the patio stones until the soles of my bare feet touch the soft grass, moist with the morning dew, and sit down.

The morning air smells different today. It smells new and fresh, and is filled with the scent of lavender from the back flower bed. It's quiet in the garden at this time, calm, with only the trees and birds and morning bees to keep me company. I try to ignore the dog as she burrows into the earth around the Persian silk tree, which is turning with the season, and instead close my eyes and remember my garden at home. A garden so rich with flowers and herbs, and memories. Memories of me, of Mother, of our life together.

I scarcely remember my life in the years between Mother leaving and returning. I only remember my years with her, and everything she told me, taught me, showed me. I fell in love with the garden because she once loved it. I grew flowers so she could pick them. I grew herbs so she could cook with them. I tended to the grass beds so she could lie on her back and gaze up at the sky with me. Everything was for her.

Now I have to find something for myself.

Epilogue

To the person who replaces me in June's life—if she needs someone, which she might not:

If you're reading this, then I'm dead. No other way to say that, I guess. But it's true. I considered pills but have decided on a trip down to the river behind Barbara's house, and I hope it wasn't too much bother to retrieve my body at the end. That river can be awfully fickle and toss up rubbish in all sorts of places. I just didn't want June to find my body in the house after work.

Don't spend too much time dwelling on this; there is nothing anyone could have done to stop me. In the beginning, everyone said it was just typical "baby blues" and I'd feel my usual self soon. I too thought it would pass, but it didn't. I am broken and have always been. But this isn't a suicide letter because this isn't about me. This is about my daughter, June. Believe me, taking this option was a difficult choice for me, but one I had to make. I didn't want to leave June, but there really was no other way, and she has seemed ready in the last two years. Please tell her I love her and always will, and that everything I did, I did for her. I can only hope she has the tools now to live without me.

Anyway, just a few things to square away because I don't have a
will or anything like that. I'm not paying those bloody solicitors to
do nothing. This letter will hopefully do.

The Funeral

June knows what to do after I die, so please follow her lead. She may
need some help with the actual organizing, but she knows the plans.
Don't tell her how to dress on the day; let her wear her wellies and
her raincoat and, if she insists, let her carry that almanac or flower
encyclopedia with her if it makes her feel better. She'll insist on
choosing the flower arrangements and that's fine, just make some
suitable financial suggestions as the service may quickly turn into a
display at Kew Gardens otherwise.

Be sure to start the service dead on 11:00 a.m. (excuse the "dead"
pun), after June's tea break, and serve lunch at exactly midday, not a
moment after.

And don't hug her and say, "Sorry for your loss." She won't like
that. In fact, don't touch her at all.

The House

Hopefully the council will let June stay in the house. We've been
there most of her life and we've kept it in good condition, so it's
only fair. I'll be sure to clean it before I go.

The Schedule

June will see to herself for her mealtimes and work schedule. Just
check in on her regularly to make sure she's okay. She's fine to shop
for herself, cook for herself, etc., but I wouldn't want her to get
lonely or for anything to happen. If the TV were to stop working,

for example, she can't watch <u>Strictly Come Dancing</u> and she'll be extremely upset.

June has a very consistent schedule, so encourage her to follow it even after I'm gone. Routines help keep her on track. She's not an emotional person, so she likely won't grieve for me in the "normal" way; however, if she's thrown off her routine, she will become very unsettled and very upset. And ensure that she keeps up with her meds, or at least consult with her GP to fade them out gradually. If she suddenly stops taking them altogether then that will likely affect her moods.

Here is a rough outline of a typical day for June:

7:30 a.m. She'll wake naturally, so you don't need to wake her.

7:45 a.m. Breakfast is a coffee with a splash of milk, plus a slice of white toast with butter (the real stuff, or she'll notice the difference). She may occasionally take a croissant with sugar-free, seedless strawberry jam. Please make sure she takes her paroxetine medication until she can see her GP. It takes the edge off her OCD.

8:05–8:25 a.m. Shower and get dressed. She'll leave just after this for the bus.

8:40 a.m. Bus into town for work (all the regular drivers know her now).

June works at Marks & Spencer. Please ensure that she remembers her packed lunch (cheese sandwich, bottle of water). On Saturdays and Sundays, she volunteers at the community garden in town from 10:00 a.m. until 2:00 p.m. She loves being around flowers. (Side note: Don't let her bring her encyclopedia of flowers and herbs to work with her no matter how much she begs. Once she forgot it in the staff room and oh my god, what a tantrum that led to. I lost three dinner plates, a ceramic bowl, and a good bottle of Chianti that evening.)

2:00 p.m.+ on weekends, June will either read or do some light gardening outside or for a neighbor until teatime.

3:00 p.m. Teatime (milky tea and a biscuit or scone of some kind—no raisins or chocolate).

On weekdays, she finishes work at 4 p.m. and will get the bus home herself.

5:15 p.m. June likes to sort the vegetables and potatoes for dinner (don't worry, she can handle the big knives).

6:00 p.m. Dinner (if you're assisting, then please make sure dinner is ready for 6:00 p.m., otherwise she gets upset).

7:00–9:00 p.m. TV time (*Escape to the Country, DIY SOS, Strictly Come Dancing,* and any gardening or nature shows).

9:00 p.m. Bedtime routines—if you can, show her how to fill a hot water bottle (I've always done it for her and then demonstrate where to place it at the bottom of the bed for warm feet).

9:30 p.m. Bedtime—she'll know herself, so you don't need to remind her of the time. She doesn't need sleep meds anymore, but do try to hang wind chimes outside her window.

June used to have episodes when she was younger, mostly angry outbursts, throwing things, etc. She's not had one in a very long time, because we keep a consistent routine at home and at work. Me being gone may trigger some of these episodes again. If they do occur, don't panic; call her caseworker, Aileen Macdonald at Glasgow City Council. She and her colleagues had some good advice for me when I was dealing with this in the beginning, such as staying calm, removing sharp or fragile objects, etc. It'll pass eventually and when June is back on routine and not thinking about me anymore, then they'll go away completely.

This may seem like a lot, but please understand—June is special. She may seem "different" to those around her, but her differences only make her more special. She has a big heart and most of the time she's sunshine and rainbows. That's why June is the perfect name for her.

June, like a warm and bright summer's day.

Acknowledgments

I originally came up with the idea of a young woman living in the garden one summer after my mother and I painted my garden shed a bright sunny shade of yellow. I joked that I might live there one day. I moved from that house two years later, sadly unable to bring the yellow shed with me, but the idea lingered.

At the same time as the yellow shed was painted, I was working on my doctorate, exploring traits associated with reactive attachment disorder and its representation in contemporary fiction. I had classroom experience working with children diagnosed with reactive attachment disorder, primarily in New Hampshire, with the support and guidance of an incredible team. When I moved back to Scotland, I continued my research into RAD as well as conversations with experts such as Dr. Helen Minnis and the Autism Research team at the University of Stirling. Shortly after, I was able to construct a tentative framework for a fictional character with RAD living with profound trauma and grief after the loss of her mother.

And so the story of June in a garden shed began to grow like the flowers in this novel, along with a deeper reflection of identity, loss, and trauma. I wrote the first draft of this story throughout my pregnancy, and after my daughter was born, I continued to work on it. Then my son was born, and there were times I truly did not think I would ever finish. But I did, eventually, and there are so many people to thank for that.

Family is a good place to start, given that it is June's objective in this story. My family supported me immensely and continues to do so as I explore more narrative journeys that speak to neurodiversity and motherhood. This book is dedicated to them—to my husband, to our parents, our children, our siblings, and all of our nieces and nephews.

The team at Peters Fraser & Dunlop is exceptional. I cannot thank my agent Silvia Molteni enough for taking a chance on this manuscript years ago when I first showed her the early chapters. Huge thanks to Silvia and Becky Wearmouth for supporting this novel and finding the perfect home for it.

That home is with the amazing teams over at Crown at Penguin Random House and with Text Publishing. Shannon, thank you so much for believing in this story and in June. Penny, thank you truly; I have fond memories of talking about sheds and flowers back when we first met. You both have transformed this novel. The cover designs for *June in the Garden* are exquisite so thank you to the designers over at Crown and Text for bringing June alive and into color. And a big thank you to everyone on the Publicity and Marketing teams.

To the experts at the Royal Horticultural Society for developing the *Encyclopedia of Gardening* and *Gardener's Almanac,* my go-to guides for building June's fascination with the outdoors and all things that grow.

To the many NHS midwives, consultants, and healthcare professionals who attempted to put me back together after a traumatic birth and postpartum journey, all while I wrote this novel.

And last, but certainly not least, I wish to thank my colleagues at the University: Liam, Kevin, Lorna, and Chris. And an extra loud shoutout to Liam and Kevin for guiding me through numerous drafts of this novel while I reframed my understanding of June's trauma.

On that note, I leave you with one final thought—neurodiversity is a celebration of different thinking patterns, some considered "unique," others considered "neurotypical," I consider myself an individual with these unique thinking patterns. Any mentions of anger and violence in this narrative refer to incidents shaped by trauma and grief, not by neurodiversity.

Thank you for reading *June in the Garden.*

Love, Eleanor Wilde x

About the Author

ELEANOR WILDE is the pen name of an acclaimed YA author. Wilde holds a master's of education and worked for several years in the U.S. public education system. She has a love of books and gardening and spends her weekends climbing hills or foraging for wildflowers in the woods. *June in the Garden* is her debut adult novel.